A DAY OF DRAGON BLOOD

A Day of Dragon Blood

Dragonlore, Book Two

Daniel Arenson

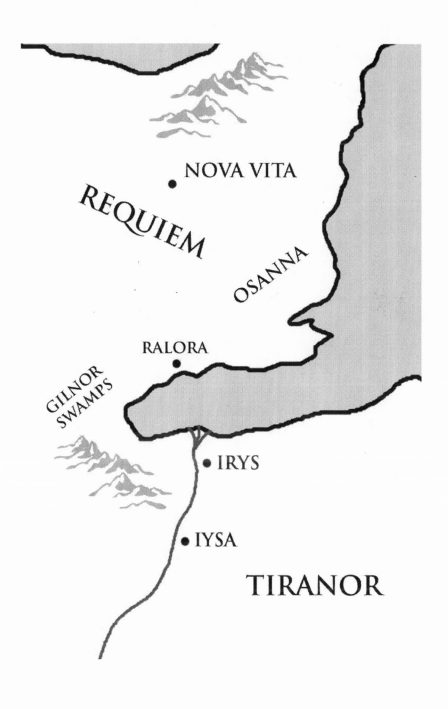

SILAS

Three dragons flew in the night, seeing demons in every shadow.

The swamplands rolled below into darkness. Mist rose from the mangroves like ghosts, only to disperse in the flap of leathern wings. The clammy scents of moss, mud, and leaf filled the dragons' nostrils, mingling with the scent of fire that crackled inside their maws. No stars gleamed above; it was a night of cloud, of fear, of a quiet before the storm.

"Where are you?" Silas whispered, scanning the darkness. His scales clanked and his scars still blazed. It had been a year since the war, a year since the Tirans had flown over these swamplands, killed his king, toppled his home, and left his body a ruin of burnt flesh and lacerations. A year--and still the scars burned, those that covered his body and those that clawed inside him.

"My lord!" said Tanin, a young dragon who flew beside him. He was a mere boy, just turned sixteen, and green as his scales. "My lord, do you see something?"

Silas grumbled. "I'm not a lord, Tanin. And lower your voice; it could carry for a mile on this wind."

Farm boys, he thought and spat. *They send me farm boys to lead in patrol.* A year ago, Silas had served among a thousand true warriors, hardened dragons who fought for Requiem's glory. Nearly all had died in the war, burned in phoenix fire over the capital or cut with steel in its tunnels.

Yet I linger. Thousands of warriors died around me, in glory and fury, and here I am... a scarred, twisted old thing serving with the children of farmers and bakers. He was barely thirty, but he felt old beside these youths--his soul like ancient leather, crumpled countless times, and his bones brittle as rusted blades.

Wings churned the mist, and Yara flew up to him, her eyes bright. A slim silver dragon, a baker's daughter, she bared her fangs.

"Silas!" she said, panting. "I saw something! A shadow in the night." She pointed her claws south.

Icy fingers seemed to clutch Silas. He looked south but saw only leagues of shadows, swirling clouds, and mangroves that swayed over mud and water.

Scales clattering with fear, Tanin snorted a blast of fire. "Where, Yara? Where?"

Silas whipped his head around and hissed. "Silence, boy! Still your tongue and your fire."

He turned his head back south. He narrowed his eyes, seeking, barely breathing. Gliding silently on the wind, he sniffed the air.

Nothing, he thought. *Nothing but leagues of these swamplands. No enemy. No--*

Beside him, the two young dragons gasped. Silas cursed and filled his maw with flames.

Damn it.

A dozen shadows swooped from the clouds, not a hundred yards away. Red eyes blazed and fangs glinted; Silas saw nothing more of the creatures but shadow. He growled, spat a curse, and blew a jet of fire.

The flames spun and screamed, and for an instant Silas saw the beasts. His blood froze. They were large as dragons, their scales metallic, their wings wide, their jaws long and sharp as blades. Human riders sat astride them, faceless behind jagged helms. Then the fire crashed against the beasts, and their shrieks shattered the night. They screeched like smashing glass, like cracking bones, like storms. Their wings thudded and they crashed against him.

Claws tore at his scales. Fangs drove into flesh. Silas growled and slashed at them, his claws screeching against scales as hard as iron. Sparks showered. He saw Yara and Tanin fighting beside him, and blood sprayed through the mist.

"Yara, fall back!" Silas howled. "Send the signal!"

One of the beasts swooped again, scales rippling and claws lashing. Silas spun, swung his tail, and hit a head of scales and spikes. Another beast flew at his right, a mere shadow in the night, and fangs dug into Silas's shoulder. Pain blazed and in a flash, Silas was back in the tunnels, back in the darkness under Nova Vita, fighting the war that had left his brothers dead and him this burnt shell of a man. Fire once more raced across him, burning as his city collapsed and all those he knew fell dead around him.

He blasted more fire. It crashed into the creatures and showered, and Silas was back above the swamps, a year later, fighting to stop this war from flaring again. In the firelight, he saw Yara retreat. The young silver dragon puffed her chest, tossed her head back, and seemed ready to send the signal for aid--three upward blasts of fire.

Before she could summon her flame, the shadowy beasts turned toward her, opened their maws, and spewed jets of pale liquid.

Heat blazed and stench flared. Silas growled. The yellow projectiles slammed against Yara and she screamed--a sound of such agony that Silas knew it would forever haunt him. The liquid sizzled across the silver dragon, eating through her scales, melting her face, and digging into flesh. Her magic left her, the ancient magic of Requiem, the magic that let their people fly as dragons. She fell from the sky as a human, a young woman burning away into bones. She disappeared into darkness.

"Oh stars, oh stars!" cried Tanin, and the green dragon turned to flee. He flew not fifty yards before the metallic creatures roared and spewed their acid. The sizzling streams crashed against the fleeing dragon, and Tanin howled and wept.

"Please!" he cried, and his voice sounded so young, the voice of a mere boy. "I want to go home, please, I'm not a soldier, please..."

He turned to look back, and his eyes met Silas's gaze. For an instant--a cold, terrible instant that lasted for ages--Silas stared into the eyes of a young, terrified boy who had believed in him... whom he had led to death. Then the acid dripped into those frightened eyes and melted them like flames melting candles. Tanin too became human and tumbled, burning into a red, bubbling chunk of meat that disappeared into shadow.

Panting, Silas beat his wings and turned to face the creatures. In the darkness, he could barely see them--only the shape of their wings, the glint of their fangs, and the red of their eyes. They surrounded him, ten or more. The riders on their backs were mere shadows. Silas's heart pounded. He knew he had to send the signal, he had to blast his fire--three blasts into the air, a cry for aid--yet if he moved, they'd kill him. He had seen enough men die to know when his own death loomed.

He tossed back his head and began to blow his fire.

The creatures swarmed.

A jet of acid flew. Silas soared and swerved. The blast slammed against his wing and he screamed. The heat blazed, enveloping him. Holes tore open in his wing; he heard wind rush through them. He flapped madly, trying to shake off the acid, but it stuck to him, eating, digging, tearing his wing apart until it fell like burnt paper shards.

He began to tumble from the sky, beating one wing.

The swamps rushed up toward him. Above him the beasts swooped.

"Take him alive!" shouted a rider. "I want him *alive!*"

The wind roared. Silas craned his neck as he fell and blew fire upward. The flaming pillar crashed against one swooping beast. It howled and pulled back. A dozen others dived down, great falling shards of black. Claws reached out and grabbed him, digging past scales into flesh.

He crashed through mangroves into mud and moss. The beasts crashed atop him. Fangs dug into him, and chains swung and wrapped around him. He glimpsed the riders leaping off their mounts, the glint of golden suns on their breastplates, and an iron club swinging toward his head.

Light exploded and darkness fell like a cloak above him.

Rain pattered.

Wind howled.

Stars swirled and Silas wandered through endless tunnels, seeking his dead brothers, seeking a way out.

LYANA

Lyana stood on the winehouse roof, watching the square below where thousands roared for death.

It seemed every soul in Irys, this lush oasis city, had come to see the execution. Men, women, and children crowded the roofs of their mudbrick homes, peering between rooftop gardens of herbs, fruit, and vegetables. Soldiers, clad in pale breastplates and armed with spears, lined cobbled streets that snaked between palm groves, silos, vineyards, and workshops. Even the River Pallan, which coiled between the city's columned temples and villas, overflowed with ships--from the simple cogs of fishermen, to the great sailed ships of traders whose holds overflowed with spices, silks, and jewels from distant desert lands.

Tiranor, Lyana thought, the sandy wind in her hair. *Scourge of Requiem--gathered here in all her glory and might, as different from my home as sunlight from starlight. I stand in the lions' den.*

It was the Day of Sun's Glory, the pinnacle of the moon's cycle; tonight that moon would be black in the sky, and tomorrow the sun would rise victorious. The people wore white and gold to worship their fiery god, and the scent of myrrh wafted through the city, thick and heady in Lyana's nostrils. She had always loved the smell, but today it smelled like corpses to her. It was a day for all great things in Tiranor, this land of sand and stone--for war, for worship... and for death.

The crowd's roars swelled when five wyverns emerged from the Temple of the Sun, a sandstone edifice whose columns and towers rose above the city, capped with platinum. The scaly beasts dragged themselves from the temple's bowels and onto the hot, sun-drenched streets. Even in the glare of Tiranor's blazing sun, their scales were midnight black, their eyes red pools like fire underground. Riders sat upon them, their helms shaped as cranes' beaks, their whips ringed with gold.

Lyana grimaced and clenched her fists. The first time she had seen the wyverns, she had thought them some strange, southern dragons--they were large, scaled, and winged like the dragons of the north. But unlike dragons, they had but two legs-- muscled and wide as their tails, with claws like great swords, twice the size of dragonclaws. Their jaws thrust out like blades, lined with teeth. Worst of all was the weapon that spewed from those jaws; Lyana had seen their acid burn only once, eating a condemned thief into bones, and it still filled her nightmares.

Chains dragged behind the wyverns. When they stepped farther from the temple, the shackles tugged their captive out onto the street: a bloody, lacerated dragon.

"Silas," Lyana whispered. Tears stung her eyes.

The wyverns grunted and trundled down the streets, dragging the chained dragon behind them. Silas breathed raggedly. His one wing was missing, burnt to nothing but a charred bone. His scales were dented, his horns sawed off. As the wyverns dragged him along the road, his blood trailed behind him. All around the crowds roared, stamped their feet, and pelted Silas with refuse and stones.

Lyana's legs shook, she panted, and her head spun.

"Oh Silas," she whispered.

She had fought alongside him in Nova Vita, battling the phoenixes over the city of dragons. He had served her father, the Lord Deramon; in her childhood, Silas often guarded her chamber at night and taught her swordplay during the day. She had to save him. She had to discard her disguise, shift into a dragon, swoop and grab him and fly with him to safety. She had to--

You have to serve your kingdom, whispered a voice inside her. *You have to stay at your post. You are a daughter of Requiem, and you serve all her people... even if you must let one die.*

It was the voice of her father, her king, and her ancestors-- the voice of her honor and memory. It was a voice she hated this day.

She adjusted the silk scarf around her eyes. The loomers of Confutatis, ancient city of the eastern realms, had woven this scarf, and they had imbued it with all their skill and magic. From one side, the cloth was translucent as summer mist; from the other, solid and thick as wool. Through the scarf, the world shone clear to Lyana; to any observer, the silk hid her green northern eyes. To this city she was but Tiana, the blind dancer of the River Spice. Her hair, once a pyre of fiery red curls, now hung smoothed and bleached a platinum blond--the hair of a Tiran. Her skin, once pale and strewn with freckles like starfields, now gleamed golden, rubbed with dyes that would tint her for moons. Once she had worn the armor of a bellator, a knight of Requiem; today she wore but strands of white silk that revealed more flesh than they hid.

I was Lady Lyana, a defender of Requiem, a warrior who could shift into a dragon and roar to battle, save Silas, and burn my enemies. She squared her jaw, heart pounding. Now she must be only Tiana-- only the blind dancer from the southern dunes, only a girl with a scarf over her eyes, a girl who could not even see this dance of blood before her. *How I wish that I were truly blind today.*

The five wyverns moved along the Palisade of Kings, a wide cobbled road lined with palms and obelisks capped with platinum sunbursts. Blood trailed behind the dragging Silas, and the multitudes roared. Cranes and ibises flew overhead, and soldiers on horseback rode behind the dragon, bearing the banners of Phoebus--a flaming sun upon a white field. The procession made its way down the palisade, under the great

Queen's Archway whose stones were carved with sunbursts, and into the Square of the Sun where thousands roared and raised their hands to the heavens. The true sun blazed overhead, drenching the city, a god of light and heat and punishment.

Across the square lay the Palace of Phoebus, a towering edifice, greater even than the palace of Requiem where Lyana served her king. Its columns rose three hundred feet tall. Stone guardians, shaped as faceless warriors, flanked its great doors; each statue stood taller than three dragons. The wyverns began climbing the stairs to the palace gateway. Silas dragged behind them; the dragon thudded against each step, groaning, smoke leaving his nostrils.

Blow fire, Silas! Lyana thought. *Blow your flame and kill what bastards you can!*

Yet he was too weak; she saw that. He was barely strong enough to cling to his dragon form. She saw the marks of whips across him. They had tortured him, forcing him to remain a dragon, though surely it took every last drop of his strength.

Lyana clenched her fists. *Queen Solina wants the mobs to see him as a broken, bloody beast, not a man.*

The doors to the palace, wrought of gold and ivory, swung open. As if summoned by Lyana's thoughts, Queen Solina stepped out of shadows, stood above the stairs, and raised her arms.

The city bowed before her, a great wave of myriads. Jaw so tight her teeth ached, Lyana forced herself to bow too.

"Blessed be the Sun God!" cried Solina. She wore steel so pale it was nearly white. A golden sun glimmered upon her breastplate, and twin sabres hung from her belt. Her platinum hair swayed behind her like a banner, and a crown of jagged, golden spikes rose upon her head like claws.

You murdered my king, Lyana thought, a sandstorm of rage flaring within her. *You murdered my betrothed. One day I will kill you, Solina.*

"Rise, children of the sun!" Solina cried, arms raised. Across the oasis city of Irys, the people rose and cried her name. "A beast we found lurking along our borders. A demon of scale and claw!"

Upon the roofs and streets, the crowd roared. Lyana looked upon the people through the silk of her scarf. She had never seen such rage, such pure, storming hatred. It suffused the faces of the men and women of Tiranor, twisting them into cruel masks. It gushed from their throats in raw howls.

We are but demons to them, Lyana thought. *We, the children of Requiem, are a noble and ancient race--a nation that lives for music, for meditation, for peace. And we are nothing but monsters here.*

"The dragons burned your fathers and mothers!" Solina cried. "Thirty years ago, when they invaded our glorious land of sunlight, they toppled our towers and drank the blood of children." Her voice nearly drowned under the roaring crowd. "But we've rebuilt! Our palace stands anew and our people are strong!" She tossed back her head and howled her words to the sun. "We will never fall!"

The roars swelled so loudly that Lyana felt them thud in her ears, pound in her chest, and shake the River Spice Winehouse below her feet.

"We will never fall!" cried the people. "We will never fall! Hail the Sun God!"

Lyana lowered her eyes. The first Tiran War had raged before her birth. Solina herself had been only a babe. Its wounds had long washed away from this city; all the fallen buildings stood again, and once more trees filled this oasis with life.

"And yet the hatred we sowed then still blooms," Lyana whispered. "And it still burns our sons and daughters."

The wyverns flapped their wings and tugged the chained dragon to his feet. Soldiers climbed the towering statues that flanked the palace doors, attaching chains to hooks. Soon Silas hung shackled between the stone guardians, a bloody dragon with one wing, displayed in all his wretchedness to the city. Solina stood before him, her boots red with his blood.

"The dragons bring drought to our land!" the queen cried. "They drink the waters that should overflow the River Pallan! The dragons eat our grain, leaving our poor to hunger! The dragons mock our lord, the Sun God who gives us life, and worship the night!" With her every word, the crowd roared, and Solina spun toward the chained Silas. "Now Requiem will learn the price of its evil. Blessed be the Sun God! His fire shall extinguish all darkness. Soon we will burn all dragons and cast out their evil with light. We will never fall!"

Fly now! cried a voice in Lyana's head. *Toss off this silk scarf, discard your disguise, and fly as a dragon to save him. You are a knight of Requiem, no blind Tiran dancer!*

Her every breath was a struggle. Her head spun. Her fingernails dug into her palms. *Oh, stars.* Her king had sent her here as a spy--to dance, to listen, to learn. *Stars, not to watch my friend killed before my eyes.*

And yet she watched, trembling upon the roof.

Solina mounted a wyvern, the greatest among them, a behemoth of iron scales named Baal. The queen cracked her whip and her mount reared. The beast roared and spewed a stream of yellow, smoking acid onto the chained dragon.

Silas howled.

Lyana wept.

I'm sorry, Silas, I'm sorry. There was nothing she could do; she knew that. If she flew, she too would die. If she flew, all her work would burn with her bones. Yet still the pain and shame coursed within her.

The acid ate through the dragon's scales, blood boiled, and Silas turned back into a man. The body hung for a moment upon the chains, then fell and broke apart. Lyana turned away and closed her eyes, but she could still hear the screams.

The crowd's roar spun around her. Vaguely, she heard Solina cry of her glory, heard her scream of offering a burnt head to the crowd; all sounds were muffled. Struggling for breath, Lyana stumbled across the roof of her winehouse, fumbled to open the trapdoor, and stepped into the attic. Once inside, she all but fell against the wall, clutched her breast, and gasped for air.

Stars, oh stars.

She forced herself to take long, slow breaths, to count to ten, to calm the tremble of her limbs.

"You will not have died in vain, Silas," she whispered. "I vow to you. I will avenge you."

I will learn about the invasion of Requiem. I will report back to my king. And I will save Requiem from the wrath of this mad, murderous queen.

She leaned against the wall until her heartbeat began to calm. Soon her eyes regained focus, and she saw sacks of grain, jugs of ale, hanging strings of dried fish, and jars of fig preserves. In the corner lay her bed, a mere pile of straw topped with a canvas blanket. Once Lyana had lived in palaces, a great knight in the courts of Requiem. But those days lay long behind her; she had lived here in Tiranor as Tiana the dancer for a year now. Today, more than ever, she missed her home and knew the worth of her sacrifice.

Downstairs in the common room, she heard the doors slam open, boots rush in, and hoarse voices cry for ale and wine. Those were the voices of soldiers; she would have recognized the gruff calls anywhere. She had heard such voices a year ago when the Tirans had invaded her realm, burned her city, and killed thousands around her.

"Come, come, sit and drink!" rose the voice of Peras, the kindly old owner of the River Spice. "Sit here, I--"

The soldiers roared below. "The dancer! Bring us the dancer! Bring us wine, old man, and bring us the girl!"

Lyana ground her teeth. Death made such men thirsty for her wine and hungry for her flesh. She would serve them wine. And she would dance for them. And one day, she swore, she would burn them all.

For you, Orin, my fallen prince. For you, Silas, whom I could not save. For the thousands of Vir Requis these soldiers killed. I will avenge you, Requiem.

She grabbed her walking staff. She stepped downstairs, silks swaying across her body, baring all but her most private parts. Staff tapping, she entered the common room. Soldiers filled it, clad in steel and leather. At the sight of her, they roared and slammed fists against the tabletops. How many of those men had slaughtered women and children in Requiem? How many more would they slaughter once the second invasion began?

Peras, kindly old keeper of the winehouse, was hobbling between the men, serving wine, platters of dates, and steaming rolls of bread. One soldier shoved the old man aside.

"Dance!" he cried to Lyana. "Dance for us, Blind Beauty! We've seen blood and death, and now we will see grace."

When they looked upon her, she knew they saw a blind girl, a scarf hiding her green northern eyes in a land of blue-eyed desert warriors. Tiana's hair was smooth and bright as beaten platinum, her skin golden as dunes--a desert daughter clad in silks, a walking staff in hand, as different from Lady Lyana as sand from snow. When she looked upon them through her scarf, she saw steel and bloodlust, a death for her people.

"Dance as we drink!" one soldier called. "Summer solstice approaches, a day of dragon blood, a day when we kill and die. Let us drink today for life!"

Her heart pounded. Today was the new moon, a day of sunfire and wine. But summer solstice was the holiest day of the Tiran year, as holy as the Night of Seven to the children of Requiem. What did this soldier mean? Would the second invasion of Requiem begin on that holiest of days, a mere eighteen days away?

"Dance!" they cried.

She walked forward and tapped her staff, feigning her blindness and meekness, and they cheered. Peras began to play his lute, and the soldiers joined in, singing and drumming upon the tabletops. When she reached the center of the common room, tables of drinking men around her, Lyana laid her staff aside. And she danced.

A year ago, when she had been a knight in Requiem, Lyana had learned to dance with her betrothed Prince Orin; they would sway among the lords and ladies of the court, lovers caught in the song of harps and pipes. Here, in this southern land of sunlight and sand and steel, she danced not like a noblewoman, but like the wick of a flame, like desert wind, like a bird of many colors rising among palms. She closed her eyes until she truly became blind Tiana, and she surrendered herself to her dance. The men roared around her like desert storms.

As she danced, she was Tiana; she forgot her true name, her true parentage, her true soul. She became the Blind Beauty, the Desert Rose, the wonder of Irys. Her body swayed and her silks flowed. She spun, arms raised.

I am a daughter of dunes, whispered her soul. *I have risen from the desert like a column of fire. I am kissed with sunlight and myrrh and pomegranate wine. I am a desert bird, flying, seeking the sky.*

At these moments, when she danced, she could almost love her enemy, almost love Tiranor for the beauty of her song, the sweetness of her fruits and wines, and the glory of her ancient towers and gold. She was Tiran. She was Tiana. She was blind and a thing of wind and sound. If Lady Lyana, a knight of Requiem, still lived inside her, she was now a scourge of cruel northern snow.

The music died.

Lyana gasped and opened her eyes behind her scarf.

Through the silk, she saw the doors of the River Spice open, and a shadow entered the winehouse and her life.

First two armored men entered the room, bearing shields and spears. Gilded masks hid their faces, shaped as the heads of ibises, the curving beaks a foot long. They moved to flank the doorway, metal sentinels, and slammed down their spears. They were the Gilded Guardians, Lyana knew--warrior priests bred to protect the highborn of Tiranor. A third man followed, entering the shadowy common room with a wind scented of sand.

He was tall--the tallest man in the room. His head was shaved bald, and his face was lined, hard, and handsome. He wore armor of pale steel, unadorned but for a golden sun upon the breastplate. A sabre and dagger hung from his belt, their scabbards simple leather, their pommels shaped as sunbursts. If not for the suns upon his pauldrons, denoting him a general of Tiranor's army, Lyana would have thought him a simple soldier.

But no, she thought. It was more than just the rank upon his armor or the Gilded Guardians who flanked him. This man did not have the eyes of a common soldier. When he stared over the room at her, she saw no lust for blood, flesh, or wine. She saw nothing at all--only blue ice, calculating and heartless.

"General Mahrdor," whispered one soldier, rising to his feet. His face paled and he slammed his fist against his breastplate. "My lord!"

The other soldiers in the room, a good hundred or more, stood at attention. Their fists all slammed against their chests. All sounds died: the music, the raucous calls, even the men's breath. Lyana stared at the general and her heart thrashed. He was staring right at her: not at her body, like the other soldiers would stare, but directly through the scarf and into her eyes.

He knows! she thought. *He knows I'm not blind. He stares through the scarf--into my eyes, into my soul.*

She dared not move, not even shiver. She struggled to calm her pounding heart; she felt that General Mahrdor would hear its beat across the room.

No, he cannot know, she told herself. *To others, the scarf is solid silk, white and covering my green northern eyes. He sees only Tiana. Only a blind dancer.*

Finally he tore his eyes away from her; it felt like he'd pulled a dagger free from her gut. He began walking through the silent winehouse, the soldiers frozen around him. He made his way to a table before Lyana. When he stared at the men who had occupied it, they bowed and retreated into the shadows.

General Mahrdor sat, poured himself a mug of wine, and stared at Lyana. The candlelight danced against his armor. When he spoke, the room remained silent. His voice was smooth as the wine, his accent highborn and meticulous; it flowed through the silent room, too loud.

"You must be this... Blind Beauty I have heard of." He took a sip of wine, sloshed it, and swallowed. "They call you the Desert Rose and say you are a dancer of much grace and beauty. I have always greatly admired and sought grace and beauty--from good wine, to fine art, and yes... though my soldiers might snicker to hear it, even dance."

Though a glimmer of amusement tweaked his lips, his eyes remained hard. Lyana barely dared breathe. A lump filled her throat, but she dared not swallow. She had heard stories of this General Mahrdor and his love of beauty. They whispered that in his villa upon the River Pallan, he collected items he found beautiful--jeweled skulls of men he slew, scrolls of human skin, and stillborn babes dipped in bronze. Lyana had always thought

those mere stories, rumors told to spread fear of the great general.
Now, looking into those cold blue eyes, she believed all those
tales.

"Well?" Mahrdor said, staring at her. He leaned back in
his seat. "Let us see the Blind Beauty. Dance for us, child."

She closed her eyes and she danced.

Old Peras played his lute, but the soldiers--who had
clapped and pounded the tabletops--were now silent. She could
hear the patter of her bare feet and the flutter of her silks. Her
body swayed. She felt his eyes on her skin, skin dyed gold to hide
her northern paleness. She was as rushes in the wind, as smoke
rising from the desert.

When her dance ended and the music died, she bowed her
head. Deathly silence filled the winehouse. General Mahrdor
stared at her--stared through her scarf, stared into her skin, stared
into her deepest dreams and fears. His eyes were bottomless and
clutching.

Without a word, he stood up and left the winehouse.

Lyana felt like an empty bellows. Her limbs began to
tremble. Around her, the soldiers breathed out shakily, emptied
their mugs, and cried for more wine. Soon cheer and song filled
the winehouse again, but iciness lingered inside Lyana.

This is what I've danced a year here for, she thought. *Stars, let
him remember my dance! Let my painted body linger in his mind! Let him
return. Let me learn what I can... if there is anything to be learned from icy,
clutching eyes.*

Night fell, wine flowed, and music swirled. Platters of
roasted fowls, served on beds of leeks and mushrooms, filled the
winehouse with their scents. Men cracked open pomegranates
and greedily scooped out tiny jewels of seeds. A few men began
playing mancala, the great game of the desert, dropping seashells
into pits in a board, then howling after every round. Lyana was
standing in the corner, singing soft desert tunes to an old soldier

with one leg, when a Gilded Guardian returned to the winehouse and approached her.

"Dancer," he said, voice echoing inside his ibis helm. The beak swooped, long and sharp as a dagger. "The General Mahrdor, may the Sun God bless him, has invited you to his villa tonight. He requests a private dance. In return he will pay you a handsome reward. Will you accompany me through the dark streets to his home of light?"

Around them, soldiers smirked and hooted.

"A private dance for the general!" one called, a man who wouldn't have dared breathe around Mahrdor. "I'd say you've charmed the old man, girl."

Another brayed laughter. "He'd like a private dance in his bed, I'd wager."

Lyana barely heard the laughter. Her innards leaped and her breath stung in her nostrils. She would enter the villa of General Mahrdor himself, chief of Tiranor's armies! Her head spun. In a year of work, listening to these drunken soldiers chatter, she had not achieved half so much. Her fingers trembled. What dark secrets would she learn in his home? Memories rushed through her: rumors of bronzed fetuses, severed heads, and parchments of human skin. But she dreamed of other treasures: of maps, of battle plans, of secrets whispered in darkness when her flesh intoxicated him and loosened his tongue.

Tiranor planned a second invasion of her home; Lyana did not doubt that. If anyone could reveal its time and location, it was General Mahrdor.

"I accept," she whispered to the Gilded Guardian.

They left the winehouse and walked through the night. On the night of the new moon, when the sky was darkest, the Tirans lit fires across the city and praised the Sun God, the banisher of darkness. Great braziers crackled atop the Palace of Phoebus, which rose to her left across the square. Torches blazed upon the columns of the Sun Temple, which rose upon a hill to the east. People crowded the streets, holding candles and chanting prayers to banish the night. Smoke rose and sparks swirled like fireflies, filling the darkness. Light and fire ruled; shadows fled.

We are shadows to them, Lyana thought. *We, the children of Requiem, who worship the stars and can fly as dragons--we are creatures of darkness for them to burn.* She swallowed a lump in her throat. These people who marched the streets, holding candles before them, did not lust for blood or death; they lusted for light. They had never met a Vir Requis, Lyana knew. They knew only the stories Queen Solina fed them: stories of wretched beasts called weredragons, demonic shapeshifters of the north who could grow scales and wings, who had toppled their temples thirty years ago.

They think us beasts, mindless killers, monsters of darkness, she thought. *They will burn us all if I cannot stop them.*

She could not stop Solina from spreading lies. But she could discover her plans. She could warn her home. She could save her people from the endless fire of Solina's wrath.

The Gilded Guardian walked silently, staring ahead through the holes in his helm; he seemed to Lyana like an automaton of metal. He took her to a dock upon the River Pallan where rushes swayed and water flowed over mossy stones, reflecting the light of lanterns like a thousand jewels. Frogs trilled and children knelt above the water, sending candles floating upon wooden toy boats, gifts to banish the darkness of the northern seas. In the water swayed a full-sized boat too, ten feet long, shaped as an ibis. Silver filigrees lined its hull, forming coiling shapes of phoenixes. The Gilded Guardian stepped into the boat, reached out his hand, and helped Lyana in. His hand was gloved in leather, icy even in the warm summer night.

He rowed. They floated down the river, soon passing the Sun Temple whose priests moved between columns, blowing ram horns. The smell of frankincense, palm oil, and charcoal filled the air. Past the temple, the river ran between the narrow mudbrick homes of tradesmen: scribes, masons, blacksmiths, and healers. Around a bend, the river flowed through a copse of palm trees, then into the wealthy quarters of merchants and nobles. Villas rose here upon the riverbanks, their gardens lush, their doorways flanked with statues. The greatest villa lay ahead, rising from a verdant paradise of palms, fig trees, and terraces of flowers. A palisade of columns led to its gates, each topped with a status of a desert animal; Lyana saw falcons, foxes, snakes, and gazelles.

They docked the boat. Three slaves waited there, clad in crimson livery, their hooded heads bowed. They accompanied Lyana through the gardens toward the villa. The song of frogs, owls, and crickets rose around her, and the heady scent of jasmine filled the air. Lyana's heart thrashed as she walked, tapping her staff before her. For a year in Tiranor, she had lurked in shady alleys, danced in rundown winehouses, and sought whispers among the common soldiers of the city's dregs. Now she walked toward the greatest house in Irys; what knowledge would she find here?

General Mahrdor waited at the villa's doors. At first Lyana did not recognize him. Instead of armor, he wore a white tunic fringed in gold, an iron circlet in the manner of Tiran nobles, and sandals. He smiled thinly, but his eyes remained cold. Again it seemed to Lyana that he could see through the scarf around her eyes, just as she could. Again a chill ran through her, but she sucked in a breath and forced herself to keep walking toward him.

For Requiem, she thought. *For my family, for my king, and for my home.*

"Tiana!" he called to her, arms outstretched. "That is your name, is it not? Come, my Blind Beauty. Welcome to my home."

He dismissed his guards and slaves, and soon Lyana found herself tapping down a grand hall, its floor a mosaic of suns and stone vultures with jet eyes. She and Mahrdor walked alone. Great statues lined the hall, shaped as nude women with the heads of animals, their fangs bared and tongues rolling. Lyana had to struggle not to shiver, not to stare at them.

You are only Tiana, she told herself. *You are only a blind dancer; you cannot see this place.*

He reached out to her. She forced herself not to flinch, to feign surprise when he took her hand. His flesh was cold like a corpse's hand.

"Come, let me help you," he said. She stared forward but felt his eyes beside her, boring into her.

Past the main hall, they climbed a stairway and entered a wide, shadowy chamber. Lyana's jaw tightened, and it took all her will to stifle her gasp.

The stories were true. Sundry items filled this place, overflowing shelves, tabletops, and alcoves. Shrunken heads, their skulls removed, hung on strings from the ceiling. Pickled hands floated in jars. A chair stood in the corner, formed from human femurs. Old torture devices, their iron rusted and dulled, hung on one wall between paintings of bloodied, broken men.

Mahrdor stood still, holding her hand. "It is such a terrible malady, blindness," he said. "I have brought you to my chamber of wonders, the place of my most prized possessions. And yet... yet to you, the world is still a pool of darkness."

She lowered her head and whispered. "Though my eyes peer into eternal night, the Sun God lights my heart."

He nodded sympathetically. "Well spoken, child. He is a merciful god to those who serve him. If your eyes are blind, your fingers will see for them. Let me guide you."

He guided her deeper into the chamber, then raised her hand above a shrunken head. When he began to lower her hand,

Lyana's breath caught and her eyes winced beneath her scarf. The shrunken head seemed to stare at her, no larger than a pomegranate. When Mahrdor placed her hand upon it, she gasped softly. The skin was smooth, leathery, and cold. Mahrdor moved her hand across it--the lips that were sewn shut, the empty eyes, the wispy hair.

Lyana gritted her teeth. *Think that you touch only old cloth,* she told herself. *Only an old, beaten tunic.*

"Do you know what this is?" Mahrdor said.

"A... a doll's head," she whispered.

He laughed softly. "Yes, child, only a doll. A doll I made myself. I have taught myself the skill, you see--to cut the neck, remove the skull, and stuff the skin with herbs. It is an art, much like dance. I am an artist too, child."

He wrapped his arm around her waist, pulled her away from the head, and placed her hand against a deformed skeleton, its bones twisted and bloated.

"I found this poor soul begging on the streets of Irys," Mahrdor said. "He was a swollen freak, his back twisted and his face bloated like a hippopotamus." He sighed. "Killing him was a mercy, but... he was such a wonder, Tiana! Such a wonder that I kept his bones. Feel them. Run your fingers across them." He forced her hands along the twisted ribs, the withered hip bones, the coiled femurs. "Do you feel the bumps, the grooves?" He sucked in his breath, seeming almost like a man in ecstasy. "They are exquisite."

She nodded, bile in her throat. "They are... fine bones, my lord."

He pulled her away from the skeleton, spun her around, and placed her hand against a mancala board. Instead of seashells or seeds, its pieces were made from dried scarabs. He made her caress the beetles.

"These scarabs ate the flesh off my skeleton," he said. "They are ravenous little beasts! Once they had their fill, and died of overeating, it was a shame to merely toss them out. Dried like this, and still stuffed with human flesh, they make such wondrous little marvels. Can you feel their claws?"

She nodded. "They feel wondrous, my lord."

Next he placed her hand upon a wide, curling scroll that covered a tabletop. Lyana gasped. It was a map! A map of Requiem! Her heart trembled like a bird trapped behind her ribs. Wooden wyverns, each the size of a thimble, stood upon the map. The miniature army was arranged as if flying out of Tiranor, across the sea, and into Requiem through Ralora Beach upon its southern shores.

The invasion plans, Lyana thought. *Stars, he's going to invade through Ralora Beach.*

Her head spun. This beach was undefended, a mere rocky shore leagues from any outpost. King Elethor had to be told. Requiem's army had to move, to defend its beach, to--

Mahrdor placed her hand upon the map, interrupting her thoughts. He moved her fingers across it.

"I made this scroll myself," he said, "from the skin of a weredragon I slew." When she tried to pull her hand back, he held it firmly. He forced her fingers across it. "Feel it, child! Do not be afraid. *Caress* it. *Luxuriate* in it. Enjoy the texture. Do you feel how smooth it is?"

Stars, the skin of a Vir Requis? Is this scroll made from one that I knew? One that I commanded in battle?

She nodded and whispered. "It is most smooth."

"Only human skin feels so smooth," he said. "It is superior to the skin of any animal. Sometimes, when I cannot sleep, I walk into this chamber and just... caress. I like to wrap myself in it sometimes, to feel close to the woman who once wore this skin." He touched her cheek, and she flinched. "Your skin is smooth too, my child."

She swallowed, heart pounding. "I would make a poor scroll, my lord. My... my skin dries easily."

He laughed softly, still holding her hand. "No," he said. "You, as you are, are a greater wonder than any scroll." He sighed. "Do you see, Tiana? Do you see why I brought you here? You are a dancer. You live for the dance! You breathe beauty, wonder, grace, the awe of art. I too am an artist. A collector." He shook his head wistfully. "The men I lead... Soldiers. Fighters. Brutes. They think I command them because I love war, love bloodshed, love killing as they do." He barked a laugh. "Love blood and killing? No. Any brute can slay a man; what is there to love of that? No. I go to war, Tiana, to *collect*, to bring back these wonders. Bones! Skin!" He sucked in his breath, eyes lit with fire. "I admire these treasures, Tiana. And you... you are among the most lovely, wondrous treasures I have seen."

He grabbed her waist with both hands and she gasped. He stared down at her, those blue eyes blazing. Through the silk scarf, he met her eyes.

No! she thought, trembling in his grasp. *No, it's impossible, my scarf looks solid from the outside, only I can see through it, he can't be looking into my eyes, can't be...*

Her limbs shook.

She had to leave this place.

She had to send word to King Elethor, to tell him of the map, to...

His fingers grabbed her silks, tugged gently, and unwrapped them like a gift. The fabric fluttered down, and she stood nude and trembling before him. She kept her chin raised, refusing to lower her head, refusing to cover her nakedness. She was only Tiana here, a dancer from the dunes, but she still had her pride.

He caressed her cheek. "So smooth..."

He led her toward a divan at the back of the room, pulled her down, and kissed her neck. His hands were confident but gentle. He knew what he wanted from her; he would take it, not with violence, not as a warrior... but as a collector. He acted, Lyana thought, as if claiming her--*owning* her--was his right, as if she would give herself to him as naturally as the night gives itself to dawn.

She had never lain with any man but Prince Orin, her betrothed whom Solina had slain. Her throat tightened and her tears burned to think of him. She closed her eyes as Mahrdor lay atop her, as his eyes closed, as he collected her. His breath was rough against her face, and she clenched her jaw.

For my home, she thought. *For Requiem.*

ELETHOR

Elethor, King of Requiem, stood upon Lacrimosa Hill before the leaders he had summoned to his council: A true dragon of the west, a griffin of the east, and a prince in armor upon his horse.

Around them, grass rustled and trilliums bloomed white. Burnt birches spread for miles, but new saplings grew between them. A flock of small, white clouds herded across the sky and distant geese honked. It was a beautiful day, but darkness lay upon Elethor's heart as he regarded his guests.

He stroked his beard as if he could draw strength from it. He had not shaved in a moon's turn, and the beard still felt foreign, too scratchy and hot and altogether not *him*. His father had worn a beard; so had his grandfather. Elethor joked that he was too busy to shave, but in truth, he had grown the beard to *feel* more like a king. On days like today, meeting these foreign leaders, it wasn't helping; he still felt too young, a mere sculptor, not a ruler of Requiem. He looked at his sister who stood beside him, a princess clad in a gown of green and silver, and drew comfort from her eyes.

If the beard doesn't help, at least I have Mori, he thought. The others might see him as too young, too callow, too weak--Elethor the sculptor, the young prince who had never wanted the throne, who had always shunned the court, and kingly beard be damned. But to Mori he was King of Requiem, as noble as their father; he could see that in her eyes, and that soothed him. He turned back to his guests.

"Friends," he said. "I have asked you to meet me here--a council of the great northern kingdoms. Thank you for taking the journey to my home in such a dark hour."

The true dragon, a salvana from the western realms, batted long white eyelashes. No wings grew from his back, yet he floated above the hill like a serpent upon water. A hundred feet long he was, with scales like disks of beaten gold. His beard was white and flowing, his moustache long, and his eyes like crystal orbs. Like all true dragons, he had no human form; the salvanae lived feral in the west, building no homes and forging no metal, but praying and singing in the wild. This salvana was the greatest among them: Nehushtan, a priest and leader of Salvandos.

"It has been three hundred years," the true dragon said, "since I flew above this place, child of stars. The seasons have turned, and once more Requiem calls for aid." When he blinked, his white lashes fanned the grass.

Elethor nodded to him, then turned to his right. A prince of griffins stood there, large as a dragon. His breast, head, and talons were those of a great eagle, noble and white as a winter sky before snowfall. His lower half was that of a great lion, larger than any true lion of the wild, and golden as bales of hay on a fall's sunset. His name was Velathar, son of King Vale, descended from the great Volucris himself, the griffin who had led his kin from captivity in Osanna back home to Leonis Isles. The griffin prince bowed his head to Elethor and gave a low caw.

Finally Elethor looked ahead. A man sat there upon a horse, his beard brown and flowing. A crown of gold sat upon his head, and he was clad in a brown robe embroidered with green trees. A sword hung upon his thigh, the scabbard filigreed with leaves. He was Prince Raelor of Osanna, son of King Aera, descended of the priest-king Silva who had raised Osanna from the ashes of its great wars.

"I have ridden hard for many days, King Elethor," said the prince. "I have answered your summons, though we in Osanna fight the darkness that grows in Fidelium. The dead rise from their tombs under the mountains, forge dark steel kissed with fire, and march across the plains. Already our northern forts have fallen. What urgent matter do you summon me here for in this time of war?"

Elethor rested his hand on his sword's pommel and raised his chin.

"It is a time of war for Requiem too. In the south, Tiranor musters a great army--twenty thousand wyverns fly for Queen Solina, mindless beasts that live for nothing but bloodshed. They are an ancient evil; for a thousand years, their eggs lay as stones in the sand, and now Solina has quickened them with the fiery seed of her lord. These beasts will fly over the sea, and they will invade Requiem, and they will burn this land with their acid. If Requiem falls, a hundred thousand Tiran troops, each armed with spear and crossbow, will follow the wyverns into this land. Solina's ambition goes beyond the destruction of Requiem; she will expand her empire here and build her forts upon your doorsteps. If Requiem should fall, no lands will be safe; not Salvandos to our west, nor Osanna to our east, or even the Griffin Isles across the sea."

Nehushtan blinked his glimmering orbs, fanning the grass with his lashes. His beard swayed and his floating body coiled behind him, golden scales chinking. He spoke in a voice like crumpling paper.

"Child of starlight, this seems to me a feud between Requiem and Tiranor alone. One might say this feud is between King Elethor and Queen Solina; a personal war. Why should we, the peaceful salvanae of the west, concern ourselves with conflicts not our own? We are a peaceful people; we true dragons live for meditation, for starlight, for prayer and wisdom. Not for bloodshed."

The prince of Osanna nodded upon his horse. "The wise salvana speaks truth. They say in my land that King Elethor and Queen Solina were once lovers, that the war between them has grown into a war between their hosts. You call us here for what-- to ask for our aid? Why should Osanna fight your wars when our own borders are threatened?"

Elethor looked at his sister. Mori stared back silently. As always, her soft gray eyes could calm the storm in his soul. He took a deep breath, then turned back to his guests.

"This war is between Requiem and Tiranor, that is true," he said. "Solina does not yet threaten your lands. For years, Tiranor has remained in the southern deserts beyond sea and swamp, and she has grown strong. A great army now lurks there, greater than any in our northern realms. What if this army left the desert? Imagine this great host--so many men and beasts--here in the north, upon your very borders, with no desert or swamp between you and their wrath. Will Solina content herself with conquering Requiem alone? Perhaps. Or would she use this land as a base for further expansion? There aren't enough farms in Requiem to feed her troops; our land is rocky, mountainous, forested and wild. There are great plains of farmland in Osanna; Solina will crave them. There are great fallow fields in Salvandos; Solina will crave them too." He gripped the hilt of his sword. "We must band together to stop Tiranor from leaving her borders. This host threatens Requiem now; it will threaten you tomorrow. Let us join our armies. Let us keep Tiranor in the desert beyond sea and swamp."

He took a deep breath. At his side, Mori nodded, silently agreeing with his words. Elethor looked at his companions: a wise true dragon of the west, an eastern king, and a griffin from distant isles. They looked at one another, silent.

Prince Velathar the griffin broke that silence. He gave a series of caws and chatters, head tilted and wings ruffling. Elethor could not speak the language of griffins, but Prince Raelor of Osanna was descended from the great priest Silva, and he could speak the tongue of beasts. He listened, stroking his beard, and translated the griffin's caws.

"This is good and well for Salvandos and Osanna, says the Griffin Prince. But what of Leonis, the land of griffins? Its isles lie across many leagues of sea, and Tiranor is no threat to them, even should it conquer Requiem. Why should griffins fly to aid dragons?"

Mori approached the griffin, raised her arm, and touched the beast's great white head. For the first time, the princess spoke. Her voice was meek at first, but gained strength with every word.

"Dear Prince Velathar," she said, "I grew up reading stories of your ancestor, the great King Volucris, perhaps the greatest griffin who has lived. When I was a girl, I loved nothing more than hearing tales of Volucris flying to Requiem's aid, sounding his cry, and fighting alongside our Queen Lacrimosa in the Battle of King's Forest. That queen fell here, where we now stand, upon this hill that bears her name. King Volucris fell here too, and we in Requiem still remember his great sacrifice." She looked from companion to companion. "Our ancestors forged great alliances. They fought together against the evil of Dies Irae: griffins, salvanae, men, and Vir Requis. Our kingdoms joined hands then to defeat the evil that roamed this land. It has been many years since those days; have we forgotten the value of friendship since?" Tears sparkled in her eyes. "If you will not fight for the sake of your own realms, fight for that old alliance: for friendship, for justice, and for memory."

She finished her speech with a shuddering breath and stood, looking from one to another. Elethor moved to stand by her and placed a hand on her shoulder. If not for the solemnity of the council, he would have embraced her.

I love you, sister, he thought. *Our father would be proud of you today.*

The guests looked at one another, and Nehushtan spoke first. His scales clinked like a chest of coins as his body undulated above the hill.

"You have spoken well, daughter of starlight, and with much passion. It is true; our four realms fought together once. I myself flew here three centuries ago and fought in the Battle of King's Forest, perhaps the greatest battle this realm has known. Queen Lacrimosa, your ancestor, was a brave and noble queen; for many seasons I mourned her passing." The old dragon sighed. "Yes, I fought alongside Requiem then. But those were different days, long ago. Only seven Vir Requis then flew, the Living Seven whose statues still stand in your city; the rest lay as charred bones upon the land. We of Salvandos could not let those last souls perish; we flew then with wrath, with lightning, with starlight. We were proud to fight at the side of Queen Lacrimosa and her daughters, the warriors Gloriae and Agnus Dei. But now, Princess Mori... now the descendants of Lacrimosa flourish. Thirty thousand dragons live in Requiem, a great host of fire and fang. We in Salvandos hate war more than anything under the stars; today you have the might to fight your war alone."

The priest tilted his head, blinked, and turned aside. He began floating down the hill, his serpentine body coiling behind him.

"Wait!" Mori cried. "Nehushtan, why do you leave us?"

He did not reply. Beard fluttering, the old salvanae rose into the sky like a plume of smoke. Soon he was but a golden thread in the distance, flying west to his ancient realm.

The Prince of Osanna spoke next. His horse sidestepped beneath him and nickered.

"The salvana speaks wisdom," he said. "Thirty thousand dragons fly here. Let them fight this war. Osanna is a great and ancient kingdom; our horses are swift, our steel is bright, and our hearts are brave. Yet when wyverns fly, let dragons fight them! We will fight our wars upon the ground." He shook his head sadly, and his voice softened. "Our kingdoms are allies; that is true. I grieve to see the blood that has spilled here... and the blood that will yet spill. Yet these are dark times, and we face our own threat in the north; we must fight our own enemies rather than yours. I am sorry, King Elethor of Requiem. We cannot help you."

With that, the prince kneed his horse, turned around, and galloped downhill. Soon he was but a speck in the distant fields, raising a cloud of dust as he rode into the east.

Elethor turned to the last of his guests, Prince Velathar. The griffin stared at him, tilted his head, and clawed the earth.

"Prince Velathar," Elethor said. He stared into the griffin's eyes. "My ancestors fought alongside yours. Will you fly with us again? Will you bring aid from your land, an army of griffins as fought here years ago? Let us join our great kingdoms again. Let us fight this evil from the south--for the sake of our old friendship."

Please, he added silently. *Without you, we are alone.*

The griffin lowered his head. He stared at the grass for a long time, perhaps thinking of his ancestors' bones that lay buried here alongside the bones of Queen Lacrimosa. The griffin raised his head and looked west at the distant golden thread--the retreating salvanae. He turned east and looked toward the horse that galloped there.

Finally he lowered his head again and nuzzled his beak against Elethor.

What does that mean? Does he mean to help us?

The griffin pulled back, and his eyes were sad. He gave a solemn shake of his head.

No.

With a great flap of eagle wings and talons that ripped the grass, the griffin soared. Soon he was flying into the horizon, a golden speck fading away.

Elethor and Mori remained upon the hill, alone in the forest. The only sound was the rustling grass. The siblings looked at each other. Mori's eyes were huge and round, the color of storm, and the wind ruffled her chestnut hair.

Elethor squeezed her shoulder. "We fought alone against the phoenixes," he said, "and we defeated them. We will defeat the wyverns too."

Mori lowered her head, held the hilt of her sword, and nodded. She did not need to speak; Elethor knew her thoughts. The same thoughts rattled through his skull.

The phoenixes killed nearly half our people. Only an ancient magic drove them away, not the heat of our fire, nor the sharpness of our fangs. Now a greater army flies against us... and we stand alone.

He pulled his sister close. She leaned against him, and the wind blew across them.

"We will fight alone," Mori whispered, "and we will defeat them. I believe. Deramon is a great warrior. So is Lyana and she will return to us. We will fight the wyverns in the air, and in our tunnels, and upon the mountains, and we will drive them back into the desert."

Elethor nodded. Deramon was a great warrior, it was true. So was Lyana. The rest of their army was composed of green youths, mere children torn from farms, bakeries, and vineyards. The wind seemed to invade his very bones, and he lowered his head.

A roar rose in the south, interrupting his thoughts. Heart thrashing, Elethor turned toward the sound. A black dragon was flying toward him and his sister, rising and dipping in the air.

When the dragon flew closer, Elethor recognized her. She was Lady Treale, the youngest daughter of House Oldnale which ruled the eastern farmlands. A youth of nineteen, Treale had begun squiring to Lady Lyana last year, training to become a knight. With Lyana away, Elethor had sent the girl to patrol the southern border; why did she now fly here outside Nova Vita?

"Treale!" he cried, pulled back from Mori, and shifted into a dragon. Brass scales clanked across him, fire filled his nostrils, and he flapped leathern wings. He took flight in a cloud of smoke.

The black dragon wobbled as she flew toward him, and puffs of weak smoke rose from her nostrils. Then Elethor saw what she carried in her claws, and his breath died.

Stars. Stars, no.

In each front claw, Treale held a body wrapped in a shroud.

They met above a forest clearing, spiraled down, and landed upon the grass. Treale placed the bodies down--the shrouds covered them from head to toe--then shifted into human form. She stood as a woman with smooth black hair, olive skin, and weary dark eyes. When she wobbled on her feet, Elethor shifted too and caught her.

"Treale," he said, examining her. Dirt and blood stained her armor. "Are you hurt?"

She shook her head, eyes haunted. "No, my lord. The blood isn't mine. It's... theirs." She looked at the bodies and her eyes dampened.

Mori came flying toward them, a slim golden dragon. She landed, shifted back into human form, and rushed to embrace Lady Treale; the two were childhood friends. Heart hammering,

Elethor looked at the bodies. The shrouds hid their faces. They seemed so small, so frail.

"Who are they?" he whispered.

Treale looked at the dead and spoke softly.

"They are Tanin and Yara, a farm boy and baker's daughter. They served my father in our lands; they grew and baked our grains. They fell at the border." She looked at Elethor, and horror replaced the grief in her eyes. "When I found them, they were burnt with acid. Their commander, a soldier named Silas, was missing. Wyverns did this, my king." She clenched her fists and her voice shook. "Solina murdered them."

Elethor held her shoulders and stared into her black eyes.

"Did you see the wyverns, Treale?" he asked sternly. "Do they invade Requiem?"

She swallowed. "I saw a dead one on the ground, charred with dragonfire--a great beast all in iron scales like armor. I ordered my men to gut it and bring it to their king; they fly a day behind me. Three live wyverns flew there. When I arrived with my men, they retreated into the south." She snarled. "The cowards invaded, murdered, and fled. I wanted to chase them. I will find them and kill them still! But... I had to bring them back, my king. I had to see them buried. I had to..."

Pain overflowed her words, and she closed her eyes. A tear drew a line through the dirt on her cheek. Elethor held her, kissed her forehead, and looked over her head to the south.

Again you bring death to my door, Solina, he thought. Rage flared within him, so hot that he gritted his teeth. He held Treale close. *Our neighbors abandoned me, but I do not face you alone, Solina. You will find that every dragon in Requiem fights you with a great roar.*

BAYRIN

He limped along the docks, hunched over, cloaked and hooded in ratty old homespun. His hand, black with dirt, reached out in supplication.

"Suns for the poor?" he croaked as sailors walked by. "Spare coins for a poor old beggar, my lords?"

The sailors ignored him and walked on, speaking to one another of finding a winehouse, soft beds, and cheap women to warm them. These ones had not seen land for weeks; they had the hungry look of men too long at sea. Bayrin could not guess what ship they had come from; hundreds lined the docks of Hog Corner. Some were mere fishermen's barges, others merchant ships with embroidered sails. Some were wide and sturdy, built for sailing north, out of the delta and into the salty sea. Others were slim and long and lined with oars, made for rowing south along the River Pallan to distant jungles of spice, jewels, and slaves. Many ships--those farther along the docks, where soldiers patrolled and no beggars dared shuffle--were military machines laden with steel and Tiran fire.

If you wanted news, Bayrin knew, you came to Hog Corner. Centuries ago, it was said, pigs would wallow here in mud, giving the place its name. Squatted upon the northern fringe of Irys, where the Pallan turned from river to delta, Hog Corner still boasted as much mud and stench as ever. Upon its hundred docks, merchants, soldiers, prostitutes, and beggars all mingled and fought and shared their tales. There were no temples in this part of Irys, no palaces or villas or nobles. In the winehouses, brothels, and alleys of Hog Corner, far from the great gilded columns of the city south, Bayrin could hear tales of sea battles, songs of distant lands, and mostly gossip. If you wanted to know which lord bedded which noblewoman, which priest was caught stealing gold, or which officer was smuggling women into the barracks, you came to this place. If the River Pallan was the artery of Tiranor, here was its throbbing heart.

"Suns for the poor, my ladies?" Bayrin croaked in his best beggar's voice. "Spare some old copper suns?"

The young women walked by, faces gaunt and eyes sunken. These ones were the dust eaters, he knew; wretched souls addicted to the southern spice. They would sell their clothes, their bodies, and their souls for but spoonfuls of the stuff. They gave him dead stares and shuffled onward, always seeking, always hunting the next taste of their elixir.

Bayrin grumbled under his hood. When he brushed dirt off his cloak, his own stench wafted and sickened him. He still could not get used to smelling this bad. A year ago, only his cloak would stink; now it seemed to have permeated his hair and skin.

Being a beggar is not my style, he thought. He was a noble son of Requiem, the personal guardian of Princess Mori Aeternum herself. He should not *stink.* A sigh fled his chafed lips.

They send my sister to be a dancer, he thought bitterly, *in a winehouse far in the clean, safe city south--right outside the palace! But old Bayrin... he gets to wallow in mud and stink like the hogs that gave this place its name.*

"Come on, Lyana," he whispered into the night. "Bring me some news of this invasion, and let's leave this cursed city."

He missed home. The memory of Requiem pounded through him every night--the rustle of birches, the beauty of white marble columns, and the loving eyes of his princess. More than anything, he wanted to see Mori again, to hold her, stroke her soft hair, kiss her lips, and never let her go.

If you saw me now, Mori, you'd wrinkle your nose and shove me away in disgust. A smirk twisted his lips. *I should return to Requiem like this, in my foul disguise, and see if your love for me is true.*

"Come on, move it, ya wretches!" rose a voice ahead. Bayrin raised his hooded head, peered into the shadows, and saw three drunken soldiers stumble down the docks. They were leaving the Black Shell, the seediest winehouse in Irys, a place where drunkards and dust eaters spent their paltry coins. Their boots sloshed through puddles, and one drew his sabre and flailed it about haphazardly. A group of sailors and peddlers scurried out of their way, and the soldiers moved on, leaning against one another. They began to sing a slurred song.

"Dragons fly
And dragons burn
Dragons scratch and bite
But Tiran men
With spear and blade
Will bloody dragons smite!"

They began to sing a second verse--this one quite ruder, detailing different parts of dragon anatomy Tiran blades would slice--when the soldiers noticed Bayrin. One kept singing. The others scowled and nudged their comrade.

"What are you looking at, beggar?" one soldier said. "Bugger off, will ya? Go!"

He marched toward Bayrin and kicked, knocking him down. Under his cloak, Bayrin wore boiled leather inlaid with steel rings, but still the kick drove out his breath and spread agony through him. He lay on cobblestones damp with water, blood, and vomit.

"Spare a few copper suns, my lords?" he said, speaking with his grainy beggar's voice. "Spare a few coins for an old, limp beggar before you sail off to smite the bloody dragons?"

The soldier kicked him again. His boot, tipped with steel, slammed into Bayrin's hidden leather armor, sending blooms of pain spreading through him. He grunted.

I am a son of Requiem. I can turn into a dragon. I can kill these men and burn every ship in this port. He ground his teeth, coughed, and forced himself to lie still. He had to wait for Lyana; she met him here every three days, and he hadn't missed a rendezvous yet.

"Pardon, my lords, pardon," he said and began crawling away. Bayrin, the guardsman from Requiem, would have fought and killed these men; here in Tiranor, he was but an old beggar, feeble and groveling.

"He thinks we're lords!" said one of the soldiers, a brawny man with a stubbly face, dented armor, and flushed cheeks. "Do we look like lords, you scum?"

Another kick sent Bayrin crashing down. The soldiers laughed. Boots nudged him and spears poked him. Under his hood, Bayrin snarled. These men were weak. Cowards. They taunted an old, defenseless beggar, yet if they knew who he truly was...

"I say we cut off his head!" cried one. "A little killing to whet the appetite before we go slay some reptiles."

"Shove your spear up him!"

"Cut his guts out!"

The boots kicked, a spear scratched his thigh, and laughter rang. Bayrin crawled along the docks. Ahead rose the Old Mill-- an abandoned mill now turned into a den of dust eaters. Coughing and grunting, Bayrin scuttled toward it on hands and knees. He crawled into the shadows behind its old bricks, leaving the sailors, dust eaters, drunkards, whores, and peddlers behind. The three soldiers followed, laughing and spitting upon him.

"He thinks the shadows can hide him, friends!"

"Good. Let's kill him nice and quiet in the dark."

Bayrin looked around him. He saw nobody but his three tormentors. Only the tallest masts of ships peeked over the roof of Old Mill. Only the loudest drunkards could be heard from behind its brick walls. Nothing but him, three Tiran soldiers, bricks, and shadows.

The soldiers raised their swords.

Bayrin stood up, doffed his cloak, and shifted.

Wings burst out from his back with a thud. Claws and fangs thrust forward. Scales rose across him. The soldiers gasped. Before they could scream, Bayrin slashed his claws. He cut through steel. Blood spurted. Two soldiers fell dead. The third tried to run. Bayrin pounced and bit, and the man's scream died between his jaws.

It took only seconds. The three lay dead and torn apart.

Bayrin shifted back into human form and looked around, heart hammering. Had anyone seen him? His palms sweated and he panted. He had never before dared become a dragon here in Tiranor, especially not after seeing what they had done to Silas.

Stars, if anyone saw...

He stood still, heart hammering, waiting for wyverns to descend upon him, for their acid to wash the flesh off his bones. When long moments passed and no enemies arrived, Bayrin breathed out in relief. From around Old Mill, the same miserable sounds of Hog Corner still rose: the squeals of the town's cheapest women, the grunts of drunkards, the songs of sailors, the creaking of ships on docks, and the peddlers crying out their wares.

With a grunt, Bayrin pulled the three bodies into deeper shadows, around a few barrels, and toward a wharf behind Old Mill. A young woman lay there on the cobblestones, deep in dust's sleep. Praying she would not wake--if she did, he would have to silence her too--Bayrin shoved the bodies into the water. They sank in their armor. With any luck, they would remain in the depths.

He stepped back toward the crowded docks, still lightheaded, to find Lyana waiting for him in shadow.

"Spare a sun for an old beggar, my lady?" he rasped, hunched over and hobbling.

His sister stood in her disguise--hair smoothed and dyed a platinum blond, her pale skin painted a Tiran gold, and her northern eyes hidden behind a scarf. A white cloak draped around her, and she held her walking staff in hand.

"A sun for a dear old man," she said, fished in her pocket for a coin, and held it out.

Bayrin approached her, took the coin, and bowed his head. He whispered. "What news, Lyana?"

Softly she said, "Not here." She raised her voice. "May I buy you a bowl of soup, old man? To warm your old bones?"

He bobbed his head. "Old Mill serves good fish and onion soup, my lady, if it pleases you."

Truth was Old Mill served the worst fish soup in Irys, possibly in all of Tiranor. That served Bayrin well; it meant the fishhouse was empty but for three dust eaters, their heads upon their tables. Soon Lyana and Bayrin sat in the shadowy corner of the common room, eating bland soup with week-old fish from clay bowls. The owner of the fishhouse, a deaf old man, sat in the corner playing mancala against himself; the board was shaped of cracked old clay, and the pieces were mere pebbles. The three dust eaters snored.

Bayrin took a sip of soup, wrinkled his face, and spat it back into the bowl. "Horrible stuff, this. I think I swallowed a few drops too." He leaned forward. "What have you learned?"

He could not see through her scarf, but somehow he knew her eyes were haunted. Her skin was dyed gold, but somehow he knew that beneath that dye she was pale. Her hand trembled around her spoon.

"Bayrin, I met him! General Mahrdor himself! I danced for him at the River Spice, and... in his home."

He slowly placed down his spoon. "You... what?"

She nodded.

Bayrin tasted the soup again and forced himself to swallow. "Lyana! For a year you've danced for a thousand soldiers, and you barely learned what hand they toss a spear with. Then one day you meet the general of Tiranor's hosts... and get invited to his house?"

She nodded. "He liked my dancing."

Excitement leaped in Bayrin. For a year, he had been sneaking between Tiranor and Requiem, delivering what paltry knowledge Lyana gleaned--what formations she saw wyverns fly in, what new names soldiers gave their phalanxes, or how many wagons of helms and spearheads she saw leave the forges. They knew Tiranor was mustering a great army, and they knew an invasion was near, but the important knowledge--the date of the invasion and its location--eluded them. Would Mahrdor deliver this knowledge to her?

Alongside his excitement, sourness spread. Lyana, his sister... dancing for Mahrdor himself in his villa. Bayrin had invited enough young women to his own home to know what Mahrdor wanted.

"Lyana, did he touch you?" he asked, eyes narrowed. He clutched his spoon like a sword. "If he did, I will... I will..."

"Will what, eat his soup?" He could feel her glare through her scarf. "Bayrin, unless you can cut through Mahrdor's breastplate with a wooden spoon, focus on what's important now. I saw a map in his villa. A map of Tiranor and Requiem with wooden wyverns arranged for invasion. Ralora Beach, Bay. That's where he's going to attack. It'll be on summer solstice; he talked of leaving that morning." She reached across the table and clutched his hand. "We finally found what we came for. Leave. Tonight. Tell Elethor the news. The invasion is only seventeen days away."

Bayrin looked around nervously. As blind Tiana, his sister was meek and quiet, but today bits of Lady Lyana flared--learned, lecturing, and *loud*. The dust eaters, however, continued to drool contentedly at their tables. The deaf cook was picking his ear while squinting at the mancala board. Bayrin let out a shaky breath and glared at his sister.

"All right, Lyana, we fly home tonight." He placed down his spoon. "Right now."

She shook her head. "You fly. I'm staying here."

He looked around again, leaned forward, and hissed. "Lyana! Forget it. You saw what they did to Silas. These people don't play games. Three soldiers attacked me tonight. Their bodies lie at the bottom of the Pallan, breastplates slashed with dragon claws. Mahrdor will notice three missing men. If he finds their bodies and sees the claw marks, he'll go hunting dragons."

His sister gave him a crooked smile. "What dragons? I am but Tiana, the Blind Beauty, the dancer from the southern dunes. And I've gained his trust--or at least his lust." She squeezed his hand. "Bay, I've spent a year working for this. I can't leave so soon. I will learn more. If I charm him, he might even take me on the invasion; generals have been known to take mistresses to war. He--"

"He wants to invade my kingdom, Lyana. I don't want him invading my sister too. No way. You agreed to dance for Requiem, not to... to..." He felt his cheeks flush.

"It won't come to that. He only wants me to dance; that is all I will do for him."

She patted his hand, but Bayrin heard the hesitation in her voice.

She's lying, he thought. *She will lie with the enemy for Requiem; she might have done so already.* The thought sickened him more than the stale soup.

"Lyana," he finally said, "as your older brother, I forbid it. You will not stay."

She scoffed, blowing out her breath so loudly it blew back a strand of her hair. "Do you? Bayrin, you might be my older brother, but I am a knight. You are not. I am betrothed to our king. You are not. And I will choose my path, not you." She rose to her feet, leaned forward, and kissed his cheek. Her voice softened. "Go home, Bayrin. Warn our people. Be safe. I love you, brother."

He stood up, still trembling. He wanted to grab her, to drag her with him, to take her away from this... this nightmare city that swarmed with hatred, blood, and acid. But before he could react, she spun and left the fishhouse, her cloak fluttering. He remained standing in shadow.

"Goodbye, Lyana," he whispered. "I love you too, sister. Be careful. Stars, be careful."

He stepped outside into a night of vomiting drunkards, sailors tugging whores, and dust eaters licking their desires with wild eyes. He stepped behind Old Mill where blood still coated the cobblestones. He leaped into the water where bodies still lay. He swam. Underwater, he could see torches flicker above, the hulls of ships, and the glint of fallen coins. He rose for air and sank again. His eyes stung and worry gnawed his bones.

Stars, Lyana. Be careful. Return to us soon.

The River Pallan flowed into a delta, thick with reeds. The lights of the city faded behind him. Flowing toward the sea, he summoned his magic.

Dark wings rose, spilling water. A shadow soared. A dragon flew in the night, flying north, flying home.

ELETHOR

He stood above the twin graves, head lowered, despair clutching at his throat.

"You fly now in our starlit halls," he said. His eyes stung. "Fly well, Yara and Tanin, warriors of Requiem."

A wave of tears spread over the crowd. Weeping rose in swells. Thousands had come to the funerals--soldiers, farmers, tradesmen, the old and the young. They covered Lacrimosa Hill where years ago Requiem's great queen had fallen in battle. They wore white robes--Requiem's color of mourning--fastened with silver birch leafs, sigils of beauty and peace. The families of the slain lay upon the graves, clutching the tombstones and crying to the sky.

Warriors? Elethor thought, looking at the families who wept--mothers gasping for breath, fathers sobbing, siblings barely old enough to fly. *No, they were not warriors. Tanin was but a farmer's boy, Yara the daughter of a baker--youths I sent south to die.*

True warriors had once guarded Requiem, thousands of men and women trained to defend their realm. They lay now in thousands of other graves, their tombstones dotting the hill like stone flowers. Grass rustled here but no more trees; the holy birches of Requiem had burned in the war last year, charred boles falling like so many bodies.

If she can, Solina will kill everyone who weeps here, Elethor thought. *If I cannot stop her, we won't even lie in graves. Our bones will lie charred among our toppled halls.*

Mother Adia, High Priestess of Requiem, stood at his side. Cloaked in white, she was a tall woman, cold and handsome as a marble statue. She raised her arms and sang above the cries of the crowd.

"As the leaves fall upon our marble tiles, as the breeze rustles the birches beyond our columns, as the sun gilds the mountains above our halls--know, young child of the woods, you are home, you are home." She raised her head to the heavens. "Requiem! May our wings forever find your sky."

Across the hill, the children of Requiem repeated the prayer. Elethor looked above to that sky and saw dragons there, hundreds of them. Nearly all the old City Guard had fallen last year. Lord Deramon had raised a thousand more recruits--youths from across the land--and they now roared above, wings beating and breath steaming. The sight of them soothed Elethor. They were perhaps merely the children of farmers and tradesmen, youths who had never held a sword or shield, but their breath was still hot, their claws still sharp.

When you invade us again, Solina, you will find us ready. You will find Requiem's roar still loud.

The people dispersed slowly, holding one another and shedding tears. Most still bore scars from the phoenix fire. Many had lost limbs, eyes, faces. Many had lost parents, siblings, children. Yet even now they mourned two more fallen. Even now they craved life and wept for its loss. Solina had not taken their humanity; that soothed Elethor as much as the dragons above.

Lord Deramon approached him, a white cloak of mourning draped across his chain mail and breastplate. His calloused hands clutched an axe and sword. The grizzled warrior, his flaming red beard streaked with white, bowed his head.

"My king," he said, "let us fly together."

Elethor nodded, summoned his magic, and shifted. He took flight as a brass dragon, flames trailing from his jaws. Deramon shifted too and flew beside him, coppery and clanking, a burly beast of a dragon. They left Lacrimosa Hill and headed toward Nova Vita, capital of Requiem, which rose white and pure from the charred forest.

"How are the new recruits?" Elethor asked him, the wind nearly drowning his words. He glided on a current.

Deramon snorted a blast of fire. "Mere youths. They are soft. They weep at night in the bowels of Castra Murus; I hear them." He growled. "But I will harden them, my lord. They will fly as warriors."

Elethor nodded, but his belly knotted. They had raised new forces for Requiem, but were they enough to hold back Solina? A thousand sentries now guarded Nova Vita, a new City Guard. A thousand more flew along the southern border, patrolling the wastelands of swamp and sea that separated Requiem from the desert. When he looked south of the city, he saw the remainder of their forces training in fallow fields--three thousand soldiers of the Royal Army drilling with swords or flying as dragons.

I lead a few thousand callow, frightened youths... against the might and wrath of a desert empire.

"Will it be enough, Deramon?" he asked. Wisps of cloud streamed around them. "Solina is raising a great host. Our spies speak of myriads of wyverns and men. Will you harden these youths in time?"

Our spies. He snorted to himself. Those spies were his best friend, Bayrin Eleison, and his betrothed, Lady Lyana. Aside from his sister, they were the people he loved most in the world, and yet he could not speak their names today. *To speak their names is too painful. Too dangerous. Today Bayrin is more than my friend, and today Lyana is more than my betrothed. They are the hope of Requiem.*

Deramon growled. Smoke rose from his nostrils, nearly hiding his head. "They will be ready, Elethor. They will fight to the death for you." The old warrior looked at the young king.

"Requiem will stand, my lord... or she will fall with a roar that will echo through the ages."

Elethor grumbled under his breath. "I prefer the former."

They reached the city. Wings scattering clouds, Elethor looked down upon his home. Nova Vita's walls rose from burnt trees, a ring of white. Dragons perched upon the crenellations, wings folded and eyes scanning the horizons. Beyond the walls, the city rolled upon hills: the palace, its columns soaring; the temple, its silver dome bright in the sun; two forts that bookended the city with towers and banners; and thousands of homes and workshops built of craggy white bricks.

Every house lost a soul, Elethor thought. *Every house mourns.*

He parted from Deramon, leaving the old warrior to clank and snort his way toward Castra Murus, the squat barracks of the Guard. Wind whistling under his wings, Elethor dived toward Requiem's palace. Even now, over a year since Solina had killed his father and brother, it felt strange to rule here. He still did not feel like a king, only the young prince. Every time he flew toward this edifice of marble, Elethor wanted to turn tail, flee into the forest, and spend his days sculpting, stargazing, and forgetting this war.

And yet every time, he tightened his jaw, narrowed his eyes, and flew between the marble columns into the hall of his fathers.

Upon the marble tiles, he shifted back into human form and walked, boots thumping. The throne lay across the hall, woven of twisting oak roots. But today Elethor did not walk toward this ancient seat. He crossed the hall, stepped through a doorway, and entered the east wing of the palace. Here, in a great chamber of stone, hung a dead wyvern.

Elethor stood before the corpse and stared.

Stars, look at it, he thought.

Lady Treale had found the creature, burnt and bloated, in the southern swamps by the bodies of Tanin and Yara. Some had wanted to bury it, others to burn it. Elethor had refused.

"Clean it and stuff it," he had told them. "Hang it up for us to study."

More eyebrows had risen when he insisted they hang the creature in the palace. Surely a dusty courtyard, or a barracks, or even a temple could store the beast? But no. Elethor had insisted. He wanted this creature here, in his home, under the same roof where he slept, ate, and waited for fire. He wanted to look at this creature every day, to stare at its fangs, its claws, its dead glare. This thing had killed two of his people; he would keep it close.

He felt so small standing before the wyvern. It hung on chains thicker than his arms. It must have been fifty feet long from nose to tail's tip; longer than but the greatest dragon. Dark scales covered it, square and metallic like plates of armor. It had only two legs, not four like a dragon, but those legs ended with claws as long, thick, and sharp as the heaviest greatswords in Requiem's armories; they made dragon claws seem like mere daggers. The beast's jaw thrust out into yet another blade, this one longer and wider than a man; Elethor imagined that it could crush through a dragon's scales like a spear into a spring doe.

Last time Bayrin had returned with news, he had reported an army of these beasts, twenty thousand strong. He had claimed they could spew acid, burning flesh off bones like fire eats leaves off trees. Elethor clenched his jaw as he stared at the great, hanging corpse.

Wings thudded and emerald scales flashed outside the window. Claws clattered against marble tiles behind Elethor. He turned to see, through the doorway, a lanky green dragon land in the palace hall.

"Bayrin!" he cried out.

His friend had been gone to Tiranor for three moons. The green dragon looked exhausted; his tongue lolled, his chest heaved, and his ears drooped. With a snort of smoke, he shifted into human form. Where a dragon had panted now stood a gangly young man, his shock of red hair wild, his eyes green and weary.

"Hello there, El," Bayrin said and walked toward the east wing. "Good to be home, and... *stars above,* what's wrong with your *face?*"

Standing in the doorway, Elethor uncomfortably scratched his beard. "It's... a beard. I figured I'd grow one."

Bayrin squinted and leaned closer. "*That's* a beard? I thought a weasel was attacking you; I was just about to tear it off." He shook his head in wonder. "By the stars, you're turning into your father, El. And what the abyss is that behind you?" He elbowed Elethor aside and stepped into the east wing where the dead wyvern hung. "Are you hiding any mistresses here, or... oh *bloody stars.*"

Facing the hanging wyvern, Bayrin gaped. A strangled cry fled his throat, and he drew his sword.

"It's dead, Bay!" said Elethor and pushed his friend's sword down. "Don't cut my head off!"

Bayrin let out a stream of curses, slammed his sword back into its scabbard, and shoved Elethor back.

"Merciful stars, El! I just spent three moons in Tiranor counting those creatures. The last thing I need is to find one here!" He gave the beast a sidelong glance. "Even if it's dead, stuffed, and hanging from chains. Stars, they're ugly critters, aren't they? Almost as ugly as that hairy thing on your face." He shuddered. "Do you remember our old nurse, the one who once slapped me for stealing her wooden teeth and stuffing them into Lyana's skirts? This creature reminds me of her." He gave

Elethor his own sidelong glance. "Come to think of it, so does your beard; I recall she had a bit of one herself."

Elethor embraced his friend. "Welcome home, Bay. Tell me the news! What did you learn? How is..." He swallowed, sudden fear twisting his heart. "How is Lyana?"

Bayrin sighed and looked back at the hanging wyvern. "She's in better shape that our friend here. But I'm worried. El, the invasion is near, and she thinks she knows where Solina will attack."

For long moments, Bayrin spoke, telling of his time in Tiranor: of the ships mustering for war in the docks; of the wyverns that drilled above Irys in battle formations; of Silas executed in town square; and of Lyana dancing for General Mahrdor, learning of a journey on summer solstice, and seeing a map of wyverns invading Ralora Beach.

When he was done speaking, Elethor stared silently at the hanging wyvern.

If Lyana is right, thousands of these creatures will fly into Requiem this moon. Memories of the Phoenix War pounded through him: burning homes, lacerated children, Solina's lips against his, and her dagger slicing his face. Her last words to him echoed.

I will kill them all, Elethor! she had screamed, his blood on her face. *I will burn them all with my fire. You will watch! And then you will crawl to me and beg to be mine.*

He left the wyvern and entered his throne room. He walked toward the Oak Throne, sat between its twisting roots, and gazed upon his hall. Bayrin came to stand before him, hair draggled and face smeared with mud.

"Am I a good king, Bayrin?" Elethor asked, voice low.

Bayrin raised his eyebrows. "You could give me a castle or two, command a few concubines to warm my bed, and I wouldn't mind a golden Bayrin statue in the city square... but otherwise you're doing fine."

Elethor sighed and looked upon the wide hall, the columns topped with dragon capitals, and the charred birches that creaked outside.

"I sent her into danger, Bay. They burned Silas in the town square. If... if they catch Lyana..."

Elethor's throat constricted. He had loved Solina for so many years, a love of fire, pain, and blinding passion. His love for Lyana was newer and had grown gradually, not a crashing flame, but warm embers that heated slowly. Would his first love kill his second?

Bayrin raised his chin and clenched his fists. "My sister outstubborns mules to pass the time. I'd drag her back in chains, if I had any." He sighed. "She will learn what more she can, and she will return. On the summer solstice our future will unfold: for Requiem, for Tiranor, for Lyana... for us. The war is coming, El. It flares again this moon."

War. Elethor's jaw clenched and icy waves rose inside him. His fingertips trembled. *How many more graves will I stand over? How many more families will I watch mourn?*

He nodded and rose to his feet. "I'll summon a council of the highborn. I'll fly to Oldnale Manor today. We will speak--the three great houses of our realm--of how to crush this threat."

Bayrin gaped at him, white showing all around his irises. "Fly to *Oldnale Manor?* Summon a council? Elethor! Solina is at our doorstep. Call the banners. Lead the Royal Army south-- today, now, right after you shave your ridiculous beard. We meet Solina over the shore. We kick her lovely golden backside back into the desert."

"No, Bay." Elethor shook his head. "I will not lead Requiem to a rushed war--not without first discussing it with the highborn."

"What's to discuss?" Bayrin raised his hands to the heavens. "Stars above, Elethor, let's fly south now. We'll fly there together.

You, me, and these three thousand toddlers you've trained into an army. It's war again and I'm not missing out on the fun."

Elethor laughed mirthlessly and traced the scar splitting his face, the scar Solina had drawn. "This is what the fun of war gave me." He sighed. "Bay, summer solstice is twelve days from today, isn't it? The flight south will take six days, seven if we're slow. That gives us some time." He bitterly twisted his jaw. "You know what Lord Yarin Oldnale thinks of me, what many of the people think too; that I'm but a youth, inexperienced and irrational. I will not fly to war on a whim." He raised his hand to silence Bayrin, who had begun to protest. "War is here, Bay, I know that. And we will fight this war. But we will meet first-- House Aeternum, House Eleison, and House Oldnale from the eastern farms--like the great councils my father would hold." He clasped Bayrin's shoulder. "Stay here, Bay. Stay with Mori. I will summon the farmlords and be back here in four days."

Bayrin's face changed like the sea in sunrise. "Mori," he whispered. "Damn it, El, I missed her." He ran a hand through his hair, sniffed at his clothes, and cleared his throat. "How do I look?"

"Slightly worse than the dead wyvern."

"Good enough!" He turned to leave, then looked back and sighed. "If I weren't eager to see your sister, I'd drag you south right now. You got lucky. Fly fast, El. Stars, you better be back here on time. Twelve days, my friend. Twelve days until twenty thousand of these buggers knock on our doors."

The two embraced--a long, wordless, crushing hug. Then Elethor stepped outside, shifted into a dragon, and kicked off the palace stairway. His wings billowed with air, and he soared over the city.

"The wait is over, Solina," he whispered as the wind whistled around him. He remembered the softness of her lips, the warmth of her body, and the bite of her blade. "You were my love. You were my life. You will die in my fire."

SOLINA

She stood in her chambers, twin blades in hands, clad in a robe of golden weave embroidered with tiny pomegranates. She stared into her tall bronze mirror and saw a queen, a scarred woman, a holy daughter of the Sun God, and a spurned soul lost in endless desert.

Around her glittered the glory of her dynasty: platinum chalices inlaid with ruby ibises, tapestries of jackals and falcons, jewelled sabres with pommels shaped as suns, and chests of gems and spices. Blankets woven of gold and silver adorned her bed of ivory. Outside her arched windows, her oasis spread to rolling dunes kissed with sunlight. By the brightest window stood the tools she had brought here for him: chisels, hammers, and three great blocks of marble.

"It was to be your nook," she whispered. "Your place to sculpt while I stood nude before you, watching you form me from stone." She touched her left blade to her lips where he would kiss her. "Oh, Elethor... this was a chamber for us."

She would bring him here. But now she would bring him in chains. Now she would hurt him. Now her soul would forever remained split like her face where the scars of fire ran.

"You could have sculpted me with hammers, but now these hammers will break your bones, Elethor. I will break your spine one segment at a time as you scream and beg me to kill you." She closed her eyes; they burned with tears. "Why did you refuse me, Elethor? Why did you drive me to this?"

She turned away from the marble and tools, walked to a window, and stood with the sunlight upon her. The steeples of

Irys rose before her, carved of polished sandstone capped with
platinum. Far in the south, past leagues of sand, she could just
make out a distant patch of green: the oasis of Iysa, a twin to Irys,
where the small oranges she craved grew in winter. Her kingdom
rolled beyond the horizon, yet what were treasure and glory worth
if she had none to share them with?

I could have shared them with...

A deep, dark memory stirred inside her, clawing at the
prison she had buried it in. She felt its cold breath in the core of
her being.

No.

She clenched her fists.

No.

That memory was still too raw, still too real, a demon
inside her that she dared not awake. She placed her hand on her
belly. She trembled, closed her eyes, and bit down hard.

That one will remain buried. That pain I dare not feel again.

She spun toward her chamber doors, intricate works of art
carved of olivewood and embossed with silver falcons.

"Ziz!" she shouted.

The doors opened and her slave stepped inside, a demure
young woman. Her platinum hair fell in braids, and her blue eyes
looked up with fear, then down at her toes. She wore a dress the
color of sand, its hems lined with blue tassels. She was a desert
child, the daughter of nomads--a good slave.

"My queen," the girl said, eyes downcast.

"Come here, Ziz. Stand beside me."

The girl crossed the chamber and joined Solina by the
window. The desert wind blew her hair. When Solina thrust her
blade, Ziz gasped but did not scream. Red bloomed across her
gown like a desert flower. She looked up, eyes huge blue pools,
wondering, betrayed. Solina held her as she died, kissed her
forehead, and laid her down at her feet. She had needed this,

needed to kill, needed to feel the warmth of blood on her fingers, see the light of life extinguished from a pair of eyes. She pulled her blade free and licked the blood from it thoughtfully. *Blood kills the memories.* She gazed upon her kingdom.

"Soon the palace will be empty of slaves," spoke a deep, smooth voice.

Solina turned to see General Mahrdor at the doorway, clad in armor, his sword at his side. His face and bald head were tanned a deep gold, and his eyes glimmered as they stared at her. Solina realized that her gown was open too far, revealing more flesh than it hid.

"You come to make love to me," she said.

He raised his eyebrows, entered the chamber, and closed the door behind him. "I come to discuss our war. I come to report of our troops' morale. I come to ask for more armor and spears. Are you so vain that you think every man at your door comes to ravage you?"

She couldn't help it. She gave him a crooked smile. "You are not every man; the others would die if they entered this chamber." She doffed her robe and stood naked before him. "Love me. I know why you're here. Do it. Roughly. Make it hurt."

He stood staring in silence. Blood pooled at their feet. She raised her chin and stared into his eyes, refusing to blink first. Finally he stepped over the body and grabbed her. He pulled her to her bed, tossed her upon her blankets of silk and golden thread, and climbed atop her. He claimed her. He hurt her. He gave her sweet pain to shout with, and she drove her fingernails down his back, and she bit his shoulder until she tasted blood. When she tossed her head back and closed her eyes, she thought of Elethor and screamed.

When he was done, she shoved him aside, rose to her feet, and grabbed her gown of white silk. She pulled it over her body; it kissed her skin with a thousand kisses.

"Come," she said, "we will inspect the lines. Show me what you've done with my army."

She returned to the window and whistled--a long, loud sound like a bird of prey. The thud of wings sounded in the courtyard below. A growl rose into a screech. With a flash of scales, her wyvern ascended a hundred feet, from the cobblestones below to her window. The beast's wings pounded the air, bending palm trees below and billowing her curtains and hair. His scales clattered, thick plates like iron armor. His eyes blazed red, his teeth snapped, and smoke rose from his nostrils. His name was Baal, and he was the greatest of the wyverns, a forge of acid, a behemoth of wrath and muscle and bloodlust.

Solina shuddered to see him, a shudder of awe and delight. For a thousand years, the eggs had lain in the desert sands, hard and polished like obsidian. For a thousand years, the priests of Tiranor, and the kings and queens of the Phoebus Dynasty, had prayed and chanted and cast their spells... and the eggs still slept.

But I... I quickened them with the seed of flame, with the life of my lord the Sun God. Her lips pulled back in a grin, and she inhaled sharply, savoring the acrid stench of the creature. *My prayers were answered; my glory flies across the desert. I am a mother of beasts. I am a goddess of wyverns.*

With her foot, she nudged her dead slave halfway out the window.

"Eat," she said.

Baal tilted his head, regarded the dead woman, then thrust forward like a striking asp. He took the body into his mouth, tossed back his head, and swallowed. His neck bulged and his scales clanked as the body moved down his throat.

"Turn," Solina told him. "I will ride you."

He turned sideways, still clinging to the palace wall. Solina climbed out her window and into his saddle. She grabbed the pole that was fastened there; it bore her banner, a golden sun upon a white field. With a crooked smile, she looked over her shoulder at Mahrdor, who still stood in her chamber.

"Ride behind me," she said.

Soon they flew upon Baal over the city. Solina gazed upon the glory of her home. From up here she could see all of Irys. The Pallan halved the city, a trail of silver-blue, a giver of life in the desert. Countless ships sailed down its waters, from the distant lands of the south, to the docks of Hog's Corner, and finally into delta and sea. Along the riverbanks rose the villas of the wealthy, their gardens lush and their columns tall. Beyond them coiled cobbled streets lined with houses and shops of mudbrick. Her palace glittered behind her, a glory of polished limestone and gold; only the great Temple of the Sun stood as tall. All around the city, her empire rolled into sand and haze and wonder.

Beyond the oasis, upon the rock and sand of her desert, her army awaited. Thousands of chariots stood tethered to horses, their wheels spiked, their riders armed with whips and bows. Thousands of soldiers bustled between tents, armed with spears and arrows tipped with poison. Greatest of all, twenty thousand wyverns stood upon the sand that had hatched them, as large as dragons, as cruel as the desert sun; they would lead the charge into Requiem, crushing the Weredragon Kingdom and paving way for her ground troops.

As she flew above, the army saw her banner, and they cried for her glory, a great cheer that rolled across the desert. Men raised spears and wyverns screamed.

"Queen Solina!" they cried. "Golden daughter of Phoebus!"

"Elethor has only five thousand soldiers," she said to Mahrdor as the wind whipped her hair. "Even if he summons every child and old woman in Requiem, small and feeble dragons in flight, he cannot stop us. We will crush them like the insects that they are."

Behind her in the saddle, Mahrdor grunted in approval. "My collection will grow. After you kill the Boy King, may I have his bones?"

She laughed. "You may have some before I kill him; I think that would amuse me. Turn one bone into a flute, and I will play it for him." She raised her banner high; it caught the wind and thudded. She shouted to the army. "Soon you will feed upon weredragon flesh! Soon you will bring light and fire to the world!"

They howled. Men clanged spears against shields. The wyverns screeched, shaking the desert. The sun shimmered, a beacon of her lord. Solina raised her head, closed her eyes, and let the light of the Sun God bathe her with glory.

MORI

She stepped into the temple, harp in hand, and took a shuddering breath. Her head swam, her lungs constricted, and the columns swayed before her. She forced a deep breath.

"Be calm, Mori," she whispered. "Be calm. Breathe. You can do this."

She took a step deeper into the temple. She had always feared this place--there were so many priestesses here, so many people come to pray, so many sick and wounded come for healing. The voices all echoed in the halls, and their feet all pattered, and the movements of robes danced like ghosts. One time all the sounds and figures had frightened Mori so much, she had run outside, shifted into a dragon, and fled the city for two days.

"But today they need me," she whispered, lips trembling. "Today I will face my fear."

She took another step.

The hall stretched before her, marble tiles white and veined with blue. Two children ran across the hall, chasing each other with wooden swords. A young priest walked between columns, carrying towels, and smiled at her. Mori's heart leaped into flight. Suddenly the priest's fluttering robes were burning. Before her eyes, they became phoenix wings, showering fire and flying toward her. Suddenly the children no longer played with wooden swords but lay bloody, steel swords buried in their bellies. Their eyes gazed at her, begging, bleeding.

"Princess Mori," said the swooping phoenix.

Mori gulped and blinked. Again she saw only a priest before her, a young man who smiled at her. She took a shuddering breath, clutched her luck finger behind her back, and managed to smile.

Only two children and a priest, she thought. *I'm safe here. I'm safe. There are no phoenixes anymore, no dead children, no war. Those days are gone.*

She kept walking.

Before the war, Mori could always retreat into the library, a great shadowy chamber underground. Only the royal House Aeternum carried the keys to the library; she could find solitude there, solace from the voices, from the movements of too many swaying cloaks, from all those crowds that spun her head. She would curl up underground with a good book, and she would read for hours. Inside the world of books, she was never afraid; she could be brave as a knight or wise as a wizard. There were no voices that were too loud, no movements too jarring, no crowds that spun around her and stole her breath.

"But now the people here need me, the people in this temple," she whispered to herself. "They need me just as much as the books do. I will comfort them however I can."

She swallowed and took another step.

Step by step, heart racing, she crossed the hall and entered the Chamber of Healing.

The domed roof towered above her, painted with scenes of stars and wise dragons of old. Columns surrounded the room, their capitals shaped as birch canopies inlaid with silver. Three rows of beds stood upon the marble tiles, and in them lay the wounded. They raised their heads, smiled at Mori, and those who still had hands waved them.

Blood rained. Fire burned. Tiran soldiers stormed the hall, plunging blades into flesh, and Queen Solina flew as a phoenix, burning bodies into ash, and...

No. Mori closed her eyes and tried to remember what Mother Adia had taught her. She breathed in slowly, filling her lungs top to bottom, held her breath, and exhaled it. She breathed deeply three times, then opened her eyes and saw no more fire, no more blood. She nodded, tightened her lips, and walked toward the wounded.

"Princess Mori," said one man who lay abed. The war had taken his four limbs; he lay wrapped like a babe in swaddling clothes. He smiled at her. "We missed you, my princess."

She smiled back. "Hello, Rowyn. I missed you too." She pulled a scroll from her pack, unrolled it, and showed it to him. "I painted these flowers for you."

He whistled softly. "They're beautiful. You know how I love sunflowers. I used to grow them before the war."

She placed the scroll by him and walked on. She reached a bed where lay Alandia, the daughter of a farmer. She had been burned so badly her face was still bloated, and her arms ended with stumps.

"Princess Mori," she whispered.

Mori knew that Alandia still lived with daily pain, even today, a year after the war. Mori produced another scroll, this one painted with horses. She knew how Alandia loved horses; she had owned two before the war.

"Here, Alandia, more horses!" she said. "See? I drew Clipper and Starshine."

The two horses now lay buried, two more victims of the war. Mori had painted them from memory a hundred times for the burnt girl. She placed the scroll on the bed.

She kept moving between the beds, handing out gifts. One child had lost his eyes and ears; she gave him a box of scented oils. If he was blind and deaf, she would let him smell a hint of life. Another man, once a soldier, had lost his sanity; he lay bound to his bed, mumbling and weeping. Mori kissed his forehead and recited old poems to him, poems he had once loved. As she whispered, she saw his face calm, and she stroked his hair until he slept. A hundred wounded filled this temple, still lingering in pain, and Mori knew these ones would stay here forever. Their bodies or minds were destroyed, their families were gone, and their houses had fallen.

Elethor can fight for them, she thought. *Bayrin can guard them. But I... I can soothe them. I can bring them some joy in their world of pain.*

When she had distributed her gifts, she began to play her harp. Lady Lyana was a great warrior, Elethor a sculptor, Bayrin a trickster; she, the young Princess Mori, had always found her talent in music. She closed her eyes as she played her harp, and she sang her song. It was an old tune of Requiem, sung among the birches for thousands of years, even in the Golden Age before the great wars had toppled Requiem's glory. It was a song of birch leaves in wind, of wings on the sky, of marble columns rising into the night... but as Mori sang, it became too a song of warmth over fear, of whispers into a pool of loneliness, of broken souls mending under a sky of fire. It was the song of her life: of her tragedy in Castellum Luna where she had lost her brother and her innocence; of her war over Nova Vita where she had seen so many slain; and of her hope for healing, her hope for a new dawn in Requiem. It was a song of starlight.

She played the last note, a haunting whisper and the flutter of dragon wings fading into nightfall, and opened her eyes. She saw that across the hall, clad in white silk, stood Mother Adia. The High Priestess looked upon her with soft eyes and smiled sadly.

"My princess," she said.

Mori approached the older woman and embraced her. "Mother Adia! I practiced the breathing you taught me last night, and I thought of birches in the wind, like you said I should, and I had only one nightmare."

A year ago, the wounds of war fresh, nightmares had twisted her nights. Until dawn, Mori would see Solina burn her brother, feel Lord Acribus grab and choke her, and see dead children strewn across Nova Vita. Slowly, moon after moon, she worked with Mother Adia to breathe, to think of birch leaves, to see stars and flowers in the night, not fire and blood.

Mother Adia kissed her cheek. "I'm glad, Mori. It will still be a while, but I hope that soon you'll sleep the whole night with no nightmares at all."

Mori nodded, feeling warm and safe in the embrace. To sleep the whole night through--without waking up breathless, trembling, and covered in cold sweat? She did not think it possible. Not now, with Bayrin and Lyana away in the south. Before Bayrin had left for Tiranor, she would sleep in his arms, and when nightmares woke her, she could huddle closer to him, kiss him, and feel safe. Now she slept alone, and she missed Bayrin so badly that her stomach ached.

"I hope so," she whispered into Mother Adia's robes. They were soft like the birch leaves she thought of at night.

Mother Adia took her from the Chamber of Healing and into halls and rooms throughout the temple. They spent an hour meeting healers in training, carpenters building new beds, and priests organizing chambers of supplies: bandages, vials of silkweed milk, needles and stitches, bone saws and scalpels, pots of healing herbs, and codices full of medical drawings that both scared and soothed Mori.

War will flare again. Bayrin spoke of armies mustering in the south, and she knew the second invasion could begin any day now. Her knees trembled, and she clutched her luck finger behind her back, the sixth finger on her left hand.

This time, when fire rains and steel bites, we'll be ready to heal the wounded. Adia will be ready with her herbs and bandages, and I'll be ready with my song and harp.

She stepped outside onto the marble stairs of the temple.
The wind pinched her cheeks and played with her hair. She
looked upon the city of Nova Vita, and peacefulness settled upon
her like golden dawn upon storming sea. The forest was still
charred, but new saplings grew between the blackened stumps.
Many houses still lay in ruin, but masons were busy as ants,
building new homes. Many graves covered Lacrimosa Hill
beyond the city walls, but many dragons still lived, gliding
overhead.

"Come back to us soon, Bayrin and Lyana," she whispered
into the wind.

The flap of wings ruffled her hair. A brass dragon came
flying toward her, scales clinking and breath snorting. Mori
shielded her eyes with her palm. It was her brother, King Elethor.
Smoke streamed from his nostrils in two trails. His claws
clattered against the temple's marble stairs, and he folded his
wings. He tossed his head, snorted flickers of fire, and shifted.

When he stood in human form, he looked *old* to Mori, older
than she'd ever known him--not old like Lord Deramon perhaps,
or like Father had been, but... he suddenly seemed closer to them
in age, no longer a youth like her. Only last year, he had been
merely her brother, the quiet Elethor who lived upon the hill.
Today she saw a man clad in steel armor, a longsword strapped to
his side, his face bearded and his brow showing the first hints of
creasing. The thin, quiet prince she had known was gone; today
she saw a king.

"Mori," he said, "Bayrin has returned from Tiranor... and he
brings news."

Bayrin is back! Mori's heart leaped with joy. Bayrin--the boy
who would tug her pigtails in childhood, who had grown into a
man who would kiss her lips, hold her in his strong arms, and
protect her. Bayrin--her guard, her guiding star, and the sky in her
wings. She wanted to run to him, to kiss him, to hold him

forever... but something in Elethor's eyes held her back. Her brother's gaze was somber and his voice low; Mori froze and stared at him.

The news is bad.

Cold, skeletal claws seemed to clutch her heart. She could barely breathe and her eyes stung. She grabbed Elethor's hands and squeezed them.

"El," she whispered, "is... is the war here again?"

Think of the leaves. Think of the wind in the birches. Think of stars at night. Don't let the nightmares rise.

He looked around him, then lowered his head and spoke softly. "Mori, do not speak of this to anyone. Not yet. I don't want the people alarmed. We think the invasion is near. We think we know where the enemy will fly." He stared at her steadily. "I need you to be strong. I need you to be brave."

Mori had expected to shiver, whimper, and see the world spin. Strangely no fear filled her, only a metallic resolve. She nodded.

"I will be brave," she whispered. "Elethor... I will be strong. I will fight."

She embraced her brother, laid her head against his pauldron, and held him tight. His armor was cold and hard against her. He kissed her head.

"Our forces are strong," he said, his arms around her. "We've trained them well. This time Solina won't catch us by surprise. This time we'll cast her back into the sea."

Mori closed her eyes. A vision flashed through her head-- Elethor lying in the temple with the wounded, his limbs gone, his face burnt like Orin's face back at Castellum Luna. She held her brother tight.

"I know, El. I know we're strong. I love you."

He mussed her hair. "I love you too, Mors." He held her at arm's length. "I fly east now, beyond the mountains, to summon the farmlords. We will hold a council of Requiem's highborn--like the great councils Father would hold. It's two days to Oldnale Manor and two days back. Sit upon the throne while I'm away, Mori. You rule in Nova Vita in my absence."

A tear streamed down her cheek. Elethor turned, shifted into a dragon, and flew across the city. Mori stood upon the temple steps, hand raised, and watched until he disappeared into the east.

BAYRIN

Sea salt, sweat, and dirt covered him. He desperately needed a good, solid soak, but Bayrin remained in the throne room, waiting for Mori.

"If she loves me when I stink, it's true love," he said to a marble bust of an old king--he thought it was King Benedictus, the great hero from the legends--who stood upon a plinth. The bust merely glowered.

Old Benedictus must smell the stink too, Bayrin thought.

He rocked on his heels, anxious to see the princess. The night they had parted, she cried and held him tight; he had barely extricated himself. He had kissed her, promised to return to her, promised to always love her. That had been three moons ago, and now Bayrin thought he could burst--he wanted nothing more than to pull her back into his arms and kiss her again.

At the same time, a sliver of ice pulsed beneath those feelings. Worry for Lyana gnawed at him. His little sister-- dancing for General Mahrdor himself! Like everyone who'd spent more than an afternoon in Tiranor, Bayrin had heard the rumors about Mahrdor. They said the man skinned humans to make scrolls, books, even upholstery. They said he collected shrunken heads, pickled hands, and bronzed fetuses he cut from living women's wombs. The thought of Lyana in his villa festered inside Bayrin so sourly that he barely noticed the palace doors open.

"Bayrin!" cried Mori. She ran across the hall toward him.

Stars, she's beautiful. Thoughts of Mahrdor's collection instantly left him. Whenever he returned from Tiranor, he realized what a beautiful woman Mori had grown into. The girl from a year ago, meek and skinny, was gone. Instead he saw a young woman, almost twenty years old, with billowing chestnut hair, wide gray eyes, and lips that smiled like all the sweetness of a fruit harvest. Despite this war and despite his worry for Lyana, he felt his heart melt, and he reached out his arms. She crashed into his embrace, and they shared a long kiss--a kiss that lasted the lifespan of oaks, the age of mountains, and the rise and fall of stars, and yet when the kiss ended, he felt it too short, like a harp's note that fades too soon.

He held her in his arms. She looked up at him, wrinkled her nose, and said, "Bay, you *stink*." She laid her head against his chest. "But I still love you."

I knew it, he thought.

"I think I got some of the stink on you too," he said. He held her hand and began leading her down the hall. "Come with me. I have an idea."

She looked over her shoulder at the throne, which was dwindling behind them. "Bay, Elethor flew to summon the Oldnales to a council. He said I must sit on the throne while he's away. I--"

"Did he say you can't sleep then, or eat, or bathe, or make love? Stars, I hope he didn't forbid that last bit." He guided her across the hall. "Come on, Mors, this throne has been here for hundreds of years. It will wait another hour for your lovely backside to warm it." He gave that backside a pat, nudging her outside the palace doors.

They stood on the palace stairway and gazed upon Nova Vita. Above the southern city wall rose Castra Draco, fortress of the Royal Army, in whose courtyard men and women dueled with swords and shields. The sounds of hammers on anvils rang; in the city's three smithies, blacksmiths were forging new breastplates, helmets, swords, and spears. For the first time, they forged armor for dragons too: great helmets the size of wheelbarrows, steel collars to shield necks from arrows, and massive breastplates to protect dragons' undersides where no scales grew. Above in the sky, Bayrin saw phalanxes of dragons swoop and blow fire, drilling great mock battles above.

War is coming, he thought. *But that is tomorrow. Today is my day with Mori.*

He shifted into a dragon and flew. With a snort of fire, Mori flew at his side, a slim golden dragon. They dived above the coiling streets. Soon they flew over King's Forest, wings bending the grass and saplings that grew from last war's ashes. They headed north toward the mountains of Dair Ranin where the Seven--great heroes of the olden days--had lived before founding Nova Vita.

They flew until the city disappeared behind, and the forests grew verdant and untouched by war. Oaks and birches spread for leagues below, their canopies an undulating green sea. The River Ranin rolled between the trees, spilling from distant misty mountains. In the old days before the wars, Bayrin would fly here with Elethor to hunt and fish and escape the court. He knew every boulder, meadow, and cave for leagues around.

"The air smells good here," Mori said, flying at his side. "Like trees and water, not... not like fear."

The two dragons, green and gold, flew around a stony mountainside and across a valley. Upon a cliff Bayrin saw the Stone Elder, a great, mossy statue of a dragon; it loomed twice his own size. They said the ancient, wild children of Requiem had carved this sentinel ten thousand years ago, long before the Vir Requis had forged iron, raised livestock, and plowed fields. The Ranin roared around the monolith and crashed down the cliff, a waterfall of mist and fury.

As Bayrin and Mori flew toward the waterfall, their wings rippled a reedy pond below, sending deer and cranes fleeing into a copse of birches. Bayrin dived and crashed into the pond, spraying a fountain.

"Come on, Mori!" he called into the sky. "It's not deep."

She circled above, looked down fearfully, then narrowed her eyes and dived into the water beside him. The pond swirled and the waterfall cascaded ahead, showering them. The Stone Elder glowered upon the cliff above. Bayrin could no longer see the forest around him, only mist and spray.

With a gulp of air, he shifted into human form. When he placed down his feet, the water rose to his chest. The waterfall seemed greater now, an angry liquid demon, and the spray pounded his weaker human form with countless watery arrows. After a moment's hesitation, Mori shifted too; the lake rose to her neck, and the spray drenched her hair.

"I'm scared," she said, voice nearly lost under the waterfall's roar. "The water is rough. Won't we drown?"

Bayrin shrugged. "Oh, I'm sure we will." He pulled off his shirt, then his boots, and finally his pants; he let them float away. He took a step through the swirling pond, moving closer to the waterfall. The spray pummeled him, turning the world white and blue.

"Finally you won't be stinky," Mori said.

He nodded. "Finally maybe you'll kiss me properly."

He pulled her toward him and kissed her--quite properly-- for long moments. When he pulled off her gown, she shivered and clung to him, and he kissed her again. She was so small against him; her head only just reached his shoulders. Their naked bodies clung together underwater, and he kissed her ear while whispering to her--endless whispers that made her laugh, and blush, and kiss him again.

War is coming, he thought, *but that is another day. Today I am happy.*

When their love was spent, they waded to the lakeside, lay upon the grass, and let the sun dry them. He held her, kissed her head, and wished he could stay here forever. The sun began to set and he closed his eyes.

Twelve days, he thought. *Twelve days until acid rains and blood washes us.* He held Mori close, shut his eyes, and clenched his jaw with the pain of old wounds and memory.

LYANA

The old man reached out and touched her bruised cheek. He clucked his tongue and shook his head sadly.

"Savages!" he said and sighed. "Beasts in armor. To strike a blind woman..." He shook his bony fist at the ceiling. "If I were a younger man, I would have given them a bruise or two!"

Lyana smiled softly. Over the past year, she had come to love old Peras, keeper of the River Spice. She lowered his hand and squeezed it.

"It doesn't hurt, Father Peras," she said. She leaned forward and kissed his stubbly cheek. He smelled of flour and dried figs. "I'm fine, and I can take care of myself."

"I saw!" he said and laughed, showing gums with only five teeth left. He shook his head in amazement. "I never would have thought a blind girl could kick so swift and hard. Now the soldier is missing a few teeth too."

She smiled softly. *But I am not a blind girl,* she thought. *I am a bellator, a knight of Requiem, a noble warrior of the north. And if I kick swiftly, and kick hard, I show a piece of Lyana, and that is more dangerous than any soldier's fist.* She took a deep breath. *I must be more careful. I will not let my cover slip and my people down.*

The crescent moon had crossed the sky outside. Dawn was near. The last of the soldiers had left the River Spice, stumbling down the street, singing the songs of their phalanxes. A dozen candles lit the winehouse, and moths danced around their flames. The orange light flickered over toppled mugs, a shattered clay plate, a half-eaten figcake, and stains of blood. Walking stick tapping, Lyana approached a broom in the corner, grabbed it, and began to sweep the floor. Peras moved around the room, collecting mugs and polishing tabletops.

Lyana loved this time of night; they were her favorite times in Tiranor. The sounds of the crowd died outside, and she could hear the wind through the palm trees, the crickets, and the frogs that trilled. She glimpsed the stars shining outside; later tonight she would climb upon the roof and try to count them all.

The Draco constellation shines here too, she thought, *even in hot, cruel Tiranor. The stars of my fathers bless me even so far from home.*

"You have fought men before, I think," said Peras, examining a crack in a mug.

Lyana smiled, broom in hand. "I am a winehouse dancer. Of course I've fought men."

I have killed men, Father Peras, she thought. *I killed them in tunnels, and in the sky, and I will kill ten thousand more if I can before this war ends.* She continued sweeping and said no more.

Peras shook his head and blew out his breath. "Men can be cruel creatures, Daughter Tiana. I have seen too much cruelty in my years... too much blood, too much hate. But not all men are cruel." He righted a fallen chair. "You should find a good man, not a soldier, not a drunkard... find yourself an honest trader or craftsman. You don't want to spend your life dancing here, do you?"

She smiled softly, sweeping shards of clay into the corner. "Dear Father Peras! I would be happy if I could forever dance in this place... though beauty does fade, and no man wants to see an old crone dance." She laughed. "I have a good man, neither a soldier nor drunkard." Her voice softened. "Back in my home far away."

Rubbing a tabletop with a rag, he looked up at her, his eyes sad. "You must miss him."

She sighed. "I was betrothed to his brother at first, a great desert warrior, the strongest man in our tribe. My betrothed was son of our chief. He owned many goats and sheep and three horses--horses that could rival those from Queen Solina's stables." She laughed softly. "It does not sound like much here in Irys, this light of the north, but in the southern dunes, a herd of livestock is worth more than gold and jewels."

She lowered her head, remembering her Orin, Prince of Requiem, a tall and handsome hero, the love of her life... a love she had buried. She took a deep breath and continued, broom still in her hand.

"One day black horses emerged above the dunes," she said. "Brigands in black rode them, sabres bright. My betrothed fought them. I did too, but they were too many. My betrothed fell and the sand ate his blood. I remember only a flash of a blade, blood on my face, and when I woke, I found that I had lost my love... and lost my eyes."

All light dimmed when you died, Orin, she thought. *All starlight faded from my nights.*

With a shake of her head, she kept sweeping. "After that, well... by the laws of our tribe, I became betrothed to his younger brother. It's an old law passed down through generations; without it, widows would be cast aside, left destitute in the desert. So as I mourned, I found myself promised to a young man named Rael." It was a common name in the deserts south of Irys, Lyana knew. She smiled softly. "Rael is nothing like his fallen brother; he is not a warrior, but a stargazer, not a hero, but a scribe of scrolls. At first I mourned, and scorned him, and wanted to flee him, but as time went by, he showed me great love--not fiery, passionate love like his older brother and I had shared, but a quiet caring, a deep respect, an ember that grows to flame. And I miss him, Father Peras."

He placed down his rag, approached her, and patted her arm. "How did you end up here, Tiana? In Irys, this city so far from your home?"

She closed her eyes behind her scarf. *Your people burned my city, killed nearly half my people, and plan to kill the rest. You are kind, Old Peras, but your queen is cruel, and her soldiers lust for blood and death.*

"A storm from the desert," she whispered. "Sand that buried our tents. A drought that killed our livestock. Brigades that murdered half our tribe. Pain, death, starvation... and so I am here. To dance. To fill my purse with bronze and copper and what silver I can earn. To return some day with life. Here in Irys, I am the Blind Beauty, a dancer from the dunes. At home, I am a shepherdess and a leader of my tribe."

Peras looked outside the window into the night. The street was silent and dark. The old man's voice was soft. "We all wear masks. I was a soldier once, did I tell you? Fifteen years I fought for Tiranor; I was an archer in the Steelmark Phalanx. Back then we used good, honest *bows*, not these clumsy crossbow contraptions the soldiers use today. I fought thirty years ago when the dragons of Requiem flew over our land, toppled our towers, and killed my king and queen. I shot poisoned arrows at them, watched the fire burn my brothers, and saw my home fall." He shook his head and closed his eyes. "The wounds I saw, Tiana... They told us war is glorious, that our light would drive out darkness with the song of the Sun God. I saw no glory. I saw blood, I saw women aflame, and I saw children burned into charred corpses. After the war ended, my family was gone. My phalanx was gone. My home was a pile of rubble. They gave me some medal of gold." He snorted. "I sold it and bought this place, named it The River Spice, and now instead of being a soldier, I serve soldiers wine and figcake." He held her arm. "We all wear masks, and we all flee our past, child. Sometimes it's all we can do to survive."

An owl hooted outside, and Peras moved his arm so that a mug slipped off a table. Instinctively, Lyana reached out and caught it.

Her heart nearly stopped.

Her breath caught.

She stood, mug in hand, eyes wide behind her scarf. She stared at Peras. He stared back, the kindly old winehouse keeper gone from his eyes. She saw the soldier there again.

He knows. Stars, he knows.

"Please," she whispered.

Never breaking his stare, he took the mug from her, placed it back on the table, and nodded.

"We all wear masks," he repeated. "Sometimes we wear scarves." He stared at her silently for a moment that seemed to last an age. Then he laughed and swept his arms around him. "Look at this place! Clean as new, and it's not yet dawn. Let's find some sleep, Tiana. Soon it will be a new night, and there will be more soldiers to intoxicate."

He left the common room and climbed upstairs, humming an old desert song.

Lyana stood alone, heart still hammering. Suddenly she felt exposed, nearly naked in her silks. She missed her armor of Requiem, missed her sword and dagger. Clad in steel, she felt so strong, so brave, a great warrior. Who was she here? A girl. Fragile. A flower to be trampled.

I want to fly home, she thought. *I want to become a dragon in the night, fly over the sea, fly back to my armor, to my city, to Elethor and Mori and everyone else.* Yet she only tightened her lips and stood in place. She had a duty here. She would remain Tiana a while longer. She had served her home with steel and flame; now she would serve Requiem with silk and skin.

As if summoned by her thoughts, the door opened, and General Mahrdor entered the winehouse.

He walked alone this night; no Gilded Guardians stood at his sides, steel birds of prey. He wore a white robe over his armor, and his head was hooded. He smiled at her thinly, but his eyes were blue shards, cold and scrutinizing. Again she felt like he could see through her silks, through her dyed skin, into her very soul.

"Tiana!" he said. "I apologize for the lateness of my visit and delight to find you still awake. I myself could not sleep. When I closed my eyes, I saw visions of you dancing; I knew I must see you dance in the flesh before your phantom twin abandoned me. Will you come to my villa, Tiana? Will you dance in the dawn?"

We all wear masks, echoed the words in her mind. *May my mask shield my pain. May the horror crash around me like a river around a boulder.*

She nodded. "I will dance for you, my lord."

The Draco constellation shone overhead as they sailed a boat down the Pallan. A crescent moon grinned. Mahrdor held a lamp before him, and the light danced upon the water like jewels.

Only eleven days until summer solstice, Lyana thought. *Eleven days until the hosts of sunfire spread to my home. Eleven days until I must kill or flee this man.*

He took her to his villa on the hill and into a hall lined with columns. Between the pillars, Lyana saw palms and rushes slope toward the Pallan, and the lights of distant homes glimmered. A hot wind blew over the water, ruffled her hair, and filled her nostrils with the scents of river and grass.

Mahrdor sat on a giltwood divan, placed his sandaled feet on a footstool, and leaned back.

"Dance for me," he said.

Again she danced for him with no music. Again her body swayed to a whispered song, the music of stars above, wind in palms, the flow of water in darkness. Her body flowed for him, and her bare feet tapped upon limestone tiles, and her eyes closed. She danced until wisps of purple dawn spread across the sky, and then Mahrdor stood and approached her, and held her, and stroked her cheek.

He leaned her against a porphyry column, kissed her neck, and made love to her there in the light of the dawn, as the River Pallan slowly awoke below them. She closed her eyes, leaned her head back, and thought of her home as he filled her. She thought of the dragons that flew above King's Forest, so high she could barely see their colors. She thought of the marble columns of Requiem's palace where she lived with Elethor, the smell of her morning bread, the calls of chickadees that always seemed to mock her. She gasped as Mahrdor loved her, and she knew she was yet another land for him to conquer, yet another trophy for him to claim, and a tear streamed down her cheek.

When he was done, he kissed her tear, stroked her hair, and whispered to her.

"You are more beautiful than this dawn, Tiana, and you are more precious than our short lives under the sun. You are like the River Pallan, a gift from the desert, and your lips are oasis fruit." He took her hand. "Come with me, Tiana. I have a gift for you, a gift as rare and beautiful as you are."

He held her hand. He took her across the hall and into a towering, domed solarium. The dawn shone through the narrow windows; they were made from true glass, a priceless rarity in Tiranor. Ferns filled the room, and a hundred cages hung between them, holding hundreds of birds: finches, macaws, conures, lovebirds, and many others Lyana could not name. They all squawked and fluttered in their cages.

In the center of the solarium stood a great, golden birdcage. It rose six feet tall, maybe taller, and its bars curved to form dragons aflight. It was empty, its door open.

"I am, as you know, a collector," Mahrdor said. He swept his arm around him. "Smell the air, Tiana! You will smell a thousand plants from all the lands of the world; I collect them.

Listen to the song of birds! You will hear a hundred different species; I collect them." He turned to face her. "And you, Tiana... you are the rarest, most beautiful of birds."

Suddenly his face changed.

Rage overflowed his eyes.

He raised his fist to strike her.

She flinched and raised her hand in defense.

As her heart hammered and her mind spun, Mahrdor nodded and slowly lowered his fist.

"I thought so," he whispered.

Terror shattered inside her.

Lyana summoned her magic and began to shift into a dragon.

He clutched her throat and squeezed, and she gasped for breath, and his fist now did strike, and pain exploded. White light flooded her. Her magic fled her. His fingers dug into her neck, and he dragged her and threw her into the cage.

His hand freed her throat. She sucked in breath and tried to shift. He slammed the cage door shut, trapping her inside. Scales flowed across her, and her body ballooned, becoming the dragon. She slammed against the cage bars and howled in pain. Her magic fizzled. She roared and clutched at it and tried to shift again, to break the cage bars, to blow fire. She felt wings sprout. Fangs lengthened in her mouth. Her body grew, hit the bars, and again her magic vanished.

She fell onto her knees, panting, a caged woman. She snarled, tore her scarf off, and glared at Mahrdor.

He stood before her, arms crossed, smiling sadly.

"Oh, Tiana," he said. "Did you truly think I did not know? Did you truly think you could fool me like you fooled the common soldiers at your winehouse?"

"My name is not Tiana," she hissed and bared her teeth as if she were a dragon. She slammed against the cage bars. They were thick and strong; gilded iron, she thought.

He shrugged. "Your name matters not. You are my pet, my trophy, the crown of my collection; that is what matters to me." He looked over his shoulder. "Come, Yarish! See her without her scarf."

Out from the shadows stepped a tall, gaunt man with white hair. Lyana growled, heart hammering. She knew this man; he was the deaf innkeeper of Old Mill in Hog Corner, the fishhouse where she would meet with Bayrin. Today the man wore no rags but donned the armor of a soldier. He gave her a blank stare; he seemed almost bored.

"Are all weredragons as stupid as this one?" he asked Mahrdor. "If so, we should have no particular problem facing them in battle."

Weredragon. Lyana growled and slammed against the bars. She hated that word--a dirty, foul word of hatred, of blood, of scorn.

"I am a Vir Requis," she said, "a daughter of ancient Requiem blessed with starlight. You will find us very problematic to kill." She snapped her teeth as if she were a dragon who could tear into their flesh; she craved to taste that flesh. "When you attack our land, you will find us ready to fell you from the sky."

The two Tiran officers looked at each other and laughed. Mahrdor shook his head. He patted the cage bars, then pulled his hand back when she tried to bite it.

"Oh, precious weredragon pet," he said. "Do you refer to the army of your King Elethor, which heads to Ralora Beach? Yes, weredragon. I know you saw the map in my chambers; I placed it there for you. I know you spoke of it to your brother, that he flew over the sea to sing the news." He gave a sad, theatrical sigh. "I think... when your King Elethor and his army arrive at Ralora, they will find only seagulls and crabs to fight."

Lyana stared, her insides trembling. Her eyes burned and she felt tears gather. She could barely breathe and her head spun. It was a ruse, had been a ruse all along. How could she have been so stupid? How could she think this disguise could fool them?

Please, stars, do not let this be... do not let my kingdom fall.

With a growl, Lyana reached out of the cage, trying to grab his arm, to pull it toward her, to bite it off. He took a step back, stared at her sadly, and shook his head.

"I will kill you," she whispered, eyes narrowed and glaring.

He smiled thinly and hunger filled his eyes, the hunger of a wolf for its prey. He licked his pale, thin lips.

"No," he said softly. "No, you will not kill me, Lyana. Nor will I kill you." He fingered a dagger that hung on his belt, its pommel shaped as a sunburst. "No matter how much you beg me to."

His grin widened.

Lyana roared and slammed against the bars.

ADIA

Without her children, her house seemed empty as a barren womb, a hall of ghosts. Most days since the Phoenix War, Adia spent her time in the temple, healing and praying; or in the tunnels stocking bandages, herbs, and supplies for siege; or in the streets of Nova Vita, visiting and comforting grieving families. But today, for the first time since the phoenixes had burned this city, Adia had taken a day for her own home.

She knelt now in her garden, stubbornly fighting a losing war against dandelions which had invaded her rows of herbs. *Even the plants fight their wars,* she thought wryly. She kept tugging at the weeds until her fingers were raw and her robes covered with soil. When she surveyed her work, she saw that she had put but a small dent into the yellow invasion.

Once children had run across this lawn, she thought. Once Lyana and Bayrin had fought here with wooden swords, their feet tearing up whatever she had planted and dragging mud into the house. Once the stray dogs Bayrin would adopt--Adia had never understood where he found so many--would dig through her flowerbeds and eat her herbs. Once laughter and light had filled these gardens. Today this was all that remained: weeds and silence.

Abandoning her floral war for another day, Adia left the garden. Sunflowers and lilac grew around her door, wild and untamed, their leaves perforated with insect bites. They too needed care she could not give them. Her door was painted green and silver--some in Requiem thought them blessed colors--and when Adia stepped through this doorway, more silence greeted her.

She walked through her house and began to aimlessly work--sweeping a corner here, polishing a mug there. As she wandered the halls, she found the silence unbearable; it engulfed her like a white demon. There were too many rooms in this house upon the hill, too many halls, too many corners where memories whispered.

Three children had once filled this house with light, she thought. But Bayrin now lived in the palace, guarding his princess; Lyana now spied in the south, in such danger that Adia lay awake most nights, struggling for breath; and her sweet youngest child, Noela, still slept under her grave upon Lacrimosa Hill. No more laughter. No more clacking of wooden swords. No more muddy footprints, or scraped knees, or nights of stargazing with cider and roasted walnuts. Only this: empty rooms and silence.

Why had she come to this place? She had work to do in the tunnels: jars of preserves needed to be labeled, and swords needed to be hung on racks, and scrolls needed to be placed on shelves. She had healers to train at her temple, young and frightened girls who had never stitched a wound, sawed through a crushed leg, or comforted a dying man. She had stars to pray to: the constellation Draco, stars of her fathers, guardians of Requiem.

And yet today she had chosen this place, this home she had shared with her husband for... how long had it been? Adia shook her head in amazement when she counted the years. Twenty-nine summers had gone by since she had married Deramon and moved into this house on the hill. She had been only a youth then, not yet twenty, and the world had seemed so bright to her, Deramon so strong, her house so full of warmth and wonder.

Empty rooms and silence; it was all that remained.

But no, she thought. Memories remained, moving through these halls like ghosts: Bayrin as a young boy, wild and impossible to tame, scratching his name into every wall; Noela first laughing, a mere moon before she had laughed no more; Lyana squealing as she tugged her brother's hair and fled when he pretended to be a griffin. Adia could still see Bayrin's name upon the walls, though it had been twenty years, and she could still hear the echoes of her daughters laughing and crying and calling for her.

She entered her bedroom, a sparse chamber of unadorned walls, a simple bed topped with white sheets, and no ornaments but for a basket of dried flowers upon a table. Adia walked to a window and looked outside at the burnt forests. She smiled softly. Those memories were kind, yet they too were fragile. Should Queen Solina fly to this hill, she would topple these empty halls and silent rooms, and then those memories too would die. Nothing would remain of this place but bricks and ash, and all the dandelions that plagued her would lie as charred dust.

She looked at the city outside; from here, she could see half of Nova Vita roll across hills to the walls and forests. She was High Priestess, the Mother of Requiem, and all those souls below were as children to her. All those memories would perish, and all those lights would fade.

"It is madness," she whispered. "Five thousand Vir Requis soldiers, most of them mere farmers, bakers, and shepherds... against myriads of wyverns and a hundred thousand desert warriors."

And yet what else could they do? Stock their supplies. Train their warriors. Pray.

"And walk through our homes," she said softly. "Relive the memories. Savor the light of life for one last day."

She heard the door open across the house, the clink of armor, and the heavy footsteps of her husband. Soon Deramon stepped into the bedroom. When Adia looked at him, she marveled at how more white now filled his beard; only last year, that beard had been bright red, and only a few white strands had invaded it. Now for every red hair, a white one grew.

Adia touched his cheek. "Deramon," she said softly and kissed him.

He removed his breastplate, then hung sword and axe upon the wall. She helped him unclasp the rest of his armor: vambraces upon his arms, greaves upon his legs, pauldrons like shoulders of steel, and a coat of chain mail. When finally he stood in nothing but a woolen shirt and pants, he looked so small to her, his arms scarred. Once she had thought him a bear of a man, a mountain of muscle and grit.

The years had softened him; they had done the same to her. For a few years now, Adia had allowed no mirrors in her home. She did not want to see the lines that grew under her eyes, the white that invaded her own black hair, and the new weight that coated her bones. When she first moved into this home--*twenty-nine years, stars!*--many called her the fairest woman in Requiem, a tall and willowy beauty with midnight hair and eyes like magic. Today her hips were wider, her legs blue with veins, her mouth less likely to smile.

Does he think me ugly? she wondered as she looked at Deramon. She knew that some lords, when they crossed their fiftieth year, took concubines--young, pretty things for secret nights. On days like these, when death loomed, would he seek out last comforts?

"It has been nearly thirty summers since we moved into our home," she said to him. "The years have kissed my hair with white, softened my flesh upon my bones, and drawn lines of memory upon my face. But today I will love you like we used to love--with all the fire we would kindle in our youth. I will take you once more into my bed, like the first time, for this may be the last time."

She doffed her robes, stood naked before him, and saw his face soften.

"The years did not mar your beauty," he said, "but deepened it. When we wed, I called you the fairest flower in Requiem; that you are still." He cupped her cheek with his large, rough hand and kissed her lips. "Now and always."

She took him into her bed. She made love to him--with the fire and passion of their youth, and with the slow burn of what they had grown for so many years. She cried out to him. Today was a last day; she savored every breath, every touch, every whisper. When their love was spent, she lay against him and kissed him.

"I love you, Deramon," she whispered. "After Noela died, I know that I forgot that. I know that my love fled you then; all love fled from me. But I love you deeply, fully; I am yours always, and I will be yours in the starlit halls. I am yours in our life and death."

The sun began to set and she slept in his arms. Tomorrow fire would burn; tonight she lived twenty-nine years of laughter and starlight.

LYANA

She slammed against the cage bars and howled.

"Mahrdor!" she shouted. Her voice filled the solarium. "Mahrdor, free me! Open this cage or the fire of Requiem will rain upon you!"

The birds that filled the aviary shrieked and fluttered. Finches bustled in their hanging cages, beeping. A macaw squawked and bit at the bars of its own prison. A horde of green conures flew from perch to perch, their cages swinging. All had smaller, humbler cages than her own. All hung upon walls or between plants in corners. Lyana's own cage stood in the center of the chamber, the golden centerpiece of Mahrdor's collection. She was his prize pet.

"Mahrdor!" she shouted.

No one but the birds answered. Lyana kept slamming against the bars, but they would not dent. When she scratched at them, the gold peeled back to reveal iron. She tried to shift into a dragon again, but as soon as scales began to cover her and her body grew, the bars shoved her back into human form.

Finally, when her body was bruised from banging against the bars, she fell to her knees. She lowered her head, letting her hair cover her eyes, and gritted her teeth. A deep terror festered inside her. Mahrdor had known--he had known all along--and now Elethor would be flying to Ralora Beach... flying to nothing but waves and sand.

He will leave only the City Guard in Nova Vita, she knew. *Only my father. My brother. A few green youths they had trained. They will die.*

The fear rose in her like flames would rise in her dragon's maw. She snarled and glared through the bars at the glass panes above. The sun was beginning to set. How long until Solina's army flew?

"I have to escape," she whispered. "I have to warn Elethor. I will not be the one who lets Requiem fall."

She slammed against the bars again. They bruised her skin. She howled in frustration and fell back down. Her eyes burned and she clenched her fists to stop them from trembling.

"I have to escape," she whispered again. "I won't let Solina murder my family. I won't let Mahrdor imprison Princess Mori like he imprisoned me." She growled. "I will escape!"

She kept slamming against the bars until the sun sank, darkness filled the solarium, and she saw nothing but a faint glimmer of moon through the glass ceiling. With a wordless shout, Lyana sat down, pulled her knees to her chest, and lowered her head.

"I'm sorry, Elethor," she whispered.

She tried not to think of home. Remembering would be too hard. Yet in the darkness, she could not stop the memories from rising like dreams. She saw the gardens of the palace, a lush haven where she would walk with Elethor and talk to him of politics and warfare and heraldry, then catch him giving her a warm look and smile. He would pull her close and kiss her cheek, and she would struggle and call him a blockhead for ignoring her words, but then capitulate and let him kiss her under the trees. She saw Bayrin again, her oaf of a brother, sneak into her chamber to draw rude pictures on her shield, place frogs in her bed, and once--she shook her head to remember it--hide a snake in her drawer of undergarments. She thought of her parents, and of her friend Mori, and her squire Treale Oldnale, and a lump filled her throat. She could not stop a tear from falling.

In the darkness, she saw the acid coat them--Elethor, her family, and her friends. Like Silas at the palace, they would scream, and their flesh would melt, until they lay as sticky bones with anguished skulls.

She placed her head against her knees. She tried to stay awake, but sleep still found her, and dreams emerged in the darkness. She no longer huddled in a cage, but hung in a cocoon of cobwebs. Nedath, Guardian of the Abyss, scuttled toward her--a rotting girl with the body of a centipede. The demon licked and bit her, and Lyana screamed and wept. She swung on the cobwebs, and dozens of creatures swung around her, shriveled skin clinging to spines, their heads shrunken like those in Mahrdor's chambers, their toothless gums smacking. *Count the screws! Grow sideways like the little hairs of skeleys.*

Cold wind blew.

A sun raced between clouds.

She walked through King's Forest outside her city, stepping daintily between conifers ancient and gnarly, her feet as snowflakes upon a carpet of fallen needles. As ten thousand magpies sang, she traversed the hilltops, and there she came upon a lion of the woods. A noble creature was he, with soft fur the color of light and paws that left no prints. She reached her fingers into his mane, and when she looked upon herself, she saw that her armor had become a pixie homespun of grass and fur, old leaves and strings of golden hair.

"O, King of all Beasts," she whispered into his ear, and lay beside him, and there he licked her lily hands and chanted blessings upon her.

"Climb onto my back, fair maiden of these pines, and lay your head upon mine," he said, and Lyana climbed onto him. He ran across the hills and took her to a faerie court where stone balustrades surrounded a pool of twigs and cyclamen petals. A sword of stone lay upon an old shield there, encrusted with kings' blood, and on its blade silver runes told of want and lacking.

King Lion laid his head upon the shield, and kissed the stone blade so that his lips bled, and anointed Lyana with a kiss. He sang.

Queen of blood
Lie upon the grave of kings
Child of shattered metal
And light

He seemed as though he would sing more. He forgot the words.

In the woods...

In the woods Lyana wept. In the woods she prayed for life, she who had been marked to die. In the woods a giant boy with the head of a moose disassembled her methodically, neatly unscrewing arms, legs, her head, laying the pieces out before him. He blinked his eyes, wet eyes the size of saucers, long lashes like oily curtains.

"Daughter of Eleison," he said, his voice like a grunt, the groan of a rutting beast. She was a tiny doll to him. His furry hands would not leave her, arranging and rearranging her pieces upon the earth of this land. This land...

So beautiful an animal...

Her blood seeped into the pinecones.

Through her city she walked, houses like boxes, stained hands, snarling teeth and fear so thick in the air she coughed, choked, and fell to her knees.

O, King Lion! King of all beasts!

She ran from door to door, but each was barred to her. She sought her mother and father, but she found only puddles on the ground full of floating teeth. In the puddles she saw the face of her dancer--hair platinum, eyes hidden behind a scarf, face dyed gold. Tiana. Her eternal twin.

The boy awaited them both, and Lyana shivered and hated and feared. She lowered her head, let her hair cover her face, and wept as men with swords marched and shouted around her, and wyverns flew over the eastern hills.

When she awoke, a cruel sun seared her through the glass ceiling. When she touched the bars of her cage, they burned her fingers. Her limbs were stiff, her head aching, her throat parched.

"Stars of Requiem," she whispered, but her lips were so dry that they cracked, and she tasted blood. She fell silent.

The birds woke, squawked, chirped, and beeped around her. The flowers growing from their vases and baskets bloomed toward the light. The room soon sweltered, and Lyana's throat ached for water, and her head began to spin. She rose on stiff limbs and began slamming against the bars again, a rhythmic beat. She threw herself against them until the gold peeled off the iron, her shoulders were raw, and bruises spread across her. She kept slamming, again and again, jaw clenched, mind blank, just to do something--anything.

"Mahrdor!" she shouted, hoarse. "Come and see me, Mahrdor! Come face me. I will kill you!"

The birds shrieked, her only answer.

He would arrive soon, she knew. He would arrive to see her, to bring her water and food, to taunt her, maybe to demand she dance, or demand she lie with him. He would not just leave her here. She kept attacking the cage as the sun moved across the sky and began to set again, and orange and red light filled the aviary.

She sat, knees pulled to her chest, and watched the sunset. Was Elethor watching the sunset too, flying toward Ralora Beach? Was Mori watching the sky, ruling alone in Nova Vita, awaiting the fire?

Her head spun and her skull seemed too tight. Her lips bled. Her throat blazed. Her stomach clenched with hunger. How long could she survive here? He would arrive soon, she knew. He would bring her water. If he did not, she would perish; he did not encage her in gold, his prize pet, to let her die. He would arrive soon--before darkness fell. He would bring sweet, cool water from deep wells, water to soothe her throat, cure her spinning head, and give her strength to fight him. The cage spun around her. She gagged and coughed.

Darkness fell.

She sat against the bars, shivering, arms wrapped around her.

He wants me to die. He will let me die here. I will die tonight. Goodbye, Requiem. I will fly to your starlit halls.

She closed her eyes and saw the pillars of afterlife.

Boots thudded across the hall.

She opened her eyes and winced. Lamplight filled the aviary, and three shadows approached her. They wore armor and helmets; she could not see their faces. When they reached her cage, one tossed a waterskin, a loaf of bread, and a wheel of cheese past the bars.

She glared at the soldiers. She wanted to shout curses at them, to try and break the bars again, to reach out and try to scratch them. One more glance at the water and food, and she chose them instead. She drank first. The water was brackish, and there was not nearly enough, but it was the best thing she had ever drunk, sweeter than wine from Requiem's vineyards. She stuffed the food into her mouth until her cheeks bulged.

Before she could swallow, the guards lifted her cage. They began to carry it toward the doors. Lyana swallowed hastily and shouted at them, voice hoarse.

"Fight me like men! Open this cage and face me in battle, cowards!" She banged against the bars. "Are you so weak that you fear to fight a woman?"

They kept walking, carrying her through the doors and into a corridor. These were no Gilded Guardians, she saw; they did not serve the General Mahrdor. Their helms were not shaped as ibises, but as falcons. Their armor was not golden, but pale platinum with sunbursts upon their breasts.

Palace guards, Lyana knew. *Queen Solina's men.*

She reached out the bars and scratched at their armor; a feeble gesture. She tried to snag one's helmet off, hoping to claw his eyes, but he caught her wrist and twisted so hard that she yelped. He released her just before her bone could crack.

"Where are you taking me?" she demanded, cradling her wrist and glaring. "I am a soldier of Requiem. You will answer to the wrath of our king."

One guard turned his head, and his falcon helm faced her. When he spoke, his voice was gravely and high-pitched, truly the sound of a steel bird. Through his visor's eye holes, she glimpsed a face hideously scarred; his eyelids were raw and hairless. This one had been lax around wyverns, she wagered.

"Queen Solina is... borrowing you for a while," the guard said, his voice as raw and twisted as the skin around his eyes. He made a sound halfway between a chuckle and a clearing of the throat. "She will return you to General Mahrdor eventually. Whether you'll return the same creature, well... that I doubt."

A hissing sound rose from his helm, and it was a moment before Lyana realized: it was laughter. The sound sent a chill through her; she couldn't help but shiver.

Solina.

Lyana had seen the queen's work in Requiem--bodies cut, burnt, killed in agony, even children. *She tortured my Orin to death. Will she do the same to me?*

She screamed in her cage and slammed against the bars.

The palace guards carried her out of Mahrdor's villa and into the gardens, where fig and carob trees rose from pebbly earth. Braziers stood in palisades, lighting the night and filling the air with scented smoke. A wyvern awaited in a cobbled courtyard, snarling at the stars. When it saw the approaching guards, it howled and bucked, scales clacking and tail lashing. Acid dripped from its maw to burn holes into the cobblestones. Its metallic scent filled Lyana's nostrils and seared her tongue.

The guards hoisted her cage onto the wyvern's back. She rolled against the bars, clenched her jaw, and snarled. They chained the cage down, and the deformed guard climbed into the beast's saddle. He grabbed a whip, cracked it, and the wyvern took flight.

The beast soared so fast, Lyana's head spun, black shadows spread across her eyes, and she nearly passed out. Her ears throbbed and her insides sank. Even as a dragon, she would never soar so quickly. She gasped for air and clenched her fists, struggling not to faint. The wyvern's girth blocked most of her view, but she could see the rims of the city around it, from the southern dunes where the torches of soldiers crackled, to the northern delta where ships sailed to sea, lanterns glowing upon their hulls. She stared across that sea, squinted, and tried to see Requiem's shores; she would draw comfort from them. Those shores were too distant and dark for her eyes, and she lowered her head.

I am alone here.

The wyvern began to descend. Streets snaked in labyrinths below, crowded with houses, palm trees, and people carrying tin lanterns--thousands of ants from up here, thousands of lives, thousands of worlds, all unaware of her pain. Lyana glimpsed the Tower of Akartum, which rose upon Phoebus Palace; they were heading there. To *her.* To the woman Elethor had loved, the woman who had murdered Orin, the woman Lyana vowed to kill.

The wyvern landed in a courtyard surrounded by walls and towers. A gateway led into the palace--a quiet backdoor. The soldiers carried her into a corridor and down a stairwell, its walls carved with suns and falcons. Their boots thudded and a thousand candles lit their way, wax melting like men under acid.

The air grew cool and musty as they descended. It seemed like they plummeted forever; the stairway coiled like a worm digging toward a man's heart. Lyana couldn't help but shiver. She crouched in her cage, snarling between the bars.

Don't dig so deep! she wanted to cry. *You will wake the creatures of the Abyss. You will free the Shrivels who hang there. You will wither with them.*

Yet a different horror dwelled in this underground. After countless steps deeper into darkness, the staircase ended and they entered the palace dungeons.

A tunnel stretched before Lyana, hewn of craggy stone. Cells lined the tunnel walls; blood trickled from between their bars, and screams rose from them, twisting in the air like demons of sound. The stench of disease, nightsoil, and fear filled Lyana's nostrils, so powerful that she gritted her teeth to stop from gagging.

The guards carried her cage down the tunnel. As they walked, Lyana stared into the cells they passed. Her stomach clenched and she could barely breathe. Inside one cell, guards were slicing pieces off a chained man as if carving a roast boar; the man screamed and writhed with every slice. In another chamber, guards smirked as they let rats feast upon a chained woman's legs; her feet were already gone. In a third cell, children hung from hooks, still alive and mewling, their bodies twisted with acid and their eyes pleading.

Lyana closed her own eyes. She did not want to see more. As the guards kept carrying her down the hall, however, she could still *hear* the torture: whips landing, hammers breaking bones, and mostly screams, horrible screams like those of the Abyss.

"I am a knight of Requiem," she whispered to herself, arms trembling. "I am a warrior. I am strong. Whatever they do to me, I can bear it."

And yet she knew that was a lie.

I cannot bear it.

If they broke her body here, they would break her mind too. If she ever returned to Elethor, she would be a shell of a woman--a cowering, mindless wretch, a fool for his court. A tear streamed down her cheek.

"I'm sorry, Elethor," she whispered. "I'm sorry, Mori."

Would they too end up here? Elethor had told her that Solina had spared his life in Requiem's tunnels; she wanted him a prisoner, not a corpse. She would bring him here, Lyana realized; she would bring Elethor to this place, and the Princess Mori, and Bayrin, and her parents, and their flesh would be sliced like roast boar, and rats would eat their legs, and...

Lyana shivered, fists trembling and tears flowing from closed eyes.

The hall seemed to stretch forever. If the Abyss loomed below Requiem, here was Tiranor's buried realm of darkness. After what seemed like hours--hours of screams, of blood, of the *crack* of bones and the *rip* of flayed skin--they reached an empty cell.

My own corner of pain, Lyana thought. *My own place of madness.*

The guards carried her cage inside and placed it on the floor. The walls closed in around her; the cell was no more than five feet wide. Its walls were carved of living rock, and manacles hung from its ceiling like iron Shrivels. In the guards' torchlight,

Lyana saw that blood splashed the walls, floor, and chains. In a corner, a rat feasted on severed human fingers.

"Remove her from her cage," said the scarred guard to his comrades. He hissed a laugh. "Hang her from the manacles."

The guards snarled, lifted chains from the floor, and began slinking them through the cage bars. Lyana snarled, grabbed the chains, and tugged them.

"Hands down!" said the guard with the burnt face. He thrust a club into the cage and rapped her fingers. She yowled and tried to grab the club, but he pulled it back. Her fingers blazed. She grabbed at the chains again, and the club slammed down a second time. Pain blazed up to her shoulder, and she thought her fingers might be broken. When the chains were slung through the cage bars, the guards tugged them. They wrapped around her body, tightened, and clutched her like iron pythons. She writhed in the trap. When she tried to tug the chains loose, the guards pulled them tighter, and the links dug into her torso.

When they opened her cage door, she tried to leap at them. The chains crushed her. She floundered like a fish in a net. When they grabbed her arms, she screamed and kicked and tried to bite them. Clubs descended; one hit her shoulder, another her wrist. A guard backhanded her twice, so that her lips split, and her jaw screamed in pain.

She howled, blood in her mouth. She tried to summon her magic, to shift into a dragon. Fire tickled her maw. Scales began to appear across her. As her body grew, the chains tightened further, cutting off her breath. She gasped for air and her magic left her. Hands grabbed her wrists and bent them. She roared; she thought the guards would snap her bones. A knee drove into her stomach and she gasped. Pain was all she knew.

They yanked her arms up, and manacles closed around her wrists. Chains tightened, pulling her toward the ceiling. She screamed. Her heels left the floor; she remained standing on her toes. The guards pulled the gilded cage outside the cell, leaving her hanging from the ceiling.

Her captors shuffled outside. All but the scarred guard with the hissing laughter remained. He stared at the hanging Lyana; his eyes were red behind his helm. She stared into those eyes and bared her teeth.

"I will kill you some day," she said softly. There was no emotion to her voice, no rage, no fear; she was not speaking a mere threat, but a cold fact.

The guard stared at her for a moment longer, then began to slowly remove his helm. Lyana grimaced and disgust swelled inside her. His head was nothing but a scar; it looked like a clump of wet, white cloth. He hissed through a toothless mouth; it looked like a mere slit in leather.

"Kill me?" he said. He laughed, a sound more like a cough. "I used to hang in this cell, girl. I hung here as they doused me with wyvern acid." He coughed and spat. "For a year I served my sentence. Now I watch others suffer like I did. Kill me? Soon you will want to kill yourself more than me."

He turned around, left the chamber, and slammed the cell door behind him.

Darkness filled Lyana's world. She heard nothing but a hundred screams.

ELETHOR

They sat in the palace war room, a towering chamber with brick walls, a shadowy dome, and an oak table so wide and heavy a dragon could sleep upon it. Torches flickered in the walls and thick curtains hid the windows. Seven seats, taller than warriors, stood around the table.

Elethor looked around the room, eying each person in turn. The highborn of Requiem sat before him.

"We have word from the south," he said. "Lady Lyana reports that armies muster, that Tiranor plans to strike at summer solstice." He jabbed his finger against a parchment map that lay across the table. "Solina will strike here, at Ralora Beach, southeast of Castellum Luna. The invasion is eight days away."

The seated highborn looked at one another, brows furrowed. At the head of the table sat House Aeternum: himself and Princess Mori. Once three more chairs had stood here: one for his father, one for his mother, and one for Prince Orin. Now only he and Mori remained, the last survivors of their ancient dynasty.

To their right sat the great House Eleison: Lord Deramon, captain of the Guard; his wife Adia, High Priestess; and their son Bayrin, guard to the princess. One seat stood empty like a missing tooth in an aching gum: Lyana's seat. When Elethor looked upon that chair, ice filled him.

At the table's left side, a man and woman shifted uncomfortably. Both wore green fabrics embroidered with the sigil of their house, a golden stalk of wheat. Both were graying, thin, and shrewd. The man was Lord Ferenor Oldnale, the woman his wife, the Lady Alyn--the parents of Lady Treale who had returned the bodies to Nova Vita. Young Treale herself sat at their side, clad in armor, her hair hidden beneath her helm. The Oldnales owned great lands outside the city; they ruled farmers and shepherds, and in the war room, they stared at one another somberly, then at their king.

"My lord," said Lord Ferenor. He rose to his feet, bowed his hoary head, and stared from under his brows. "We have suffered greatly in Requiem. Two wars against Tiranor already... I fought in the first one thirty years ago. My two sons fell in the second last year." He shook his head, his voice cracked, and tears filled his eyes. "We cannot bear a third war. Fly out to Tiranor! Meet its queen. Sit with Solina at her table and treat with her. The time has come for peace."

Lord Deramon, burly and bearded, rose to his feet so roughly his chair nearly toppled over.

"Treat with the woman who burned our city!" he blustered. "Make peace with... with that devil who slew our children underground?" He pounded his fists against the tabletop. "Lord Ferenor, your sons were honorable men. I mourn them. But your mind has gone soft with your grief! Let warriors speak here tonight, not farmers."

Ferenor stiffened and his cheeks flushed. "Lord Deramon, calm yourself. Warriors have ruled over Requiem for long enough. What have you warriors brought us? Not surprisingly: war. Perhaps now is the time for farmers' counsel." He smoothed his tunic. "Yes, Solina burned our city and slew our children. Did we not do the same to Tiranor thirty years ago? She is an enemy, yes. You make peace not with friends, but with enemies."

Deramon growled so loudly he could have been standing in dragon form. "Where were you, Ferenor, when Solina's men poured into our tunnels? Where were you when she was burning our children, when I was swinging my axe and sword into the skulls of her men? I did not see you in the battlefield. After you've faced ten thousand men with hatred in their eyes and blades dripping Vir Requis blood, come to me and speak of making peace."

"And I suppose you want to face ten thousand more men!" Ferenor said, pulling himself as tall and straight as he could. "I suppose you want to see more blades dripping our blood! Put down your sword and axe, Deramon. Lift a plow and a pitchfork; our people need them more than your weapons."

Deramon reached for that sword and axe, which hung on his belt. Bayrin leaped to his feet and grabbed his own sword's hilt. Treale cried out in horror and tried to pull her father back into his seat. Before steel could be drawn, Elethor rose to his feet and raised his hands.

"Calm yourselves!" he demanded. "Deramon, Bayrin, sit down! Ferenor, you too. We've come here to talk, maybe to shout, but not to fight. Down, all of you."

Their eyes shooting daggers, they sat down, though Deramon kept his hands clenched around his weapons. Bayrin sat grumbling, his face nearly as red as his hair. For a moment, everyone sat stewing and staring at one another. Elethor continued.

"Three thousand warriors of the Royal Army train here in Nova City," he said. "Most are young and green, yes, but they will fight bravely. I will lead them to Ralora Beach and meet Solina in battle."

Again the room rose in shouts.

"This is madness!" said Lord Ferenor, leaping to his feet again. "Three thousand warriors? They are mere boys and girls!"

Bayrin actually jumped onto his chair, pounded the air, and shouted. "Boys and girls with more courage than you, Ferenor!"

Ferenor's wife, the Lady Oldnale, was shouting at Bayrin to
sit down and stop making a fool of himself. Deramon was
growling. Mother Adia raised her hands and cried for calm. Mori
cowered in her chair and whimpered, and Treale rushed over to
comfort her. Elethor clenched his fists at his sides and closed his
eyes. The voices rang through his head, spinning like the voices
of the creatures he had seen in the Abyss.

We must turn the screws, skeleys! the shriveled creatures had
said, mere spines wrapped in skin. *We must count the hairs that grow
sideways!* They all spun around him, laughing and smacking their
gums.

No one will know, Elethor thought. *No one will know of those
nightmares Lyana and I saw. No one can know the true darkness of the
world but me and her.*

He felt a hand on his shoulder. He opened his eyes to see
Mori at his side, looking at him in concern. He patted her hand
and looked back at the council.

"Lord Ferenor," he said to the blustering lord. "I
understand your concern. Truly I do. Your daughter serves in
the Royal Army. My betrothed does too; so did my brother. But
I know Solina. She will not offer us peace. She comes to kill us.
She comes to kill every last Vir Requis and topple our halls.
There is only one thing we can do against the tide from Tiranor;
face it in battle."

Bayrin shouted approval and slammed his fist into his palm.
Ferenor, however, seemed unswayed. He raised his nose and
snorted.

"Solina cares not about my daughter, nor my farms, nor
your fine halls of marble." He pointed a shaking finger at Elethor.
"She hates *you*, Elethor. You alone, you and your family. Why
should my farms burn and my daughter fight for a feud between
you and her?" He raised his voice above the shouts around him.
"She killed your father and you want revenge! That's all this is

about. And the sons and daughters of Requiem will die for your pride!"

Everyone shouted so loudly Elethor could only make out random words. Deramon shouted something about Ferenor being the greatest coward in Requiem, while Lady Oldnale cried that Deramon was a bloodthirsty brute. Robes swaying and hands trembling, Ferenor was shouting at Elethor; he could hear only "warmonger!" repeated over and over.

Rage boiled in him. Elethor clenched his fists, wishing Lyana were here with him; he thought that his betrothed could outshout them all. *But for now you are away, Lyana, so I'll have to do the loudest shouting.*

"Settle down!" he cried. "Sit down, everyone! Deramon! Bayrin! Sit down and take your hands off your swords. Ferenor, calm yourself! *Warmonger* you call me? War is coming whether we like it or not. A host flies to Requiem; what would you have us do rather than face it? Cower in our holes and wait for death?"

"I would have you make peace!" Ferenor shouted. "I would have you solve your conflict with Solina using words, not fire and steel. You will doom us to more death! When children die, their blood will be upon you!"

With that, Ferenor Oldnale kicked his chair down. It crashed to the floor. With a flourish, he wrapped his cloak tightly around him, spun on his heels, and marched out the door. His wife followed, snorting and giving the council a last dirty look before disappearing outside. Lady Treale bit her lip and lowered her eyes as she trailed after the pair; she looked back at the council guiltily, whispered an apology, then followed her parents outside. Bayrin shouted after them, shaking his fist and cursing their house, and it was long moments before those remaining in the room settled down and stewed silently.

Peace, Elethor thought. *Could he make peace with Solina? Could he meet her at Ralora Beach, treat with her, and avoid this war?*

He looked at Mother Adia, who had mostly remained silent. She stared at him, her eyes deep pools. Again she reminded him of the marble statues he would carve, stoic and pale and strong.

"Adia," Elethor said, "you are a priestess, a healer, a woman of peace. What do the stars tell you? Can we truly avoid this war?"

She stared at him steadily, and starlight seemed to swirl in her eyes. She stood straight and tall, then spoke in a voice like the song of the sky.

"I saw the bodies of children torn apart. I saw the men who slew them. I saw Solina burn the wounded I tried to heal. Elethor, there will be no peace with this queen. She flies here with one purpose: to kill us all." She reached across the table and grabbed his hands. "You must stop her from reaching this place. You must meet her in battle, crush her host, and cast her back into the desert."

"Stars yeah!" Bayrin said and pounded the tabletop. "It's wyvern killing time."

Elethor looked at the map on the table. He ran his fingers across the mountains, valleys, and seas. *Ralora Beach. That is where I'll see her again--Solina, love and bane of my life. The woman I kissed so many times, the woman I sculpted and pined for... the woman I must kill.*

He looked up at what remained of his council.

"Deramon and Bayrin. Stay here with the City Guard. Protect Nova Vita." He turned to Adia. "Adia, pray for us. Prepare to heal us." Finally he looked at his sister, and his voice softened. "Mori, while I fly to the south, you will be the only Aeternum in Nova Vita. Sit upon the throne until I return. You rule in my stead."

She nodded, lips trembling but eyes staring at him steadily. He turned to leave, but Mori caught his arm, then pulled him into an embrace.

"Be careful, El," she whispered. She looked up at him with wet eyes. "Please, El. Please be careful. Be strong. I will pray for you. I will protect our city while you're away."

He held her tight and kissed her forehead. She felt like a trembling leaf in his arms. She was his last living family, his most precious soul.

"I'll be back soon, Mori. I promise you." He held her hands tight and looked into her eyes. "I promise."

Long arms wrapped around them and squeezed--Bayrin joining the embrace, tall and knobby, his shock of red curls pressed against their faces. Elethor was short of breath before he freed himself from the crushing hug. When he did, he and Bayrin clutched each other's shoulders.

"Fly high, El," his friend said, eyes somber. "And if you see Solina, by the stars, this time just kill her quickly."

He sighed, remembering the time he had let her scar his face, let her escape from him. "I will." He squeezed Bayrin's shoulder. "And you, Bay, guard my sister well. If you don't, I'm going to hang you up beside that dead wyvern."

Next he shared a crushing handshake with Deramon; the burly lord grumbled something about killing a few dozen Tirans for him. Finally Elethor embraced Mother Adia, who was as soft and warm as Deramon was cold and steely. The priestess kissed his forehead and whispered a prayer.

"May you always find Requiem's sky, my king." Adia smiled and touched his cheek. "I will await you upon the walls of your city, son of Draco, and I will pray for you."

Her embrace was like starlight wrapping around him in a cocoon, forever warm and guiding his way. He ached for it when they parted.

His throat tightened and his eyes stung. He turned and left the chamber.

Outside the palace, he shifted into a dragon and soared into the night. He let flames fill his maw, and he shook his body to hear his scales rattle. The city rolled beneath him, silver under the moonlight. Elethor looked upon the rows of homes and workshops, the palace below him, the temple ahead, and the white walls like a crown rising from King's Forest.

"I won't let you fall again, Nova Vita," he swore into the wind.

He descended toward Castra Draco, fortress of the Royal Army, whose four towers rose white and tall, their banners undulating. Elethor flew above the battlements and roared his call.

"Warriors of Requiem!" he cried. "Soldiers of the Royal Army! The time has come to spread your wings, to blow your fire, to fly to war. Sound the horns of battle! Arise, warriors of Requiem!"

Atop the four towers great horns blew. The sound keened across the city, deep as the years of Requiem--a peal of ancient song, of runes in stone, of the age and light of stars.

"Arise and fly, dragons of Requiem!" Elethor called as the horns of Requiem blew.

Armored men and women began streaming from the fortress. In the courtyard, they shifted into dragons and soared, firelight dancing between their fangs. Elethor growled and began flying south, wind roaring beneath his wings. He blew flame in the night, a beacon of war. Behind him, hundreds of dragons flew, soon thousands.

"Fly, Royal Army! We fly south! We fly to war."

The dragons soared. Flames rose in pillars. The city turned orange below them, and people emerged from their homes to wave and sing prayers.

Elethor dived into the night. Behind him, thousands of dragons flew and roared their song.

SOLINA

As she descended the stairs, rage simmered in her, a white-hot forge. She clenched her fists, gritted her teeth, and her breath hissed.

"Lyana," she whispered, almost able to taste the name's foulness on her tongue; it tasted like congealing blood.

At the bottom of the stairway, a doorway led into her tunnel of triumph. As she walked, boots clanking, she smiled to hear the screams, to see the twisting bodies, to smell the acid that ate through flesh and bone. Her enemies twitched and begged for death in every cell: those nobles foolish enough to oppose her plans, and those soldiers too weak and slow when she had drilled them. Their families too hung here, flayed and whipped and cut and burnt, wives and children alike.

Good, Solina thought, smiling as she walked by cell after cell. *They suffer for their disobedience, and Lyana the weredragon will suffer most among them.*

A child screamed from one cell; he hung from the wall, body blackened.

"Please, my queen," he begged. "Please."

She nodded to him as she walked by. "I will give you mercy, child. I will let you die once your body can bear no more."

The child was a fellow Tiran. Even if his father was a traitor, his blood was pure, and he deserved eventual death. But Lyana... Solina snarled and dug her fingernails into her palms. Lyana was a weredragon, a filthy shapeshifter. She deserved no such mercy. She would live to a ripe, miserable old age.

Finally she reached the weredragon's cell, the smallest and darkest cell in this dungeon. Solina opened the heavy, blood-stained door and stepped inside. Her snarl turned into a smile.

A single torch flickered upon the wall, casting orange light against the beast. Lyana hung from the ceiling on chains, head lowered, her hair dangling. More chains wrapped around her torso and legs, keeping her in human form. She stood on her toes; her shackles would not let her heels touch the floor. Tatters of a silk garment covered her, barely concealing her bruised flesh.

"Lyana," Solina said softly.

The weredragon raised her head and stared. A bruise spread across her cheek, and her lip was swollen, and yet she glared with blazing hatred.

Solina's smile widened. "You still have your spirit," she said and drew a razor from her belt. "That's good... that's good. I will enjoy breaking it."

Solina inhaled deeply, savoring Lyana's scent of fear. The memories swirled in the darkness like ghosts. *Can't you fly, Solina? Can't you fly?* The little girl with red curls laughed and danced around her. *Look, I can become a dragon! Can't you fly too?*

Solina clenched her jaw and raised her razor. The torchlight blazed against it, and a flicker of fear filled Lyana's eyes.

Good, Solina thought. *Good.*

"Your hair," she said. "You have straightened your curls. You have dyed them platinum. You try to appear as a Tiran, but we smelled your dirty blood. You mock our pure, noble race with your treachery." She took a step forward, razor raised. "I will strip you of this mockery."

She grabbed Lyana's hair, pulled it, and began shearing. She gritted her teeth as she worked, tearing nearly as much hair as she cut. She moved the razor roughly against Lyana's head, scraping her scalp; blood beaded upon it. Lyana glared and snarled, but said nothing. Rage simmered in her eyes, amusing Solina; she smirked when she examined her work. Lyana stood bald before her, head bloodied.

"Much better," she said, nodding. "The world will see you for what you are: a filthy creature. I've stripped you of the hair that mocks us. I will now remove that glare from your eyes."

Solina reached into the pouch on her belt. She withdrew a glass vial. The liquid inside swirled, milky white tinged with green tendrils. She broke the wax seal with her thumb, and a scent like vinegar and apples filled her nostrils, sour but not unpleasant. Lyana, however, winced and bit down hard, and her fists clenched.

"Do you know what this is, Lyana?" Solina asked, holding the vial out. When it neared the chained Lyana, the weredragon hissed and turned her head aside. "It is a rare herb, one that grows in Osanna across the sea. Laceleaf, they call it there; they use it in their cooking. The weredragons have a different name for it, don't they? *Ilbane* you call it, I am told. A poison to your wretched kind. They say just the touch of its leaf can burn you; here I carry its pure latex."

Lyana snarled and looked aside, eyes reddening. "Ilbane has not grown in the world for hundreds of years."

"Then this should not harm you in the slightest."

She splashed the vial onto Lyana's face.

The weredragon clenched her jaw and growled. Her fists shook and her body writhed. Her skin reddened where the liquid touched her. She hissed, sucked her breath, then finally tossed back her head and howled. Solina watched, smiling softly.

"It burns, does it not?" She shook her head sadly. "I would use acid on you, child, were not my Lord Mahrdor so smitten with your pretty face." She caressed Lyana's cheek. "For now I will leave your face pretty... but I will hurt you. I will hurt you badly. You will scream for me like nobody has screamed before."

She pulled another vial from her pouch. A dozen more clinked inside. Lyana saw the collection, paled, and closed her eyes. A tear flowed to her lips.

"Solina, please," she whispered.

Solina laughed. "You are begging so soon?" She shook her head sadly. "I begged too as a child when you mocked me, when you called me a stranger. I begged the Sun God to free me from your prison. I begged too as a woman when your betrothed burned me and left me scarred. And I begged Elethor. I begged him to be mine, to rule with me in Tiranor... but he chose you instead." She broke the seal off her second vial. "From my childhood until today you hurt me, weredragon. You mocked me. You stole my love. And now you spy on my kingdom. And yes, you will beg now. You will beg all night and for every night hence."

She smiled and raised the second vial.

For an hour she worked--spilling the sap across Lyana, watching it burn her, hearing her scream. She forced it down her throat. She splashed it into her eyes. She smeared it across her until the weredragon shook and wept. When finally her vials were empty, she unlocked the chains that bound Lyana to the ceiling. She watched the wretched creature fall to her knees, trembling and smoking.

"Guards!" she cried.

She stood smiling, hands on hips, as her guards entered the room and lifted the weredragon. Solina began walking upstairs, out of shadow and into sunlight. As the guards dragged Lyana behind her, the chained wretch barely struggled. Her feet dragged and blood trickled down her chin. Even if chains were not still binding her, Solina doubted the girl could muster enough strength to become a dragon now.

They dragged Lyana out of the palace, through a garden of fig trees, and into a courtyard. A snowy mare waited there--White

Flame, Solina's favorite mount, the finest beast from her stables. The horse nickered and tossed her head, chinking the golden rings that filled her mane. Lyana slumped, the guards holding her up. She coughed weakly and spat blood.

"Chain her," Solina said.

The guards pulled Lyana's arms forward, manacled her wrists, and ran a chain between them to White Flame's saddle. Solina mounted her mare, stroked her mane, and kneed her.

White Flame began to walk. Solina smiled upon the saddle. Lyana shuffled behind, coughing and struggling for breath.

"Weredragons think themselves a noble race!" Solina said. Her guards marched at her sides, spears thudding against the cobblestones. "Look at this one. Look how she walks behind me, chained and bruised. How noble she is!"

They crossed the courtyard, rode through a vineyard, and entered the sun-drenched streets of Irys.

Thousands of men, women, and children roared--they crowded the streets, covered the roofs, and stared from their windows. They howled at the sight of Solina and the chained weredragon. As Solina rode and Lyana limped behind, the people shouted and jeered.

"Weredragon!" one cried.

"Murderer!"

"Monster!"

Somebody tossed a rock. It struck Lyana's shoulder and drew blood. Another tossed a soiled swaddling cloth. Soon hundreds were tossing refuse at the chained, limping weredragon. Solina smiled as she rode, keeping the chain tight; it was long enough that none of the trash could hit her. She kneed her horse to a faster clip. Lyana fell, was dragged several feet, and barely struggled back onto her feet. Blood trickled down her elbows.

She is no longer screaming, Solina thought in distaste. Her lip curled. *She will scream more before this day is over. The entire city will hear it.*

As she rode, she thought of Elethor--her pure, handsome prince, the love of her life, the fire of her youth. He had rejected her, swung his sword at her, cast her out... and chosen this Lyana, this filthy weredragon, instead. Solina growled. She was a great queen, a beautiful monarch clad in gold and splendor and sunlight. Behind her dragged a bloody, filthy wretch, half alive, a mere creature, not a woman to love.

"You will see, Elethor," she whispered. "I will bring this Lyana with me to Requiem, and you will see her filth, her monstrosity. She will be broken when you see her again, a crushed insect, and I will be glorious."

She rode all morning as the crowds jeered. Lyana coughed and struggled for breath, her feet bloody, her eyes rolling. When the sun hit its zenith and her lord's fire burned brightest, Solina rode across the Square of the Sun, heading back toward her palace. The Palace of Phoebus, her ancestral home, loomed above her--an ancient edifice of towers and battlements. A limestone staircase, fifty feet wide and glittering white, led from the courtyard toward the palace gates, where two faceless stone warriors stood, a hundred feet tall. At the foot of this staircase she halted White Flame and dismounted.

Lyana collapsed onto the cobblestones. Thousands of people filled the square, howling in rage, tossing rotten fruit onto the weredragon.

"Stand her up," Solina said to her guards. "Take her up the steps to the Faceless Guardians where we burned the last one."

A smile on her face, Solina began walking up the steps of her palace, heading toward its gates. Behind her, her guards grabbed Lyana under her arms, hoisted up the bloody creature, and dragged her upstairs. As Solina climbed, her smile grew, and her lord's light filled her eyes. The glory of Tiranor and the Phoebus Dynasty rose above her, stone kissed with gold. Sunbeams flared around the Tower of Akartum, the tallest steeple in Tiranor, blessing her.

Finally they reached the Faceless Guardians, two statues of stone that protected her home; they had stood here for three thousand years, and even the dragons of Requiem had been unable to topple them. The guards chained Lyana between the two statues, one arm bound to each, so that she stood stretched between them. The weredragon's head hung low, and blood trickled down her chin.

Solina approached her captive, touched the blood on her cheek, and leaned close.

"This is where we killed your friend Silas," she whispered. "Are you frightened, Lyana?"

The weredragon looked up. Pain filled her eyes... but rage too. Deep, simmering rage, two forge fires. Blood and bruises covered her face, but Lyana managed to growl.

"You may kill me," the weredragon said, "but the wrath of Requiem will fly upon you, Solina. You will burn forever in the flames."

Solina laughed. "So much spirit still left to break; it is a wonder. You are making this day more enjoyable than I could have imagined." She whispered into Lyana's ear. "And your spirit *will* break, Lyana. It will break today. I was merciful to Silas; I let him die. You will receive no such mercy, not for many years." She turned toward her guards. "Beat her. Beat her so the city hears her screams."

She stepped back. The guards stepped forward, whips in hand. And they beat her. And she screamed. And the city heard.

The crowds howled. The whips lashed. Blood fell upon the stones of her palace.

When Lyana fell unconscious and her guards lowered their lashes, Solina glared at them.

"You will beat her until I tell you to stop."

The beating continued. The sunlight flared across them, a blaze of glory and justice.

ELETHOR

As sunset spilled over the field, the sounds of the camp rose like music: soldiers talking and coughing, spoons clattering in bowls, and ravens cawing as they circled overhead. Three thousand Vir Requis sat upon boulders and grass, eating and drinking, boasting of how many Tirans they'd kill, laughing at rude jokes, and remembering their homes. One man began to sing Old Requiem Woods, an ancient song; others soon joined him, and the song swept through the camp, and even the most dour and frightened hummed and smiled.

"Two days from Nova Vita," Elethor whispered. "Four days from the sea where I'll meet Solina again."

He stood upon a hillock, apart from the others. He was not much older than these soldiers--a young king of only twenty-six summers, his father fallen too soon. And yet he felt decades more ancient, an old man with the weight of an ancient race upon his shoulders. The wind tousled his hair and filled his nostrils with the scents of cooking meats, strong ale, sweat, and grass. He looked upon this camp and thought about Lyana, and the summer night felt cold.

"Fly back to us," he whispered. "Be safe."

A young woman detached from the camp and came walking uphill toward him. She wore a breastplate engraved with a stalk of wheat, and a sword hung from her hip. When she came closer, Elethor recognized her smooth black hair, olive skin, and dark eyes: the Lady Treale Oldnale, squire to Lyana. When she reached him, she held out two steaming bowls of stew.

"My king," she said and bowed her head. "I thought you might be hungry. Please, would you eat with me? I have some bread in my pack too and a full wineskin."

She looked up at him expectedly. A short and slim girl, Lady Treale was of an age with Mori--not yet twenty--and a friend to the princess. As Elethor watched her, he remembered fighting Tiran soldiers in the tunnels--towering men twice Treale's size, bloodlust in their eyes. How long would Treale last in battle against them, and if they let her live, would she beg them for death? An image flashed through his mind: young Treale trapped underground, sliced with swords, screaming as desert warriors mounted her. He clenched his jaw, banishing the thought.

He sat down and patted the grass beside him. "Come, Lady Treale. Sit beside me. Let us share a meal and wine."

She sat beside him in the grass and wriggled until she was comfortable. They ate silently for long moments, watching the camp. The singing below died, soon replaced with gales of laughter over rude jokes.

"Not much like my father's army," Elethor said with a sigh. "Those were hard men; they ate with grim purpose, fuel for battle. I rarely heard them laugh."

Treale chewed a crust of bread. "These ones are nervous. I lead a phalanx of a hundred warriors; they are younger than me, and I'm not yet twenty. Most have only held plows until this year; others have only held quills. Several of my warriors are fifteen years old; some of the boys are too young to shave." She heaved a sigh. "Let them boast of the Tirans they will kill, my lord. Let them laugh at their jests and sing their songs. It drowns their terror." She looked at him, and he could see her own fear behind her eyes. "It is better than terror."

Elethor sighed too. He placed his spoon down in his empty bowl. "Your father thinks me a fool. He tells me to make peace with Solina, not lead these youths to war. When we meet

Tiranor's army, we will not face the children of farmers. We will meet hard men from a cruel land, bred to kill for their Sun God; women too, brides to the blade, desert warriors who shave the sides of their heads, pierce their lips with rings, and lust for the blood of dragons." He looked at Treale. "They do not tell jokes around their campfires this night. They do not laugh nervously to hide their fear. They do not sing old folk songs. They sharpen spearheads and howl for blood. Each of these warriors will ride a wyvern, cruel beasts with scales harder than ours and acid crueler than our fire. They will fly in perfect formations. They will not scatter in battle. They will each fight to the death."

Treale paled and clutched her spoon as if it were a sword. She tightened her lips and raised her head.

"Do we stand a chance?" she whispered.

Elethor looked down at the camp. Two boys were chasing each other around a fire, swinging swords in mock battle. They laughed, the high laugh of youths; they were barely old enough to even be called youths.

"I don't know," he said softly. "Your parents think not. What do you think, Lady Treale? Your father calls for me to make peace; by that, he means me to surrender. And yet you are here, clad in armor, fighting for your king. Tell me your thoughts."

She placed down her empty bowl, uncorked her wineskin, and drank deeply. "I'm frightened," she finally said. "And I don't know if we can win this war. But..." She looked into the night, for a moment lost in thought. She looked back at him. "My lord, my brothers fought for King Olasar. They died over King's Forest. It broke my father's heart; mine too. It's been over a year, and I still weep for them most nights. They were raised to be farmlords, not warriors, yet they fought for their king." The firelight danced in her eyes. "I will fight for mine."

He reached out and clasped her hand around the wineskin. His eyes stung. "You are brave, Lady Treale. You are brave like the knight you squire for. I am honored to fight by your side."

She smiled and rolled her eyes. "Brave like Lady Lyana? That I am not. She is a great warrior and a true bellator! The last of her kind. My brothers were knights too, and they often spoke of her courage; they said she could best any man in swordplay. You walked with her through the Abyss itself! A land of horror." She shivered. "I can only wish to be as brave; my insides quiver now to think of it. You are most lucky to be her betrothed."

Elethor took the wineskin from her and drank. It was good, strong wine from the southern vineyards on the coast; dry and warm in his throat.

"Lyana is strong," he said, "and wise, and brave. She is our greatest warrior. My brother Orin was such a warrior; his men adored him. I did too, as did Lyana." He drank again.

Treale reached out, hesitant, and touched his arm. Her eyes were soft. "You are a good man for her, my king. You too are strong and brave; you will be a fine husband to Lady Lyana."

He raised his eyebrows and blew out his breath. "Oh, Lyana needs no good man, nor fine husband; not since Orin died. But the land has its laws; I am to care for her after Orin fell. Do you know why such laws exist, Treale?" When she shook his head, he continued. "In the old days, the women of Requiem had less power than today. They could not serve in the army, nor own land, nor possess wealth. They were dependant on their fathers and then their husbands. Widows could become destitute, and so living brothers took them as wives--to protect them. Lyana does not need my protection--she's always been strong--but the old laws remain. We both respect them. And I love Lyana; I can think of no better queen."

She kept her hand on his arm. "And yet... you once loved another," she whispered.

Her eyes were soft, her lips parted. Elethor knew then that she too had once loved and lost; perhaps a young man fallen in the war.

"Yes," he said softly. "I once loved another."

I loved Solina like wine, like sunrise after darkness, like fire in the cold. For years she lit my life; for years after she left Requiem, the pain of losing her hollowed me.

Yet he could not tell these things to Treale, just as she would not speak of the lost love that filled her own eyes. She gazed at him softly, then shook her head wildly and rose to her feet. She brushed crumbs off her as if trying to brush off memories.

"I'm betrothed in an arranged marriage too," she said, "to some horrible, pompous farmlord." She thrust out her chest, swung her arms, and walked in an exaggerated swagger. Then she sighed and her arms drooped. "And he's nearly twice my age! Oh, my stars; sometimes I wish I were a commoner, not the daughter of a highborn father." She gave him a sidelong glance. "Don't you ever wish the same, my lord? To... to marry whoever you truly loved, not whoever the laws of the land require you to love?"

He thought of Solina: the flame of his youth, the light he had carried for so many years. She had been passion and sweet unending pain. She had been forbidden and banished. Lady Lyana... did he feel the same toward her?

It had been a year since he'd seen Lyana, and he missed her, and he loved her--he knew that he did--and yet... he could not stop the doubts from whispering. As Requiem's ancient laws decreed, men inherited the wives of fallen brothers--to protect and provide for them. Yet Lyana needed no protection from him; she was wiser than him, stronger in battle, and just as wealthy. How could he defend her, be a strong man she could depend on? He respected Requiem's laws, and he would marry his dead

brother's betrothed, and Lyana told him that she loved him, but...
did she truly? Before Orin's death, Lyana had glanced his way
only to lecture him; was her love for him now true, or forged by
ancient creed?

As these thoughts filled him, he couldn't help but notice
Treale's beauty; her lips were full, her skin smooth, her hair a
cascade of midnight. Her armor fit snugly against her body,
hinting at the curves beneath. She looked at him with huge,
admiring eyes, a young woman in the presence of her king. What
would it be like, Elethor wondered, to choose a bride himself--a
bride like Treale, a pretty young maiden who looked up to him?
Could he have been happy with her? Treale saw him as a great
king, a leader, a strong man, not the younger brother of a fallen
prince, not some... consolation prize.

He thought of Bayrin, his closest friend. Bayrin had such
a love--he had Mori, a woman who adored him, a soft and loving
woman to protect. With somebody like Treale, could Elethor
have that too? With Lyana, he always struggled to appear strong
enough, wise enough, noble enough... and he always felt like he
failed, like no matter what he did, he fell short of Orin, fell short
of the hero Lyana deserved. As Treale looked at him with her
large eyes, he understood how Bayrin felt with Mori; he felt
strong, a powerful man with a woman to defend.

And she wants me, Elethor thought, staring into Treale's
eyes; she stared back, lips parted, chest rising and falling. *I can see
it in her eyes. If I want her, she is mine.*

He lowered his head, tearing his gaze away. Guilt flooded
him. Lyana was spying in Tiranor, risking her life for him; how
could he think such thoughts? And yet he thought them, and he
could not speak of them--not to Treale, and perhaps not to
anyone.

He looked back at the young squire. "I love the Lady
Lyana. She is strong. She is wise. She will be a fine queen."

Treale bit her lip and nodded. She sat back down and lowered her eyes. "Yes, she is all those things. I love her too! Truly I do. It's an honor to squire for her." She looked back up at him. "I'm sure she will be a fine queen for you and that your love will grow. You both deserve it, my lord; I know how much you suffered."

He leaned back and let his fingers play with the grass. He watched the campfires below, hundreds of flickering stars.

"I never wanted to be king, you know," he said. He laughed softly. "Shocking, I'm sure; the whole kingdom knows it, I reckon. I wanted to be a sculptor. I *was* a sculptor. But Lyana... this is what she was born for. I've known her all her life; from the time she could talk, she spoke of being a knight, and a heroine, and a queen someday. She is those first two things already; she will be the latter soon enough." He turned his head and looked at Treale. The firelight painted her face and danced in her eyes. "What of you, Lady Treale Oldnale? Did you always dream of being a knight?"

She smiled softly. "Oh stars, no. I never held a sword until a year ago. Not what you want to hear on the eve of battle, I'm sure, but it's the truth. I always wanted to be... oh, it's terribly silly." She blushed and stared at him pleadingly. "Promise you won't laugh if I tell you. Will you promise? All right. I always wanted to be... a puppeteer." She made a soft squealing sound and covered her face. "Horrible, isn't it? But..." She peeked between her fingers. "I've always loved puppets. I used to watch them as a child at the farm fairs--the puppet shows with Kyrie and Agnus Dei, who would always fight and bicker, but loved each other dearly. My mother used to tell me I looked like Agnus Dei-- the real one from the stories, not the puppet. Do you know? Our family is descended from her and Kyrie, that's what Father says."

Elethor nodded and sighed. "Oh, I had to spend many painful hours studying lineage in my youth, tracing the lines of the families from the Living Seven. My teachers used to bore me half to death with tales of Agnus Dei's grandson moving east, settling the plains, and founding your house. Dreadfully dull lessons."

She snorted a laugh. "They are less dull when puppets perform them at farmers' fairs. I still remember the taste of blackberries, and the sound of the flutists, and how my brothers would insist we go see the cattle. But I always wanted to watch the puppets. I was only eight years old when I sewed my own Kyrie and Agnus Dei dolls--I made them from my old dresses and pillows--and my parents roared with pleasure when I put on a show. I knew then that I wanted to do nothing else. I wanted to make puppets--rooms of them, *castles* full of them--enough for countless fairs." She sighed and her eyes saddened. "But then... then the war broke out. The phoenixes invaded, and my brothers fell in battle, and... well, it seemed wrong to sew puppets when war raged. So I took my oldest brother's sword and shield, flew to the capital, and well... here I am today." She played with a blade of grass. "It's not much of a story, my lord, not as impressive as yours or Lyana's. I did not walk through the Abyss nor fight in the tunnels. I switched a needle for a sword, farmlands for barracks; that is my tale."

The sun had disappeared beyond the horizon while they spoke; only a dim glow now painted the west. The stars winked between clouds; Elethor could see only the tail of the dragon, the last few stars of the Draco constellation.

Below in the field, the soldiers were unrolling their blankets and lying down to sleep under the stars. The night's first guards shifted into dragons, took flight, and began circling over the camp. Weariness crept over Elethor; they had flown hard for hours and his body ached.

"This hill is a good place for sleep," he said. "The grass is soft, the air fresh, and guards patrol above us." He yawned and stretched. "If you've not found a place to lie down, share the hill."

Treale yawned magnificently, a yawn that flowed across her body from toes to outstretched fingertips. She unbuckled her breastplate, unclasped her sword, and kicked off her boots. She hesitated for a moment, looked down and up again, then leaned forward and kissed his cheek. Her lips were soft and warm. Then, blushing, she lay down at his side, placed her cheek upon her hands, and was soon asleep.

Elethor watched her for a moment, smiling softly. He remembered a day long ago when Treale and Mori--mere children then--had placed a toad on his dinner plate, then fled the hall giggling and shrieking.

Mori would always delight in the Oldnales visiting Nova Vita, he remembered. *She would speak for days of her friend Treale coming to see her and would cry whenever Treale flew home.*

It did not seem so long ago; the years had gone by in a daze, and now Mori sat upon the throne, and Treale flew to battle at his side. Elethor lay down beside the young noblewoman, looked up at the stars, and found that his weariness had left him. How could he sleep with all these souls--his sister, his soldiers, and his people at home--depending on him? How could he lead them to war like his father had?

He rolled over so that he faced Treale. He drew comfort from the peacefulness of her slumber--the smoothness of her face, the rise and fall of her breast, and the breeze in her dark hair. He closed his eyes and finally sleep found him too, and he dreamed of hot desert winds, thrusting spears, and sandstone towers rising from dunes.

MORI

Whenever Lord Deramon entered the palace hall, Mori felt faint. Today he stormed in with all his usual bluster, bowed curtly, and stomped toward her. Sitting on her brother's throne, Mori cowered and wished the chair's twisting oak roots could swallow her. Her heart thrashed and she felt a trickle of cold sweat trail down her back.

"My princess!" Deramon called, a great bear of a man, his beard a red flame, his axe and sword clanking against his armor.

Mori's head spun as he approached. It was not that Deramon was a bad man--and after all, he was father to Bayrin and Lyana, two of the people she loved most. It was just that...

Oh stars, does he have to walk so fast? And do his eyebrows need to be so red and bushy? She tried to imagine those eyebrows not as flames that could burn her, but as two friendly caterpillars crawling above his eyes. The thought calmed her, and she even managed a tremulous smile.

"Lord Deramon," she said in a small voice.

He had soon crossed the hall and bowed, hands on his weapons. "My princess, the work on the tunnels is complete. Come with me; I will show you the fortifications."

Mori didn't want to go with him. She wanted to stay here, in the safety of the palace, with only columns of marble around her and Bayrin at her side. She looked over at Bayrin now; he stood as always by her throne, his armor bright and his sword at his side. He placed a hand on her shoulder and spoke softly.

"Are you ready, Mors? I'll be with you."

Mori looked between him and Deramon and shuddered. The city was just so... so *busy*, all bustling with masons and healers and carpenters. There would be wagons of bricks, and mules carrying lumber, and peasants storing food, and the sights and sounds would spin her head. She knew they would; they always did. Here in the palace there was silence, there was safety, there was soothing marble and the song of harps. She gave Bayrin another pleading look, but he only patted her shoulder and smiled comfortingly.

Mori lowered her head, bit her lip, and nodded. "I'm ready," she said in a small voice.

I am Princess of Requiem, she thought. *I will do my duty. With Elethor away, I rule here. I must protect my people, even if the city sounds will make my knees shake and my belly twist.*

They left the hall, stepped outside the doors, and stood for a moment on the hill. Mori gazed upon the city that rolled around her. She heard the sound of hammers on anvils, forging armor for men and dragons. Smoke plumed from smelters and dragons dragged wagons of iron ore from the mountain mines. Farmers wheeled carts down the streets, carrying preserves, wineskins, and dried fish into the tunnels. Dragons perched upon every wall, and men-at-arms guarded every street. The smells of smoke, oil, and sweat filled the air.

War, Mori thought. She took a deep breath, clutched her luck finger behind her back, and began walking downhill. *I will be brave. I will stand strong for my people.*

As they walked through the city, people bowed their heads and whispered blessings upon them. Hands reached out to touch Mori's gown; she knew these were signs of respect for their princess, but their touch frightened her. So many still bore the scars of last year's war. So many had burnt flesh, missing limbs, haunted eyes that spoke of their pain, or no more eyes at all. They spun around her, and her breath felt tight, and her chest ached, and again she saw him--Orin, charred and dying, his innards spilling, and Acribus grabbing her, and--

No, Mori, she told herself. She shut her eyes and forced a deep breath. *Don't think of that. Breathe. Just breathe.*

She forced herself to focus only on that breath--good, healing air entering and leaving her lungs. She focused on the feel of cobblestones beneath her feet and the light breeze on her face, and slowly her heartbeat slowed, and she opened her eyes. Once more the city was steady, and no more fog covered her vision.

Soon they reached Benedictus Archway, which rose from a cobbled square, leading into the tunnels. Two guards stood before it, spears crossed. They bowed their heads and parted for Mori. She stepped between them onto a steep, narrow staircase that plunged into darkness.

Deramon walked at her side. "The staircase is too narrow for wyverns, my lady. We made damn sure of that." He gestured at his feet. "And the stairs themselves are narrow, as you can see. If any Tirans charge down, they will crash in their armor."

As Mori descended and shadows spread, she found herself soothed. Her head cleared and her fingers no longer trembled. There was safety here underground, surrounded by stone. She kept walking, a hundred steps or more, until she reached a doorway. The doors towered above her, carved of oak banded in iron.

"If the Tirans invade, this is the first obstacle they'll face," Deramon said. "No battering ram will break through these doors; they're solid oak and iron, a good foot thick."

"Almost as thick as Lyana's head," Bayrin spoke up behind them.

Deramon pounded on the doors. "Open up, men!"

As the doors began to creak open, Bayrin muttered, "Solina won't need a battering ram; she just has to knock."

When the doors had opened, Mori saw five guards bearing pikes and shields. Longswords hung at their waists, their pommels shaped as dragonclaws. Deramon nodded to them and turned to Mori.

"If the Tirans invade the city, I'll place a hundred of these pikemen here. Even if Solina does break through these doors, she'll face blades of sharp, cruel steel."

"Almost as sharp as Lyana's tongue," Bayrin said. "And just as cruel."

Past the doors and pikemen, they walked down a tunnel. Its walls were craggy, and Mori ran her hand across the stone, drawing comfort from its cold roughness. Candles burned in alcoves, and pikes and swords hung from hooks. As they walked, Mori imagined thousands of people fleeing here into darkness, and she took deep breaths and bit her lip.

This is a safe place. A safe place.

The tunnel stretched two hundred yards, maybe more, before it reached another staircase. The steps were so narrow, Mori had to hold the wall for support. Finally they reached a portcullis, its bars shaped like dragon teeth. Beyond these iron jaws she saw more guards; they wore plate armor and bore crossbows and swords.

"If the Tirans claim the top level, they will be stopped here," Deramon said, voice a low rumble. "If war reaches this city, I'll place two hundred men here armed with enough crossbows and bolts to slay an army. The Tirans will pile up dead."

Bayrin tapped the jaw-like portcullis. "I like it. Judging by how crooked these iron teeth are, Lyana obviously modeled for them. Let's see what's next."

Deramon gestured at the guards, who pulled the portcullis open. Beyond the iron teeth, they walked down more tunnels, these ones so narrow they had to move single file. Mori walked between the two men, barely as tall as their shoulders. She wished she could spend her life here underground, Bayrin at her side, maybe with a good book too, one with maps. The air was cool here and the noise of the city gone.

If ever this war ends, she thought, *I will fill this place with books and scrolls and come here to read every day. Nobody can hurt me here.*

As they walked through this second level of tunnels, Deramon gestured at walls stocked with spears, crossbows, and shields. He spoke about filling this place with guards who would slay any Tiran warrior who reached this deep. Finally they reached a third barrier: great doors carved of solid bronze. More guards stood here, and when they pulled the doors open, Mori saw a cavern that plunged into darkness.

She entered and looked around, hands clasped behind her back. The cavern loomed around her, nearly as large as the palace throne room. Its walls and ceiling were craggy, still showing the claw marks of dragons. A hundred candles burned here. Alcoves in the walls held supplies: jars of apple preserves, strings of sausages, jugs of wine and ale, skins of water, and sacks of grain. Other shelves held more weapons: arrows and bows, swords, and spears. Through narrow passageways, Mori glimpsed more chambers, similarly sized and stacked.

"And this chamber," Bayrin said, "is as big and hollow as Lyana's head."

Mori explored the chamber. She ran her hand over the supplies and weapons, peered into the other chambers, and drank from an underground stream she found. It reminded her of Crescent Isle's great caves, the place where she had met the Children of the Moon last year; it seemed lifetimes ago. She knew what this place was for. The soldiers would guard the top two levels. Here the young, old, and wounded would hide.

"Here we will survive," she whispered.

She closed her eyes. She remembered fleeing into the dungeon of Castellum Luna as the phoenixes flew; they slew her brother there. She remembered fleeing into these very tunnels as the phoenixes burned the city; Solina had shattered their defenses and slain thousands. When she opened her eyes again, Mori's heart nearly stopped.

Twenty thousand bodies filled the chamber, twisted with acid, their skin like wet cloth. A few twitched and begged for death; most already lay dead. Blood sluiced her boots and Solina laughed, hands on her hips, like she had laughed when killing Orin. The dead reached out to Mori. Melting hands clutched at her gown, and faces like dripping wax begged her.

"Please, Mori, please, save us, kill us, please..."

They pawed at her, their skin melting, sticking to her, and dripping off their bones to stain her gown. Mori closed her eyes again.

No. I won't look at them. I will breathe like Mother Adia taught me.

She opened her eyes again and they were gone. She saw only Bayrin and Deramon standing several feet away, pointing at a blade and arguing about whether it was a longsword or a bastard sword. Finally Deramon snorted in disgust, shook his head at his son, and turned to Mori. He called her over, and she approached hesitantly.

He took her to a tapestry upon a wall, one she had sewn throughout her sixteenth year. Upon its blue fabric, embroidered dragons flew between silver stars, and white birches of glistening thread rose below them. Mori remembered working her fingers raw on the tapestry; it had taken her countless hours to make, and she had given it to Orin to hang in his chambers. She remembered how his eyes had widened to see it, how he had hugged her, and how they had flown that night to Lacrimosa Hill to gaze upon the real stars.

And now my tapestry too hides underground like all the memories of my life.

When Deramon pulled the tapestry aside, Mori's own eyes widened. A narrow tunnel gaped there, just wide enough for a man to crawl into. Mori peered into it; she could not judge its length, but when she called out, her voice echoed deep.

"My men have been carving this tunnel since the winter," Deramon said, standing behind her. His voice, normally booming, was strangely soft. "If all else fails, Mori--if the wyverns slam at the doors of these chambers--you will crawl into it."

She pulled her head out from the tunnel, turned toward Deramon, and shivered at the sight of his eyes; she had never seen the gruff old warrior look so sad.

"Where does the tunnel lead to?" she whispered.

Still holding the tapestry back, Deramon stared into the tunnel's darkness. "To the wilderness. To hope and exile. To life." He shook his head softly. "It will save you, Mori; it will take you from this city, from war, from death. You will spend a long time crawling through its darkness. When you emerge, you will fly... fly as far as you can and never look back."

Mori stared into the tunnel. The darkness seemed to stare back, an abyss peering into her soul. Bayrin came to stand beside her, placed his arms around her, and held her close.

So that would be my fate, Mori thought. *Should the Tirans break through, I would be doomed to forever flee, to hide, to survive in pain while my people lie dead behind me, their ghosts crying to me.*

Deramon seemed to shake himself from a dream. His armor clanked, he grumbled something under his breath, and he let the tapestry fall to hide the tunnel.

"But it won't come to that," he grumbled, all the grit back in his voice, and again he was the same gruff old lord. "If the Tirans are foolish enough to invade, we'll smite them dead."

The lord turned aside with another grumble, marched toward a rack of swords, and stared stubbornly at them. Bayrin went to his side, and soon the two were arguing again. Mori remained by the tapestry. She stared at it: the lush blue fabric, the dragons of golden thread, the thin silver birches, the stars she had stabbed her fingers so many times to sew. As she looked upon the scenes, the embroidered dragons almost seemed to fly and the stars to shine: a scene of Requiem in the night, peaceful and glittering.

But now a new night falls, she thought, *and when its darkness spreads, will I dare do what I must? Will I dare enter this tunnel, crawl to life, leave the others to die? With Tirans in the hall, their steel slaughtering us, how many would flee behind me? Five? Six? Would the rest remain here in their tomb?*

She shut her eyes and turned away. She walked toward Bayrin and Deramon, stood at their side, and listened to them argue about steel and forging and the shapes of crossguards. She missed Orin and Father and Lyana, and she could not shake the trickling, icy fear that filled her belly.

MAHRDOR

He walked through the night, flanked by guards. Alongside the alleyways, the walls of workshops and winehouses closed in around him like a prison cell--craggy, hard, unyielding. Lord Mahrdor hated walls around him. He hated these narrow burrows of the commoners.

This city is a prison, he thought, mouth twisting bitterly, *and I am a hunter of the desert.*

He gritted his teeth as he walked, as around him soldiers marched, as before him commoners scuttled into their homes. He yearned to leave this cesspool, to mount his wyvern, to fly across sea and plain, to hunt in the great northern wilderness. He licked his lips, imagining it. So many creatures there to catch! So many bones to study. So much skin to peel, and screams to hear, and jars to fill.

"Let Solina crave her glory," he whispered into the night, the walls closing in around him. "Let her worship the sun. I will have my prizes of the night." He looked up at a sky strewn with stars. "The sun fades in the dark, but my collection never dies."

In his left hand, he carried a sack with three dripping lumps. With his right hand, he reached into the pouch on his belt. He fingered the treasures he kept there, teeth he had collected from the old man's sons. How they had screamed! The memory of those screams warmed his blood, and the cold, hard feel of the teeth steadied his head. Soon the alley walls no longer seemed to trap him.

There is power in my trophies. There is glory in the night. There is safety.

The alley opened into shadow, and soon they walked
across the Square of the Sun, boots thudding against its
cobblestones. Lingering peddlers and wandering youths saw the
soldiers and scurried into shadow. Clouds flowed across the
moon. Mahrdor took sharp, deep breaths, as if he could inhale
the night itself. Soon, he thought, he would carry more teeth in
his pouch--the teeth of Lyana. He decided to take her treasures
slowly, to savor them: first a toe, then a finger, eventually her foot
in a jar. He would keep her alive for as long as he could; for
decades. She was his greatest prize, his rarest of birds, and he
would make her last.

Finally he saw the winehouse again. It rose tall and narrow,
built of rugged mudbrick. A sign hung above the door, painted
blue and gold, featuring an oared ship and the words "The River
Spice".

Mahrdor turned toward his men. The Gilded Guardians
stood frozen, staring at him through their ibis helms. They
gripped their swords.

"You know what to do," he told them.

They moved forward, automatons of steel and gold. One
kicked down the door, and they streamed into the winehouse.
Mahrdor stood at the doorway, smiling softly, watching them
smash jugs of wine, crush tables, and shatter plates and mugs.
Wine thick with clay shards sluiced around his boots.

"What are you doing?" cried a crinkly voice from the second
story. "What do you want?"

The old winekeeper rushed downstairs into the common
room, hair wild. Peras was his name, Mahrdor remembered.

Foolish man, the general thought. *You should be fleeing across the
rooftops, not charging into your death.*

One Gilded Guardian grabbed the old man. The other
drove a gauntleted fist into his stomach, then backhanded him.
Blood filled the old man's mouth, and his scream faded into a

gurgle. The guards shoved him down, and one kicked him. Coughing blood, Peras crawled into the corner and shivered. He tried to reach for a fallen knife, but a guardian stepped on his hand, then raised a fist above him.

"Enough," Mahrdor said.

The Gilded Guardians froze. The winehouse lay in ruins, and the only sound was Peras's hacking breath. Mahrdor approached the fallen, bloody man and opened the sack he carried. He held it upside down, and three heads rolled onto the floor.

When Peras saw the toothless heads of his sons, he tossed back his own head and howled. He leaped up and clawed at Mahrdor, crying in agony. Blood stained his tunic and tears filled his eyes.

"My sons! My sons! They were winemakers, only winemakers." He grabbed the fallen knife and slashed the air. His eyes were red, his face torn. "Damn you, Mahrdor! May the Sun God burn you!"

Mahrdor stepped back, dodging the knife, and drew his sabre. He thrust the blade. Steel gleamed in candlelight. The sabre drove into Peras's belly so smoothly Mahrdor barely felt any resistance; it was like skewering a slab of butter. He stepped closer, driving the blade down to the hilt, smiling softly. Peras gasped and blood trickled down his chin.

"You harbored a weredragon," Mahrdor said to the dying man. "I do believe it will be *your* soul that burns."

He shoved Peras back and pulled his sword free. The old man fell, whispered a last prayer to his god, and died between the heads of his sons.

Mahrdor stared down at the body and the heads. His lips curled in disgust. The remains looked to him like crushed worms. Briefly he considered taking a trophy from Peras too, but the man had only several teeth, and the rest of him was wretched. Bile filled his throat, and Mahrdor turned away.

"Burn them," he said to his guards. "Burn everything inside this place. It sickens me."

He stepped outside into the night and sucked the air. When his head stopped spinning, he spat and walked into darkness.

I don't need that old, shriveled body in my collection, he told himself. *Soon we fly to Requiem. Soon I will have Lyana. Soon I will have all the trophies of a god's dreams.*

DERAMON

"Into the tunnels!" he shouted, flying above the city. "Single file! Walk, don't run. Keep moving!"

Below him, the people of Nova Vita shuffled down the streets. Youths were snickering with their friends; Deramon saw one boy pinch a girl's backside, making her squeal. A few old women stood chatting in the corner. Deramon fumed and smoke blasted from his nostrils. Only a year had passed since Solina had burned this city, and already these people forgot the horror of war?

"Into the tunnels, come on, you lazy bastards!" Bayrin shouted, flying beside Deramon. The young dragon blasted fire across the sky. "If this were a real invasion, you'd all be charred bones by now. Move it! Move!"

The people below hastened their step and moved down the streets. They began snaking into the three archways that led underground: one marble archway at Benedictus Square, a second by the temple, and a third behind a copse of trees by the city walls. Clad in steel, men of the City Guard lined the streets, guiding the people into safety.

As Deramon flew above the city, his belly knotted.

"They're too slow," he muttered. "Damn too slow."

Beside him, his son sighed and shook himself, clanking like a bag of dice. "They'll move faster next time, or I swear, I'll start roasting people from above." He looked at Deramon. "Father, I've seen these wyverns fly. They're fast. Damn fast. Faster than Mori with a snapping turtle chomping her tail. If any show up here, the people will have to do better."

Deramon cursed under his breath, and so much smoke left his maw it nearly blinded him. Over the past few moons, every mason and carpenter in town had been working in the tunnels. After Solina had destroyed the underground labyrinth last year, Requiem had rebuilt it stronger and safer, but that wouldn't help if the people couldn't enter fast enough.

"Move it!" he shouted at the streets below where a few stragglers shuffled toward the tunnels. Finally--it seemed like ages--the last laggard disappeared underground.

"City Guard!" Deramon shouted; a thousand of the guards still lined the streets. "Shift and fly! Battle formations!"

At his order, a thousand men and women shifted into dragons and soared. Their roar shook the city. Four phalanxes-- each with a hundred dragons--moved to perch upon the city walls. Four more phalanxes landed upon the palace, the Temple of Stars, and the city's two forts. The remaining dragons circled above Nova Vita, howling and roaring fire.

It wasn't perfect. Some dragons bumped against one another as they flew, and some seemed hopelessly confused, not sure if to perch upon a building or soar. Some phalanxes flew in tight formations, divided into battle flights of four dragons--two leaders flanked by two defenders. Other phalanxes flew in a confused cloud.

Bayrin grunted. "They're bloody farmers, Father. Look at them. Half of them look like they've never flown in their life." He sighed. "The wyverns will tear through them like Lyana's cooking through my bowels."

Deramon was busy howling commands. "Dragonclaw Phalanx, bloody stars, form rank! Flights of four, go!" He whipped his head around. "You! Where are you flying? What phalanx are you? Go, down there, guard the temple, girl!"

The groan that escaped his son's throat was loud as a roar. "Merciful stars, we're in trouble. Look at that one, Father. She's

barely fifteen if she's a day, I reckon. And she's in the City
Guard?" He panted and glared at Deramon. "Father, if Solina
reaches this city, she'll be flying with thousands of wyverns--tens
of thousands--each bearing a seasoned rider. How are these...
these farm girls and bakers' boys going to stop her?"

Deramon was wondering the same thing. Last year, he had
commanded a thousand tough, gruff men. All but two hundred
had burned, and half of those survivors now guarded the southern
border. *Damn it, I need more time,* he thought. *I need another year to
turn these youths into warriors.*

"It'll have to do," he said. He flapped his wings, rising
higher, and waited until his guards finally manned their posts.
"It's what we have, Bayrin. And they will fight when the time
comes. They might be youths. But they can still blow fire. They
can still slash claws. They will fight and they will protect our city."
He cracked his neck. "At least, Bayrin... let me pretend. It's
better to have hope than to despair." He blasted fire and howled
to the city. "Drill's over! Return to your homes! City Guard--
shift and regroup in the fortress courtyard!"

The tunnel doors opened and the people began streaming
back into the streets. A few looked around nervously, possibly
imagining the coming war. Others still laughed and gossiped as
they went. Many were wounded, still carrying the scars of the
phoenix attack; these ones limped and stared with haunted eyes.
Others ran and laughed, the scars of war gone from their bodies
and souls.

As the people returned to their homes and workshops, the
dragons of the City Guard flew to their garrison, the squat Castra
Murus by the northern wall. The thud of two thousand wings
sent saplings bending, cloaks fluttering, and dust flying across the
fort's battlements. When the dragons landed in the courtyard,
they shifted into armored men and women bearing swords; they
would need their steel should the battle move underground.

Finally, after long moments of bumping into one another and Deramon shouting himself hoarse, they stood in formation--ten phalanxes, each commanded by a survivor of the old City Guard. They stood in rows, stiff, heads raised. One man scratched himself, then froze when Deramon scowled.

Finally, when all stood at attention, Deramon shifted too and stood before them in human form. Bayrin stood at his side, shaking his head sadly.

"Farm girls and bakers' boys," the young man repeated and sighed.

Deramon grumbled as he stared at his warriors. Elethor had drafted every healthy Vir Requis over fifteen years old, but some here looked younger. A few girls were so short and skinny they looked barely old enough to fly, let alone fight a wyvern. Some boys looked so green, Deramon half expected them to be chewing straw and herding sheep right here in the courtyard. Some were scrawny, others fat. A dozen or so were old graybeards with bent backs. Some had the pale look of scribes or priests, others the tanned look of farmers. They all had but one thing in common. They all looked scared.

"They sent me boys and girls!" Deramon shouted at them. He spat noisily. "They sent me the sons of farmers, boys who had never held a sword. They sent me the daughters of seamstresses, girls who had only wielded needles. They sent me weak, frightened children!"

They stood at attention, stiff, a few trembling. Deramon growled and continued.

"But now war is coming. Now you are no longer youths." He raised his voice. "Now you are men and women of the City Guard! Now you are warriors of Requiem!" He stared from one to another, scowling. "I once led a thousand seasoned fighters; they fell. You are here to continue their fight. You are here to honor their memory." He paced the courtyard, moving across the lines. "But when Queen Solina invades our city, you will not fight for honor. You will not fight for glory. You will not fight for gold, because I'm not going to pay you." He stood still and faced them. "You will fight for farmers and seamstresses, for scribes and masons, for winemakers and shepherds. You will fight for your fathers, your mothers, your siblings, your grandparents. You will fight for your homes, because if you don't, Solina will destroy those homes and kill those families." He drew his sword and raised it. "Today you are warriors! Today I am proud of you. Raise your swords, City Guard!"

They roared. A thousand blades rose like a steel forest. At his side, Bayrin was grinning wildly and raising his sword so high, his arm looked ready to dislocate.

The roaring continued for long moments. When Deramon stalked off to his chambers, he heard the guardsman swing blades, cheer, and speak of slicing Solina to ribbons. They laughed. The fear had left them.

But fear still dwells inside of me, Deramon thought. He closed the door to his small, shadowy chamber in the heart of Castra Murus. The air was cold and damp, and Deramon poured himself a mug of strong spirits. He drank; it burned down his throat. When he closed his eyes, he saw the faces again--the faces of his dead men, staring up at him as he shoveled dirt into their graves.

"They're only youths," he whispered in the dark. "Only children. Stars, don't let them die under my command." He lowered his head and his shoulders shook. "Stars, don't let me lose these boys and girls too."

He looked out the window at the sky. Night was falling. War was near.

ELETHOR

"Come on, Elethor!" she said. She tugged his hand and they ran through the forest. Solina laughed. "Come on, you turtle!"

Leafy branches slapped them. Moss and dry leaves flew from under their boots. Finally they emerged from behind alders thick with lichen, beams of sunlight fell, and they beheld the waterfall. Solina gasped and squeezed Elethor's hand so tightly she nearly crushed it.

"Beautiful," she whispered.

The water crashed down a cliff into a pond, spraying mist and foam. A great, mossy statue of a dragon perched atop the cliff, guarding the waterfall. The ancient children of Requiem had carved it, legends said, thousands of years before King Aeternum had raised the palace of Requiem.

Solina spun toward Elethor, teeth sparkling in her smile, her eyes glittering blue. Her chest rose and fell as she panted.

"Come on," she said, "let's get closer!"

Elethor stood before the pond. The waterfall's spray wet his face. "Why don't we just admire it from here, we can--"

With a snort, she leaped into the water, dragging him with her.

Water flowed over him and entered his nostrils. He thrust his head out and took a breath, only for Solina to splash him, filling his mouth with water.

"Elethor, come on. Closer! Right under it." She pointed at the waterfall that crashed ahead into the pool. Her hair turned dark gold with water, and her freckles shone like stars. She turned and began swimming toward the waterfall's wrath.

"Solina! Can't we just swim here?"

She turned back toward him, gave him a toothy grin, then began to swim toward the waterfall again. With a sigh, Elethor followed. The spray soon rose so thickly he could see only a foot ahead. The water crashed so loudly, his ears ached. Water kept filling his mouth, eyes, and nostrils.

"Solina, where are you?" he shouted and spat out water.

He looked around but saw only the mist. Currents swirled around him, and when he put his feet down, he could no longer feel the pool's floor.

"Solina!"

A hand reached out from the mist, grabbed the back of his head, and pulled him forward. He found himself pressed against Solina, her mouth against his, her hands in his hair. They kissed for long moments. The water crashed around them.

She shoved him back. "Get *off.* Come on, follow me." She mussed his hair, then vanished into the spray.

He caught her on the lakeshore. She stood before him, dripping wet, her tunic clinging to her. With a crooked smile, she stripped off her clothes and shook her hair. They made love there in the sunlight, until dirt and grass and dry leaves clung to their wet bodies, then lay holding each other and watching the water. She nestled against him, and he kissed her head. The autumn leaves rustled and the blackbirds sang.

"I don't ever want to go back," she whispered. She tightened her arms around him, laid her head against his chest, and closed her eyes. "I don't ever want to return to Nova Vita. I want to stay here with you, Elethor. Just you and me here in the forest. I love you so much. I hate all the other ones. I hate them!" She opened her eyes, revealing tears. "I hate Lyana, and I hate her father, and I hate all the rest of them." She growled, then sniffed, and her tears fell onto his chest. She held him tight. "I love you so much, El. You are the only one I love. Let's never go back."

He kissed her head and held her close. Her naked body was warm against him.

"Lyana can lecture a lot; I know it! She does the same to me, but she means no harm. Mori can seem to pity you; I know that too. But she only tries to comfort you, not hurt you. You know this, Solina; I've told you many times. Please let go of your anger." He pulled back an errant lock of her hair. "Never go back? Requiem is our home; it's your home too now. Will we live as beasts in the wilderness? Hermits clad in leaf and fur?"

"I don't need any leaf or fur." A deep light filled her eyes. "I am no beast, no hermit. I am the last survivor of the Phoebus Dynasty. Let us flee Requiem! Come with me to Tiranor, El. I will rally my people. I will raise the palace anew, that palace your father destroyed. We will rebuild the desert, El! You and I. We will become great rulers, an empress and emperor in a magical realm." She clutched his shoulders, digging her fingernails into them. "It will be our secret world, a world of steel, spice, and sunlight." Her eyes shone.

Elethor sighed. "Solina, I wish I could go there with you. Truly I do. But... what lies there for us? A ruined, toppled city. A desert of sand and death." He shook his head. "How could I leave my family? How could I leave Orin and Mori and Father and the rest of them?"

She snarled. Her fingernails drove deeper into his shoulders, so painful that he winced.

"To the Abyss with them," she snarled. "I don't care about them, El. They don't understand us. They don't know what it's like to be us. They don't know how much we love each other." She rose to her feet, walked toward the lake, and stood with her back to him. She gazed at the waterfall. "One day they will see,

El. They will see my strength, and they will see our love, and we will no longer have to hide."

He walked toward her and embraced her. She laid her head against his shoulder, and they stood holding each other, watching the water crash.

He turned around.

Below the hill, his army stood--three thousand dragons clad in armor, snorting fire and smoke. They covered the valley, scales chinking, the heat of their flames filling the air. Elethor stood above them, still in human form--no longer a skinny youth, but a bearded man in armor, a sword at his side, his face scarred with war.

It's been eight years since that day, he thought. And even now he missed the touch of sunlight, the kiss of her lips, and her hair between his fingers.

She was different then. I was not wrong to love her then.

He lowered his head and closed his eyes. The guilt clawed inside him, clutching his innards. She had been his love--his life. *It's me she wants. It's our war--hers and mine.* He gritted his teeth. *And thousands will die for us.*

He turned away from his army and looked south. Mountains spread into a horizon of dark clouds. Ralora Beach lay beyond the shadows; from there she would emerge.

Is Lord Oldnale right? Do I lead us to destruction? Will Requiem burn for the love and hatred of me and her?

Staring into the southern clouds and rain, he remembered Solina killing the children in the tunnels, burning the city, screaming that she would slaughter them all. He clenched his fists.

No. Oldnale is wrong. Solina would destroy us--for the death of her parents, for her captivity, for her madness.

He shifted into a dragon, flapped his wings, and rose into the sky. He roared a pillar of fire.

"Dragons of Requiem!" he called. "We fly! We fly to war!"

They howled behind him. Their wings beat like war drums. Their flames rose. The Royal Army of Requiem took flight. Elethor soared into skies of cloud and rain, and his army followed with howls and fountains of fire. As he dived through the storm, Elethor remembered swimming after Solina as the water pounded him, chasing her, seeking her through mist and spray. He had caught her and kissed her that day; now he would meet her again... and kill her with steel, flame, and blood.

SOLINA

She stood upon the Tower of Akartum, the tallest spire of her palace, and caressed the chains embedded into the limestone.

"Soon you will hang here, Elethor," she whispered. She imagined caressing his face like she caressed the chains, kissing him, and leaving him to wither in the sun. "Soon you will scream here upon the city your father burned."

At her feet, five vultures cawed in an iron cage. They bit at the bars, screeched for food, and clawed the air. She had been starving them, tossing them enough raw meat to keep them alive but always hungry, always vicious. She cooed to them.

"Soon, my darlings. Soon, when he hangs here, you will feed upon his flesh."

The smiled softly, imagining it. How he would writhe! How he would beg! When the vultures tore into his flesh, he would weep for forgiveness. When the vultures tore out his eyes, he wouldn't even be able to do that. But he would scream.

"Oh yes, you will scream, Elethor." Solina licked her lips. "The entire city will hear it."

She swept her arms around her, spreading her light across Irys. The city rustled around her, the palms and figs swaying, the cranes and ibises singing, the River Pallan flowing like a string of silver. The sandstone temple rose before her, kissed in sunlight. The villas of the wealthy lined the riversides, while behind them stretched thousands of brick homes, silos, and shops. Far north, the city melted into Hog Corner and finally to delta and sea.

"I will fly across this sea for you, Elethor," she whispered. "And I will bring you home."

The vultures bit at their cage, screeching for blood.

Smiling softly, Solina turned south and faced the desert. Upon the dunes stood her army. Twenty thousand wyverns screeched and clawed the sand, a host such as the world had never seen, twice the size and might of the phoenix army she had led last year. Men and women sat upon them, clad in steel, their shields like twenty thousand suns, their spears like rising sunrays. Solina raised her arms and cried to them.

"You will slay dragons!" she shouted, and her riders raised their spears and howled. The wyverns tossed back their heads, jaws rising like blades, and roared. The city shook with their cry. It was a cry of war, of death, of light and victory and her eternal glory. It was a cry that thudded in her chest, blazed with light across her eyes, and filled her mouth with the taste of blood.

"You will topple the lizard courts, avenge your fallen brothers, and bring the Reptile King in chains to die in sunfire!"

Their howl swept over her like wind from the desert, like the breath of her lord. She whistled, a sound like a bird of prey, and her wyvern took flight from the courtyard below. The beast's wings thudded, bending palm trees and sending sand flying across the palace. His scales, square plates like armor, clanked and glimmered. His eyes blazed red, his black teeth snapped, and smoke rose from his nostrils. Baal, the king of wyverns--a forge of acid, a deity of wrath and muscle and bloodlust.

When he reached the tower's battlements, Solina climbed into his saddle. She grabbed the shield and spear that hung there and raised them--sun and sunray. She dug her heels into Baal, and the wyvern's wings beat like a storm into sails. The beast soared, wind streamed Solina's hair, and she snarled.

"To war!" she cried and raised her spear higher. The tip glinted, a beacon of fire.

"To war!" howled twenty thousand riders behind her, and wyverns screeched, and wings thundered. The city streamed beneath her, trees bending and leaves flying under the blast of leathern wings. When she looked behind her, she saw her army following, a sunlit host, a light upon the desert, a fire to burn out the darkness of dragons.

"To Requiem!" she shouted.

"To Requiem!" rose the cry behind her.

They streamed over delta and sea. To war. To Requiem. And to Elethor.

"We will meet again, my love, my life," she whispered, remembering those days long ago when she would love him in darkness. Soon no more darkness would hide him. Soon he would hang upon her tower, and her lord's light would strip him bare, and his bones would be her toys.

The wrath of Tiranor flew, and Solina smiled.

LYANA

Pain burned across her like scarabs ripping flesh from bone. Every flap of the wyvern's wings shots bolts of fire through her. She sat in the saddle, chains clutching her in an iron embrace. All around her, the army of wyverns flew, a storm of scales rising and falling. Wind gusted, rain fell, and the wyverns soared. Lyana winced, her stomach rising and falling like a dead jellyfish on a storming sea. She felt a stitch on her back open and blood trickle to her tailbone. She closed her eyes and let out a soft moan.

"Silence," said Mahrdor. He sat in the saddle behind her, his arms reaching around her as he held the reins. "Make another sound, and I'll cut off your hand and gag you with it."

She fell silent. They had stitched the raw, bloody lashes across her body, but not before rubbing ilbane into them. The poison still burned, spreading through her. Every jostle in the saddle felt like whips beating her anew. She opened her eyes once more, saw the wyverns rise and fall in the rain, and swallowed to stop from gagging.

Oh Elethor, she thought and her eyes stung. *I failed you.*

He was waiting at Ralora Beach, she knew--hundreds of leagues away. Because of her... because of her. She grimaced and cursed herself, the anguish a claw inside her. She had fallen into Mahrdor's trap so easily. She had doomed her people to death-- sweet Princess Mori, her dearest friend; her family, whom she loved more than life; Elethor, her betrothed and king. *I doomed them all.*

A gust of wind blew rain across them. The wyvern bucked and howled, and Lyana dug her fingernails into her palms. She felt another stitch open, and she trembled with the pain. *What I must look like now...* Her face felt swollen; she could barely see through her puffy eyes. Her torso bore a network of long, raw welts still oozing blood between the stitches. The chains dug into her, working their way through her skin. Her scalp still felt raw and bare. If her family saw her now, would they even recognize her, or see only a bloodied, beaten wretch?

A thunderbolt crashed and the wyverns screeched. A few spewed acid into distant forests below; where the foul liquid landed, the trees crumbled. Lyana looked around her, trying to place her location. She could see almost nothing through the storm: trees below, the shadow of mountains ahead, a river to her west. They had crossed the Tiran Sea yesterday, but Lyana did not know this land.

This is not Requiem, she thought. She had flown over Requiem countless times, traversing it north to south, east to west. She knew every mountain, river, and forest in Aeternom's Kingdom. She breathed out sharply through her nose.

Of course.

She shook her head. How had she not guessed it? Solina's army would not invade Requiem's southern border; a thousand dragons patrolled it, from Gilnor's swamps in the west to Ralora Beach in the east.

"We're flying over Osanna," she whispered as thunder rolled.

Osanna. Ancient realm of men. Empire of steel and stone. Its soldiers rode horses, unable to become dragons like Requiem's children; they could not stop an army of wyverns. Osanna's border stretched across the east of Requiem, from the snowy mountains of northern Fidelium and down hundreds of leagues to the southern sea. Not with every dragon alive could Requiem patrol that great wilderness of forest, mountain, and plain.

Lyana gritted her teeth. She had to escape. She had to warn Elethor. Images of the Phoenix War swam before her: burning people in the streets, children torn in two, severed limbs littering the underground. *I can't let my city burn again.*

The fear and anger pounded through her, overpowering her pain. She looked down at the irons binding her: they wrapped around her torso and clasped her wrists behind her back. Her armor and sword were as parts of her; they could shift into a dragon with her. But these manacles were foreign constraints. If she shifted now, they would dig through her enlarged body, shoving her back into human form.

Her mind worked feverishly. Mahrdor would have the keys. She knew such men; he wanted to control her, to own her, to have power over her enslavement and freedom. Even if he intended to never unlock her, he would keep the keys on him. *Part of owning someone is having the power to free them... and refusing to.*

She would kill him, she swore. Even if they flew at full speed, it would take several days to reach Nova Vita; she would kill him before that time. She would kill him tonight, or next night, or while they rode this wyvern, or outside the very walls of Nova Vita, but she would kill him. She would not let him reach her city. She would not let him bring death and blood to her people.

He will pin me down tonight, she thought. *He will shove himself inside me as I lie chained, as he proves his dominion. And I will bite out his throat.* She snarled into the rain. She could not grow dragon fangs while chained, but her teeth could still shed blood.

They flew for hours. They flew through wind and lightning, over forest and glen, over forts and snaking walls where men scurried like ants. They passed out of the storm into a red sunset, and the wyverns screeched, a sound like cracking mountains, like dying worlds. Thousands of the creatures howled in the red light, flies bustling in a puddle of blood. Solina rode at their lead, all in gold, her banner raised. The queen began to descend toward a field of rocks and wild grass, and the others followed. Air shrieked around Lyana, her head spun, and her stomach lurched. She had flown for countless hours as a dragon; flying in human form was new, and she gritted her teeth to stay conscious.

The ground rushed up to meet them. The wyverns filled their wings with air and landed, claws kicking up earth and grass. They tossed back their heads and shrieked to the sky, and the world seemed to shake. Mahrdor landed atop a hill, and when his wyvern bucked, Lyana fell back against the general. Her back blazed, an inferno of agony. His breath filled her ear, scented of wine and the honeyed scarabs he ate.

"Tonight you will dance for me again," he whispered.

His wyvern lowered its wing, forming a ramp to the ground. Mahrdor dismounted, grabbed Lyana, and pulled her to the field. She stood chained beside him, watching the army set camp, and tried to judge their location. Bayrin had said that, flying as hard as he could--pushing himself to the very limits of his strength--he could travel from Irys to Nova Vita in five days. If these wyverns flew as hard, they were in south Osanna now, somewhere west of Altus Mare port, but still south of the great city of Confutatis. The plains rolled for leagues around her, fading into mist and the shadows of jagged mountains.

Soldiers bustled about, their steel red in the sunset. As darkness fell, they lit torches and fires. Commanders marched around the camp, shouting orders as lower ranks unpacked supplies from their wyverns. Tents began to rise, squat and tan for the common soldiers, tall and embroidered for the officers. Around the campfires, the troops began to eat their battle rations: flat breads dipped in palm oil, dried fish, tangy cheeses, and dried figs and dates. Where the officers camped, cooks prepared more lavish meals: water fowl brought live in cages, slaughtered fresh, and roasted upon coals; platters of pomegranates, olives, and small hard apples; and soft breads cooked upon iron disks. Wine and beer flowed through the camp, and as darkness fell, soldiers sang of the conquest to come. The wyverns fed from sacks of rotten meat bustling with flies, and they too shrieked as if singing for war.

At the far side of the camp, upon a boulder the size of a house, stood a tall shadow--a woman holding a banner, her hair flowing in the night.

Solina. Queen of Tiranor.

Lyana gritted her teeth, staring at the queen over the army of man and beast. Was Solina staring back at her from the darkness? Lyana thought of how Solina had seduced Elethor in his youth, kissed him, made love to him in Nova Vita. The rage simmered inside her. This desert tyrant had tainted Lyana's betrothed, burned her home, and killed so many of her people.

I will kill you too, Solina, she thought, fists clenched behind her back. *I will kill you and Mahrdor. I vow it. I vow it by the stars of my people.* She raised her eyes, seeking those stars, but clouds covered the night. *First night from Tiranor. How many more nights are we from my home?*

Armor creaked and Mahrdor placed a hand on her shoulder. His fingers closed around it, too tight, driving pain through a welt that rose there. He gazed upon the camp with her. His face was blank, the face of a golden statue. Lyana stared at his belt where hung a ring of keys.

Those keys are for my shackles, she knew. *And he wants me to see them. He wants me to know his power over me.*

"You will dine with me tonight," he said. "Come, my tent is ready for us."

He gestured at a lavish tent, as large as a commoner's house, which rose upon a knoll. Its black canvas walls were emblazoned with golden suns. Gilded Guardians surrounded the tent, bearing spears and shields. Despite her fear and wounds,

Lyana found that her belly grumbled. She could not remember
when last she had eaten.

Clutching her shoulder, Mahrdor led her into the tent.
Inside, his men had set an oak table, a bed topped with
embroidered blankets, and iron candelabra holding a score of
candles. A meal steamed upon the table--a honeyed roast duck on
a bed of sliced limes, a platter of flat breads dipped in oil, stewed
greens topped with sliced garlic and almonds, and a bowl of
miniature oranges from the southern city of Iysa. A golden jug of
wine stood by two jeweled cups. Two chairs stood at the table,
their olivewood engraved with scenes of ibises flying over rushes.

"Sit," he told her, led her to a chair, and shoved her into it.
"Eat."

He sat across the table from her, took a knife, and began
to carve the duck. The skin *cracked* when he cut into it, and the
meat's scent filled Lyana's nostrils. Despite herself, her mouth
watered. She sat, wounds blazing, wrists bound behind her back.
When he placed morsels on her plate, she leaned forward and ate.
The meat was fatty and tender, the bread still steaming and
dripping olive oil, and the stewed greens so soft they almost
melted on her tongue. When he poured wine into her mug, she
grabbed the rim with her teeth and drank; it was strong, dry wine
that spun her head.

For a long while, they ate silently. Mahrdor watched her
during the meal, eating little himself; he merely nibbled the odd
morsel. His eyes never left her, but Lyana didn't care. She was
famished and she ate whatever he gave her. She would need her
strength to kill him. She would need her strength to flee this
place.

Finally, when the duck lay as barren bones, Mahrdor
sighed.

"It is a pity," he said. He reached across the table and caressed her raw scalp. "You had such beautiful hair. Dyed a Tiran platinum, I presume? Do I detect red stubble growing?"

She swallowed a bite of bread, glared at him, and said nothing.

He sighed. "Lyana, you misjudge me. That is your name, is it not? Lyana Eleison, a lady of Requiem's court?" He sipped his wine. "I care not that you are a weredragon. I knew you to be one the very first night I saw you. Did I hurt you then?" He shook his head. "I am not Solina. I wish not to torture you, nor beat you, nor parade you through the streets as the commoners pelt you with their trash. I did not give you your wounds; the queen did that. I did not place these manacles around you; she did."

She growled at him. "You caged me."

He raised his eyebrows. "Caged you? Yes, that I did. I caged you in a gilded work of art, its bars shaped as dragons--a home for a rare bird, for a beloved pet. Manacles of iron? Crude things. They do not befit one so fair."

"Then remove them from me."

"And see my rare bird fly away? No, I dare not. Not here in this camp." He picked an olive from a dish, placed it in his cheek, and sucked it. "I do not crave war, Lyana; it is a barbarous thing. I do not crave blood, nor the torture of my enemies; those are things for brutes, for lesser men. I am--"

"A collector, yes. So you have said."

He laughed--a cold, brief sound. "I do repeat myself, don't I? A fault I should remedy. But yes, Lyana, I am a collector of fine things. The map you saw in my chamber was set there to trap you; my other prizes are true trophies. Oh, I could make some trophy from you too; a shrunken head, perhaps, or a chair from your bones and skin. I would enjoy carving you into a piece of art, but I think you, Lyana, are a greater prize when living. I will modify you; a few changes here and there with knife and hammer. But aside from those, I will keep you as you are--a rare bird, a pet for a golden cage. Surely that is a better fate than what Solina can offer you; she would offer you only the dungeon, the lash, and the poison." He caressed her cheek. "I will protect you from her, Lyana, and you will be mine. A true weredragon noblewoman--the crown of my collection."

She raised her chin and glared. "You will not call me that word. I am a Vir Requis. I am descended from Terra Eleison himself. I am--"

"...in no position to make demands," he finished for her. He spat his olive pit into a handkerchief, folded it neatly, and placed it by his plate. "Are you done eating? Good, Lyana. Good. The food has done well with you; the color returns to your cheeks and the fire to your eyes. Soon your wounds will heal, and your hair will grow, and you will be as fair as before. I will see to it."

He rose to his feet and began to remove his armor. He placed his breastplate, vambraces, pauldrons, and a dozen other pieces of steel upon a table. When he stood clad in nothing but his tunic and breeches, he moved to stand by the bed.

"Now," he said, "dance for me. Dance like you danced in my home. Dance and you will see that home again--and never more Solina's dungeon."

She stared at him. He stared back, digging his gaze into her. *For Requiem.*

She rose to her feet so suddenly her chair fell back and nearly knocked over a candle. Her chains clanked. Never removing her eyes from his, she danced.

Once she had danced in silks; today she wore chains and tatters. Once she had swayed like a desert wind; today she moved like a trapped bird fluttering against the bars of its cage. He eyed her hungrily. As she swayed near him, he tugged at the rags she wore, tearing a strip of cloth. He bared his teeth, a rabid wolf eyeing his prey.

As she danced before him, chains chinking, he reached out like a striking asp, grabbed her, and pulled her onto the bed. He shoved her facedown onto the mattress, and when she looked over her shoulder, she saw him undoing the laces of his breeches.

When he mounted her, she closed her eyes, gritted her teeth, and buried her face in the bed. She wanted to do it now, but forced herself to endure him. He was lustful now. He was strong now. He would be weak soon. He had known her twice before; she could endure it again. She closed her eyes and thought of the skies of Requiem, the sound of harps in marble temples, and the thousands of dragons who flew like shards of colored glass under the stars.

When he was done with her, he rose to his feet, breathing heavily. He approached the table, yawned magnificently, and began to pour more wine.

"By the Sun God, Lyana," he said, "you do take the strength out of a man."

Quick as a juggler, Lyana shoved her bound wrists under and around her legs; her arms were now bound before her, not behind her back.

She leaped toward him.

She wrapped her chains around his throat and pulled.

The jug of wine fell and shattered.

Their lovemaking had weakened him; it had strengthened her. He made a choking sound, struggling for breath and finding none. She dug her heels into the floor, growled, and pulled back with all her might, willing the chains to dig into his neck. He reached over his back, and his fingers grazed her scalp; he could have grabbed her hair, had Solina left her any. She tugged the chains with all the strength she still had.

"I am Lyana Eleison, daughter of Lord Deramon and
Mother Adia," she hissed into his ear. "I am a knight of Requiem.
I am a daughter of starlight. You will die today."

He stumbled back to the bed, clawing at her. He was a tall
man; she was slight. She clung to his back, tugging, grinding the
chains. Blood dripped down his chest. He croaked for breath.
They slammed into a candelabrum; the candles fell onto the rug.
He stumbled toward the tent walls. She dug her heels and pulled
him back.

Die already! She gritted her teeth and hissed as she pulled
the chains. He took a step toward his armor and sabre. Snarling,
she tugged the chains mightily; they dug into his throat. He kept
walking. Another candleholder fell and the rug began to blaze.
His hand reached for his sword. He grabbed the hilt.

Lyana twisted the chains and gave a mighty tug. Mahrdor
drew his sword, gasping for breath. She pulled him back. He
raised the blade. His bare feet stepped onto the burning rug, and
with a choked mewl, he fell forward.

He crashed to his knees, and Lyana tugged backward,
growling and straining, until he gave a last gurgle, and his head
slumped forward.

Crouched above him, Lyana snarled and looked around the
tent. The flames had spread to the walls and crackled, raising
black smoke. Shouts rose outside. She heard soldiers clanking
toward the burning tent. She straightened, panting and growling,
a feral animal. Her arms and legs were still manacled. Gilded
Guardians burst into the tent.

With a shout, Lyana slammed her fists against a burning
chair, sending it flying. It crashed into the guardians and blazed.
There were three of them, their blades only half-drawn.

Stars of Requiem, be with me.

Lyana crouched, grabbed Mahrdor's sword, and wrenched it
free from his grip. Was he dead or merely unconscious? She had

no time to check. Wrists bound, she swung the sabre with both hands. She drove the blade down, hitting one guardian where his pauldron met his neck; her blade drove several inches down his torso. She pulled it free, swung again, and cleaved the neck of another guard.

The third managed to draw his own sword. Lyana swung, parried, and drove the blade forward. It clanged against the guardian's armor. The tent blazed. Lyana swiped her sword across the tabletop, sending burning scraps into the guardian's face. When he fell back, she drove her blade down hard, cleaving him.

Outside, she heard more soldiers shouting and running uphill. Smoke filled the tent now, so thick that she coughed and could barely see. She leaped over a flaming rug, knelt by Mahrdor, and grabbed the keys from his belt. Frantically, she twisted her fingers; with her wrists bound, she could not fit the key into the manacles' lock.

Soldiers burst into the tent.

Lyana swung around, lashed her sword, and tossed a flaming table against them. Key in hand, she leaped over fire, through tent walls, and out onto the hill. She rolled in the night, still chained, toward an army.

Soldiers came rushing up toward her. With her mouth, Lyana thrust key into lock and twisted. The manacles around her wrists clanked open, revealing bloodied flesh. The soldiers ran, shouted, and began drawing their blades. Teeth bared, Lyana thrust the key into the chains around her legs. The lock clinked. The chains fell. The soldiers reached her.

She swung her sword, parrying one weapon. A second sabre nipped her shoulder, and she screamed. She raised her blade, parried, and thrust. Blood splashed. Lyana leaped back.

Pain exploded when she summoned her magic. Her head spun. She could barely cling to it. She was too wounded, still coughing, still too weak. Scales appeared and disappeared across her. A sabre swung down, and she raised her blade, barely parrying. Wyverns shrieked around her and the clouds above swirled. Two of the scaled beasts came swooping toward her. The world burned and spun.

Requiem! May our wings forever find your sky.

Her mother's words spoke in her mind, deep and strong, comforting her.

This is not me. I am not a wounded creature who lies in the mud. I am Lyana Eleison. I am a knight of Requiem, daughter of a great priestess. I walked through the Abyss itself. I fought in the Phoenix War. I am Vir Requis and I will find my sky.

Blades lashed down toward her.

They clanged against scales.

Her wings beat like war drums, sending smoke and dirt flying. With a great roar, a *dragon* roar, she soared. Her claws lashed men. She flew higher. Wyverns swooped toward her, and she blew her fire. The jet of flame roared, lighting the night, and slammed into the beasts. They howled and bucked, and Lyana shot between them.

She flew straight up, moving so fast that her head spun. She dared not look behind her. She crashed through clouds until the stars burst into light above. The Draco constellation shone, the stars of her fathers. She flew toward it.

Shrieks sounded below her. She looked down to see wyverns--a hundred or more--burst from the clouds toward her. Riders sat upon them, and their crossbows fired. Lyana howled and banked, and the bolts shot around her. One scratched her shoulder. Another pierced her wing, and she roared in pain. She rained her fire, hit one wyvern, and flew southward.

The beasts shrieked. Jets of acid flew.

Lyana soared, neck craned back, so fast she nearly blacked out. The acid flew beneath her; she flapped her wings mightily, but drops still sizzled against her tail. She howled. It felt like a hundred arrows slamming into her.

I am a bellator of Requiem. I am a warrior. I walked through the Abyss. I will fly!

In the south, she saw the storm still brewing. Lightning burst inside the clouds, stains of light. Lyana growled and flew toward the tempest. An army of wyverns flew behind.

Acid sprayed. Lyana swooped and shot forward, narrowly dodging it. A drop splashed her wing and ate a hole through it, only coin-sized but blazing with agony. Wind whistled through the opening. She roared and flew forward, straight as a javelin.

When she looked over her shoulder, she saw more wyverns; hundreds now flew behind her. Their bolts and acid flew. Lyana gritted her teeth, beat her wings mightily, and shot into the storm.

Thunder boomed. Lightning blazed around her. Rain pounded her, aching against her wounds. The winds billowed her wings; she nearly tumbled. She narrowed her eyes and gritted her teeth. Despite the agony, she flew on. Lightning crashed and the clouds roiled like smoky demons.

I will never stop flying. Not until I reach Elethor.

If Bayrin had delivered the message, Elethor and his Royal Army waited at Ralora Beach. It lay hundreds of leagues away.

I must find him. I must summon him back to Nova Vita. If the wyverns reach the city before us, Requiem will fall.

Lyana snarled and flew.

MORI

Silence filled the royal hall.

Beyond the marble columns, silence filled the city.

Mori sat upon the Oak Throne, barely wanting to breathe, and prayed for some sound, anything to break this emptiness. She wanted to hear armor creak as soldiers rushed outside, or dragons roar above, or minstrels play, or children laugh, or... anything other than this silence that rang in her ears.

Outside, the guards manned their posts, perched upon wall and roof. Their family members, those too young or old or wounded to serve, huddled in their homes. Barely a breath stirred across Nova Vita, jewel of the north, capital of Requiem.

We all wait, Mori thought, *with bated breath, with tight hearts, with tingling fingers. We wait for the storm to strike. Stars of Requiem, look over my brother. Bring him home to me safely.*

She turned to her left, and the fear in her heart softened. Bayrin stood there, the only other soul in the hall. Her guardsman held the hilt of his sword, and a helm covered his head of shaggy red curls. When he saw her looking at him, he tilted that head to her, gave her a crooked smile, and winked.

"You look quite comfortable in that throne, little one. I think when Elethor returns, he might find a contender for the crown."

She gave him a shaky smile; the sound of his voice was desperate relief, a breath of air for a drowning woman.

"I wish I never had to sit upon this throne," she said. Her smile faded and she looked at her feet; she was short enough that they did not reach the floor. "I miss the days my father sat here.

I miss the days Orin filled the seat when Father was away. I..."
She sighed and clutched her luck finger. "I never thought Elethor
and I would be the ones ruling here."

Bayrin cleared his throat theatrically. "*Elethor and I*, is it?
Mors, my sweetness, dear old El rules alone; he is our king and
tyrant, as tragic as that is. *You* are a seat filler." He gave her a
penetrating stare. "At least you are quite prettier to look at than
Elethor; guarding him is a real eyesore."

Mori lowered her eyes. She wished she could laugh at
Bayrin's words. More than anything, she wanted to lie in his arms
in some fluffy bed, to watch the clouds outside the window, to
laugh at his prattling until her cheeks hurt. She wanted little else
from this life; not a throne to fill, not gowns, not power... only a
warm bed, an open sky, and a man who loved her. She sighed. If
Solina reached this city, even those humble dreams would be lost.
Solina would burn them with the rest of this city.

Before her eyes, she saw the Phoenix War again: Solina
raining fire upon the city; children running burning through the
streets; men crawling through tunnels, bleeding, missing limbs;
and more painful than all, she saw her brother burnt and cut on
the ground, entrails spilling, as Lord Acribus hurt her. She closed
her eyes, as if she could banish those visions in darkness, but they
still danced.

Breathe, Mori, she told herself. *Like Adia taught you. Breathe
and be brave.*

Standing at her side, Bayrin took her hand and squeezed it.
"Don't be scared, Mors. If any wyverns enter this room, I'll give
them a taste of my fire. It doesn't taste quite as bad as my
mother's porridge, but it'll do the trick."

But Mori wasn't scared for herself; she had fought in a war
already, and she was ready to fight another one. She was scared
for her people: the farmers and tradesmen, the merchants and
miners, the children and elderly. If Elethor did not return--she

trembled to think of it, but knew that she must--she would lead what remained of Requiem. Could she and Bayrin truly fight Solina and all her hatred?

She looked at Bayrin. He smiled at her, hand on the hilt of his sword.

And if the time comes, she thought, *will he draw that sword for my last mercy? If our city walls lie fallen around us, and Solina's men pound at our doors, would Bayrin find the strength to plunge his sword into my breast, then fall upon it?*

She left her throne and walked across the great hall of Requiem's kings. Its marble columns towered, the tallest structures in Requiem. As she walked, Mori touched every pillar she passed. She had studied many scrolls about their history. Three hundred years ago, Queen Gloriae had risen from the ashes of war and built forty-nine of these columns. The fiftieth, which Mori now approached, was thousands of years old; the first King Aeternum, father of the dynasty, had carved that column in the days when Vir Requis still lived wild. In the books, it was written that even Dies Irae the Destructor, who had killed a million Vir Requis, could not topple that column.

When Mori reached the ancient pillar, she placed her palm against it, lowered her head, and closed her eyes.

"Please, King Aeternum," she whispered, willing her voice to travel past the ages, through generations of monarchs, to the first king of her land. "Please, my king, give us strength. Watch over us this hour. I will not let your column fall."

She tried to imagine the old monarchs of Requiem standing here and praying: King Aeternum who raised this column millennia ago; King Benedictus who led Requiem in war against the griffins; the great Queen Lacrimosa who fell in the Battle of King's Forest; Queen Gloriae who raised Requiem from ruin and founded Nova Vita; Queen Luna the Traveler who had written many books and scrolls; and her father, King Olasar, the greatest man she had known.

And now Elethor and I, the young prince and princess, are the last of our dynasty. Now we must pray, and we must fight.

She opened her eyes, left the column, and approached the doors of her hall. They stood open before her, revealing the city. Mori stepped under the gateway, stood above a great marble stairway, and stared upon her realm. Cobbled streets snaked among young birches, spreading to white walls; beyond lay forests, mountains, and an orange sky. The wind billowed her hair.

Bayrin came to stand beside her and held her hand. They stood together, silent, watching the long night fall.

ELETHOR

They perched upon the cliffs of Ralora Beach, three thousand
dragons with smoke in their nostrils, fire in their maws, and fear
in their hearts. Smoothed stones and seashells, white and indigo
and deep purple, formed a mosaic upon the shore below,
appearing and disappearing as the waves raced, crashed against
the cliffs, and retreated in an eternal assault. Beyond this shore of
stone and shell, the sea stretched into the horizon, a gray carpet
patched with metallic blues and greens. The sky above mirrored
the waters, roiling with clouds that veiled the sun.

"Where are you, Solina?" Elethor whispered. He stood atop
a towering boulder, the highest point on the cliff. Around him,
his army spread like scaled crenellations--a dragon on every patch
of bare rock. Behind them, where the cliff sloped to a landscape
of hills, more dragons waited. Their eyes all stared. Their nostrils
all smoked. Not a tail flapped nor a wing shrugged. Their bodies
were tense, their scales silent, their fire simmering and ready to
blow.

"Come on, Solina," Elethor spoke to the sea. "You wanted
to see me again. I'm here, waiting for you."

When he narrowed his eyes, he saw nothing but the endless
sea. The waves crashed. Foam sprayed. Clouds swirled. No
wyverns, no Tirans, no old lover and desert queen.

It was the summer solstice. If Lyana had been right, the
Tirans would invade here today.

When the sun dipped toward the horizon, the dragons
began to move restlessly. A few blasted snorts of smoke, and

Elethor heard scales clink. He grumbled and dug his claws into the cliff.

"My lord, what should we do?" said Lady Treale, who perched upon a boulder beside him. The black dragon was staring into the horizon, her fangs bared. She was young, but she was of noble birth and a knight in training, so he had stationed her at his side. With every knight but Lyana slain in the Phoenix War, Elethor could not afford to turn squires away--not even the youngest daughters of farmland lords.

It's not because of how she kissed my cheek, he thought. *It's not because of her soft face smiling by my side at nights, nor the starlight in her hair, nor the light in her eyes.* He grumbled low in his throat. *Lyana is away--my betrothed, the woman I love. Treale is the closest thing here to a knight, and I need her near. That is all. That is all. And her pretty smile be damned.*

"They'll be here," he said to the young dragon, trying his best to ignore how large her eyes were. "I trust Lady Lyana. She's never let us down. If she says Solina will invade here today, it will happen."

Treale shifted her lower jaw. "My lord, the sun begins to set. What if..." She swallowed a puff of smoke. "What if we're in the wrong place?"

Then Requiem is defenseless, he thought. *Then nothing but a small, green City Guard stands between Solina and Nova Vita's fall. Then we are cursed, and only dusty old scrolls will remain to tell of our glory.*

He said none of this.

"I trust Lyana," he repeated instead.

But did he trust her? Lyana was his betrothed, his love, the woman who had walked through the Abyss with him. To him she was a paragon of strength, wisdom, and courage. Was he blind to her faults? Maybe Treale's father had been right. Maybe he should never have flown to war, but instead met with Solina, treated with her, maybe even surrendered to her. Every wave that crashed sounded like the moan of a dying man, and as the sun set, every sunbeam looked like a bloody spear.

Whispers rose behind him and voices cried out.

"Lyana!" cried one of the dragons upon the hills. Others echoed his call.

"The Lady Lyana! Lyana returns!"

Elethor spun toward the hills, heart thrashing. A blue dragon was flying from the north, roaring fire.

Lyana.

"Stars," Elethor whispered. He took flight, wings beating so mightily, the air bent down Treale's neck. He soared over his army, away from the sea and toward the flying blue dragon.

"Elethor!" Lyana cried to him.

She was hurt, he saw. He gritted his teeth. Blood covered her scales, and she flew with a wobble.

"Elethor, they're behind me! Wyverns!"

She still flew over a mile away. Before she could reach him, a dozen wyverns plunged from the clouds into open air. More followed until a hundred swarmed after Lyana, their stench carrying on the wind. The beasts screeched, blew jets of acid, and shot toward the Royal Army.

Stars. Fear, sharp and cold, thrust into Elethor like a spear. For an instant he froze, wings still, staring at the creatures. Teeth bared, he forced the fear down and roared.

"Dragonbone Phalanx!" he shouted to the dragons below him, a group of farm boys with wide eyes. They would have to fight as men today. "Fly, to my left!" He looked to his right where stood a hundred slack-jawed dragons, the sons and daughters of traders. "Firespear, fly! To my right!"

The wyverns shot toward him with blazing eyes, a mile away, then a hundred yards. Riders sat upon them, clad in steel and clasping crossbows and shields. They were but a drop from the sea of Solina's army, but they were a drop of acid.

Lyana reached him, bloody and panting, and spun to fly by his side.

"Dragonbone!" Elethor shouted hoarsely. "Firespear! Fly! Fly!"

Two hundred dragons clumsily took flight. A few yelped in fear, and others blew fire too soon, scattering their flames into empty air. Dragons from other phalanxes soared too and came to fly behind him, a jumbled crowd. Treale shot forward to fly at his side, roaring fire, and Elethor growled and summoned his own flames.

The wyverns crashed against them.

Elethor had never seen a living wyvern, only a hanging corpse. Now a horde howled before him; it was like facing charging bears after studying a harmless rug. A jet of acid flew toward him and Elethor banked. The spray hit a dragon behind him, and the young soldier screamed. Elethor saw his scales bubbling, and then the dragon lost his magic; he fell, a screaming boy, his clothes and skin sizzling. Crossbows fired and bolts flew; one slammed into Elethor's leg and he yowled. Ten more wyverns swooped above him, and acid rained. Elethor reared, flew backward, and hit a dragon behind him. With a roar, he shot flames in a fountain. They crashed against the wyverns. The creatures screeched, heads tossed back, and Elethor soared toward them. He blew more fire, then lashed claws and fangs.

He howled. It felt like biting iron; the beasts had scales like the thickest armor. When he clawed them again, sparks rose; he could not reach their flesh. One of the creatures thrust forward and bit, a striking asp. Fangs dug into Elethor's shoulder, just missing his neck, and he roared. He lashed his tail madly, hit the beast, and its jaw opened. Elethor roasted it with fire.

The wyvern's rider blazed, screamed, and fell from the saddle into the night. The wyvern itself roared, confused, consumed with bloodlust. Without its rider, it was but a mindless beast. Elethor clubbed its head with his tail, again and again, until it fell from the sky.

"Aim for the riders!" he shouted to the dragons around him. "Kill the riders!"

He looked around wildly, surveying the battle. He could not see Lyana. Far to his right, Treale was shooting between wyverns as fast as a scurrying bee, blowing flames. Hundreds of dragons flew haphazardly, abandoning all the formations he had taught them; they fought not as an army, but as a mob. Wyverns crashed between them, clawing and biting and blowing acid. Dragons turned into young men and women all around and fell screaming, acid eating through them. Bodies littered the hills below.

A fountain of acid poured toward him. Elethor growled, banked, and crashed into a second wyvern. Droplets blazed against his wing, and he howled. He flapped that wing madly, shaking the acid off, but already holes were tearing open. The wyvern he'd crashed into clawed his shoulder, drawing blood. With a growl, Elethor bit into its neck. He thought his fangs could break off, yet he grimaced and shoved them deeper, until he bit through the wyvern's scales and tasted flesh. The creature roared, and Elethor pulled his jaw back, a scale in his maw like an iron shield. He spat it out and blew fire in a curtain, holding back the other wyverns; a dozen flew toward him, eyes red and maws dripping.

"My king!"

Treale swooped from above, claws outstretched, and slashed at the wyverns. She joined her fire to his. Ten more dragons flew from below, showering flame. Atop the wyverns, riders burned and screamed. A few were still firing crossbows even as they blazed. Elethor soared, swooped, and lashed his tail. He tore one rider near in half, showering blood like red mist, and roasted another. Their riders dead, the wyverns fought wildly, driven by pure instinct. The dragons crashed against them. Fire and acid filled the air. Claws and fangs lashed. Bodies fell.

Finally only a handful of wyverns remained. Screeching, they turned and began to fly north.

"Don't let them flee!" Elethor shouted. He looked around, seeking Lyana, but couldn't see her. Fear gripped him, but he growled and began flying north in pursuit; seeking Lyana would have to wait.

Treale and several of her troops, dragons from her father's farmlands, flew with him. They were young, fast dragons, grown strong from hunting over the plains. They caught the wyverns a league from the beach, slew them with fire, and roared in triumph. When the beasts hit the ground below, their acid spilled like juice from cracked melons, eating into the earth.

When the last wyvern was dead, Elethor found himself trembling.

Lyana. Stars, Lyana, where are you?

As Treale and the others howled around him, he spun and began flying back to the beach.

Stars, Lyana, if I find you dead, I'm going to kill you.

He returned to hills littered with death: bodies charred black, their bones peeking from cracked skin; strewn limbs and severed heads, ripped from torsos with claw and fang; and clumps of raw flesh leaking from blackened armor, mere vestiges of humanity. Blood soaked the grass. Among the dead, wounded men and women screamed, some missing limbs, some burnt black and red, some futilely clutching at their spilling entrails. Elethor saw one girl, sixteen if she were a day, weeping in blood; her legs were gone, burnt away to stumps.

Nausea rose in Elethor. His head spun. Lord Oldnale's words returned to him. *The sons and daughters of Requiem will die for your pride!*

Elethor clenched his jaw, lungs tight, barely able to breathe. The death and blood whirled around him.

They had brought a dozen healers from Nova Vita--young women trained by Mother Adia in the temple. These healers now rushed among the wounded, pressing bandages to cuts and burns. Dozens of dragons still flew above, having abandoned their phalanxes; they looked like headless chickens flapping around a coop. The rest of the army perched atop the cliffs, some staring back at the hills, others still watching the sea.

A hundred wyverns nearly tore through us, Elethor thought, stomach churning. *What will twenty thousand do when we meet them?*

Then he spotted Lyana, and all thoughts but of her faded from his mind.

He had not seen her in a year, and he barely recognized her. She lay on the ground in human form, wearing tatters of silk. Lashes covered her body, stitched but still raw and red, and her head had been shaven so roughly scratches covered her scalp. Her eyes were closed, her body limp. Several soldiers surrounded her, staring down with pale faces. Elethor landed by them, nudged the young men aside with his wings, and shifted into human form.

Stars, oh stars, Lyana, what did they do to you?

He knelt above her and checked her pulse. Her heart still beat, and she still breathed, but that breath was shallow. Bruises covered her face, and fresh blood beaded along her stitches. They had beaten her within an inch of her life. One of the lashes looked particularly raw and swollen; Elethor thought it might be infected.

"Lyana, I'm here," he whispered. He lifted her head gingerly, leaned down, and kissed her forehead. "You're safe now. We'll heal you."

Along with his worry, shame filled him. How could he have doubted his love for her? How could he have spoken to Treale of being forced into marrying Lyana... thought of Treale herself as a woman to love? He clenched his fists and his head spun. Here in his arms lay Lyana--imperious, headstrong Lyana, beautiful and sad Lyana, the woman he loved more than the sky, than the rustle of birches, than the stars themselves--a new light in his life.

Healers soon knelt above her, rubbed herbs into her wounds, and let her drink medicine from a vial. Still Lyana slept. She was barefoot, Elethor noticed in a daze, her soles cut and red. He touched her forehead and his eyes stung.

"Lyana," he whispered as healers tended to her. "Do you remember what I told you in darkness, when we walked through nightmares we thought we could never wake from?" His memories returned to the Abyss and the disease that had infested her there. He caressed her cheek. "I told you that I would heal you, that I would bring you home. I told you that I'm always yours. I still am."

Treale approached in human form, damp eyes peering from an ashy face. Mud and soot covered her armor. She knelt by Lyana, touched the knight's cheek, and then looked up at Elethor. Worry filled her eyes.

"My lord, the wyverns... they flew from the north," the squire said. She looked at the storm clouds whence the beasts had emerged. "Where did they come from? What does this mean?" She looked back at him, eyes haunted. A bloody cut ran down her arm.

Still holding Lyana, Elethor looked at a dead wyvern that lay a dozen yards away, burying its rider. His belly knotted and an invisible claw clamped his skull. He looked back at Lyana.

"Wake up," he whispered to her. "Wake up, Lyana, and tell us what you know."

She lay in his arms, eyes closed, breath shallow.

"The Lady Lyana will sleep for a day and night," said one of the healers, a young woman with dark braids and white robes now blood-red. "We gave her silverweed wine. It will heal her, but she will not wake until tomorrow."

With a stab of memory, Elethor recognized this healer; she was Piri, the daughter of a winemaker, a girl whom Bayrin had boasted of kissing in the forest three years ago. He remembered her brother too; the man had fought by his side in the Phoenix War and fallen underground. Elethor closed his eyes, his belly sinking. His breath felt like smoke in his lungs.

"Place her on a litter, Piri," he said. "We fly with her."

Piri looked at her fellow healers and nodded. Two of the robed women fetched a litter, placed Lyana gently upon it, and strapped her down. Piri shifted into a slim, lavender dragon with silver horns; the litter was fastened onto her back like a saddle. Elethor ached to see his betrothed lying there, so small upon her mount.

He turned away to face Treale and hundreds of other soldiers; they stood in the dirt, watching him, awaiting orders.

"These wyverns were but a drop from the sea of Solina's army," Elethor said. "Lyana was their prisoner; her wrists and ankles are chafed from chains. She escaped them. She flew here; the wyverns we slew were sent to catch her." He looked south toward the crashing sea. "Solina will not invade from the south." He clenched his fists. This beach lay only a league from their eastern border. *Bloody stars, how could I be so blind.* "She already flies in Requiem. She invaded from Osanna... from the northeast."

Ash covered Treale's face, but he could still see her blanch.

"Stars," she whispered. "The border with Osanna... My parents..." She shifted into a dragon and took flight, her wings raising clouds of dust. "She will be burning Oldnale Farms. We must fly!" The black dragon blew fire. "Fly, dragons of Requiem! Fly!"

Elethor shifted too, flapped his wings, and took flight. Night had fallen. He soared higher until the air grew thin and cold and the hills became mere lumps across a rolling land. He tossed his head back. He roared the signal: three diagonal blasts of fire. A pause. Three more blasts tilted like falling columns. A pause. Three more. All dragons across the border, which stretched from here to Gilnor in the west, were trained to know this signal.

Fall back.

Fall back to Nova Vita.

He stared to the west. The next guard post lay several leagues away; three dragons patrolled there. Elethor stared, barely daring to breathe. What if they could not see him through the clouds? What if they had fallen? Finally, in the distant darkness, he saw the signal returned.

Three diagonal blasts of fire. Fallen columns.

Fall back.

Fall back to Nova Vita.

Even farther away, so far he could barely see, the next outpost raised the signal too. The alarm would stretch across the border for hundreds of leagues, from soldier to soldier, until it reached the swamps of Gilnor where the last dragons flew.

Fall back.

Fall back home.

Elethor descended until he flew a hundred yards above his army. Men were already digging graves for the fallen. Elethor roared to the army.

"Fly, dragons of Requiem! Shift into dragons and fly! Into your phalanxes. Fly in formation. Leave your dead. We fly to war!"

Fire streamed between his teeth, impossible to contain; he blew a stream into the sky. He began to fly north, eyes narrowed and belly roiling. Soon three thousand dragons flew behind him, their wings and howls a storm. Treale flew at his side, panting and snarling.

"We must fly to Oldnale Manor, my lord!" she said to him, eyes flashing. "It lies on the border with Osanna. If Solina invades there, she will burn every farm my family owns."

Elethor cursed himself. He cursed the wyverns. He cursed Solina and all her men. He had left the dead to rot behind him. He would now leave the living too, and the fires of sacrifice burned through him.

"We do not fly to Oldnale Manor. If wyverns flew there, Treale, we must trust that your family fled. Twenty-five thousand souls live in Nova Vita; that is where Solina heads. That is where we head too." He growled and blew a blast of fire. "We failed to block her passage into Requiem; we can no longer save the countryside. We fall back to the capital."

Treale gasped and tears filled her eyes. She shook her head mightily and roared her fire.

"My king! I cannot abandon my family. I cannot leave them to die." She glared at him, fire sparking between her teeth. "I must fly to them, my king."

He glared back at her, eyes narrowed. "You are a soldier of Requiem, Treale Oldnale. You train for knighthood. Your duty is with your king." He lowered his head, chest aching, and his voice softened. "I lost my family to Solina; I know the pain of loss. But our duty now lies at the capital; it is Nova Vita we must defend now. And you will fly there with us."

Treale gave him a long stare, rage and tears mingling in her eyes. Then she blasted fire, spun around, and began flying east.

"I go to warn my family!" she said. "That is where my duty lies. Goodbye, King Elethor! We will meet in our starlit halls of afterlife!"

With that, she disappeared into the clouds, roaring fire.

Elethor watched the clouds, throat tight.

Her family will die, he knew. *She will die. Her home and people will burn. All of Requiem will rise in flame again.* He howled, letting rage overflow his terror. *But I will save my city. If Requiem burns around us, I will save our last bastion.*

"Fly!" he cried. "Fly with all your speed!"

They flew through the night, three thousand strong, sons and daughters, a young king, a bloodied knight. The darkness spread endless before them and the winds of war screamed.

SOLINA

He entered her tent clad in armor, clutching his throat and still wheezing. He took slow, confident paces and held his back straight and shoulders squared--a pathetic attempt to restore some pride. He had lost their catch; no steel armor nor strong stance could save his pride today.

Solina sat in her chair, feet upon a footstool. Around her draped the walls of her tent--thick red cloth embroidered with golden suns. Candles burned upon giltwood tables around them. Solina sipped wine, then placed her goblet down. She gave Mahrdor a long, silent look. He stared back steadily, blue eyes emotionless, but his fingers still clutched his throat, and his lip gave a twitch.

Solina sighed. "You let the bird fly."

When he spoke, his voice was but a hoarse whisper. "A dragon, my queen, not a bird; a dragon who nearly clawed my throat out." He pulled his hand back, revealing a neck scratched red and raw. Blood still dripped from it.

Solina laughed. "The Lady Lyana Eleison. I grew up with her, Mahrdor--a pampered girl born into splendor. I saw her cry once when a bee stung her in the gardens. And this rich, spoiled spawn of a lordling, born with a silver spoon up her backside, nearly clawed out the throat of mighty General Mahrdor, Lord of Tiranor's Hosts?"

As stiff as he stood, he managed to stiffen further. "My queen, the girl you knew has grown. She is a vicious beast now, a creature, a--"

"Was she a dragon in your tent?" Solina asked.

Mahrdor began to say something, then closed his mouth. He inhaled sharply through his nostrils. "My queen? I--"

"You claim she is no bird, but a creature, a... how did you call it? A vicious beast? Your tent still stands, does it not? Charred, yes, but still standing. I saw it from the hill. Surely a vicious *dragon* would have torn your tent to shreds."

Something cold and dangerous filled his eyes. She had never seen him stare at her like that. Quick as it kindled, the blue fire in his eyes died. He raised his chin. "She shifted into a dragon outside my tent."

"And yet..." Solina crossed her legs upon the footstool. "And yet you were found gasping and croaking *inside* your tent, clutching at your throat. You were dragged from the smoke nearly dead. Curious thing, is it not? One could almost think--it's a long stretch of imagination, to be sure, but hear me out--one could almost think that a chained, pampered, utterly defenseless girl choked you... not a dragon." She raised her palms, as if weighing one enemy in each. "Vicious dragon? Chained girl? Which was it, Mahrdor? Which of these horrible enemies did this to you?"

His lips pulled back in but the slightest snarl, and his hands formed fists at his sides. "A girl who can *become* a dragon, a--"

"A girl who became a dragon *after* choking you." She rose to her feet and approached him. "Mahrdor, you lead this army. You command the hosts of the Sun God himself. You are, supposedly, the greatest soldier in my kingdom. And this..." She touched his neck. "The work of a chained, pampered girl from a soft northern land."

He stared at her silently. She could see his emotions: rage, shame, and finally... finally the blank duty of a soldier. He lowered his head, jaw clenched.

"I failed you, my queen." Fists clenched at his sides, he knelt before her. "Forgive me, your highness."

She sighed again, stepped aside, and looked at the back of the tent. A clay jug sat there, a cloth atop it. When she sniffed the air, its scent tingled her nostrils. She turned back toward her general. He looked at the jug, paled, and returned his eyes to her.

"My queen. I..." He breathed sharply. "I beg you."

"Beg me?" she said and snorted a laugh. "I begged too, Mahrdor. I begged the weredragons to spare my parents' life. I begged them to release me from my northern captivity. I begged so many times." She touched her line of fire, the scar that ran down her face, neck, and chest. "But they scarred me, Mahrdor. They deformed me. It was Lyana's betrothed who gave me this scar, the lover of the woman you freed." She pointed at the jug. "Now you will carry scars too. Do it silently. Your left hand; the one you tried to conceal your neck with. Make not a sound. If you scream, your right hand will follow."

His lip curled. "And if I refuse?" he rasped.

She shrugged. "Refuse then. Storm out of my tent and try to escape; we will hunt you. Try to kill me. You could not defeat a chained girl; you will not defeat me."

He took a step toward her. His eyes blazed. "If I escape, you will hunt me, but you will not catch me."

"Perhaps." She sat back down and sipped her wine; it tasted of berries, oak, and a hint of spices. "You could perhaps evade us for a while. You could seek exile in some distant land, a sojourner. Instead of your villa upon the River Pallan, you could squat in alleys in Confutatis, or live feral in Hostias Forest, or become a hermit in some western mountain in Salvandos. You could forsake your servants and fine meals; you could eat squirrel dung if you like. It bothers me not; it would, in fact, amuse me. Then, a few years down the line, I will find you with a long beard and some ratty cloak--a pathetic disguise--and I will dip your head into my vase. Or..." She raised her left hand and flexed the fingers. "You can do this quickly, you can do it silently, and we can keep flying to Nova Vita."

He stared at her. Their eyes locked for what seemed the turn of seasons. She saw the madness there, that madness he kept hidden, that drove him, that would have him prove his loyalty today. She herself would have run, but he would be too stubborn, too proud.

He tore his eyes away, walked toward the jug, and thrust his fist into the acid.

His jaw clenched and his body shook, but he did not make a sound.

ELETHOR

They flew through the night, thousands of dragons with blazing eyes. Clouds hid the stars and rain fell. Only the fire in their maws lit the darkness. Their wings glided upon the wind. Below them, red firelight raced against mountaintops and cliffs.

"Be strong, Mori," Elethor whispered into the wind. "I'm coming home."

When he looked northeast, he saw the distant red glow. It still lay many leagues away, but rose like a dawn. Firelight. The wilderness of Requiem burning. *Solina flies there.*

He looked over his shoulder. His army stretched for a league behind, the slower dragons dragging like a wake. Elethor cursed. They were only as fast as their slowest soldiers.

"Fly, dragons of Requiem!" he shouted in the night. "Fly with all your might!"

He looked back into the northern darkness. Nova Vita lay there beyond mountains, forests, lakes, and fields. Hundreds of leagues still lay between them and their home. Elethor had been flying for a day and night, and his wings ached, and his lungs burned, and dull pain throbbed in his chest. He forced himself onward.

Soon true dawn rose in the east, as red as the distant fires. Clouds stretched across the sky like bloody fingers. When Elethor looked at his army, he saw dragons panting, wobbling, and falling out of formations. Behind him, the stragglers were nearly too distant to see. Many of the dragons who had guarded the border--those who had been stationed closest to Ralora--had joined them. The others were making their own way to the capital; it could be days until they began to arrive. Elethor ground his teeth, spat flame, and cursed some more.

"We must rest, my lord," said a lavender dragon who flew by him--the young healer Piri. Like all healers, she wore a litter over her back; upon it, fastened with ropes, Lyana lay in human form. The knight's eyes were still closed, her wounds still raw.

Smoke rose from Elethor's mouth, nearly blinding him. He wanted to keep flying. How could he stop when Solina burned the farmlands, when her army flew toward Nova Vita, when the last Vir Requis faced the wrath of twenty thousand wyverns? He growled and forced his wings to keep flapping. He had to save Mori. He had to save Treale if he still could. He had to stop Solina from felling the city his ancestors had built.

"My lord!" said Piri. Her tongue lolled and her eyes rolled back. She wobbled as she flew, jostling Lyana upon her back. "Please, my lord, we must rest."

The lavender dragon looked ready to fall from the sky; if she fell, Lyana would fall with her. How long had they been flying? A day and night, or was it two nights? Elethor could no longer remember; he could barely form thoughts. All he knew was pain--the blaze in his lungs, the throbbing of his wings, the stabs in his chest. Exhaustion overwhelmed him, numbing even this pain. He felt like he could fly forever until he collapsed at the gates of Nova Vita.

"Solina," he managed to whisper. "Solina, I am coming for you."

Yet how would he fight her, sapped of strength, his army close to collapsing? Piri was right. They had to sleep, eat, and regain their strength. Even if they could reach Solina without rest, they would reach her exhausted; she would crush them.

He nodded and tossed his head to scatter the smoke from his nostrils. "We set camp." He raised his voice. "Dragons of Requiem, we land."

He began spiraling down toward a valley between rolling mountains. A river pooled there into a lake, its shores grassy. A few feet above the lakeshore, Elethor filled his wings with air, reached out his claws, and landed with a groan. As soon as his wings stilled, pain blazed across them, down his chest, and into his jaw. He felt like he would never fly again. He looked above him to see thousands of dragons land around him, moan, and collapse.

Elethor shifted into human form. At once sweat covered him. He wiped it from his eyes, approached Piri, and helped unload the litter Lyana lay on. He laid his betrothed upon the grass and knelt over her.

"Lyana," he whispered and held her hand.

Her eyes fluttered opened; she seemed just now to be rising from her long silverweed sleep. She blinked at him, then gasped and tried to rise, but straps still held her to the litter.

"Elethor!" she said. "El, the wyverns, they--"

"I know, Lyana." He touched her forehead; it was hot. "We've been chasing them north for two days. You drank silverweed and have been sleeping." He began unbuckling the straps that held her onto the litter. "We're in Cela Mountains, a third of the way to Nova Vita."

As soon as her straps were opened, she sprang up, crashed into his embrace, and held him tight. She sniffed and her fingers dug into his back.

"Oh, Elethor," she whispered. "I'm sorry. I'm so sorry."

He closed his eyes and lowered his head. She felt so thin in his arms, frailer than he'd ever known her. He held her awkwardly, daring not touch the stitches that ran across her back. He wanted to stroke her head, but her scalp was still raw; red stubble covered it. He gently kissed her forehead.

"You need not be sorry, Lyana," he whispered. "*I* am sorry, though. I sent you into danger. I let this happen to you.

I'm sorry, Lyana. I will never send you away again." He raised her chin with his finger and kissed her lips. "I'm not letting you get into any more trouble."

She laughed weakly and tears sparkled in her eyes. "My parents could never keep me out of trouble; you won't either." Then she sniffed again and touched his cheek. "Did you grow a beard, Elethor? It suits you. You look like your father."

He snorted. "You lose hair, I gain it." Then he pulled her close again, nearly crushing her against his chest. "You scared me, Lyana. Stars, I'm glad you're back. I--"

I love you, he wanted to say. *I love you like a new spring after winter. You are the strongest, bravest woman I know.*

Yet as he held her, he could say none of those things. He could still feel the touch of her lips on his. And he still thought of Orin, the man she had loved, the man they had lost. He still thought of Solina, whose kisses never felt like this, warm pecks of the lips, but like spirits shooting through him. He loved Lyana; he knew that. How could he not? Lyana was wise and strong and beautiful. And yet... and yet...

I hold her because Solina left. I hold her because my brother died. He looked away.

Soldiers approached them, carrying battle rations: dried meats, kippers, bread rolls, and jars of apple preserves. Elethor accepted the food gratefully, both for his hunger and the awkwardness of his embrace with Lyana. He released his betrothed, and for long moments they ate in silence.

The commanders of his phalanxes approached. Most were survivors of the old City Guard--seasoned warriors. A few were minor nobles--one an Oldnale, an uncle of Lady Treale, another a distant cousin of Bayrin and Lyana. Elethor gave them their orders:

"We sleep for five hours. Then we fly again."

Within moments, the soldiers of the Royal Army lay with closed eyes; those who had followed him to Ralora Beach, and those who had joined them from the border stretching west. Elethor lay upon the grass, looking up into the clouds. Lyana nestled in his arms, her head against his chest, her breath soft. She slept, mumbling and holding him. He kissed her cheek.

Dawn rose around them, blood red. In the northeastern horizon, distant fires glowed.

Be safe, Treale, Elethor thought, staring to her distant home. *Come back to us.*

As he held Lyana, he thought of Treale's soft hair, her dark eyes, and her warm lips against his cheek. He thought of Solina, the love of his youth, who flew from the north. He wanted to think about nobody but Lyana, nobody but this perfect woman in his arms--and she was perfect, even with her hair sheared and her body bruised. And yet his belly knotted, and his thoughts swirled like ghosts rattling in his skull. Finally he slept, Lyana warm in his arms.

TREALE

She had left the Royal Army two days ago and soared over the wilderness. She was young and slim and fast as roaring wind. The army had long disappeared behind her; the plains lay ahead, rolling green toward distant fires.

Oldnale Farms. Burning.

Her wings, lungs, and chest blazed with pain. She howled and blew fire. She had forced herself to sleep last night and to hunt a deer, but exhaustion still tugged on her like chains. The thought of the two graves outside Oldnale Manor--the graves of her brothers, slain fighting the phoenixes last year--rattled through her mind. She would not let her parents lie dead beside them.

The plains spread beneath her for leagues. Wild grass and reeds swayed. A river cut through them, bustling with cranes and geese. Hills rose every league, bristly with elms and beeches and maples. In the distant northwest, Treale could just make out Amarath Mountains, a white hint upon the blue sky. When she looked east, she saw red and black clouds claw the sky; her home lay there.

"Mother," she whispered, eyes stinging. "Father."

Her shadow raced across the grasslands below; she had never flown faster. Memories flowed through the mists of pain. Treale saw the great, scarred table in the manor hall where she and her brothers would play with wooden soldiers; the apple pies her maid would bake, and how Treale would sneak into the kitchens to steal a slice before dinner; the spears and arrows she would carve from fallen branches in the grove outside their home, pretending to be a warrior; and the hundreds of puppets she had sewn and placed upon a dozen shelves.

"My home," she whispered into the wind. "All my memories, my heartbeat, the sky of my wings."

Did the fires now claim it?

She flew, plains racing beneath her, wind howling across her scales. She blew fire. She flew for hours, a small black dragon in an endless world of grass and distant flame.

The sun hung low and red in the west when she saw the Tiran army.

A cry fled her throat.

Treale knew then: There was no hope for her family, for her king, for her army, for her race. Requiem would fall, and her children would burn or scatter in the wind. There would be no victory against these invaders from the south, only acid, blood, and death.

They covered the sky like a black cloud. Countless wyverns swarmed there; from this distance, they were mere specks, but Treale had seen enough up close to imagine their metallic scales, their red eyes, their chins that thrust out into blades. Upon their backs, she saw the glint of armor and streaming banners. Even from leagues away, she heard the shrieks and war drums, a song of death. Smoke unfurled above them, turning the sky black, and shadows spilled across the land like ink. Behind them fires blazed across the prairies. As Treale flew, she saw wyverns dipping from the mass, swooping to the lands below and kindling them. The fires raced across field, meadow, and forest. As every new blaze crackled to life, the wyverns shrieked with new vigor.

They did not come here to conquer, Treale thought. *They did not merely come here to kill. They came to destroy the very land that bred us.*

She dived down so fast her head spun and her belly lurched. She landed in swaying grass, shifted into human form, and knelt. The wild grass rose around her, five feet tall. Grasshoppers and crickets bustled. Treale pulled her knees to her chest, shivered, and whispered prayers.

"Please, stars of Requiem." She hugged herself so tightly her arms ached. "Please don't let my parents lie dead; they are all I have left. Don't let these wyverns reach our city; it is all Requiem has left. Don't let King Elethor lose his courage; he is our last hope."

She looked up at the sky. Smoke was spreading above, blocking the sun, turning blue to black. The wyvern shrieks tore across the land. She could hear men now too; they shouted orders to one another, voices as cruel as the wyvern cries. Would they fly here too? Would they burn this grass she hid in?

She sat shivering, peering between the blades of grass, until the cries of the swarm moved westward and dimmed. Treale stood, only her head rising from the tall grass. The wind streamed her hair, and when she stared west, she saw the wyverns flow into the distance.

"They're heading for Nova Vita," she whispered. "Fly fast, Elethor. Save whoever you can... and flee this land."

She leaped, shifted, and flew east. A wall of fire rose before her.

Treale dived through smoke, coughing, eyes narrowed and watering. Soon flames were racing below, baking her belly. She swerved, rose, and dipped, seeking pockets of air. The fire crackled and roared. The sky churned black and red. She felt as if she flew through a furnace, and she yowled. She wanted to rise higher, to escape the smoke, but dared not. She had to stay here near the ground, seeking her home.

Soon the land below her changed. These were no wild grasslands that burned, but ploughed fields. The wheat and barley--lush green when she had left her home--now blazed. Barns rose in flame and collapsed. Treale could not even cry; the heat seared her tears dry. She howled. She kept flying.

Finally she saw it ahead, red on black--Oldnale Manor burning.

"Mother," she whispered.

She shot between columns of smoke. She swerved between walls of fire. A blast of flame from trees below licked her claws, and she screamed and drove onward. She crashed through fire, dived toward the hill Oldnale Manor rose upon, and landed in the courtyard outside the manor gates.

Cobblestones covered the courtyard, searing hot against her claws. Three guards lay dead before her, flesh charred black; if not for their armor, the wind would have scattered them into ash. Around the hill, trees crackled and flames blazed. Before her, the doors of the manor stood burning. She saw more flames through the windows above.

"Mother!" she cried. "Father!"

Still in dragon form, she ran toward the doors and slammed through them. The wood crashed with a shower of burning splinters. Inside the main hall, tapestries and rugs burned and smoke swirled. Treale crawled, head against the floor where less smoke flowed. If she became human now, the heat would bake her flesh; even her dragon scales felt close to melting. She coughed and kept moving.

"Mother! Father!"

She could see barely a foot ahead. She reached out her claws, scratching the floor. She hit a fallen chair, shoved it aside, and kept moving. Her tail flapped behind her. She coughed and roared for her parents.

She crawled another foot through the smoke... and found herself staring at a burnt body.

Treale screamed.

The flesh had blackened and shriveled, clinging to bone. The skull gaped and the fingers thrust up like burnt twigs. Shreds of charred cloth clung to the body, and around its neck hung a talisman shaped as a sheaf of wheat.

It was her mother.

Tears filled Treale's eyes. She shivered. She froze for a moment, then with a cry, she scurried two feet away. Her throat burned. She could barely breathe. She hit something soft and hot, turned her head, and saw a second body. It too was charred black, little more than crisp flesh clinging to bones in armor. She knew the breastplate it wore; this was her father.

Treale howled. She wept. She had to take the bodies from here; she had to bury them. Weeping, she clutched her father with her claws. His body came apart in her grasp, falling from his armor like ash from a pipe, and Treale closed her eyes and trembled.

A rafter cracked above. Flames showered. The beam crashed before her and fire roared. Treale coughed and had to close her eyes against the heat. She pushed herself back, spun, and ran toward the doorway. She burst outside into the courtyard and took flight.

"I'm sorry, Mother," she whispered. "I'm sorry, Father."

She soared until she burst from smoke into clear sky. She coughed and trembled in the air. When she looked below her, she saw nothing but the inferno. A chunk from Oldnale Manor's roof collapsed, and soon nothing remained but brick walls, a shell of death and memory.

A fiery trail led west, stretching from the manor across the land. The flames trailed behind the wyvern army, moving fast, moving to Nova Vita.

When they reach our city, all there will die, Treale knew. *My friend Mori will lie charred in the ruins of the palace. Twenty thousand dragons-- children, elderly, the wounded of the last war--they all will die.*

Treale tossed back her head and roared, a great howl that seemed to tear the sky, a howl of rage and loss. She was but a small black dragon, a single voice in the flame, but she thought her howl could rise to the stars.

If they die, I will die with them. I will go down fighting like my brothers did. She snarled and blew flame. *And I will take some wyverns with me.*

Roaring, she flapped her wings and drove through the air, following the wyvern army. The lands burned behind her, and tears flowed from her eyes--tears of farewell for her home, her parents, and the green lands she had loved.

BAYRIN

He was flying over the eastern forests, the city walls a distant crown behind him, when he saw the shadow. Bayrin cursed and spat fire.

The darkness spread over the mountains, a hundred miles away--as far as his eyes could see. At first he thought it a cloud, but it moved too swiftly. It looked more like a great flock of ravens, but ravens would be too small to see from here. Bayrin growled deep in his throat.

Wyverns, he thought. When he sniffed the air, he caught a hint of their stench; they stank like vinegar and sulfur.

"Damn it, Elethor, where are you?" he muttered, gliding on the wind. His king had gone south to stop these beasts from invading; now they flew from the east. A chill ran through Bayrin, rattling his scales and rippling his tail. Had these beasts skirted the Royal Army... or crushed it?

"Well, the fun begins," he said, turned around, and began flying back to Nova Vita. "El, if you're alive, you better get back here soon to join the party."

As he flew, he tossed his head back and blew blasts of diagonal fire--the shape of falling columns. Patrolling several leagues around the city, his fellow outflyers blew their own blasts and began to fall back to the walls. The walls themselves brimmed with dragons, a good five hundred of them, wearing the armor their smiths had been forging all year.

Will the acid eat through steel as through flesh? Bayrin wondered. He growled again. *We'll soon find out.*

As he approached the city, he roared the call. "Enemy at the gates! City Guard, man your posts!"

Roars and blasts of fire rose from the dragons upon the walls. The city erupted into chaos. Guards streamed out of craggy Castra Murus, shifted into dragons, and flew to perch at their posts: fifty dragons upon the palace, fifty on the Temple of Stars, and hundreds more spread across the walls. A hundred guards marched down the streets in human form, clad in breastplates and holding swords and shields. Their faces were hard as iron masks.

"People of Nova Vita!" Bayrin cried as he circled above the city. "Evacuate into the tunnels. Walk calmly in single file--like we drilled. Into the tunnels!"

Families began leaving their houses, frowning at the skies. A few children were laughing and elbowing one another; they thought this too was a drill. Others sniffed the air, seemed to detect the distant stench of the wyverns, and their eyes darkened. The people began to snake down the streets--some limping, others moving on crutches, the stronger helping the weaker. Soon they were filing into the three archways that led underground.

Bayrin looked over his shoulder toward the east. He flew too low to see the shadow now, but the acrid stench still wafted on the wind. He thought he could hear a distant buzzing like a cloud of locusts. He cursed under his breath as he flew over the city.

"Damn it, Elethor, where are you?"

As people streamed through the streets below, Bayrin flew toward the palace. He landed outside its doors, shifted into human form, and ran into the main hall. Several guards stood upon its tiles; behind them, Mori sat upon the Oak Throne.

The princess looked at him over the guards, and Bayrin's breath caught and his heart twisted. *Stars,* he thought. Her eyes seemed to drown him, gray pools of infinite depth. Mottles of sunlight kissed her pale cheeks, and her chestnut hair cascaded. Such sadness clung to her that Bayrin ached; with only a look across the hall, her eyes spoke of Orin's death, of the fall of Castellum Luna, of their kiss in the mists of northern isles, and of the wildfire that raced toward them. For the length of her stare he froze, unable to move or speak or breathe. A guard in the hall stirred and his armor creaked, drawing Bayrin's gaze. He cleared his throat and scowled.

"Men!" he barked. "Into the tunnels. Guard the people underground. Move! I'll lead the princess to safety."

The guards bowed their heads. "Yes, Lord Bayrin," they said and raced outside, drawing their longswords.

Bayrin looked back at Mori; they were alone in the palace. She rose from her throne, face blank. She wore a gown of bluish gray--the color of her eyes when she cried--and a sword hung from her waist, its pommel shaped as a dragonclaw. Bayrin crossed the hall, walked up the marble stairs to the dais the throne stood on, and reached out his hand.

"Come, Mors," he said softly. "Let's get you into the tunnels."

She stood frozen before her throne. Between the eastern columns, she could see the city where dragons perched upon roofs and walls. The sky was turning red; distant fires blazed.

"Where is Elethor?" the princess whispered. "Where is my brother?"

Bayrin took her hand. He spoke softly. "I don't know, Mori. Come, we must go."

She turned to meet his gaze, and again the sadness of her eyes flooded him. Her lips parted, pink in her pale face like a flower in snow. Her hair swayed in the wind that blew between the columns. She seemed to him almost a figure of starlight, a ghost in the hall. He tightened his hand around hers, and she raised her head, took a slow breath, and nodded. He helped her down the stairs of the dais, and they crossed the hall in silence. The columns rose around them, and Bayrin wondered if this was the last he'd see them standing.

Outside he found a sky the color of burnt flesh. Hundreds of dragons of the City Guard perched atop roofs and walls, staring east with narrowed eyes. Smoke rose from their nostrils in hundreds of plumes. On the cobbled streets, people were still moving toward the tunnels; guards in armor guided them. Bayrin saw an elderly woman limp forward, leaning against her daughter. One child pushed a wheelbarrow where lay his legless brother. Many people still bore the scars of last year's war, limbs and faces twisted with old fire.

Stars, haven't these people suffered enough? Bayrin thought, sudden rage finding him. He clenched his fist around the hilt of his longsword. *We barely survived Solina once; now she comes to burn us again.* He wanted to shift into a dragon, fly into the wyvern army, and slay Solina with all his fire and fury. For a year now, sadness had filled this city--had filled Bayrin too--as they healed, as they rebuilt, as they still wept for the dead and wounded.

Now this desert queen brings her steel and fire here again. Bayrin growled. *Now she seeks to undo all our healing.*

How could such cruelty exist? How could one queen feel such hatred, such rage, that she would seek to crush an entire race? Bayrin could not understand it. This felt like something from the old stories, the ones where King Benedictus fought as the tyrant Dies Irae slew all but the Living Seven. Bayrin had never imagined such terrors could truly exist outside of dusty old books, yet now he smelled them on the wind, and he heard their shrieks in the distance coming closer.

They reached a tunnel entrance. People were moving under the archway, down the stairs, and into shadow. The archway guards bowed their heads.

"Princess Mori," they said. "Lord Bayrin."

Mori bowed her head to them. She touched each guard on his shoulder and kissed his cheek. Their eyes were solemn, strong but frightened.

"Thank you, my friends," Mori whispered. "Thank you for your strength, for your steel, and for your courage."

Bayrin led the princess onto the narrow, candlelit staircase. Last year, the people had rushed into these tunnels, burning and terrified. Today they walked somberly, and every few feet, guards stood with spears, crossbows, and shields. At the bottom of the staircase, a heavy door waited, and more guards stood here to usher them through. Down the tunnels Bayrin and Mori walked, passing more and more guards, under the portcullis, and past doors of bronze.

Here spread a network of chambers where Requiem's people hid. Thousands of men and women--those too young, old, or wounded to fight--huddled here. Word had spread that the war had truly come, that this was no drill. Tears filled eyes, mothers embraced children, and whispers rose like maelstroms. In every chamber, three guards stood armed with steel.

"The Princess Mori," whispered a few people. More whispers rose through the tunnels. "The Princess Mori! Stars bless you, my lady."

Bayrin led Mori to the deepest chamber. The walls and ceiling loomed, carved with dragon claws. The air smelled of moss, soil, and fear. They moved to stand by a wall where candles burned in alcoves. Mori looked at Bayrin, held his hands, and her lips parted as if she would speak but could not find words.

"Mori, I return to my post," he said softly. "I will watch upon the walls, and I will fight in the sky above our city." He looked at the wall where hung a tapestry, its threads forming scenes of dragons flying under stars. "Mori, if I fail... if they break down the doors... you know what to do."

She looked at the tapestry and clutched the hilt of her sword.

"I know," she whispered.

He nodded, throat tight. "It will not come to that. Not so long as there is fire in my maw, strength to my claws, and wind in my wings. I promise you, Mori."

She lowered her head and nodded, bit her lip, and looked up at him. Tears trembled in her eyes, and she touched his cheek, then wrapped her arms around him. She held him tight.

"Be careful, Bay," she whispered. "I love you."

She looked up at him, and he cupped her cheek and kissed her--a long kiss that melted into rivers of mist. Bayrin closed his eyes, and again he lay upon grass in the Crescent Isle, the place where he had first kissed Mori. He could smell the pines and mist. He could feel the cool, damp air against his skin and Mori's soft hair in his fingers. She had been a mere girl then, frightened and meek, and he a lowly guard; the past year seemed like a lifetime of healing.

"I love you too, Mors," he whispered and held her close. He kissed her forehead. "I will come back to you. Always. Always."

He left the tunnels, her kiss still warm on his lips and the softness of her hair still tingling his fingers. When he emerged onto the city streets, he found them deserted; every last guard aboveground perched as a dragon upon the walls and rooftops. He shifted and took flight, wings raising demons of dust. He landed upon the eastern wall and stared into the distance.

The shadow was closer now. Fire raced below it, consuming the countryside, and smoke unfurled like wings. Bayrin could just make out the glint of distant armor and spearheads, just hear war drums on the wind. He shifted his jaw and fire sparked between his teeth.

Twenty thousand wyverns, he thought. *A thousand dragons of the City Guard. Stars, Elethor, where the abyss are you?*

Wings beat like more war drums, air blasted Bayrin, and his father landed beside him. Lord Deramon was a burly beast of a dragon, all clanking copper scales. The stone walls moaned below him, and so much smoke rose from his maw it hid the landscape.

"Any sight of the Royal Army?" Deramon asked, voice a grumble like gravel under boots.

Bayrin shook his head. "Nobody has seen Elethor. No word from him." He looked at his father and his stomach knotted. "We are alone."

Had Elethor fallen? What about Lyana? Bayrin's eyes burned and terror swelled inside him. He clutched the battlements, his claws digging into the stone. He forced himself to think of Mori's eyes, her lips on his, and the softness of her hair. If his king and sister were dead, he still had to fight--for Mori and for all the others underground.

The smell of smoke and acid filled his nostrils. The eastern shadow shimmered and grew.

SOLINA

Night began to fall when she saw the City of Dragons ahead. She bared her teeth and snarled. Her wyvern howled beneath her and clawed at the sky. Baal's scales clanged and as his tail lashed, Solina bounced in the saddle, pushed her knees against it, and smiled.

"Nova Vita," she whispered and licked her lips.

A year ago, she had ravaged this city--ripping dragons upon the streets, crushing houses, and burning the holy birches of Requiem. And yet these walls still stood. *Now is the time to finish the job.*

"Mahrdor!" she shouted, voice rising on the wind. "Divide them up! Invasion formation. Go!"

When she looked over her shoulder, she saw him flying there upon his wyvern. His left hand was wrapped in leather, and his right hand clutched a sabre. Behind him flew two hundred phalanxes, each a hundred wyverns strong. Every wyvern howled for blood and clawed the air. Every rider raised a spear and cried for glory, for Tiranor, and for Queen Solina. The roar shook the sky. Every phalanx flew in formation, their banners sporting their sigils: bloody claws, flaming hearts, crossed sabres, blazing suns, and dozens of others.

"Phalanxes!" Mahrdor shouted, voice hoarse and deep in the wind. "Invasion formation! Sunfire! Bloodspear! To my right, move. Wyvern Claws, Heartflame, Sabre Steel--fan out, go!"

The general flew between the lines, arranging the phalanxes for invasion. From the border, the army had flown in a line--an arrow of glory. Now they spread out like a claw opening to clutch the city. They would encircle this pathetic Nova Vita, crush it in their grip, and claim its spoils.

"Soldiers of Tiranor!" Solina howled, riding at their lead. She grabbed the banner pole from its ring on her saddle and raised it high. Her standard blew wide and long--a golden sun upon a white field. Her soldiers howled for their queen.

"Queen Solina! Queen Solina! For the glory of Phoebus!"

Even in the wind, their voices reached her, so loud and deep they thudded in her chest. They gained speed. Below them the lands streamed, and the wind shrieked, and the clouds swirled, and Solina howled for the glory of her lord.

"Soldiers of Tiranor!" she shouted again, banner held high. "Tonight your wyverns will feast upon dragon flesh!" The riders howled and the wyverns shrieked. "Tonight the light of the Sun God will banish the darkness of reptiles!" The soldiers roared and brandished their sabres. Solina screamed hoarsely. "Tonight every phalanx will prove its glory and strength! The phalanx that kills the most weredragons will enjoy the greatest spoil: the Weredragon Princess for its men's pleasures!"

The riders howled their approval. The phalanx commanders raised their banners high and chanted their names.

"Sunfire!"

"Bloodspear!"

"Sabre Steel"

Two hundred banners flew. Two hundred phalanxes roared for their glory.

"We fly to war!" Solina howled, raising banner in one hand, sabre in the other. She cried out the Old Words of her people. "We will never fall!"

They answered her call. "To war! To war! We will never fall!"

The city loomed near now--so near that she could see the dragons upon its walls.

"Destroy this city!" she shouted and the army roared.
"Bring me the king and princess alive! Slay every other reptile you
find!"

They shot through the wind. Their banners streamed.
Their wyverns cried. They crossed fields and flew over burnt
forests, moving closer, until the city loomed three leagues away,
then two, and Solina snarled. She reattached her banner to her
saddle and grabbed her shield. She held sword and shield before
her. *Soon I will lick blood from this steel.*

She was snarling, already tasting the coppery sweetness,
when roars rose in the south.

She turned in the saddle and saw him there.

My love. My youth. My sunfire.

"Elethor," she whispered.

She knew it was him. From here the dragons were but a
distant cloud, a shimmering shadow of color and flame, but she
knew that he flew there. She could feel him on the wind, hear
him in the distant roars. Once more she heard his cry--echoing
from eight years ago--as he stood upon the walls of Nova Vita,
calling her name.

"Solina!" His voice had been raw and torn. "Solina!"

She had wept that day, burnt and bleeding and alone. She
had left him, going into her exile. She had fled into the sand,
raised her kingdom from ruin, raised this army, raised this glory to
light the world. And now he would shout again above the walls
of Nova Vita. Now again fire would burn and blood spill.

"Elethor," she whispered again, "you have come to me."

How many times she had kissed him! How many times
she had loved him in the dark! Today he would be hers again, not
a lover, but a prisoner. Today he would cry her name again, not
in love, but in agony as she ripped into his flesh.

"Elethor..."

She clutched her sabre between her teeth, grabbed the reins, and pulled her wyvern around. The beast banked, tilting so steeply that Solina nearly fell from the saddle. She snarled and began flying south.

"Riders of Tiranor!" she cried. "Assault formation! Form rank! Follow me--we fight in the sky!"

The other riders noticed the distant cloud too. From here the dragons were a mere smudge in the sunset, a shimmer of scales, blue and red and green. Fire rose from them like sunbeams. Their howls rolled upon the wind. Solina led the charge, sabre raised, shouts ringing hoarsely. When she looked over her shoulder, she saw her army change formation; now they formed a great fist in the sky. Her strongest phalanxes flew at the vanguard, armed with spears and crossbows. Their wyverns filled their maws with acid; the sharp stench filled Solina's nostrils and burned her lungs. She inhaled deeply, savoring it.

"For the Sun God!" she cried and her army echoed her call. "Banish their darkness with our light!"

The two armies streamed toward each other. When the dragons came nearer, Solina bared her teeth in a grin. At most four thousand dragons flew toward them--probably fewer. *We outnumber them five to one.*

"For Requiem!" rose their distant cries, deep and echoing against the stony mountains below. "Requiem!"

The sunset blazed red, casting beams across the land like spilling blood. The mountains below kindled in the light. Dragonfire rose in pillars. Wyverns screeched. Soon only a league separated the armies, and Solina raised her blade and cried to her love.

"Elethor! Elethor, we meet again!"

He flew at his army's lead, a brass dragon with fire in his maw. He sounded his roar, and his dragons answered the call.

"For King Elethor!" the dragons cried. "For Requiem!"

Fire blazed toward her. Her wyvern's acid blew. Above the mountains, the armies clashed with blood and screams.

ELETHOR

Roaring fire, he flew at Solina.

Sunrays blazed around him. His fire streamed forward, crackling and spinning. From the inferno, a stream of acid hissed. Elethor howled and banked, dodging the acid. The drops sizzled against his side, jabs of agony like arrows tipped with poison.

"Elethor!" rose her voice from the smoke and flame. She laughed maniacally. "We meet again, Elethor, King of Lizards!"

He growled and flew toward her; he could just make out her form among the smoke. All around them, dragons and wyverns clashed. Fire and acid sprayed, blood spilled, crossbows fired, and bodies rained. Elethor blew fire and Solina raised her shield. The flames bathed it, white-hot, and Solina screamed.

Her wyvern, the great beast Baal, lashed claws the size of men. Elethor pulled back, dodging the blows. Baal's neck thrust forward, jaws snapped, and a fang tore at Elethor's leg. Blood splashed, and Elethor soared just as the beast spewed acid.

He swerved, dodged the sizzling fountain, and swooped. Before he could muster fire, Baal barreled into him. Fangs drove into Elethor's shoulder. He roared. Acid filled Baal's mouth, spilling across Elethor; he screamed in agony.

"You scream like a sow in heat, Elethor!" Solina shouted, grinning wildly. She raised her crossbow, loaded a bolt, and aimed. "You will scream for me in Tiranor soon."

Nearly blind with pain, Elethor swiped his tail.

The crossbow thrummed and a bolt glanced off Elethor's horn.

His tail hit Solina and she screamed.

The blow knocked her sideways--nearly off her saddle. The reins tugged tight, and Baal released Elethor and fell into shadow.

"Elethor!" Solina screamed, and then a horde of dragons and wyverns rolled between them, and she vanished into clouds of fire and blood.

Elethor's shoulder blazed; acid drenched it. He slapped his claws and blew his breath at the foul liquid. The last drops fell, revealing a steaming wound; the acid had eaten through three scales and left his flesh raw and red.

He looked through the flames, seeking his fellow dragons. They flew all around him, four thousand strong; nearly all the dragons who had guarded the southern border, from Ralora to western Gilnor, now flew with him. They were roaring battle cries, blowing flames every which way, and scattering and reforming in chaos. Some howled in fury; others wailed in fear. As he watched, acid sprayed several dragons. They became men and women in midair, screaming and clutching at their melting faces; they fell into darkness.

"Dragons of Requiem!" Elethor cried. "Form rank! Into your phalanxes. Fight them! Kill the riders! Burn them down--"

Two wyverns crashed into him. Their fangs and claws tore at his scales. Acid sprayed and Elethor howled.

He soared, claws lashing, and crashed between them. Above them, he shook himself and bellowed. The acid was already eating at his scales; as he shook, it rained upon the wyverns below. Their riders screamed as the acid seeped through their armor.

Even as they burned, the riders raised crossbows. Bolts flew. Elethor swerved. One bolt shot through his wing, and he crashed into a wyvern at his side. Another beast dived above. Elethor could see no end to them. He spun in all directions, spraying fire and holding the creatures back.

"Solina!" he shouted.

Where was she? He dived between raining bodies, seeking her. Smoke blinded him. Wyverns and dragons shot in every direction, flashes of scales. Human bodies thumped against him, rolled off, and hit the mountains below.

"Form rank!" Elethor shouted. "Dragons of Requiem! Fight them!"

He looked from side to side, panting. Acid coated them. They screamed. Their magic left them; they became men and women and tumbled. *No, not men and women,* he realized. They were mere boys and girls--farmhands, weavers, and shepherds. They cried for their mothers. They fell, flesh melting, screams echoing in Elethor's ears.

This is no battle, he thought. *It's a slaughter.*

The wyverns flew in perfect formations, attack flights of four--two attackers flanked by two defenders--swarming from phalanxes of a hundred. They undulated into the distance; Elethor saw no end to them. Most had not even fought yet, but howled for blood, awaiting their turn to kill. They formed a ring of metal and acid around the dragons, picking them from the sky one by one.

"Dragons, fly in your phalanxes!" Elethor cried. "Kill the beasts!"

Blue scales flashed below. From a ball of fire and smoke soared Lyana. Flames streamed from her maw and crashed against a wyvern above her. She spun, lashed her tail, and tore off a rider's arm; it tumbled with a spray of blood. She looked from side to side, clawing the air. Elethor flew toward her, roared, and flamed a wyvern. Soon the two dragons, brass and blue, fought side by side. Wyverns flew from all sides.

"This is a bloodbath!" she shouted at him. "Elethor, we must retreat!"

Crossbows fired. One bolt glanced off Lyana's back, and another pierced her wing. A spear slashed Elethor's burnt shoulder and he howled. Wyverns dived from above and acid rained. Elethor and Lyana scattered, dodged the burning rain, and soared. They blew fire, slashed claws, and felled wyverns from the sky.

The bodies of Vir Requis tumbled all around them, returned to human forms. One girl slammed onto Lyana's wing, still alive and screaming, then plummeted into darkness. A boy fell before Elethor, a writhing mass of flesh that twisted and steamed with acid. His screams died before he could hit the mountains below.

"We cannot let them reach the city!" Elethor shouted. He lashed his claws, blew fire, and tried to find Solina. Was she dead? Did she still fight?

Wyverns dived toward him. Blood and acid filled the sky. The sun disappeared behind the horizon, and dragonfire lit the night. Screams and shrieks rose, and the dead fell in darkness.

DERAMON

He stood upon the walls, a coppery dragon spewing smoke, and growled at the distant battle. From here, he could see nothing but bursts of fire, fluttering shadows, and glints of steel. He could hear only distant screams and muffled commands. Deramon fumed and gripped the crenellations.

"It's a bloodbath," Bayrin whispered at his side, tail slapping the wall. He snorted a flicker of fire, then looked at Deramon. "Father, let us fly to them."

Deramon grumbled under his breath. He was commander of the City Guard; never had his force left Nova Vita to fight the battles beyond the walls. For three hundred years--under his father's command, and his grandfather's, and his ancestors' going back to Terra Eleison himself--the City Guard had manned its post.

"We have our orders," he said gruffly. "We protect the people of Nova Vita. We will not leave them in the tunnels."

Bayrin fumed. Smoke rose between his teeth in curtains. He shook his head wildly and slapped his tail. "Father, I can hear them screaming from here! Those are our men screaming. Stars, they're dying out there. They need us."

Deramon glared at his son, a gangly green dragon. "The people of this city need us. Twenty thousand seek shelter in the tunnels; we'll not abandon them. This is our post."

Snorting and shifting his claws, Bayrin looked back and forth between his father and the battle. A separate battle seemed to rage within him. Finally he leaped from the wall, filled his wings with air, and began flying south.

"To the Abyss with my post!" he called back to Deramon. "I'm flying to Elethor."

The young guard growled, blew fire, and soared into the night. Soon he was but a sliver of scales flying toward the storm of battle. Deramon watched from the walls, growled, and cursed. He shook his head mightily, scattering fire, and his claws dug ruts into the battlements. Finally he let out a string of curses, flapped his wings, and rose into the air.

"Stars, I'm going to regret this," he muttered. He looked over his shoulder and howled to his men. "Temple Guard! Palace Guard! Northern Wall! Barracks Guard!"

The dragons of those posts stared at him, eyes glowing in the night--three hundred warriors in all. *Damn buildings are empty anyway,* Deramon thought with a grumble. He raised his voice again.

"Fly--with me! We fly to war." Deramon roared fire and glared at the rest of his Guard, those who manned the remaining walls and streets. "The rest of you miserable lot--man your posts and don't let any bloody wyverns in, or I'll flay your hides!"

With that, he flapped his wings, howled to the sky, and flew into the southern darkness. Behind him, four hundred dragons roared and followed. The wheat and barley below bent under the beat of their wings, and their flames lit the darkness.

"For Requiem!" one guardsman cried behind. The others answered his call. "Requiem!"

They cut through the night. The wind roared around them. Four hundred dragons--flying toward a storm of fire, acid, and death. The fire of battle lit the night. When they drew closer, they saw thousands of wyverns--tens of thousands--surrounding the Royal Army. Their scales clattered, their claws shone, and their acid felled Vir Requis from the sky. Bodies rained and slammed into the mountains below.

Deramon growled. Ice seemed to spread through his gut like the fingers of ghosts.

My men don't know I too feel fear, he thought, jaw clenched and eyes narrowed. *Not I, the great Lord Deramon Eleison.* And yet as he flew, his belly twisted with terror, and he howled to let his fire melt the ice.

He flew for glory. He flew for death. This would be the last battle of his life, the battle where he fell, where his son fell, where his men fell with a roar to enter legend. He sounded that roar now.

"Requiem!" he called to the sky.

The wyverns ahead spun to face the new dragons, reforming rank in the clouds. They bared teeth like swords, their eyes burned red, and their riders fired crossbows. Bolts streamed through the night, shards of lightning. Two dragons howled, turned to humans, and fell from the sky. With shrieks and battle cries, a thousand wyverns flew toward the City Guard.

The sky exploded with fire, acid, and blood. Deramon roared his flames, burning three wyverns. He lashed his tail, slamming its spikes into another's eyes. His dragons roared around him, and fire spouted and rained to the mountains below. The wyverns filled the night. Sprays of acid rose and fell around him. Deramon skirted between them, growling and beating his wings, trying to fan the acid aside.

One spray glanced off his side and he roared; it felt like spears slashing across him. He growled and swooped toward the wyvern that had burned him. The beast reared and bit the air. Deramon lashed its head, but his claws glanced off scales, raising sparks; those scales felt harder than the thickest breastplate in Requiem's armories. The wyvern shrieked, a deafening sound, and shot more acid. Deramon dropped in the sky, flew under the beast, and rose behind it. He snapped his jaws at the rider, catching the man as he spun to aim his crossbow. Deramon's teeth punched through armor and tore the Tiran in two. He spat out half a corpse, then bathed the screeching wyvern with flame.

Still the beast flew and roared. Deramon clutched its back, bit its neck, and clawed its flanks. It bucked beneath him. Deramon was among the largest dragons in Requiem; this beast made him seem like a scrawny child just learning to fly. Its tail lashed and slammed into Deramon's back, cracking scales. Shrieks sounded above, and more wyverns dived, maws opening to reveal pools of acid.

Deramon cursed, tugged sideways, and flipped the wyvern over. He held the struggling beast above him, and the acid cascaded onto its belly. It roared. Its legs kicked the air. The acid seeped through it scales, and its blood rained.

"Father!"

Bayrin's voice rose through the battle. The green dragon shot through fire and smoke, roared, and slammed into the wyverns above Deramon. They howled. More dragons flew into them, showering them with fire.

Cursing, Deramon tossed off the mewling wyvern he clutched; it tumbled from the sky. He flew up and joined Bayrin, and they lashed their claws, felling another beast. When Deramon looked around him, he saw a sea of wyverns; thousands encircled him, his son, and what remained of the dragons he had led to battle. Perhaps fifty still flew; the rest lay dead on the mountainside.

"Elethor!" Deramon howled. He stared south over thousands of wyverns and dragons, clouds of fire and acid, and spraying blood. "Elethor, get your dragons out of here! We fight underground!"

A brass dragon rose from fire, perhaps a mile away-- Elethor Aeternum, King of Requiem. Blood stained his muzzle, and he spat a legless Tiran rider from his mouth. He nodded at Deramon and shouted to those of his dragons who still lived.

"Royal Army!" he cried. "To the city! Fall back to Nova Vita. To the tunnels!"

Dragons began rising from the fray and flying north. Deramon cursed and felt those old, icy fingers reach through him. Four thousand dragons had flown south with the Royal Army; he saw several hundred who still lived.

It's a massacre, he thought. His innards burned and shook. He saw the images again: his men dead underground, his king burnt, the bodies of children strewn around him--children he had vowed to protect. Beyond those shadows, he saw an older ghost: the body of Noela in her crib, a mere babe. He had shaken her, pleaded with her, raised her above his head and howled in grief. He had buried her. He had wept for days, mourned for years.

How much death can we endure? he thought in a haze. He could barely hear the battle anymore. The screams were muted. The acid and fire gave no heat. The bodies on the mountains below gazed up at him--young eyes, scared, the eyes of sons and daughters, husbands, wives.

You failed us, Deramon, those eyes said to him. *You vowed to protect us. Won't you save us?*

Deramon shut his eyes. The children in the tunnels would die too. They would die like Noela. But he would not bury them; he would die in acid at their side.

"Father, fly!" rose a voice. Deramon opened his eyes to see Bayrin hovering before him, his scales burnt with acid, his flank slashed and bleeding. His son slapped him with his wings. "Father, fly with me."

With a howl, Deramon flew.

The dragons of Requiem raced over the mountains.

The wyverns chased.

When Deramon looked behind him, he saw Elethor leading ragtag survivors in flight. Wyverns dived all around them, spraying them with acid, picking them off one by one. With every

flap of dragon wings, another Vir Requis turned human, screamed
and clutched melting skin, and tumbled into darkness.

"Fly, dragons of Requiem!" Deramon shouted. He dived
back toward Elethor, roasted a wyvern, and flew by his king. The
lands streamed beneath them. The wind roared. All around
them, countless wyverns shrieked, and riders chanted, and acid
flew, and crossbows fired, and everywhere--everywhere in the
night Vir Requis fell dead. Wherever he looked, he saw them
burning, saw their pleading eyes.

Deramon! You vowed to protect us!

"Fly, dragons of Requiem!" cried King Elethor. "To the
city! To the tunnels!"

Deramon sought Nova Vita in the darkness. He could not
see the city. Flying to battle, the flight had seemed so short, a
mere dash across field, forest, and mountain. Now the miles
stretched endlessly. Now the fields and forests drank the blood
of dragons.

"Father!" rose a pained cry, and a blue dragon streamed
toward him.

Pain drove through Deramon like a spear in his chest. His
eyes stung. *Lyana!* Lyana flew there, his daughter, the light of his
life. She was wounded, her scales chipped, her eyes narrowed
with pain, and her body thin.

"Lyana," he whispered.

Again he held Noela's body, his youngest daughter. Again
he wept over the babe. *Stars, don't let me lose Bayrin and Lyana too. If
you have any mercy, stars of Draco, let me die before them.*

A phalanx of wyverns, bearing banners of red swords,
swooped from above. Crossbow bolts ricocheted off Deramon's
back and he roared. Acid rained. He banked, knocked into
Lyana, and shoved her aside. The acid streamed around them.
Deramon howled, raised his neck, and flamed the beasts. Lyana
soared and slashed at the wyverns' bellies, tearing saddles loose

and sending riders tumbling. Yet for every Tiran they slew, three Vir Requis screamed, burned, and fell.

It seemed like hours before they saw Nova Vita ahead. The city rose from a scorched forest, crackling with torches. Deramon howled and flew as fast as he could.

"To the tunnels!" he shouted. "Flee to the tunnels, flee underground!"

He looked around him; only dozens of dragons still flew. He looked behind him; the wyvern army filled the night. Countless red eyes blazed and countless fangs glistened in the firelight.

The surviving dragons, burnt and bloody and roaring, flew over the city walls. Those dragons still on the battlements and roofs took flight, roared fire, and crashed into the wyverns. A few died. A few fled north.

"Into the tunnels!" Deramon cried. "City Guard, we fight undergrou—"

Three wyverns crashed into him, cutting off his words. Acid doused his scales and fangs bit. He howled and spewed fire, driving them back. All around him, dragons and wyverns crashed above the city, fangs biting, claws lashing. Death rained. Claws and tails lashed at buildings and walls, and bricks fell. Columns crashed. Screams filled the night as the city of Nova Vita, fair capital of Requiem, crumbled below.

SOLINA

Her hand blazed. She snarled. When she raised her fist, her glove was charred and torn. Through the rents, she could see raw, red flesh. She clenched her fist tighter.

You did this, Elethor, she thought. She howled in rage. Ignoring the pain, she twisted her burnt fingers around her banner pole. She lifted it high, letting her standard unfurl. She flew above the battle, watching the wyverns and dragons clash above the city below.

"Level this city!" she shouted. "Leave no building standing! Bring me King Elethor alive."

Nova Vita was a small city--a backwater village compared to the glory of Irys. Her cloud of wyverns covered it entirely, a black fist from above. Barely a hundred reptile warriors still lived; more fell dead every moment. Some were landing on the streets, shifting into human form, and racing into the tunnels.

"Where are you, Elethor?" Solina whispered.

She dug her heels into her wyvern. With a scream, the beast swooped so fast that Solina's stomach lurched. She narrowed her eyes, snarled, and grasped her sword and banner tight. In the rushing dive, the wind lashing her, she could barely feel her burnt hand.

Wyverns parted to let her dive until she flew mere feet above the city's roofs. Below in the streets, weredragons clanked in armor, racing toward the tunnels. Solina howled, tugged her reins, and flew above them.

"Burn them, Baal!" she cried.

Her wyvern sprayed the street with acid. Weredragons screamed and fell. They tried to slap the acid off, but it seeped through their armor and began eating their flesh. One man clawed at his face; his eyes were already gone. Solina grinned, soared upon her wyvern, and flew across the city amphitheater and public baths; beyond them more weredragons were racing down the streets toward a second tunnel entrance. Solina swooped, splashed the street with acid, and soared as the men below screamed and fell. Baal's claws crashed against the tunnel archway, and its stones cascaded and crushed weredragons. The beast's wings beat, sending debris flying across the city.

Solina soared higher, seeking more dragons. She could see none. With their fire gone, the night was dark; she could barely see fleeing shadows. Her wyverns spread around her, flying in rings. Their riders held torches and howled for blood.

"Destroy these buildings!" Solina cried. "Let no column stand!"

The wyverns roared, dived, and began lashing the city buildings. A year ago, she had led ten thousand phoenixes to this place; their bodies had been woven of fire, and they had burned many trees and doors and bodies, but left the city's masonry standing. Today she had brought twenty thousand wyverns, each a behemoth of rippling muscles under metallic scales. Buildings collapsed under their blows like houses of cards.

"Level this city! Bring it down!"

Bricks tumbled and columns cracked. Dust rose in clouds that flowed across Solina. She dived toward the Temple of Stars, which rose upon a hill. She tugged the reins left, and her wyvern spun. His spiked tail--wider and stronger than a battering ram--cracked a column. He lashed the column again and again until it shattered. Soon the entire temple was collapsing. Solina soared higher and smiled as the dust flew and the bricks fell.

"You prayed here to your stars," she said. "But they cannot save you now. Not from the glory of my lord."

The weredragons cowered in their tunnels, daring not fight. Solina spat in disgust; they were vile creatures, too craven to defend their home. Truly they were shadows of the night, slinking things that wilted in the light of her lord.

She tugged the reins, directing Baal to fly over the Weredragon Palace. The edifice rose three hundred feet tall, its marble columns capped with dragon capitals. Solina snarled to see it. Eight years ago, the Weredragon Prince had burned her here. The scar blazed across her body now, a searing memory. The line of fire ran from her forehead to leg, from that year to this day. This cruel palace, disguising its evil with marble grace, was where the weredragons had torn her apart from her love, exiled her, and sealed their doom.

"You burned me here," she whispered through clenched teeth. "Now these ruins will scream for ten thousand years."

She reached into the pouch that hung across her saddle. She withdrew two clay balls wrought with red runes. A smile spread across her face.

Tiran fire.

The liquid inside these clay balls burned brighter than streams of dragonfire, than pools of acid, than the smelters of southern Iysa where her blades had been forged. For a year, a thousand men had labored in her barracks, distilling this liquid ruin and blessing it with the wrath of the Sun God. Today their work would blaze in glory.

She circled around the palace, rose high above its roof, and dropped two clay balls. As they fell, she saw the runes upon them glow red. Then they hit the palace, and her glory covered the city.

The Tiran fire exploded with blue light. The inferno burst out, great disks of white flame. Bricks shattered, columns cracked, and smoke filled the sky. Solina screamed to the Sun God, pulled out two more clay balls, and dropped them too.

The explosions rocked the city. Two columns shattered and fell, and then the roof caved in. Solina could barely see through the smoke and dust and flame. Laughing madly, she wrenched the pouch off her saddle and held it upside down. Ten more clay spheres tumbled onto the palace.

The air itself seemed to crack.

Ringing filled her ears over a sea of muffled susurration.

Fire thrashed the sky, and columns fell, and clouds of smoke rose; she could hear nothing but the ringing, a song of angels. She laughed, though she could not hear her own voice, and soared higher. Wind blew, kissed her cheeks, and streamed her hair. Below, the dust rolled across the city, burying the houses, the amphitheater, the barracks, and the collapsing temple. When the dust settled, Solina howled and laughed.

The Weredragon Palace was gone. Only a single column remained standing, rising from rubble.

"There is only one monarch of Requiem, Elethor!" she cried, her voice but a dim, distant whisper under the ringing in her ears. "I am queen of this land. You are but a cowering reptile. Emerge from your hole and face me!"

Thousands of wyverns howled below her, flying across the city and tearing it down. A hundred of the beasts slammed into the towers of Castra Draco, garrison of the Royal Army; the towers tumbled. Claws tore down homes. The walls crumbled, and beyond them in the farms, acid poured across the crops, until nothing but scorched earth remained.

"Tear down every last wall!" Solina howled. "I want to see nothing but rubble!"

All night the wyverns flew, screeching and destroying. Their riders chanted and laughed and sang the songs of their phalanxes. The weredragons remained hidden underground, if any still lived. It was a night to banish all nights, a battle to end all darkness.

When the sun rose, it rose upon glory. Its beams lit a world cleansed of evil. Solina raised her sword to the light and cried to the Sun God, and tears streamed down her cheeks.

"We bring your light to the world, Sun God!" she cried. "Hail the Light of Tiranor!"

Her army roared the prayer. Sunlight glinted on bright armor, spears, and swords. Their banners streamed in victory. Below them, where a city had stood, a single column rose from a ruin of rubble, dust, and bones.

TREALE

As she flew toward the city, she watched it fall.

Her eyes stung, her lungs ached, and a cough still lingered in her throat. Her scales and wings were singed, and it was all she could do to keep flying. The lands of Requiem burned around her in the night: farms, grasslands, forests, all crackling and raising red pillars in the night. Before her, across the leagues, she saw Nova Vita, and she saw its towers fall.

The cloud of wyverns clutched Aeternum's City, a black claw from the south. The beasts kept swooping and knocking down homes. A great wyvern, bearing the banner of Queen Solina, unleashed balls of fire that rocked the city. As Treale flew, she watched the Temple of Stars shatter--the place where she'd been born. She watched the palace crumble until only one of its columns remained. She watched the walls themselves--the fabled white walls of Nova Vita, which Queen Gloriae herself had raised to defend her city--collapse.

"Requiem," Treale whispered. "Land of dragons. Realm of Aeternum. I watched your towers fall, and I shed tears, and I cried to the stars for your glory lost."

In her old books, King Benedictus had spoken those words--centuries ago when the griffins had toppled their forest halls. King Benedictus had borne the rare, black scales Treale too possessed. She was descended from him through his daughter, Agnus Dei, who had survived the slaughter.

And now I fly here, and now I watch the slaughter, and now I watch your towers fall, Requiem.

Treale flew closer to the city, then paused and hovered. Tears stung her eyes. The shrieks, war cries, and booms of shattering stone rose ahead. They slammed into her. The smell of acid burned her nostrils.

"What do I do?" she whispered, head spinning. Her breath quickened into a pant. Her chest ached. The cries slammed against her: the roars of wyverns, the chants of Tiran men, and beneath them... could she hear screams of pain, of her dying brothers and sisters?

What do I do?

Dawn began to rise around her, red and gray, and her eyes blurred. Hovering in midair, she looked aside. What would her ancestor Agnus Dei have done? In all the stories, Agnus Dei was a great warrior, a fiery dragon who charged recklessly into the hordes of the enemy. In old paintings and statues, she looked like Treale too--with dark fiery eyes and black hair.

"She would not run," Treale whispered. "She would roar her fury, blow her fire, and charge at the enemy. She would kill many wyverns until they finally tore her down."

And she would have died, whispered a voice inside her. *She would have died and never given birth to her son Ben, and House Oldnale would never have been. I would never have been.*

Treale turned and began flying north, heading toward the distant forests beyond fire and death. She could hide there. She could try to find other survivors. She could continue the battle from the wilderness. Her throat tightened as she flew, and tears flowed from her eyes.

The faces of her parents, charred and gaping, filled her eyes. Thousands of souls now burned in the city, crying out to her, begging for aid.

With a yelp, Treale spun and began flying toward the city again.

They need me. I can't leave them. I must save them!

She howled as she flew, a black dragon in the blood-red dawn. Soon the city was closer, rising from inferno. The eyes of the wyverns burned. Their banners flapped. Their songs rose-- songs of glory, light, and death. No more dragons flew. The wyverns were swooping and tearing down the last trees, homes, and statues. The sun rose, its red light falling upon little but rubble.

They're all dead, Treale thought as she flew over blazing farmlands. *Stars, they're all gone, they're all fallen.*

She mewled and spun around again. Once more she began flying north. She had to hide. She could no longer help her people. If she died with them, her bones would lie here forever, useless. In the forests of the north she could survive, she could seek survivors, she could...

I am a coward. She growled and her eyes burned. *I am a soldier, yet I flee from battle.* She looked up, seeking the stars of Requiem, seeking their guidance. Yet she could not see the sky, only smoke and ash, black and red. No more starlight fell upon Requiem. Voice torn, fire in her maw, she cried out the prayer of her people.

"Requiem! May our wings forever find your sky." She howled as she flew. "I will find your sky again, Requiem. I vow to you."

Shrieks of rage flared behind her.

She turned to see a dozen wyverns tear themselves from the army over Nova Vita, howl at the sky, and fly toward her.

Treale cursed. She cursed Tiranor, she cursed the Sun God, and she cursed herself for her stupidity. They had heard her cries, seen her fire, and now she too would die, and her bones would not even rest among her comrades, but burn in the wild.

She could charge at them, she knew. For death! For Requiem! For eternal starlight--to die in battle, to rise to the starlit halls in a final blaze of glory.

Instead, she kept fleeing toward the northern forests.

King's Column still stands in the ruins of our palace, she thought. The legends whispered that it would stand so long as a single Vir Requis lived. If she was the last one alive, she would not die here, she would not let that ancient column fall.

The world burned. She flew over the ruin of her home. The wyverns howled behind her. When she looked over her shoulder, she saw their eyes blaze, their riders aim crossbows, and their maws gape, full of acid. A dozen flew there, maybe more, black and red and golden in the clouds of smoke.

She shot through ash until the cries of the city faded behind her. She burst through flame and flew through smoke, coughing, blinded, the heat searing her belly. When she looked behind her, she saw only black and red swirls, a nightmare world, the Abyss itself risen to fill Requiem. Yet still she heard the wyvern cries. Still they followed her. Crossbow bolts whizzed through the smoke around her, and one grazed her tail. She bit down on a scream.

They can't see me. If they can't hear me, they will lose me.

She swallowed. She blinked. She shoved down the horror that filled her. She flew.

Treale no longer knew north from south. She saw nothing but smoke around her, smoke above her, and fires below her. The world spun. Was she still flying to the forests, or had she changed direction in the inferno, and was flying back toward the ruin of her capital? She heard the shrieks behind her, distant and echoing.

Just keep those shrieks behind you, she told herself. *Just fly away from them as fast as you can.*

She trembled. Her scales felt hot enough to melt; they expanded in the heat so that she could barely move. Her lungs and throat blazed as if she had swallowed lava, and she did not know how much longer she could fly. Yet she forced herself to

keep flying, one flap of her wings after another. She tried to keep
her body slim, to leave no wake through the smoke. Yet she must
have been leaving a trail, for the shrieks still sounded behind her,
and more bolts flew toward her. One lashed her side, and she bit
down on a yelp. She gritted her teeth, blinked her eyes, and flew
onward.

"I'm sorry, Elethor," she whispered. "I'm sorry I could not
fight by your side, could not die by you."

In the haze of smoke and fire, she lay by him again upon
the hill. She talked to him of their pasts, and kissed his cheek, and
slept by his side--young and scared, but feeling safe by her king.
It was a last, kind memory and she let it fill her. If nothing else--if
all the halls of Requiem fell, and she died here in the wilderness,
and jackals ate her bones--she still had that memory. She had still
lain upon a hill with her king, and talked to him of old manor halls
and puppets and dreams. She still had one dream of soft, quiet
camaraderie to soothe her in the flames.

It seemed like she flew for hours. Her head was muzzy, and
a deathly haze had begun to drown her pain, when finally she
emerged from the smoke. An ancient forest rolled before her,
spreading into red dawn, a tangle of shadows and secrets.

Before the wyverns could emerge from smoke behind her,
Treale swooped. She all but crashed into the forest, snapping
branches and slamming, half dead, onto the hot earth. She shifted
into human form at once. In her smaller, weaker body, she
trembled so violently that she could only lie shaking. Ash covered
her. Welts rose across her skin. She coughed on the ground,
gasping for breath.

"Please, stars," she prayed. "Let me live. Let me *live*. I
cannot die here, away from my people, shameful. Please don't let
me die."

She could not stop shaking. The trees rose above her,
labyrinths of wood. She coughed and sucked the hot air for

breath, and her eyes rolled back, and the haze of death spread across her. *No! No.* She clawed the ash. She bit her cheek and pain flared. She forced a deep, raw breath, and her lungs screamed in agony. She tried to remember that night--the night she had lain by Elethor upon the hill--and draw strength from it, to once more taste the clear air and feel brave.

The wyverns roared. Their cries nearly shattered her ears.

"Stars, give me strength."

Burnt and shaking and gasping for air, Treale Oldnale pushed herself to her feet. The forest spun around her, and she had to grab a bole to stop from falling. She looked south and saw a wall of smoke like a shimmering tapestry. The wyverns shrieked within it. As she stood trembling, she saw them burst from the inferno and fly above the forest.

Treale ran.

She ran between the trees and leaped over roots. Above in the canopy, the wyverns overshot her. They appeared only as shadows against the smoke and clouds, black against black. Their cries rang out.

"Find the weredragon!" cried one rider, voice distant and echoing. "Tear down the trees! The creature shifted and runs as human. Find it!"

Treale's boots hit a root, and she fell. Her cheek slammed against the earth. She lay trembling, eyes burning. The wyverns soared overhead, bending the trees. She felt the blast of their wings. Droplets of their acid pattered around her, raised smoke, and began to eat into the earth. A few droplets hit Treale's boot, and she winced and gritted her teeth, struggling not to scream. She kicked the boot off, pulled her knee to her chest, and slapped at her foot. The flesh felt hot and raw.

"Please, stars of Requiem, please. Let me live. Shine on me this red dawn."

She looked up but saw no stars, only the canopies of trees, a sky of ash, and the shadows of wyverns that circled and screamed.

Tears of pain streamed down her face. She did not know if any other Vir Requis still lived, or if she was the last. Her body shook so badly, she did not think she could rise. She gritted her teeth so hard they ached. She growled. Arms like wet towels, she managed to grab a branch. She pulled herself up. Her lungs burned and her knees shook wildly; she did not think she could still run.

But Treale ran. She ran through the forest, not knowing what direction she moved. She could see only several feet ahead, and the trees rose like twisted goblins around her, their branches reaching out to snag her, to tear her clothes, to scratch her face bloody. She tasted the blood and sap on her lips. Still she ran, the forest spreading endlessly and the scourge of her people howling above.

ELETHOR

They stood behind the doors, swords drawn, and waited.

The tunnel walls rose around them, craggy and black. Only several candles upon the walls lit the darkness; their light flickered and cast shadows like dancing demons. Elethor gripped the hilt of Ferus, his ancient sword. With narrowed eyes, he stared at the doors before him. He tightened his lips. He breathed slowly. He waited.

His warriors stood around him. Lyana stood at his right, sword drawn in her right hand, dagger in her left. A helmet hid her stubbly head, the Draco stars carved onto its brow, and the candlelight danced against her breastplate, the ancient breastplate of a bellator. At his left stood Bayrin and Deramon, clad in the armor of the City Guard and clutching their own blades. A hundred other warriors--survivors of the battle over the mountains--filled the tunnel behind them, blades orange in the candlelight.

A hundred souls stood in silence, staring at those doors. A hundred souls waited for death. Beyond those doors, a staircase rose narrow and steep toward the fallen city. The candles flickered with their every breath. Not a piece of armor clanked.

Stars, be with us today, Elethor prayed silently.

The doors before him were a foot thick, carved of oak bolted with iron. Great beams stood in brackets. No battering ram would break these doors, Elethor knew. A wyvern's tail perhaps could shatter them, but Elethor had ordered the doors built a hundred yards down the narrow staircase; no wyvern could fit down here to reach them.

Behind him, the tunnel sloped into silent darkness. Beyond tunnel, portcullis, and more doors loomed the chambers where his people waited, where Mori waited, where the last light of Requiem glowed.

All that separates them from their fall is me, my warriors, and a whisper of starlight.

He flexed his fingers around the hilt of his sword, reminding himself that he had prepared for this day.

We are safe here, he told himself. *They will not claim these tunnels. We will hold back the enemy.*

A smaller, cold voice whispered in his head. *But for how long?* They had food and water for a year. It was a long time, but eventually their supplies would run out. What then? Would they starve here underground? He squared his jaw and clutched his sword tighter. Had he led his people into a tomb?

A great boom shook the tunnels. The candles flickered and dust fell. Above, through many feet of stone, he could hear the distant cries of wyverns. Elethor narrowed his eyes and sucked in breath. A second crash shook the tunnels, and again the wyverns wailed, a distant sound like ghosts. Elethor snarled. When he looked at his sides, he saw Lyana, Bayrin, and the others clutch their swords tight. More booms sounded. More dust rained and the candles danced. Muffled voices rose in song: the battle songs of Tiranor, songs of triumph and bloodlust.

For the first time somebody spoke. "Bloody stars," Bayrin muttered and spat. "They're destroying the city. Bastards."

Lyana looked at her brother, then turned toward Elethor. Their eyes met. Any other day, Elethor would have expected to see Lyana roll her eyes, scold her brother, and launch into a lecture. Today she only stared silently, and new ghosts haunted her eyes. Elethor remembered holding her in the Abyss as Nedath's curse spread across her, as her body wilted and her teeth fell. They had emerged from darkness. They had defeated ancient evils underground. The memories pained Elethor but comforted him too; they had faced darkness before and defeated it. They would face this new darkness together too.

"Elethor," she said, pale. "Bayrin is right. I know he rarely is, but... they aren't leaving one building standing."

Elethor nodded, fist clenched at his side. He spoke in a low voice. "I know. But I would rather them crush buildings than bodies." He shook his head, struggling to drown panic. "Stars, Lyana, they ripped through our army. They were like hawks in a cloud of sparrows."

Lyana looked behind her where warriors filled the tunnel. "There are twenty thousand wyverns above us. They outnumbered us over the forest." She looked back at him, eyes dark. "Elethor, we have twenty thousand Vir Requis in the lower chambers. One dragon for every wyvern." She bared her teeth. "Let us fly! Let us fly in battle, the great last stand of the Vir Requis. Let every child, grandparent, and wounded son of Requiem fly to war today. We will make such a roar."

Her eyes glistened in her pale face, and her hands gripped her weapons. *She is a warrior,* Elethor thought, *raised on tales of knights and epic battle. But I am a king.*

"Lyana, these wyverns crushed soldiers--dragons trained to fly in formation, to blow fire from above, to slash claws, to lash tails. My soldiers trained for a year, and these wyverns tore through us." He shook his head. "Thousands of survivors hide below us, it's true. Children. Mothers and babes. Old men and women. Cripples." He sighed. "Even as dragons, their fire is weak, their claws soft, their hearts frightened. Many of them have lost their fangs to old age; many others haven't even grown theirs. No, I will not lead them out to die in the skies. There is safety underground."

Her eyes flashed. "Elethor! Last year they tore through these tunnels like--"

"Last year this place merely stored grain and wine. Last year no doors stood here. We have thick doors now and strong men to guard them; three levels stand between the Tirans and our people. They will not break in so easily this time."

Bayrin, who had watched the exchange with dark eyes, let out a slow breath. Dirt smeared his face and hair, and a wound spread across his arm.

"Famous last words, El," he muttered. "Bloody stars, but for the first time in my life, I'm going to agree with Lyana. We--"

Battle cries surged behind the doors, cutting off his words. Armor and weapons clanked above, and soon Elethor heard boots thudding down the staircase, rushing from the city into the tunnels. The cries of Tirans rose, hoarse and crude. Above them rose a shrill voice; it made Elethor close his eyes, grind his teeth, and cringe with old pain.

"Kill the weredragons!" cried Solina behind the doors. "Bring me the Reptile King alive! Slay the others."

The boots thudded and the Tiran voices rose in wordless, enraged shouts. With a boom that shook the tunnels, they crashed against the doors.

Elethor tightened his grip on his sword. His hand was sweaty. Why hadn't they carved this tunnel wider, wide enough for a dragon to blow fire? Why hadn't they made the doors thicker, or carved them with arrow slits? They hadn't had enough time! Not enough time to dig, to prepare, to--

The Tirans slammed against the doors again. They creaked, and Elethor found himself snarling.

Deal with this now. You cannot change the past. Face them down as you are.

He looked to his left at Bayrin and Deramon. They stared back and nodded.

"We fight with you, my friend," Bayrin whispered.

Deramon growled. "We kill for you, my king."

When Elethor looked to his right, he saw Lyana glaring at the doors, blades raised. She spared him a quick glance, eyes blazing with green fire, and smiled crookedly.

"I'm ready to spill blood," she said. "Keep count, El; I bet I can kill ten times more than you."

Elethor nodded at her, silent. *Good.* This was the Lyana he wanted to see, not the Lyana with sad eyes, but the knight with the fiery stare.

The doors shook again and splinters cracked. The Tirans howled behind the oak and iron. Again and again the doors shook, and every boom rolled through the tunnel, louder than thunder. *Thud. Thud.* The Tirans howled. Solina screamed. *Thud. Thud.* Splinters flew.

"Break them down!" Solina shouted.

Her men roared. *Boom. Thud.* Splinters flew. Candles fell around Elethor. He stood still, staring at the doors, waiting. His warriors stood around him. *Boom. Thud.* Again and again. Screams and shrieks. *Thud. Thud.*

"Requiem," Elethor whispered. "May our wings forever find your sky."

His men repeated the words around him. The Tirans screamed for blood. Their shadows danced under the doors. *Boom. Thud.* Screams and splinters.

And then... silence.

Ragged breath, curses, and grumbles sounded behind the doors. Boots stomped upstairs and Solina's shrieks faded. Soon the sounds of her men faded too, moving back to the city above.

Elethor released the breath he hadn't realized he was holding. He squinted at the doors.

What are you doing, Solina?

"Stars yeah!" Bayrin said at his side. He grinned wildly. "The doors stood! The bastards couldn't break them. This time we were ready for them!" He growled at the doors. "Pity, almost; I was looking forward to shoving my sword up Solina's backside."

When Elethor looked at Lyana, he saw less hope there. The knight was still staring at the doors, her eyes narrowed and her lips tightened.

"I don't like this," she whispered.

Bayrin snorted. "Why, Lyana? You were worried you couldn't kill as many men as me? The cowards gave up! They thought they'd find undefended tunnels like last year. Well, they--"

Elethor interrupted his friend. "They'll be back, Bay. Keep your sword drawn. Get ready. Wait."

Silence fell.

They stood, gripping weapons, breath soft.

Above, the sounds of collapsing buildings faded, and even the wyvern shrieks died.

Elethor caught his breath. In the silence, his ears rang.

With a swell like a typhoon, a thousand wyvern shrieks rose above. Elethor grimaced. The sound was so loud and shrill he couldn't help but cry out. Bayrin snarled and winced, Deramon cursed, and Lyana growled. It sounded like the entire army of wyverns cried above the stairs. Acrid stench flared, so hot it burned Elethor's nose, eyes, and throat.

Lyana straightened and her face paled. Her eyes widened and she shouted, "Back! Everybody back!"

Confusion reigned. Lyana began retreating, trying to herd soldiers back into darkness. Elethor stared at her, then back at the doors. The stench of acid intensified. His eyes stung so badly, he could barely see. The wyverns above howled. A sound like a river roaring plunged beyond the doors.

Smoke and stench exploded, and the doors began to sizzle. Acid seeped around and under them.

"Stars," Elethor whispered. He spun and began running. "Back, everyone! Deeper into the tunnels--move!"

Acid sluiced around his boots. The soles began to sizzle. He cursed and ran. A hundred soldiers raced before him. Bayrin and Deramon ran cursing at his side. When he looked over his shoulder, Elethor saw the doors splintering. A hinge fell. Acid burst through a hole and shot into the tunnels. The doors looked like a dam holding back a river--a dam about to collapse.

Elethor looked back ahead and ran, teeth bared and eyes burning. The darkness swirled. Behind him, he heard the doors shatter.

MORI

They huddled in the chambers of the third level--twenty thousand souls, weeping, shaking, and praying. Mori stood by the tapestry she had woven, struggling to calm her beating heart. The sea of people rolled around her. Wounded soldiers, survivors of the battle, writhed upon the floor, their flesh twisted with acid. Children screamed and clung to their mothers. What soldiers could still stand manned the doors, swords drawn and faces hard. From above, Mori heard faded echoes of battle: wyverns screeching, buildings collapsing, and men howling. With every boom of a collapsing tower, the people shivered; some wept and trembled.

"Be strong, Elethor," Mori whispered, clutching her luck finger behind her back. "Be strong, Bayrin and Lyana."

She missed them. Her chest ached for them. She wished she could be with them now, guarding the upper tunnels, a sword in her hand. She was no warrior, but surely anything was better than this--waiting here in the darkness, only a few candles lighting the chambers, surrounded by tears and wails and the stench of burnt flesh.

One wounded guard moaned only several yards away, his face melted away, his eyes gone; he gaped with empty sockets. Mother Adia knelt above him, her robes stained with blood and death. Younger healers, her pupils, were moving between the other wounded, applying ointments to wounds, pouring silkweed into mouths, and praying. Yet even the healers trembled, and even their faces were pale.

They are all scared, Mori realized--healers and guards, the wounded and the strong. So many, even those untouched by acid, still bore the old scars of the Phoenix War. *There is no hope here, only fear.*

Mori tightened her lips. No, she was no warrior, but she was a leader to these people. She was a princess of House Aeternum, an ancient dynasty that had ruled in Requiem for millennia. She would help her people in her own way.

"Children of Requiem!" she called. Her voice was small at first, nearly drowned under the sounds of battle and weeping. She called out louder. "Vir Requis! Hear me, my people."

They looked at her--children, the elderly, guards, healers and wounded. Many still wept and trembled. Mori forced herself to stay strong, to calm the thrashing of her heart. So many eyes upon her spun her head, but she clutched her luck finger, and she spoke loudly so that her voice carried through the chambers.

"My brother, King Elethor, protects us. His sword is sharp, his armor thick. Our soldiers stand at his side; they are brave and strong. We are safe here." She turned to look at Adia who still knelt above the blinded man. "Mother Adia! May I lead the people in prayer?"

Holding the wounded guard, Adia stared across the people at Mori. Her eyes were deep, dark pools reflecting the candlelight; the shadows of memory and loss danced in them. She nodded silently. Her lips twisted but she said nothing.

Mori began to sing. She was no priestess, but she loved the temple services; she would always sing the prayers along with Mother Adia, voice quiet and shy, but pure. Today she let her voice sing out loudly for all to hear; it still sounded high to her, too high, not deep and sonorous like Adia's voice. Yet it carried through the chambers, and the people sang with her.

"As the leaves fall upon our marble tiles, as the breeze rustles the birches beyond our columns, as the sun gilds the mountains above our halls--know, young child of the woods, you are home, you are home. Requiem! May our wings forever find your sky."

As they sang, the fear seemed to leave the people; their trembles eased, their tears dried, and their backs straightened. They had sung these songs a year ago in the Phoenix War. The Living Seven had sung these songs three hundred years ago, fighting Dies Irae and his griffins. Three thousand years ago, King Aeternum himself--the first king and Mori's ancestor--had carved these words into King's Column, which still rose above them.

In generations to come, Mori thought, *the Vir Requis will think of us--of me and my people--singing our words underground. We will survive. We will pass our song on, a torch of starlight, a dream to forever find our sky.*

Screams echoed through the tunnels above.

Mori's voice died.

The people began to whisper and weep again. The guards at the doors clutched their swords and looked around with narrowed eyes. The screams rolled above them, torn in anguish. The stench of acid hit Mori's nostrils, so sharp it burned through her nose down to her throat and lungs.

"Stars," she whispered. She looked over the crowd of survivors at Mother Adia. The priestess met her gaze, eyes wide with terror.

Boots thudded outside the doors. Men screamed. The smoke and caustic stench swirled. Voices cried in anguish. Fists began pounding at the chamber doors. She heard them cry of Requiem, cry for starlight, cry for their king.

"Open the doors!" Mori cried to her guards. "It's our men! Open the doors!"

Her guards, faces pale and jaws clenched, lifted the bar from the doors' brackets. At once the doors slammed open. The smell of acid flared. From the darkness, a Vir Requis guard ran into the lower chambers, screaming. His flesh twisted with acid. Mori screamed too. He looked, she thought, like tallow melting in a suit of armor.

The burnt man ran five paces into the chamber. His eyes had burned away. His mouth screamed, a gaping hole in his ravaged face. People scurried aside, wailing. The guard fell to his knees, gave a last cry, then fell forward and lay silent.

Through the doors, acid began to trickle into the chamber.

Mori stood frozen for an instant. In her mind, she saw everyone in these chambers--thousands of them--melting and burning, screaming, pawing at her, weeping as they died around her. For that instant, her heart froze and no breath found her lips.

She clutched her luck finger.

Panic later, Mori. Fight now.

She ran toward the shelves of supplies. "Grab sacks of grain!" she cried. "Pile them at the door! Soak up the acid!"

She grabbed a sack of wheat, dragged it toward the doors, and tossed it down. She drew her sword, slashed the sack open, and grain spilled. The wheat began to soak up the flowing acid. Some sluiced around her shoes, and her soles began to steam.

"Grab the grain!" she cried. "Stop the acid!"

Around her, some people wept and shivered, curled up into balls. Others began to pull more sacks of grain, slash them open, and spill their contents onto the acid that trickled from above. As they worked, more guards began running into the chambers. Some were so burnt, they were unrecognizable; they were but living wounds. Others suffered milder burns; they too began slashing open sacks of grain.

Stars, where is Elethor? Where are Bayrin and Lyana and Deramon?

Mori growled and kept working. Why had they not foreseen this? Why had they not carved drainage holes into the tunnels? She winced, cursing herself but knowing she could not change the past. *Fight now. Save these people now.*

The acid flow strengthened from trickle to stream. Mori dragged more sacks, slashed them open, and spilled more grain. People wailed around her. Some acid flowed around the grain and began eating at people's boots.

Elethor, where are you?

As she dragged a sack forward, she saw Adia dragging the dead man away, the one who had first burst into the chambers. His flesh dangled through his armor, and sudden horror pulsed through Mori. Was that... was that Elethor? Was that wounded, wreck of a person Bayrin or Lyana?

No. No! It can't be. Tears stung her eyes and she slashed another sack open. The acid was pouring more powerfully now. People were screaming. Several children shifted into dragons-- they were but the size of horses--and clung to the ceiling.

"Do not shift!" Mori shouted. If they all became dragons, they would crush one another and breathe all the air. "Move into the deeper chambers. Go!"

They began to move through the network of chambers, pushing deeper, but acid kept pouring. More and more grain spilled. The acid began to eat through Mori's shoes; they were falling apart. She grimaced and kept working even as her soles began to blaze.

"Mori!"

She looked up and tears filled her eyes. Bayrin came running through the doorway. Behind him ran Lyana, Elethor, and Deramon. Acid was steaming on their boots and armor, but their skin was still smooth. Mori cried out to them, a tremble seizing her.

They leaped over the sacks of grain, which were still soaking up the acid, and began kicking off boots, unclasping armor, and removing gloves. They tossed the steaming leather and steel aside, then began slapping at their bodies.

"Merciful stars, this stuff is hot!" Bayrin cried. He pulled his tunic off and tossed it aside, remaining bare-chested. He slapped at his torso, searching for droplets of acid.

Mori rushed toward him. "Bayrin! The Tirans! Are--"

Eyes dark, he spat. "They haven't entered the tunnels, but they've got every last bloody wyvern flooding us with acid, I reckon."

Lips tightened, Mori turned to look at her brother. Elethor's shoulder was burnt, his jaw was tight, and his eyes blazed red and hard. He clutched his longsword Ferus.

"Keep stacking the grain!" he shouted to the people. "Every last sack--I want it blocking the doorway!"

They kept working. Soon a great pile of sacks--enough grain to feed hundreds--filled the doorway and half the chamber. The survivors huddled deeper against the walls, pushing into the further, deeper chambers, a sea of living flesh filling this labyrinth of stone. Mori stood huddled between Bayrin and Lyana. She reached out and clasped their hands--Lyana with her right hand, and Bayrin with her left hand, the one with her lucky sixth finger.

If we die, she thought, *I die with those that I love.* A bitter smile touched her lips. *That is not a bad way to die.*

She looked up at Bayrin. He met her eyes and squeezed her hand tight. They stood together--a king and princess, healers and wounded, nobles and commoners. They watched as the sacks began to melt, as the heat and stench rose. One man began to sing, voice hoarse, the old songs of Requiem. Hesitant, a woman joined him, and soon they all sang together--thousands of voices rolling through the tunnels, thousands of voices calling out the cry of starlight, the song of dragons.

Acid saturated the grain. The sacks melted away. The distant shrieks of wyverns sounded, and the acid grew to a river... then came gushing into the chambers.

MAHRDOR

Pain.

Pain tore through him like a horde of scorpions in his veins.

He twisted his left hand into a trembling fist. The black leather glove he wore clung to the ruin of his flesh, sticking to blood, fat, and muscle. The pain flared from fingers to elbow and coursed through his body. Blood pounded in his ears. A red veil seemed to cloak the world.

She did this to me.

He sat upon his wyvern, a beast named Phel born with four leathern wings, having absorbed her sibling in the egg. One eye, one nostril, and three teeth of that twin thrust out from Phel's cheek, twitching with anguish; the rest of the parasite rotted inside her. The twisted wyvern perched upon a hill, claws digging into a fallen column. From his saddle of leather and steel spikes, Mahrdor stared down across the ruins to the archway; Solina sat there upon her own wyvern, goading the beast to spew more acid into the darkness below.

She burns the weredragons like she burned me.

He snarled. Even the movement of baring his teeth sent pain blazing, and he nearly lost consciousness. He clutched the reins.

I should kill her now, he thought. Rage crackled through him. Fire blazed across him. *I should slay her with my sword. I should peel back her skin, eat her flesh, and carve her bones with my name.* Blood and fire painted the world. His head spun. His fingers trembled, and he gritted his teeth so hard he chipped a tooth and spat out the chunk. He licked his lips and imagined the taste of Solina's organs bursting between his teeth.

He tugged the reins. His wyvern cawed, leaped over a pile of bodies, and landed ten feet closer to Solina. Mahrdor glared at his queen. She sat upon her mount, her back to him, her hair billowing, a banner of gold in the dawn.

Mahrdor grabbed the glove on his left hand. He peeled the edge back, snarling. The pain exploded like Tiran fire inside him. Through the veil of red, he stared at the flesh beneath: twisted, soft, barely clinging to the bone.

I will burn her too, he swore. *Slowly. Inch by inch. Year by year. She will grow old in my dungeons, screaming for me. She will live a long life.*

Why had he taken the ancient punishment? Why had he dipped his hand into the acid? He could have killed her then. He could have slain her in her tent; he was strong enough, and she was but a woman, weak of flesh and mind. And yet... and yet he had shoved the hand in. He had taken the pain. He had drunk it up eagerly, savoring it, a pup begging for forgiveness.

For what? The mercy of a queen? The honor of his post, a lord of hosts? He snarled, choked, and coughed. He spat a glob of phlegm and blood. What did he care for honor or power?

"All I ever craved was my collection," he said through a tight jaw. "All I ever wanted was to *create*."

He was an artist first, a warrior second. How he would have created art from Lyana, a true knight of Requiem! He would have molded her body, painted and pierced it, broken and healed it, shattered her bones and reshaped them until they mended into the forms he desired. And he would have molded her mind. He would have turned her from a proud, strong warrior into a mindless slave, a cowering creature, an animal that knew nothing but fear and pain and drool. She would have been his greatest creation, his gilded bird.

That is why, he knew. *That is why I drove my fist into the jug. Never forget. Never forget why you are here.*

He growled at the sky where red clouds churned. He would find his Lyana again. He would return her to his villa in Tiranor. He would break and reshape her. If he had to sacrifice a hand, well... let his hand be as a work of art too.

He ripped off the glove.

He screamed.

He held the deformed hand before him in the dawn. When he flexed the fingers, flesh tore and pain blinded him, rivers of red and white. He found himself laughing through his screams.

It is beautiful, he thought.

His queen had done this to him, and he laughed, realizing his folly. How could he have hated her for this? She had made his hand beautiful. She had molded him. She had *collected* him. She had turned his flesh into a work of art, into rivulets of scars, into *beauty*.

Maybe one day he would return the favor. He would scar her with beauty too. But not yet. Not yet. First he would take what was his: a horde of weredragons to collect, a knight, a princess, a king too if Solina would allow it.

"They will all be my treasures," he whispered to his ruined hand. "They will all be beautiful like you, my love."

He tugged the reins, pulling his wyvern away from Solina. He dug his heels into the beast and Phel soared, four wings beating in unison. Soon Mahrdor was circling above the city, nostrils flared, taking in the scent of death. In the dawn, the devastation rolled below him, a tapestry of triumph. The walls of Nova Vita lay fallen, bricks strewn across the smoldering forest like scattered teeth. The temple lay shattered, its columns snapped like bones. The palace lay in rubble; only a single column, hundreds of feet tall, rose from its ruin. Homes, shops, statues--all lay smashed, white with ash and red with blood.

Such pathetic creatures, the weredragons, Mahrdor thought. He had fought in the war thirty years ago, a mere youth clutching a spear for the first time. He had watched the dragons destroy Irys, kill his parents, torch the palms and boil the River Pallan. How they fell now! They had not lasted a day.

Mahrdor thought back to that war thirty years ago. He remembered finding his family crushed and burnt in the ruins of his house. He remembered lying by their bodies for days, staring at their gaping wounds, watching the flies feast, smelling them rot, admiring their beauty. When finally priests had found him in the ruins, they had thought him mad, had shaken their heads at his smile, at the blood on his lips.

But is it not better to smile than weep? Mahrdor thought as he flew above, admiring the death and destruction. *Is it not better to admire beauty than mourn loss? To collect art rather than cry over blood?*

He began circling down toward the city square, where Tiran warriors guarded a pile of wounded, whimpering weredragons. Some Tiran soldiers stood afoot, aiming spears or crossbows at the prisoners. Others sat upon their wyverns, ready to spew acid. The weredragons lay in human forms, clad in chains and splashed in blood.

Mahrdor landed his wyvern in the square. The beast's claws dug ruts into the cobblestones. She tossed her scaly head back, nostrils flared to inhale the scent of weredragon blood, and howled to the sky.

"Be calm, my girl," Mahrdor said and stroked Phel's nape. "Soon you will feast upon their bodies. Once they tell me all they know, their flesh will be yours."

The wyvern mewled, slapped her tail, and beat her four wings. Her drool splashed the cobblestones and began eating through the stone. The third eye on her cheek blinked and shed tears. Sometimes it seemed to Mahrdor that this absorbed twin, only hints of it showing, craved flesh and blood just as much.

Stroking the beast, Mahrdor dismounted. When his boots hit the cobblestones, pain flared through him, racing through his bones to the fingers of his ruined hand. As he walked toward his men, he saw their eyes shift to that hand, saw horror and disgust fill them. When he gave them cold stares, they stiffened and saluted, banging their fists against their breastplates.

"How many prisoners are there?" he asked one of the soldiers, a phalanx captain with golden skulls upon his pauldrons.

The man looked at the pile of chained, bloody weredragons and snarled. He was missing a tooth, and a scar ran across his head, cleaving his platinum hair like a red snake.

"Fifty in that pile, my Lord Mahrdor," he rasped. "Ten of them are dead already. A dozen more will be dead by nightfall." The captain snorted. "The rest will live a little longer if you wish it, my lord, though they will envy their dead."

Mahrdor stood and examined the creatures. One looked like a pile of rotten cornmeal, moaning and still smoking with acid. A few were children. A few were dead. Chains bound them in a pile of flesh, blood, and tears. Mahrdor pointed at one.

"There, bring me him, the brute with the black hair. That one is a soldier."

The weredragon sat hulking, head lowered, his wrists and ankles bound with manacles. Burns spread across his arms, and his left eye was swollen shut. He wore a breastplate emblazoned with the Draco constellation; a man of the City Guard, Mahrdor knew.

Two Tiran soldiers approached the pile of prisoners and jabbed the burly guard with spears.

"Up, weredragon," one said with a grunt. "On your feet."

The wounded guard grunted and remained with his head lowered. His helmet had been knocked off in the battle, and blood matted his head. One of his ears was a lacerated mess.

"Can you hear, lizard?" the Tiran said. "Get up, damn it."

The two Tirans grabbed the weredragon and began pulling him up. Finally the beast seemed to awake. He tossed back his head and howled, the wordless cry of an animal. He spun, lashing his chains at the Tirans. The men cursed and thrust their spears. One spearhead slashed the weredragon's leg, and the creature howled and swung his chains again. More Tirans rushed forward. It took ten men to subdue the weredragon, chain his wrists to his sides, and shove him forward. When finally the brute stood before Mahrdor, blood stained his teeth and dripped down his leg.

Mahrdor stood, examining the weredragon. Held in the grip of two Tirans, the weredragon stared back from his one good eye; that eye blazed with hatred.

"Good," Mahrdor said. "Good, you have spirit. That means you'd have risen high in the Weredragon Guard. You'll have the information I need."

He reached out his burnt hand. When he uncurled his fingers, they blazed with pain and made a sickening, crackling sound like old parchment unfolding. He caressed the weredragon's bruised cheek and swollen eye, letting wound touch wound.

"My hand," Mahrdor said, "is a work of art, a landscape of pain and punishment. I will turn you into a work of art too. Piece by piece, I will make you beautiful."

The weredragon growled, but fear filled his one good eye. Mahrdor nodded. Smiling thinly, he turned to his men. "Bring me jugs of acid. We will see if he learns to speak."

Two men brought forward the acid.

Two others shoved and held the weredragon down.

Mahrdor began to work.

As the weredragon screamed, Mahrdor smiled. As flesh burned, he licked his lips. He created. Even here, in the rubble of battle, he was an artist. He shaped flesh. He wove symphonies from screams.

"There is an escape tunnel underground," he said as he worked, trickling acid against flesh. "The Weredragon King would have carved one. Where does it lead?"

The weredragon only screamed. His left leg was gone already, a sticky mess of flesh barely clinging to bone. Behind him, the other weredragon prisoners wept and wailed. Mahrdor clucked his tongue and kept working.

"Speak and your pain will end," he said. "Speak and I will create something from your corpse rather than your living flesh. It would be easier for you, I think." He poured more acid and the man's howls rose. "I have escape tunnels in my villa in Tiranor. My queen does in her palace. Every ruler of importance has some path to flee an underground tomb. Where does the Lizard King's tunnel go?"

Mahrdor worked and the man screamed.

He screamed of his phalanx.

He screamed of his commanders.

He screamed for his wife and mother.

He screamed until he was a useless, burnt chunk of flesh, and Mahrdor kicked him aside. He licked his lips and grinned.

"This one knows nothing," he said. He pointed at a second chained weredragon--a young woman in the steel armor of a soldier. "Bring me that one."

He cracked his neck and kept working. Soon this one was screaming too.

It was three more weredragons before one finally screamed, face sizzling under acid, of the escape tunnel underground.

"It leads to the eastern hills!" the creature cried, its eyes eaten away. "It emerges between three boulders on a hillside--five hundred yards east from the walls. Please... please..." The creature sobbed. "Please kill me. Give me death. Give me mercy."

Mahrdor kicked the wretch aside.

"Give you mercy?" he said to the twisted beast. "But you already gave me what I want. Why should I dirty my sword?"

He turned, leaving the burnt weredragon to writhe and wail on the ground. He mounted Phel again and soared, smiling thinly.

From behind him rose the screams of the prisoners and the laughter of his men. Below him rolled the destruction: piles of rubble, smashed columns, and the corpses of wyverns and weredragons. Two archways still stood, the entrances to tunnels; at each one, wyverns lined up to spew acid underground.

By nightfall the tunnels will be overflowing, Mahrdor thought. He licked his lips, imagining the beautiful screams and stench and death below. He looked at his left hand and shuddered to imagine all the flesh that was now sizzling below the earth, hidden like the curves of a woman under a dress.

He spotted Solina in a square, still sitting atop Baal, her behemoth of a wyvern, the greatest of the beasts. She had moved aside, allowing a lesser wyvern to spill acid underground. The fumes stung Mahrdor's nostrils and eyes. His arm blazed in pain as if remembering the heat of acid. Gritting his teeth, he landed his wyvern upon the smashed cobblestones by his queen. He bowed his head to her.

"Queen Solina."

She looked at him, amusement in her eyes. She raised her eyebrows, stretching the scar that halved her face.

"Your hand," she said. "Will you not bandage it? I do not wish to look upon this thing."

Phel grunted and sidestepped beneath him. The twisted beast was smaller than Baal, but Mahrdor thought his girl just as mean. He patted her scales until she calmed.

"You created this hand, my queen," he said and raised it in salute. "Don't you wish to remember your power over me? Don't you wish me to always remember my sin and your might?"

"I care not," she said. "You are a soldier. A tool. That is all." She looked at the tunnel entrance. Heat and distant screams rose from it. "I care about the Weredragon King. I care to see his body burned and writhing, not yours."

Mahrdor allowed himself a thin smile. "I can give you the Weredragon King. You may burn him yourself if you please."

She snarled at him. "I asked you to bring me the whore Lyana, and you let her free. What nonsense do you spout now?"

Upon his wyvern, he sketched an elaborate bow. "No nonsense, my queen, only information. I persuaded our prisoners to impart it. There is another doorway to these tunnels; it lies outside the city. The weredragons carved it as an escape route." He looked at the acid pouring underground. "They will be escaping now, I presume. Your Weredragon King, his sister, and probably the lords and ladies of the Reptile Court--including my beloved bird--are likely crawling out from the city as we speak."

She reeled Baal toward him. The beast snarled and his drool spattered. Solina herself looked nearly as beastly, her eyes blazing and her lip curled back.

"Where does this tunnel lead to?" She raised her sabre. "Speak, Mahrdor, or by the Sun God, your right arm will burn too."

Mahrdor laughed and flexed his ruined fingers. The pain flared, turning his laughter into a grimace. He coughed blood and smiled. "I will lead you there, my queen. I will lead you to the Weredragon King." He kicked Phel, driving her closer to Solina. He glared into his queen's eyes. "But I want my Lyana. And I want the Weredragon Princess. Give me those two rare birds, so that I may reshape them and turn them into pets of my own. You can keep the king and do with him as you please."

Staring at him, her eyes blue ice, she tugged Baal's reins. She spun the beast around until wyvern pushed against wyvern.

She leaned sideways in the saddle toward Mahrdor, sword drawn and eyes narrowed.

"Show me there." She kicked her wyvern, soared, and howled. "If the king is mine, his women will be yours! Now fly!"

Mahrdor smiled and flew.

ELETHOR

The acid kept pouring. Wails rose through the chambers. Acid pooled and people huddled atop boulders and clung to walls. More acid streamed from above and sizzled. Droplets splashed onto flesh and burns spread. Feet melted. Children wept. An old man cried to the stars and leaped into the stream, a vain attempt to hold it back with his body; the acid ate through him and kept pouring.

"Elethor!" said Deramon, face red. He moved through the crowd, grabbed Elethor, and pulled him toward the wall. "This is it, Elethor. It's time to leave--you and Mori."

Eyes somber, Deramon gestured at the tapestry Mori had woven, which hung upon a craggy wall. Elethor knew what lay behind it--the escape tunnel carved for his family, a snaking pipe that led outside the city.

He looked back at the crowd of survivors. Many had begun to dig, forming holes for acid to fill and mounds to stand on. Others stood upon corpses. The acid kept flowing around them, moving from chamber to chamber.

"There are thousands of people here," Elethor said. "I won't leave them to die."

Mori stood by his side, face pale but lips firm. She nodded, head raised. "I'm not leaving either, Deramon," she said with a voice soft but steady. "I am princess of this realm; I go down with the ship."

Deramon scowled, looking from king to princess. His eyes darkened and his lips curled back in a growl. "You and Mori are the last Aeternums, a dynasty that has ruled in Requiem for three thousand years. I loved your father, Elethor, and I loved your brother. I won't let you and your sister die too. I am sworn to guard your house; I will not let it fall."

Elethor glared at the older man. "And I am sworn to guard this realm, and I will not let it fall." He grabbed the tapestry and pulled it free, revealing the tunnel. He turned to the survivors and called out, voice echoing. "Mothers and babes--to me! Mothers and babes only--through this tunnel! It will lead you to safety. Mothers and babes only!"

The people wailed. At once it seemed that everyone was charging toward the tunnel. One man slipped and fell into streaming acid; he screamed and burned. Bayrin stood in the crowd, holding men back, shouting for mothers and babes. Adia was praying and guiding mothers forward. People were weeping.

Elethor clutched Mori's hand. He looked into her wide gray eyes. She stared back steadily, clutching his hand.

"Are you sure, Mori?" he whispered. "I will send you through this tunnel if you wish it. There are thousands of people here; it would take hours for everyone to crawl out, and we have only moments before the acid overflows us."

Her eyes flashed. Her lips tightened. Suddenly Mori looked as fierce and strong as Lyana.

"I stay," she said. "With you. With my people. If we go to the starlit halls, we go together." She raised her voice to the crowd. "Mothers and babes only! Move, to us!"

Soon the first mother appeared at their side, weeping and clutching her newborn. Adia, her white robes tattered and burnt, helped guide the young woman and her babe into the tunnel. Soon they disappeared into the darkness.

"Keep crawling!" Elethor called into the tunnel. "Crawl for an hour--until you reach the forest--then fly! Fly east and don't return."

Bayrin and Deramon were moving through the chambers, guiding mothers and babes through the crowd. Adia helped each pair enter the tunnels and prayed for them. Some older men tried to shove their way through, to enter the tunnels themselves; Bayrin and Deramon held them back.

"Mothers and babes only!" Elethor shouted. Only ten pairs had entered the tunnel so far; countless still remained. "Into the tunnel. Crawl and then fly!"

Wyvern shrieks echoed above with new vigor. The flow of acid intensified. People screamed and scrambled onto one another. The holes they had dug filled up, and the mounds began to melt. The acid began to consume Elethor's boots and sting his feet. He breathed sharply through clenched teeth. Mori clasped his hand so hard she nearly crushed it. In the far side of the tunnel, where the floor sloped, people wailed. The acid rose past their ankles, then reached their knees. They began to fall and burn away.

"Into the tunnels, go, my child!" Adia cried to a mother and babe, helping them climb into the darkness.

We're not going to last another moment, Elethor realized. How many had they saved? Thirty people? Forty? *The rest of Requiem will die in these tunnels, the end of our Second Age.*

Lyana moved through the crowd toward him. Her face was pale, her eyes wide. She clung to his arm.

"Elethor," she whispered. "Elethor, I will fly with you. I will roar by your side in the starlit halls. We fly there together." She growled at him. "Don't you leave me there!"

Elethor growled too. The acid blazed against the soles of his feet, and he pushed himself to the wall. Panic swelled in his lungs.

No. No! I won't let Requiem fall on my watch. Not for my war with Solina.

People fell and screamed and melted before him. They reminded him of the bodies he had seen last year in the Abyss, but back then, hope had awaited them. He and Lyana had freed the Starlit Demon. They had driven the beast through the earth, carving a great shaft out into the sky.

What I would give for such a tunnel now! I--

Elethor froze.

He snarled. He looked at Lyana who clung to his left. He looked at Mori who clung to his right. He loved them both so much that he shook with it. He nodded. His eyes stung.

For my father. For Orin. For the light of our stars and the sky in our wings.

He looked at Mother Adia. "Adia, I need you to stay here. I need you to keep leading the mothers and babes through the tunnel; once they've all escaped, you will crawl after them, and you will lead them to safety." He turned to Deramon. "You too, Deramon; they will need your strength. You and Adia will lead the survivors."

They all stared at him. Adia sucked in her breath.

"What are you planning, Elethor?" the priestess whispered.

He turned away from her. He looked between Lyana and Mori, who both clung to him, and at Bayrin, who approached with somber eyes.

"Fly by my side, Lyana and Bayrin," he whispered. "Fly by me, Mori. Whatever happens, we fly together."

They looked at him, lips tightened. They said nothing.

If we die, we die together, Elethor thought. *If today I fall, I fall with those whom I love.* He squared his shoulders and raised his head. *But I won't fall without a battle for the poets to sing of.*

He faced the crowd and roared.

"People of Requiem!" he shouted. "Hear me, Vir Requis! I am your king, Elethor Aeternum, Son of Olasar. Hear me today!"

They turned toward him, and he saw the fear in their eyes. *I am their king; let me be a pillar to them.* He raised his head and spoke in a voice deep and clear.

"We are in darkness," he said. "We are in the pit of despair. But I do not lose hope. I do not stop fighting. Even in the most dark, hopeless cave a light shines somewhere; we will find that light and crawl toward it." He pointed to the tunnel behind him. "Mothers and babes--Adia will lead you to safety. She will lead you to light. Follow her through darkness and into the wild."

The mothers kept moving toward the tunnel, clutching their infants. Some moved on burnt, twisted feet. Adia and Deramon continued helping them into the tunnel, blessing them with prayers. Elethor raised his voice louder.

"The rest of you!" he shouted. "We will find our light too. We will find our sky. I promise this to you. Today you are soldiers! Today you are all warriors of Requiem. Young and old, children and elders, you now fight for the Royal Army! You can fly as dragons. You can blow fire. You can slash your claws. Today we all fight with one roar! Today we are all warriors of starlight! Stand back, people of Requiem, hear my roar and answer my call!"

He let go of Lyana and Mori.

He leaped through the people toward the flowing acid.

In the chamber of stone, he shifted into a dragon.

People screamed and scurried back. Elethor's claws reached out, hitting the walls. His wings hit the ceiling. In dragon form, he nearly filled the chamber, nearly crushed the people beneath him. They ran and leaped over acid. With a great dragon roar, Elethor began to slam his tail against the northern wall.

This is where the Starlit Demon flew, he remembered. He had seen the tunnel maps. This was the place--beyond this wall. Here had the Starlit Demon carved its cavern. Here awaited their sky. He slammed his tail and chunks of rock fell.

"Requiem!" he cried, fire in his maw. "Our wings will find your sky!"

He slammed his tail again. Cracks raced. Rocks plummeted. The wall collapsed outward, revealing a gaping shaft--a hundred feet in diameter--full of wind and rain and echoing wyvern cries.

"Fly, dragons of Requiem!" Elethor shouted and leaped into the great shaft. He beat his wings and soared toward the sky. Walls of stone raced at his sides. "To death! To blood! To glory! Today we all fight; today we roar as one!"

With a roar that could deafen gods, the dragons of Requiem soared behind him--out of darkness and into the light of battle and song.

SOLINA

Outside the city the forests burned. Solina flew upon her wyvern, savoring the smell of smoke. It was a dry summer; Solina had kindled these flames only yesterday, and they now raced across Requiem, eating all in their path. She smiled thinly as she flew over the burning landscapes. Should any weredragons escape Nova Vita, they would find little sanctuary here. No places remained for them to hide. All the weredragon lands now blazed with the light of her lord, casting out the reptilian darkness.

She looked behind her. Lord Mahrdor flew there upon his own wyvern, and behind him flew fifty of his men, each armed with crossbow, spear, sword, and shield. Their wyverns screamed and their wings roiled the smoke from the blazing lands below. Behind them, Nova Vita lay as a black smudge upon the land, bustling with wyverns like flies over a carcass.

Her smile widened. *You will flee that rotting carcass of your city, Elethor,* she thought. *You will flee into my arms.*

Mahrdor flew up beside her. He pointed his ruined hand below.

"There, my queen. Three boulders by a hillside. That is where the weredragons will emerge." He licked his lips. "That is where Lyana and I will meet again."

Solina imagined what he would do to Lyana, and laughter bubbled in her throat. She had seen Mahrdor's work before. Truly, the man was an artist. She had seen the scrolls he made from human skin, the chairs of bones, the shrunken heads, the pickled hands. And she had seen worse: the sniveling, pathetic creations he kept in his deeper chambers. Those ones were his

greatest treasures, living works of art that he had created--
breaking and reshaping bones, sewing flesh to flesh, twisting and
burning and molding his prisoners into creatures of haunted
beauty.

That is what awaits you, Lyana, Solina thought. *That is what
awaits you, Mori.*

She began spiraling her wyvern down toward the boulders.
Her men descended around her, wings fanning the forest flames.

"But you, Elethor," she whispered. "You will be *mine* to
torment. I will break you myself. I will wield the hammers that
nail you to my tower, that shatter your bones, that make you
scream and weep and beg. I will stand there, glorious in the light
of my lord, and watch my vultures feast upon your living flesh."
She clenched her fists. "The entire kingdom will watch, and the
people your father orphaned will cheer!"

She landed in a patch of burnt grass and hot stones. Baal
screeched at the flames that surrounded them; the wyvern was
skittish, bucking and whipping his tail. Solina patted his scales.

"Hush, Baal!" she said. "The fire of our lord cannot hurt
us. Hush! Lower your wing."

The beast calmed, though his eyes still blazed red and his
tongue still lolled, dripping acid that burned holes into the earth.
When he lowered his wing, Solina climbed down to the forest
floor. Grass smoldered beneath her boots. Before her in the
hillside loomed the black mouth of a tunnel.

Solina grabbed the crossbow that hung across her back.
She loaded a bolt and twisted the crank, pulling the string taut.

"Load crossbows, men," she said over her shoulder. "We
enter the darkness."

Mahrdor and the others were dismounting their wyverns.
The firelight blazed against their armor. They grabbed their own
crossbows, and the sounds of twisting cranks filled the forest.
Swords hung from their waists and spears hung across their backs.

"Let us slay some dragons," Solina said.

She turned back to the tunnel, and was prepared to enter it, when she saw two weredragons emerge. A grin split her face.

The female weredragon was halfway out the tunnel when she noticed the Tirans, paled, and froze. She held a babe in her arms; the little beast began to wail. Solina loosed her crossbow into the spawn; its wails died at once.

The mother screamed. Mahrdor's crossbow thrummed. Its bolt slammed into the mother's throat, and the wench fell, gurgling, still clutching her babe as if it still lived. Solina drew her sabre and landed two blows, finishing the job.

"Where is the Weredragon Princess?" Mahrdor demanded. "Where is the Lady Lyana?"

As Solina was loading another bolt, a shadow stirred in the tunnels. Solina saw a second mother and babe crawling forward. When the mother began to flee back into darkness, Solina shot her crossbow again, hitting the creature inside the tunnel. Her men shot their crossbows too, until the wailing babe inside silenced, and blood trickled out.

Solina sighed. "Oh, Elethor. You fool." She shook her head sadly and looked at Mahrdor. "The weredragons carved an escape tunnel... but send mothers and babes out, rather than their monarchs." She spat onto the body at her feet. "Noble halfwits. It will be their death."

Mahrdor cleared his throat and stared down at the bodies in distaste. "I care not for mothers and infants. I want a knight. I want a princess. I want my birds of paradise."

Solina loaded another bolt and stepped toward the tunnel. "You will have them, and I will have my king, though their feet might be a little burnt. They still cower inside as our acid flows." She entered the tunnel; it was only four feet tall, forcing her to crawl. She held her crossbow before her. "Follow, men! We slew them in the sky, and we will slay them underground."

She had crawled a dozen feet when she saw candlelight ahead. Yet another mother crawled there, clutching her wailing offspring. Solina shot them, loaded another bolt, and wriggled over their bodies. The babe was still alive and squirming; she slew it with her dagger. Every ten or twenty feet, she had to shoot another spawning beast and her get. The blood flowed across the tunnel.

She had crawled for what seemed like an hour, and she was down to only three crossbow bolts, when she saw firelight and heard screams ahead.

She grinned.

When she crawled closer, she saw a scene of ruin. A great chamber loomed ahead; in its walls, she saw passageways to other chambers. Bodies littered the floor, nearly covered with acid; most were nothing but bones now. A handful of survivors--more spawning mothers--crowded upon a mound of earth, waiting to enter the escape tunnel.

Solina licked her lips, leaped from the darkness, and landed among them.

The babes wailed. The mothers screamed. Behind her, her men began leaping from the tunnel, and crossbows fired, and mothers fell dead.

A roar echoed.

Solina spun around to see a great, coppery dragon in the chamber. She inhaled sharply. Lord Deramon! The beast stood before a wall that had collapsed. Through the gaping hole, Solina saw a shaft leading upward; she recognized the passageway the Starlit Demon had carved last year. Wyverns were flying down the shaft; Deramon was holding them back and blowing flames. Acid blazed across him, eating through his scales, but still the dragon howled, blew fire, and lashed claws. The wyverns were trying to enter the chamber, to attack the mothers and babes; the dragon flamed them.

Solina smiled, raised her crossbow, and pointed it at Deramon.

"Goodbye, old friend," she said with a crooked smile.

When she pulled the trigger, a white figure leaped forward and slammed into her. The bolt whizzed and ricocheted off a wall. Solina snarled and fell several steps, nearly crashing into the rivers of acid. She spun to see Mother Adia, the woman's eyes wild and her teeth bared.

The priestess was unarmed and still in human form, but she looked every inch a beast. Her eyes blazed with condemnation. Her hair flurried. Her fingers curled as if they bore dragon claws. She leaped again at Solina.

"Stars of Requiem!" the priestess cried and drove her fingernails toward Solina--her only weapons. "You will die here, Solina, and may your Sun God forever burn your soul."

Solina sidestepped, amused. With a snort, she drew her sabre. The curved blade flashed, arcing out of its sheath and into Adia's flesh.

The priestess froze.

Solina's smile widened.

With a snarl, Solina pulled the blade back. It emerged bloody from the priestess--a giver of hot, intoxicating blood, the blood of her enemies, the blood of her glory and triumph.

Adia stared silently, red spreading across her white goan like a field of poppies growing in snow. Her eyes were deep pools, emotionless. Her lips whispered silently.

"Weredragon," Solina said to her, disgust dripping from her voice. She spat. "Fall at my feet and beg for a quick death."

Adia held the wound that sliced her belly; she was calm, like a mother holding her babe. The priestess stared at Solina, and still no pain filled those eyes, no fear, no anger... and as Solina stared into those eyes, it seemed to her that starlight glowed inside them, not blazing and furious like the light of her lord, but soft and mysterious like the night sky. And suddenly Solina herself was afraid, for she saw a power in those staring eyes, in those pools of night--a power she could not understand or burn.

"Child," Adia whispered. Blood stained her lips. "Poor, wayward child... what have we done to you? How did we hurt you so? Why does such pain fill you?" She reached out a bloody hand. "Would you forgive us, child, for the pain we gave you?"

Solina sucked in her breath. That pain danced inside her, gripped her, and spun her head. Her eyes stung with it. Suddenly she was a youth again, frightened and lonely, seeking comfort in Elethor's arms. Suddenly the courts of Requiem seemed so large to her, the dragons so cruel, their fire so hot, their stars so beautiful and foreign to her--stars that would never bless her, a lost desert child. She wanted to weep. She wanted the priestess to embrace her, to pray for her, to be her mother too, as she was a mother to all of Requiem.

No! No.

Solina's fist trembled around her sword. *No, that is not me. It was never me!* She snarled. Her flesh burned with hatred. She did not need their pity. She did not need their love.

She howled in the chamber. "May your pathetic stars burn your soul, Mother of Reptiles!"

Screaming, she thrust her sword. It drove into Adia's chest. Hot blood stained Solina's fingers. When she pulled her sword free, the blood sprayed her, and Adia fell to her knees.

The priestess gave Solina one last look--a look of sadness and of love. The starlight in her eyes dimmed and she fell.

A howl rose behind Solina, deafening, filling the chamber like a storm.

Blood on her hands, lips curled back, Solina turned to see Deramon. The dragon roared--the roar of hearts rending, of forests burning, of towers crashing. It was a roar like the ghosts of a drowned city calling from the ocean depths, like a dying race that would forever cry from lost graves, like children lost in flame, like the sound her own heart had made when they tore her from Elethor. It was the roar of a man for the woman he loved, of a grief and pain too great for any mortal body to hold, too wrenching for any mind to contain. It was grief itself--primal, pure, and deeper than all the seas and tunnels in the world.

Solina froze in wonder, in fear, in awe. Tears filled her eyes. *I made him roar this sound,* she thought. *I had the power to create this.* Here in this cave, before this dragon and this howl, it seemed to her a greater triumph than all the towers she had raised, the armies she had led, and the dragons she had slain.

I made something pure. I created this roar and it is the greatest, saddest, and most perfect thing I ever did.

The great dragon's scales blazed with light. His claws rose like swords. His fangs shone like the whetted blades of demons. The wyverns outside the cavern, freed from his flames, spewed acid. The streams crashed against Deramon, drenching him, eating away at him. His scales began to shrink and twist, revealing raw flesh beneath them. Yet he did not fall. He rose tall in the chamber until his head nearly hit the ceiling. His wings unfurled like a dark sky. And he roared his fire.

The stream crashed toward Solina.

She screamed.

She remembered Orin's fire--the fire that had scarred her body and soul, that tore her from Elethor, that placed this flame in her heart. The old pain clawed inside her. Solina leaped aside. She nearly crashed into the acid. The flames blasted the rock where she had stood.

"Your soul will burn with hers!" Solina shouted and fired her crossbow.

The bolt slammed into the dragon's flaming maw.

The dragon reared. His fire hit the ceiling and rained. With a cry, Solina drove forward. She shoved into a mother and babe, knocking them into a stream of acid. She leaped onto their bodies, sprang toward the dragon, and swung onto his leg. She scurried up the scales until she clung to the beast's back.

He bucked and roared. His wings flapped. Solina snarled and clung to him. The dragon leaped, slammed against the ceiling, and Solina screamed. If not for her armor, she'd have been crushed between scale and stone. Acid sizzled across the dragon, eating at her breastplate, her boots, and her gloves.

"Die with your whore, reptile," she said. Tears stung her eyes and she could not breathe. "You tore me from Elethor. You told your cruel king of our love." Suddenly she was that youth again--afraid, angry, and weak. Her tears streamed and she roared, her own roar of pain and fury and loss. "You drove me to this, Deramon! You brought this death upon your land! Look around you. Look at the dead. Look at the corpse of your wife. Die knowing that you did this, beast! Die knowing that you killed her!"

Blinded with tears, strong with her fury, Solina reached around the dragon's neck. She swiped her sword. His scales were weakened with acid; her blade tore through them and into the flesh.

His roar died upon her steel.

The beast fell.

With a shower of blood, fire, and acid, the great Deramon Eleison--Guard of Requiem, slayer of many Tirans, Lord of Dragons--fell in darkness and light. His head hit the floor, and his wings fell limp, and the fire drained from him. Bloodied, he returned to his human form--a grizzled man clad in armor, body scarred and eyes dim.

Solina stood and stared down at the man. In her youth, he had always seemed so frightening to her, a mountain of hair and muscle and steel, all booming shouts and clanking weapons, twice her size and ten times as loud. Now he seemed so small to her--

too thin in his armor, his beard more white than red, his booming voice silenced. He was still alive. He crawled across the mound of earth and stone. He reached out to the body of his wife.

His hand, bloodied and scarred, clasped the hand of Mother Adia. The priestess's hand, pale and lifeless, seemed so small and fair in Deramon's grip, a white flower in the paw of a lion.

"Adia," he whispered, voice hoarse, nearly silent. "Adia, my love. Do you see them? Do you see the white columns, the starlit halls of our fathers?" He clasped her hand, his eyes dampened, and a smile trembled on his lips. "We fly there together; we will dance and sing there always, my love. We will see our Noela again."

Solina drove her blade down into his back.

He gave a last gasp.

His eyes closed and he lay still, holding the hand of his wife.

Solina stared down at their bodies. Her lips curled back in disgust. When she looked up, she saw her men staring, silent. The last bodies of mothers and babes lay strewn at their feet, pierced with bolts. When fighting above Nova Vita, her men had cheered and howled for every dragon slain. Now they only stared.

She ignored them. She skirted a pool of acid and approached the shaft the Starlit Demon had carved last year. Wyverns fluttered up and down the chasm. Solina placed her fingers into her mouth--they tasted like sweet blood--and gave a loud, long shriek of a whistle.

A screech above answered her. Wings blasted air, each flap a thunderbolt rank with death. Baal, the King of Wyverns, dived down the tunnel and faced her. The beast hovered before the collapsed wall. Acid dripped between his teeth. Solina leaped through the opening, swung around Baal's neck, and climbed into his saddle.

"Grab those bodies," she told the beast. "Grab them and fly."

The wyvern reached into the collapsing cavern. He grabbed the body of Adia with one clawed foot, the body of Deramon with another. The beast licked his lips and looked over his shoulder at Solina.

"No, Baal," she said and stroked him. "You will not feast upon these ones. Not yet. We will first flaunt them before the city." She kneed him. "Fly! Into the sky!"

They soared.

Walls of stone blurred at their sides. They rose from underground into a city of ruin, then into a sky of smoke, ash, and fire. Twenty thousand wyverns screeched and spat their acid. Twenty thousand dragons flew around them--children, old toothless beasts, and cripples missing limbs. The mob of Requiem, an untrained mass, bustled and roared fire and slashed claws. Solina inhaled sharply.

It's beautiful, she thought. *A great tapestry of glory.* She had never seen so many beasts flying and killing under one sky; it seemed to her like the great stories of old, the ones where griffins toppled the mythical halls of Requiem's golden age.

Blood rained. Blood coated her. She licked blood off her lips and sword, savoring its coppery taste, the taste of her might. It was a day of dragon blood, a day of sunfire, a day of triumph.

When she looked across the battle, she saw him there--her king, her love, the jewel she sought.

"Elethor!" she cried and flew toward him.

MORI

The battle was lost. Mori could see that. She shot through the chaos, eyes burning. Blood and acid rained. Everywhere she looked, clouds of wyverns and dragons fought above the fallen city. Bodies crashed down into the ruins, and their blood flowed across the strewn bricks, smashed mosaics, and shattered columns of her home. Wind roared and clouds of ash roiled above her.

Only a single column rose from the devastation, a great pillar of white marble, three hundred feet tall and kissed with a beam of sunlight: King's Column, raised by King Aeternum himself millennia ago. Swarms of wyverns were attacking it, lashing their claws and tails, but could not break it. Mori knew the legends. The old scrolls wrote that so long as a single Vir Requis lived, King's Column would not fall. Looking around the battle, Mori realized with a chill: the column might fall this day.

The wyverns were everywhere. Two swooped toward her, the sun at their backs. Mori screamed, dodged their streams of acid, and soared above them. She roasted their riders with fire. The Tirans screamed and burned, and the wyverns crashed down. Three more wyverns flew to her right, and Mori shouted and dived under them, then spun and blazed them. She had always been so fast, the fastest dragon in Requiem; these burly wyverns were clumsy around her. Yet other dragons were faring less well. So many were elderly, wounded, or young. Dozens were mere toddlers, no larger than ponies, their wings weak and their fire mere sparks. They fell around Mori, burning with acid and peppered with crossbow bolts. When they hit the ruins below, they returned to human forms and lay dead--slashed, burned, torn apart.

Mori growled. She flamed another wyvern. Acid splashed her tail and she howled. She soared higher, crashing through wyverns and dragons, and surveyed the battle. Barely any soldiers of Requiem now flew; their army was now comprised of the old, the weak, the frightened. The wyverns were tearing through them like a pack of wolves in a chicken coop.

She looked around for Elethor, Bayrin, and Lyana, but could not see them. Had they fallen too? Did she now lead these ragged, dying remains of her people? She growled, eyes stinging, fear an inferno in her belly.

We cannot win, Mori thought. *We must flee.*

"Dragons of Requiem!" she cried to the battle. "Flee! Flee into the forests! Flee to the east and west. Leave this city!"

When she looked below her, she saw a group of young dragons flying over the ruins of the temple. Wings batting madly, they cried out for their mothers. A wyvern shrieked and shot toward them. Acid streamed, crashed against one young dragon, and the child fell dead and twisted. Three more wyverns charged, their own projectiles spraying. The young dragons wailed and another fell, the acid eating through her scales like a swarm of ants on meat.

With a growl, Mori swooped.

She crashed between three wyverns fighting a few older, toothless dragons. With a howl, she rained fire upon the beasts that burned the children. They shrieked and turned toward her, acid sputtering. Their riders burned and screamed.

"Flee, dragons!" Mori cried down to the children. "Flee to the forests!"

Two of the wyverns began soaring toward her, their riders flaming. Several young dragons wailed and began fleeing, only for wyverns to pursue them. Crossbows fired. Another dragon fell dead.

Mori roared her fire. The flames crashed against streams of acid that rose toward her. The blasts exploded, spraying flames and acid. Mori howled, dived, and closed her jaws around a rider. She tore the man in two, then spat out his top half. It tumbled, entrails dangling like the tail of a comet. The second wyvern rose toward her, a crossbow thrummed, and a bolt slammed into Mori's shoulder. She blew her fire and swiped her tail. She knocked the rider half off the wyvern; the reins pulled taut and the wyvern banked. Mori bathed it with fire until it fell.

"Flee, dragons of Requiem!" she cried to the children. They were flying around confused, calling for their parents. Wyverns were tearing them down one by one. Mori flew, flamed a wyvern, and herded the children forward, wings spread wide. When wyverns shot toward them, she blew a ring of fire, lashed her tail, and thrust her claws.

"Together, here, with me!" Mori cried to the surviving children. Her wings opened wide, as if she could shield them all. She drove them forward, nipping at them with her teeth and goading them with her tail. "Fly! Fly into the forests and hide! I will find your parents and send them there too. Now fly!"

Wailing, tears in their eyes, the children fled. Soon they flew over the fallen walls of Nova Vita and headed toward the burning forests. Three wyverns began to chase them, and crossbows fired upon another child, sending the girl falling into the flaming trees.

Roaring, Mori flew over the crumbling walls. She crashed against the three wyverns. Fangs bit her tail. Acid blazed against her wing. She blew flames against the riders, soared higher, and swooped again, raining more fire. The wyverns fell.

"Fly!" she cried after the children; the survivors were distant now, mere specks over the blazing landscapes. "Fly and never return!"

She panted. Blood trickled down her scales, and wind roared through a hole in her wing. She turned back toward the city and grimaced. The wyverns flew like storm clouds over the ruins, raining their acid. Only a handful of dragons were fleeing over the toppled walls, wyverns in pursuit. Some dragons still fought but were falling fast. Mori growled. She began flying back to the city. Her wing ached and she wobbled. Her body burned, and she realized that acid had eaten through the scales on her back leg. A bolt thrust out from her shoulder, a demon of steel eating away at her.

Yet still Mori flew, eyes narrowed and breath blazing. She had to save whoever she still could. She had to find her brother, to find her love Bayrin, to find her dearest friend Lyana. And so she flew back to the inferno, blood and fire streaming behind her, death blazing before her.

She flew over the ruins. The battle raged around her. A great wyvern soared ahead, the largest she had seen, rising from darkness like a demon from the Abyss. Its rider glittered, a deity of gold holding a banner of a blazing sun. The rider's cry rang out above the battle, high and beautiful like the cry of a goddess.

"Elethor!"

Mori snarled.

It was Solina.

The Queen of Tiranor rose higher. Her wyvern's wings thudded, two hundred feet wide, spreading debris across the ruins below. Her gilded armor shone, a second sun in the sky. Her hair streamed behind her, a second banner of gold.

"Elethor!" she called again. "Your city is fallen, Reptile King! Fly here and beg me to spare those of your vermin that still live."

Mori wheeled her head around. Across the city she saw her brother, and tears filled Mori's eyes. Elethor rose from smoke, a great brass dragon roaring fire. Mori remembered him as a gaunt youth, a dragon barely larger than herself; now muscles rippled beneath his scales, his flames burned white-hot, and his eyes blazed with the fury of a king. Suddenly he was not merely Elethor, her sad brother, but a great king of Requiem, as powerful and noble as her father.

Wyverns surrounded him--hundreds of them--a fortress of iron scales and spraying acid. Inside the ring, two more dragons rose from smoke: Bayrin, his green scales splashed with blood and ash, and Lyana, her blue scales dented but her wings still beating strongly. The three dragons fought back to back, blowing rings of fire, holding the wyverns back.

Mori wanted to fly to them. They were the people she loved most; without them, there was no reason to live. She wanted to fight by them, to die by them if she must. She took a deep breath, flapped her wings, and prepared to charge and fall with them in the ring of iron and acid.

Before she could flap her wings again, she saw from the corner of her eye that Solina's wyvern clutched two bodies.

Mori's breath died.

She looked closer and felt her world collapse.

Solina's wyvern held the bloodied bodies of Adia and Deramon.

A mewl left Mori's throat, a cry of pain soon rising to a roar. Tears filled her eyes. Fire blazed in her maw. Mother Adia--her greatest teacher, her guiding star, the Mother of Requiem and like a mother to her. Lord Deramon--greatest warrior of Requiem, the bright blade of her people. Fallen. Their lights dimmed.

That day returned to her, that day worse than any other, a cold day in a far southern fort. She again saw Solina smile as Orin lay burnt at her feet, again saw the queen slash her blade, slice

Orin open, savor his screams. Again Mori lay upon that table as
Lord Acribus invaded her, and again Solina watched and laughed
as Mori's body and soul and innocence shattered. That had been
over a year ago, but now it bloomed within her, and rage filled
Mori, a rage hotter than dragonfire, a rage that spun her head and
overflowed her grief.

I was a child then, Solina, she thought. *I was scared, young, and
alone. But now you will find my fire bright and my soul hardened. You gave
me this pain. You gave me this strength.* Her dragon roar pealed across
the city. *Now you will die in my flames.*

She drove through smoke and over ruin toward the Queen
of Tiranor.

Solina spun toward her. "Mori!" the queen cried in delight.
"My sweet little bird!"

The queen's crossbow thrummed.

Mori snarled and banked. The bolt grazed her leg, and she
kept flying. The devastation blurred below her. Wyverns flew at
her; Mori shot above, beneath, and around them.

Orin always said I could fly like a bee, she thought. *He always
said nobody could catch me. You killed him, Solina. Now you will die here--
in the city where he lies buried.*

She soared over the shattered Temple of Requiem and
roared her fire.

Solina's wyvern, the great beast Baal, howled and reared. A
sizzling jet spewed from his mouth. Acid crashed against flame.
The streams exploded and rained upon the ruins.

Mori beat her wings madly. The left one throbbed, holes
spreading through it, but Mori ignored the pain and growled. She
shot over the crashing inferno and rained her fire upon Solina.

The queen raised her shield. The flames engulfed her,
exploding around the shield and cascading upon her wyvern. The
beast screeched and bucked, and more acid spouted, a geyser of

heat and stench. Mori banked, dodging the stream. Drops splashed her and she roared, swooped, and lashed her tail.

Solina still lived, clasping her charred shield. With a howl, Mori slammed her tail down.

Light flashed. Solina's blade rose. Steel slashed Mori's tail and blood sprayed.

She screamed. The pain leaped through her, a striking asp. She blew more fire, but Solina flew beneath her, and her wyvern rose higher, a wall of scales and claws. The beast dwarfed Mori, twice her size. Its maw opened and its cry shook her, and its maw boiled like a smelter. Acid spewed toward her.

Mori soared. Acid splashed her back legs. She cried. She tried to blow more flame, but only sparks left her maw. The pain tugged at her magic like hands trying to rip off a gown; she struggled to stay in dragon form.

No! Don't fall. Fight her! Kill her! For Orin. For your people who lie dead beneath you.

Mori drove toward Solina and lashed her claws.

One claw slammed against the queen's shield and shattered it. Splinters showered. Mori's second claw slammed against Solina's blade. Steel rang and Mori howled. She leaned down to bite the queen.

Solina rose in her saddle and thrust up her sword.

The steel sliced across Mori's cheek, screeching and shedding sparks.

Mori screamed, pulled back, and heard wyverns swoop behind her.

She spun to see them. Their claws reached out and their riders shot crossbows. Bolts slammed into her.

"Take her alive!" Solina screamed somewhere below. "Chain the beast!"

Mori could barely see. For an instant she lost her magic, tumbled as a woman, then regained her dragon form and flew again. Smoke and fire and cloud swirled around her. Her wounds blazed. She tried to flap her wings, but a spear shot through the left one, where a hole already spread from the acid. She spun and did not know up from down. Blood flowed into her left eye.

"Elethor!" she called out. "Bayrin!"

She could not see them. She saw nothing but the blazing eyes of wyverns, claws that clutched her, and chains that swung around her.

"Bring her down!" rose Solina's voice from the haze. "Chain the beast!"

A claw slammed into Mori's back, driving through scale into flesh.

A cry fled her lips--a cry of pain, of fear, of a girl who was lost in Castellum Luna and breaking apart in the darkness.

Her magic left her.

She plummeted through the sky, a human girl, until claws caught her. The great shards wrapped around her, nearly crushing her ribs. More wyverns rose and chains swung around her.

"El!" she tried to cry, but her voice was only a hoarse whisper. "Bay... Lyana..."

She tried to shift into a dragon again, but could not. The wyvern claws nearly crushed her, keeping her in human form, and the chains tightened around her limbs. Wyvern scales surrounded her; between them, she could catch only glimpses of fire and ruin.

"Take her south!" rose Solina's voice. "Take her to Tiranor and chain her in my dungeon. I will come to her soon. Fly now! Fly south with the beast!"

A stream of scales flowed beneath her. Wyvern wings flapped around her. Mori struggled in the grip. She tried to cry out, but she could barely breathe. Soon the wyverns parted below, and she saw fallen walls and then flaming farmlands. She looked up to see a burning horizon flowing to distant, shimmering light.

The cries of dying dragons faded behind her. The lands streamed below. Mori's eyes closed and she knew nothing but pain, smoke, and the cry of wyverns.

LYANA

No. Stars, no. Please stars, let this be a dream. Let me wake.

She saw Queen Solina rise over the ruins. She saw the queen smirk. She saw the bodies of her parents fall from the wyvern claws.

Mother. Father. Tears filled Lyana's eyes. *Stars, please stars, no. They're dead. She killed them.* Her body trembled and she could barely keep flying.

A roar sounded behind her, torn with pain. Bayrin howled and blew fire.

"Solina!" he cried, voice hoarse. He soared, slashing and biting, a wild beast wreathed in flame. Lyana had never seen her brother like this. Blood and cuts covered him, and everywhere wyverns flew around him.

"Scream for me, beast!" Solina called across the battle. The queen laughed. "Die screaming for the reptiles that spawned you!"

Lyana's head spun. The grief seemed too great to bear. She howled to the sky. Around her, so few dragons still flew--a mere scattering of survivors. There were almost none left to save. Lyana sounded her cry: the cry of a warrior, of a knight, of a daughter grieving.

You took everything from me, Solina, she thought, tears in her eyes. *You took my city. You took my Orin. You took my parents.*

Even her rage could not rise above this grief, this great cry of loss, this falling of a kingdom and race. She howled with her grief and she flew toward Queen Solina through fire, acid, and blood.

I will kill her. I will kill our nemesis, then fall dead upon the ruins of the city I loved. My bones will rest forever by my parents, and I will walk with them in our starlit halls.

She saw the queen ahead. She narrowed her eyes. She flew with an empty, cold shard in her chest. She flew to kill and die.

A storm of wyverns rose from the ruins below. Bolts flew. Acid sprayed. Solina's voice rang across the battle.

"She is yours, Mahrdor! Enjoy my gift to you."

Lyana snarled. She saw the lord there. Mahrdor flew upon his four-winged wyvern, leading five more beasts. He clutched a crossbow in one hand; the other hung scarred at his side. Disgust flooded Lyana to remember how she had lain with him in his villa upon the Pallan, letting him invade her among his trophies of flesh. She drove toward him and blew her fire.

Mahrdor banked, and her jet of flame hit a wyvern behind him. Lyana soared. Fire and acid exploded. Crossbow bolts slammed into her; she barely felt them. She shot toward the sky, then swooped with the sun at her back, claws outstretched and fire raining. Another wyvern fell. Lyana howled.

For Requiem. For my parents. For the souls of my ancestors who watch from above. For the glory of our fallen columns and our stars.

Her fire bathed the battle. Her fangs bit through armor. Her claws painted the city with blood. She was Lyana Eleison, a knight of Requiem, a broken woman. She was a girl running through glittering halls to her parents. She was a youth gasping in wonder under blankets at old books of adventure. She was a glowing woman, betrothed to her prince, a lady of the courts. She was a warrior. She was a killer. She was flame and fang, claw and blood. She was Lyana Eleison and she was the wrath and agony of an ancient, fallen kingdom, the shattered notes of a dying song.

The wyverns fell around her, torn and burnt. Only one rider and beast remained before her: Lord Mahrdor.

Around her, the battle for Nova Vita raged in a haze. Some dragons were still fleeing, others still fighting and dying. Wyverns still swarmed around them. But here, in this pocket of silence above the ruins of her temple, it was just her and her enemy, her and the man who had invaded her body, caged her, and destroyed her home. She drove toward him, howling and blowing her flame.

Dragon crashed against wyvern. Fangs bit. Acid and fire roared. They tumbled, clawing and biting, and crashed into the ruins below. A fallen column cracked beneath them, and the wrath of Tiranor shrieked above.

Pain exploded through Lyana. Her back leg blazed; she thought the bone might be broken. Growling, she pushed back, untangling herself from the wyvern that writhed and snapped its teeth. Mahrdor rose from the saddle and drew his sword. Bricks, corpses, and puddles of blood spread around them. The stub of a column rose twenty feet beside her, ending with a crown of jagged marble.

Her head swirled. Lyana flapped her wings once. She struggled to her feet. She summoned fire into her maw.

Mahrdor's crossbow fired.

The bolt slammed into Lyana's neck.

She fell back, gasping for breath. The pain tore her magic from her like claws pulling her heart from her chest. As she shifted, the bolt clanked bloody to the ground. She found herself gasping in human form, on her knees, clutching her neck. She looked up, wincing and dizzy, to see Mahrdor walk toward her. Ash covered his armor, and half his face was gone, burned into a mess of red and black clinging to his skull. Eyes blank, he raised his sabre above her.

Lyana could barely move. The pain twisted through her bones like a horde of demons. With clenched teeth, her gloved hand closed around the hilt of Levitas, her ancient sword. She drew the blade as Mahrdor's sabre drove down. Steel clanged against steel.

The battle still raged above, but its sounds seemed muffled to her, the beasts blurred. Vaguely she heard her brother howl, heard Elethor cry for Requiem, heard Solina scream--but their cries seemed to rise from beyond distant dreamscapes she could not grasp. Her world had become this stage: half a column, bricks, and a cruel desert lord.

His blade flashed down again. Lyana parried. She pushed herself up, parried again, and thrust her blade. Steel clanged.

They moved in a slow, lumbering dance of pain. His flesh sizzled, dripping off his cheekbone. No emotion filled his eyes; they were blue ice, the eyes of a corpse. He swung his blade. Sparks showered.

"I will twist you," he said, lips bloody. His voice was gravely, a sound like bones crushed under boots. "I will shape you into a treasure. You will be the jewel of my collection, and you will *live*." He swung his blade. "I will never let you die. I will never let your pain end."

His sabre slammed against her breastplate, knocking the breath out of her. She swung her sword down and cleaved his pauldron. Blood spilled down his shoulder. He snarled, revealing a mouth full of shattered teeth. Their blades clashed again.

"No, Mahrdor," she whispered; it was as loud as she could speak. She felt blood trickle down her neck into her breastplate. "You will never more hurt anyone. You destroyed us, but you will fall with us. The one you sought for a trophy will be your death."

Her blade flashed. Levitas was an ancient sword, borne by Terra Eleison himself, a knight of Requiem, the hero of the great war against Dies Irae. Today she, his descendant, was the last of the bellators--perhaps soon the last of all dragons.

I still swing your sword, Terra, as you did. I still wear the armor of our order. I still fight for the bellators, even as they have all fallen, and I still swing Levitas for Requiem, even as she lies in ruin. I will soon dine at your side among our celestial columns.

She howled as she swung that old blade. She howled for her ancestors and for her king--a last battle cry. Levitas shone with starlight. The ancient steel drove through Mahrdor's breastplate, into his heart, and crashed through his back. With light and blood and metal, she drove her fury through him. She screamed with the might of her stars.

He gasped. He stared at her, skewered on her blade. They froze, eyes locked.

"I am Lyana Eleison," she whispered, clutching the sword inside him. Her voice trembled. Tears and blood ran down her face; she tasted both on her lips. "I am a knight of Requiem. I am a daughter of starlight. May your lord burn your soul in his fiery halls."

With a scream, she pulled her sword back. The blade retreated from him with gushing blood. He remained standing for but a moment longer, then fell forward. He lay dead at her feet.

Lyana shifted into a dragon. She took flight. She soared above the ruins. Thousands of wyverns howled, flapped wings, and dived toward her.

ELETHOR

Children lay dead upon the fallen palace. The corpses of elders, their white hair stained red, lay broken upon the shattered amphitheater. The body of a mother huddled under an orphaned archway, clutching the charred remains of her babe. As he flew between wyverns, searching for survivors, Elethor saw only death-
-thousands of corpses, extinguished stars.

"Mori!" he cried. "Mori, where are you?"

He could not see her. Night was falling, a sunset of fire and smoke and cloud. Shadows cloaked the city like a blanket. It began to rain. The drops pattered against the ruins, washing away the blood and acid. Distant thunder rolled and countless wyvern eyes burned red in the darkness.

"Mori!" he shouted. He had not seen her since bursting from underground in a shower of light. Had she fallen upon the city? He dived and flew between shattered columns, seeking his sister. So many dead--he saw corpses everywhere. They lay upon bricks, in puddles of acid, upon fallen walls. Some were mere skeletons, flesh eaten away and ribs cracked like the city's columns. Others were torn apart, limbs scattered. *Is one of those charred remains my sister?* Elethor's eyes burned as he called for her.

The rain fell in silver curtains. Nothing but bodies. Nothing but ruin.

And so it ends, Elethor thought in a haze. *So does Requiem fall, as it fell in the days of King Benedictus.* His eyes stung and smoke streamed between his teeth. *I'm sorry, Requiem. I'm sorry, Lyana. I failed.*

"Fly!" Bayrin cried in the distance. "Go, into the forest, fly!"

Elethor looked up to see his friend. Blood covered Bayrin's scales, but he still flew, herding a group of ragged, lacerated dragons. The survivors--there were a dozen or more--were taking flight from a collapsed house like crows rising from a disturbed tree. Wyverns spotted them, shrieked, and began to chase.

Growling, Elethor flew toward them. His body ached. The bolts of crossbows dug inside him, and burns stung across his scales.

Some still live. Some I can still save.

King's Column rose before him, a pillar of moonlight rising from darkness. It glowed in the rain. So long as it stood, there was hope, Elethor knew. So long as that column rose, he would fly. He would fight. He would seek the sky beyond wyvern and cloud.

He flew around that column, heading toward Bayrin and the others, when a great wyvern rose before him from the ruins. Its wings unfurled, black shrouds for the death of a god. Its eyes blazed, two red torches. It blocked the sky, a demon of darkness and iron. Atop its back rode a deity of gold, her banner streaming, her sword raised. The Queen of Tiranor cried out to him in the night.

"Elethor! Elethor!"

He reared before her, wings wide and fangs bared. "I'm here, Solina."

She raised her sabre high. Lightning flashed and slammed into the blade. Solina laughed--an echoing laughter that rang across the city like funeral bells.

"Hello, my love! Hello, my king!" Wyverns rose around her, black ghosts in the night. Solina pointed her blade at Elethor and called to them. "Grab the Reptile King! Bring him to me in chains."

The wyverns surged.

Elethor soared.

He rose through rain and cloud. Lightning crashed around him. Thunder blasted him and he howled in the darkness. Wyverns shrieked below him, and pillars of acid rose around him, a temple of corrosion. The clouds covered them. Elethor could see no more than several feet in any direction. He kept flying higher through the storm. The wind howled and shards of lightning exploded. One lightning bolt hit a wyvern; the beast screamed and fell.

"Catch the reptile!" Solina's voice stormed somewhere below him. "Chain the--"

Thunder boomed over her words. Elethor leveled off and dived through the clouds. He tried to fly north, to head into distant forests where he could hide between smoldering trees. He could only guess the direction. He saw nothing but clouds, heard nothing but thunder, rain, and shrieks. Acid sprayed to his left, nearly searing him. He banked right and flew higher.

He had to find Mori. He had to find Lyana and Bayrin. Were they still alive? Was anyone still alive? He ached to cry to them, to roar their names, but dared not; wyverns flew everywhere in the clouds. One appeared before him, emerging from darkness ten feet away. Elethor dared not even blow flames lest the other wyverns see; he drove forward and lashed his claws, tearing the rider apart. The wyvern fell. The rider's limbs tumbled.

Pain drove through Elethor. His eyes stung. Smoke blew around him, searing hot. He wanted to still his wings, to fall upon his realm, to lie forever as charred bones.

I failed my kingdom. I failed Lyana. I'm sorry, Father. I'm sorry, Orin.

He looked at the sky, seeking the halls of his fathers, but saw only cloud and rain. He rose higher. His wings blazed and wind howled around him. Ice began to spread across his scales, and the thin air spun his head, and yet still he soared. *Requiem. May our wings forever find your sky.* The clouds broke, and he emerged from the storm. Below him, the clouds and rain and lightning swirled, an orchestra of water and fire. Above him spread the night, ablaze with countless stars. The Draco constellation shone, glittering so brightly it nearly blinded him. He flew, caught between storm and star.

"I fly to you, Father," he whispered. All sounds faded; he could barely hear the storm beneath him. He looked up at the stars. "I fly to you, Queen Gloriae. I soon will dine in your hall, King Aeternum."

Will Mori await me there? Will Lyana forever sit by my side as the celestial columns rise around us? Will the great kings of old scorn me for my failure, for our ancient realm that fell under my reign?

A voice spoke behind him, clear in the night, as if answering his thoughts.

"You did not fail, Elethor."

He turned to see Solina upon her wyvern. The beast flapped its wings languidly, hovering before him. The golden queen regarded him, a visor hiding her face.

Elethor wanted to rage. He wanted to howl. He wanted to blow fire, to fight, to kill Solina and then crash dead with her to the ruins below. Yet no rage found him now, only grief that dampened his eyes, churned his gut, and swelled in his throat.

"I let Requiem fall," he said. He hovered before her. The night seemed so silent; only dim rumbles of thunder rolled below. No more wind blew. He hovered before his old love in soft darkness and starlight.

She shook her head. "No, Elethor. You could not have stopped me. Your father and brother could not stop me either; they fell before my flame. You fought me for many days, Elethor, and you led your people with honor. They are not ashamed of you, Elethor. You fought nobly and you are stronger than you know. Your father and brother were worshipped as warriors; they saw you as a sculptor, a stargazer, a lesser prince. But I knew who you are, El. I always knew. You showed your strength to me and to your people."

She lifted her visor. Her eyes were solemn. He remembered those eyes. With stabs of agony, he remembered marveling at their beauty, staring for hours into their depths. This was the woman he would kiss, the woman whose naked body he held under blankets, whose hair he would stroke--the woman who had claimed his soul and even now, even here, held it in her hands.

"My people are dead," he said. "Solina, what strength can I show them now?"

She pointed above to the Draco constellation. It seemed impossibly distant, impossibly large, great suns of distant fire.

"They watch over you, Elethor. The souls of your people whisper there; so do the souls of your father and brother. I sent them there, but I need not send you." She reached out to him. "It's not too late, Elethor. I love you. I've always loved you. Requiem is gone; I crushed it so we might be together again. Return with me to your home. Return with me to the desert; we were always meant to rule there together." Tears sparkled in her eyes like more stars. "Elethor... I hate you. I vowed to destroy you. But now I look upon you and I love you." She reached toward him. "You and I were always meant to fly here, to hurt each other, to love in pain. Blood and fire have always been ours; we have beaten blood and fire before, and I returned to you. It's time to go home."

Soft light glowed around her, and she seemed to Elethor not the Queen of Tiranor, not the tyrant and slayer of his people, but the Solina who would hold him in caves and forests, whisper of secret magical kingdoms, and cry onto his shoulder, then laugh and kiss him.

"I never wanted anything but this," Elethor said softly. "A quiet place. The light of stars. You and I. For years that's all I dreamed of."

Her wyvern's wings rose and fell like a silent midnight sea. Solina reached out toward him from the saddle. "That is what you have! That is what I brought us. Let your magic go, Elethor. Turn into the man I love, ride with me in my saddle, and we will live like this forever. No more fire or blood--just you and me."

He laughed weakly. Smoke rose from his nostrils. "That is not what you said last year when you drove your dagger down my face. You spoke of torture then. You spoke of making me beg for death." He sighed. "Solina, the days when we could have been like this, here in solitude, are gone. Too much blood has spilled. Too many stones have shattered. Too many lights have gone out."

She shook her head. "There is only this, Elethor. Don't you understand? There is no more Requiem for you to return to." Her wyvern lowered its head, its dark body nearly disappearing into shadow. Solina seemed to float before him, a golden queen in the night. "All has fallen. All has been laid to waste. The land where we grew up is gone, Elethor, swept away in this rain like the last snows of winter. Let spring rise from its ashes. With me, Elethor. With me."

He looked below him. The storm swirled silently, a sea of gray and red and blue, flaring every moment with the faded glow of lightning. Requiem had fallen; there was no more home beneath those clouds. All was gone: the temple where he would pray with his people, their song rising between the columns to the stars; the house where he would sculpt and whisper Solina's name in the night; the gardens and hills where he would laugh with Bayrin; the palace where he had grown up with Orin and Mori.

Gone. All is gone.

He looked back up at Solina. "Where is Mori? Where is my sister?"

Something crossed Solina's eyes, the flicker of deep fire. Her voice hardened. "I spared her life. I did not kill her. She lives, Elethor. She lives. She will be allowed to live in our realm."

Yet there was no warmth to her voice; the shadow of her rage now filled it. He looked into her eyes and saw the madness there. The old Solina still lurked inside her, crying out to him--the Solina he had loved for years, the Solina whom he still loved, even now. But that fire burned now across her soul, the fire that had burned her body and twisted her mind, that perhaps had always simmered deep within her. He could not rid her of it, he knew. He could not undo her deeds, could not cleanse her of her crimes.

A peace settled upon him then, and the starlight warmed him. He knew, perhaps for the first time, that she was gone from him; like never before, he knew that Solina--*his* Solina, the one he had loved--had fallen too, as ruined as the city below them.

"I will not join you in your desert court," he said. "You may fight me; you may try to chain me. I will die fighting you above the earth of my home, in the light of my stars." He smiled softly. "It will be a good death."

Solina stared at him a moment longer, silent. Tears flowed down her cheeks.

"Goodbye, Elethor," she whispered.

Lightning flared and thunder boomed.

Solina screamed.

She drove her wyvern toward him.

Elethor spread his wings and bathed her with fire.

She screamed. The fire flowed across her. He shot forward and his claws lashed. She swung her sword; the steel sliced his claw. He tried to bite her, to crush her between his teeth. Her wyvern swooped. Elethor followed, lashed his tail, and tossed Solina from her saddle.

She tumbled.

Her hair burned.

"Elethor!" she screamed, falling into darkness. "I carried your child, Elethor!"

She laughed and wept, hair blazing, arms reaching out toward him. Elethor inhaled sharply and dived after her, eyes narrowed.

"Solina!"

She laughed as she fell through cloud and rain, hair alight.

"I carried your child when Orin burned me!" she shouted, tears streaming. "I lost the babe in his fire. The kingdom you fight for, the family you love--they murdered your child!"

He reached out his claws.

He tried to grab her.

Stars of Requiem, stars, no. Please, stars, no.

He screamed, diving as fast as he could. He stretched out his claws. He grazed her fingertips. Screaming and laughing, her hair crackling like a torch, she vanished into cloud and rain

"Solina!" he howled and roared fire.

Stars, our child... stars, no.

He roared for her, voice torn, like he had called for her eight years ago from the walls of his city.

"Solina!"

He dived through the storm. Rain pounded his face. A lightning bolt slammed down by him. Wyverns rose from darkness and crashed into him. He tumbled. Scales flashed.

"Solina!"

My child.

"Elethor!"

The voice rose below, muffled and distant. A bolt of lightning slammed against a wyvern's rider and exploded. Fire burst. The beasts screeched. Elethor drove upward and through them.

The distant voice cried again. "Mori! Mori, where are you? Elethor!"

Lyana!

Elethor howled. He flamed two wyverns, clawed a third, and drove through the storm. Wind pushed against him, and rain lashed him, but he kept flying. He wanted to seek Solina, to dive through the clouds, to slay her if she still lived--but Lyana needed him.

"Lyana!" he shouted into the storm.

Lyana--his betrothed. Lyana--of steel and fire. Lyana--of red hair that would never fall the way she wanted; of green eyes that would mock him one moment and love him the next; of wisdom and strength, of softness and joy. A knight. A betrothed. A woman who had walked with him to the Abyss and back. She cried to him now. *Let me seek her now. Let Solina go.*

"Lyana!" he cried again. The wyverns streamed around him. "Lyana!"

Her voice called from the distance. "Elethor! Stars, Elethor, where are you?"

He dived lower. When he emerged from the clouds into rain and smoke, he cried out to her, and she answered his call, and he flew over ruin, over fallen walls, over charred forests. He saw blue scales ahead and he drove toward her, eyes stinging.

She flew and all but crashed against him. A green dragon emerged from shadows by them, the rain washing blood from his body: Bayrin.

Wyverns swarmed upon them. The three dragons blew fire, holding them back. A stream of acid fell, and they scattered, blew more flames at the beasts, and regrouped.

"Lyana, where's Mori?" Elethor demanded. Spears rained, and one lashed across his shoulder.

"We thought she was with you!" she said.

With a chill, Solina's words returned to him. *She lives, Elethor. She lives.*

More wyverns emerged from the clouds. Elethor cursed. He flapped his wings and soared back into the cloud cover. Bayrin and Lyana flew by his side, blowing fire at the wyverns.

"Bayrin, fly north!" Elethor shouted. "Lyana, fly east! I go south. We must find Mori."

A wyvern shot between them, showering acid. They scattered and Bayrin slew the beast with claw and fang.

When it fell, the green dragon cried, "And what then, El? The whole bloody kingdom is burning!"

Acid rained. They rose higher in the clouds. Lightning flashed and thunder boomed.

Stars, she was carrying my child...

"When the sun sets again, fly to Sequestra Mountains!" he shouted. "If you find Mori, bring her there. Now go! Find her, Bayrin!"

The green dragon cursed. His wings were charred and his scales bloody, but still he blasted fire. He turned and began flying north, calling her name.

Lyana remained at Elethor's side. Acid had spilled down her left flank, withering the scales. She stared at Elethor, her eyes haunted. She hovered before him.

"Oh, El," she said softly.

He growled. A lightning bolt crashed, illuminating a sky full of wyverns; thousands still flew.

"Go, Lyana!" he shouted. "Fly east! Fly now!"

She looked ready to weep. Her eyes watered. A howl left her throat. Her fire blazed. She spun around, roaring Requiem's call, and flew into the east. Soon she vanished into the clouds, wyverns in pursuit.

Stars, Mori, where are you?

He roared her name. He flew south. The fury of Tiranor flowed around him, and the bodies of his people littered the farmlands below.

TREALE

"Please let them fly away," she whispered, shivering on the ground. "Please, stars. *Please.*"

The charred trees rose above her, their leaves burnt white, their branches like fingers groping at the sky. The rain pattered down, swaying in the wind. Beneath the clouds flew the wyverns, grunting and screaming like rutting beasts.

"Don't let them see me, stars," Treale whispered.

She huddled in the mud between the trees. Ash and rain covered her hair. A glob of acid sprayed down ahead and began eating through a tree. Burns spread across her thigh and she grimaced; she had not imagined any wound could hurt so much. Her lungs still ached with smoke, and she wanted nothing more than to cough, but forced herself to hold her breath. She pushed herself down into the mud under the trees.

The wyverns flew in formation above; there were eight. When Treale peered between the branches, she could see that their riders bore banners sporting a golden sun on a white field-- Solina's personal guard. The lead wyvern carried a bundle in its claws, and Treale glimpsed flashes of muddy blue.

She gasped.

Despite the ache in her wound, and the fear in her breast, she pushed herself up against the bole. She peered between the charred branches and leaves.

"Stars," she whispered.

The beasts overshot her, but Treale had seen enough. The wyvern held a woman in its claws, her blue dress tattered and bloody, her limbs chained.

Blue fabric was rare in Requiem; it came all the way from the southern sea, where divers collected the mollusks which leaked the indigo dye. Even House Oldnale, the wealthiest family in Requiem after the royal Aeternums and noble Eleisons, owned no blue fabrics. That was the color of royalty. That was a gown of a princess.

"Mori," Treale whispered.

The wyverns vanished overhead, flying... Treale did not know which way. How could anyone tell north or south with these clouds and this rain? Gritting her teeth against the blazing pain, she clutched the tree and began to climb. Soot covered her hands. The tree was wet but still hot from the fire. She grimaced. Her wounds burned like ten thousand suns, shooting pain through her limbs, into her fingertips, even into her teeth. She groaned and kept climbing. When she reached the treetop, she straightened. So much mud and soot covered her, she imagined that she looked like yet another branch. Squinting, she stared after the retreating wyverns. The blue gown flapped in the leader's claws, and Treale thought she could hear a muffled cry-- the cry of a young woman. The rain kept falling, and even the shrieks of the wyverns sounded dim.

It's her. It's Mori.

Treale trembled and nearly fell from the tree. She clutched its branches so tightly her fingers bled. Mori had been her dearest friend since childhood; the two had been born mere days apart. Treale had grown up yearning for every harvest, when she could travel to Nova Vita and spend several joyous days with Mori-- reading books in the library, teasing the princes with giggles and secret words only she and Mori understood, and going to the warrens behind Castra Murus to feed the rabbits. Every winter, when the Aeternums visited Oldnale Manor for the Feast of Stars, Treale would let Mori sleep by her side in her great canopy bed; the two would stay up nearly all night, whispering of the knights they would marry someday, what new pups they would adopt, and all the other secrets of youth.

Lyana would often spend time with them too, but Lyana was two years older and so much wiser, so much stronger; the knight had always seemed closer to the adults, more like Prince Orin. *But Mori and I were always as sisters--two young girls of great families with great older brothers.*

Now none of that remained. No more canopy bed or farms or... maybe not even any more Vir Requis.

"But you live, Mori," Treale whispered, eyes damp.

Shame burned inside her, as cold as her wounds were hot. She had defected from King Elethor's army. She had fled from Nova Vita at the sight of its ruin. Tears burned in Treale's eyes. *I am a coward. I wanted to be like Lady Lyana, a brave knight, but I fled from battle.*

She growled low in her throat. She narrowed her eyes and watched the wyverns flee.

"I abandoned my king, my lady, and my kingdom," she whispered, a lump in her throat. "But I won't abandon you, Mori."

The wyverns were soon distant specks in the storm, and she could no longer hear their calls. Treale knew what fate awaited Mori if she could not save her: the princess would be imprisoned and tortured, and when her body was broken, she would be burned in the city of Irys among the dunes.

I won't let that happen.

In the treetop, Treale shifted and tested her wings. She rose into the storm, a black dragon with dented, charred scales. The wind and rain lashed her, and she could barely flap her wings, but she growled, she snorted fire, and she flew.

"I will find you, Mori." Smoke streamed between her teeth. "I will follow you to the desert itself if I must."

They had no home to return to. Requiem lay in ruins, her halls fallen like so many old stones. But so long as Mori lived, there was hope. Treale sniffed and realized that tears filled her eyes.

We will flee into the wilderness, Mori, you and I. We'll find a cave to live in, or a green forest that no fire has touched, and we'll whisper and laugh together again. If everyone else is fallen, we will still have each other.

The wyverns flew ahead, flecks on the horizon. Fire flickering in her mouth, her wings roiling the clouds, Treale Oldnale followed through the ash, rain, and ruin of the world.

SOLINA

She stood at a towering window in her chambers, its archway large enough for a wyvern to fly through. A wind from the desert blew, billowing her white silks and platinum hair. Her golden jewels chinked, and the coppery taste of sand flickered across her lips. She gripped the hilts of her twin sabres and gazed upon her home.

Cranes and ibises flew above her oasis, singing to the sun. Date and fig trees rustled. Men labored across the city of Irys, sweat glistening on their golden skin: tending to vineyards, hammering swords on anvils, and raising statues and columns for her glory. Ships sailed up the River Pallan, overflowing with spices and gems from Iysa, Jewel of the South and a twin to Irys. From the north, wyverns were flying over the delta and landing in Hog Corner. Upon their backs, they bore the trophies of Requiem: longswords of filigreed steel, statues of marble from Requiem's temples, sacks of golden coins, and chests full of books and scrolls and artifacts.

"All your glory is mine, Elethor," Solina whispered into the desert. "All that you had is gone from you."

She winced in sudden pain. It had been a moon's turn since she had fallen over Nova Vita, since her wyverns had caught her tumbling and burning. Her chest still hurt sometimes, though her healers insisted her cracked ribs had healed. Her hair had burned; she had shaved it off that day, and it was still short under the wig she wore.

"And soon I will bring you here too."

Ten thousand wyverns still flew over Requiem, burning
what forests remained, slaughtering whatever dragon they found
cowering in the wastelands.

"All but you, Elethor," she whispered. "They will not
slaughter you, no." She drew Raem, her blade of dawn, and held
it aloft. "They will bring you here alive, and it will be this blade
that you scream for, this blade that I will hold above you, as you
weep and beg me to stab your heart." She snarled. "But I will
not, Elethor; I will not show you any more mercy. You turned
down my mercy. Now you will *live*."

She shut her eyes and winced.

I spoke to him of my secret. I spoke of our child.

She clenched her jaw so hard she felt her teeth could crack.

No. No. That will remain buried. She clutched her swords so
tightly, her fists trembled. *I will never remember that pain again.*

She turned from her window. Trophies of her conquests
filled her chamber. The sword of Lord Deramon, its blade
engraved with the Draco constellation, hung upon her wall. The
brooch of Mother Adia, a silver birch leaf, shone upon a plaque
carved from the Weredragon Temple's marble. Below these
spoils stood the Oak Throne of Requiem, the soot sanded off the
twisting roots that formed it. Around the throne, covering the
tiles of her floor, lay jugs of weredragon gold and jewels, helms of
fallen knights, and blades of northern steel.

"I will sit upon this throne as I watch you scream," Solina
whispered. "I will place my feet upon the helms of your warriors,
and I will laugh as my vultures feed upon you."

Still clutching her swords, she left her chamber. Her
sandals thumped against the stairs leading down her tower. She
walked across corridors with tiles so polished her reflection
walked beneath her, clad in white silks and gold. She crossed her
grand hall where a hundred guards stood armored in platinum,
their visors shaped like the heads of falcons, and her throne rose

glittering, a monolith of ivory and jewels. She descended dark stairs into the underground, where the air was cold and damp even as the sun pounded the desert above. She walked down tunnels, sloping ever deeper, until all scent and sound and memory of the world faded into darkness.

She grabbed a torch that burned upon a craggy wall. Dust carpeted the floor. Cobwebs, old blood, and chained skeletons covered the walls. Still she walked, going deeper, until the tunnel narrowed to a mere burrow, and the air was so cold even the Sun God could not warm it.

She approached the chamber that lay ahead. Her torchlight flickered. She stepped through the doorway and snarled a grin.

The creature hung there from the ceiling, wrists chained. The pathetic, beaten thing did not even look up. Blood trickled from its wrists, and cobwebs filled its dangling hair. It was a wretched being, emaciated, its skin lashed and raw. When Solina approached and the torchlight blazed against the beast, it gave a low mewl and swung on its chains; it was too weak to do anything else.

Solina caressed the creature's cheek. It shivered under her palm. She stroked its hair and kissed its forehead.

"Hush now," Solina whispered. "Soon he will be with you, my sweet Mori. Soon your brother will be with you again."

ELETHOR

He stood inside the cave and stared out upon the forest. The trees rolled into misty horizons, their leaves golden and red. A cold wind blew, ruffling his hair, and ravens circled under the veil of clouds. A drizzle fell, deepening the colors of the world until all became a smudged painting of brown, orange, and silver. Elethor held Ferus's hilt. He could barely see Requiem from here, only a distant haze of smoke. The burnt lands of his fathers lay beyond the leagues, ravaged and swarming with wyverns.

Elethor lowered his gaze to the camp below the mountain. Men and women moved between the trees, clad in leaf and fur and mud. A few men were skinning a deer, and two children ran around a tree, banging wooden swords they had carved. A mother nursed her babe, and an old man sat upon a boulder, reading from a scroll of prayers. Four Vir Requis stood in dragon forms, guarding each corner of the camp; mud covered their scales to dull their shimmer.

Ninety-seven souls, Elethor thought. *Fewer than a hundred survivors from a realm of fifty thousand.*

As he stood in the cave upon the mountainside, looking down at this ragged camp, he thought of Mori.

"Do you too hide in some distant camp beyond our borders?" he whispered. "Do you have someone with you, someone to protect you?"

He looked over the forest, as if she could emerge any moment from the distance, a golden dragon--haggard but smiling, *alive.* Every day he waited here in this cave, watching the horizon for wyverns, watching for Mori. They had lived here for two moons now, and still she did not arrive.

Elethor lowered his head. *Maybe you lie among the ruins of Nova Vita, resting by the bones of Orin and Father. Maybe you now sing with them in the starlit halls. I love you, sister. I miss you.*

A blue glimmer flew upon the horizon. Elethor stood watching, the wind in his hair, until the sapphire dragon emerged from the distant mist and flew toward the cave. Lyana landed on the mountainside and looked up at him. Smoke rose in curtains from between her teeth.

"Lyana," he said. He approached as she shifted into human form. She stood before him with somber eyes, still clad in the silvery armor of the bellators.

"I'm sorry, Elethor," she whispered. She removed her helm, embraced him, and laid her head upon his shoulder. "I'm so sorry, my king. I searched Fidelium in the north, and the plains of Sequestra, and sought her among the cities of Osanna. None have seen the princess."

He held her. Her hair had grown an inch, and the fiery curls brushed against his face. He cupped her cheek and kissed her forehead. Her eyes were deep green pools.

"Maybe Bayrin found her," he said softly, but heard no hope in his voice and saw none in Lyana's eyes.

They stood upon the mountainside, watching the forest until emerald scales shimmered in the north, and Bayrin flew toward them. The green dragon landed outside the cave, panting and cursing. He spat a flicker of fire.

"Bloody stars!" Bayrin said. "The north is swarming with those wyvern bastards." He raised his tail; an ugly welt rose across it. "One gave me this before I roasted him." He whipped his head from side to side, then lowered his eyes. "I... I was hoping Lyana had found her. Oh, stars."

He shifted into human form. Red rimmed his eyes and ash filled his hair. His gangly frame was thinner than ever, stubble was thickening into a beard across his face, and soot covered his breastplate and scabbard. He looked down, tightened his jaw, and clenched his fists. Elethor saw a tear on his chin.

He approached his friend and held his shoulder. "We'll find her, Bay. We won't rest until we do. For as long as it takes, I will send out dragons to every corner of the world, and we will find her."

Yet in the cold pit of his stomach, Elethor knew there was only one more place they could search, one more hope to save her... to save everyone who still lived here among the trees.

He turned to look south. The forests rolled for countless leagues, finally fading into a yellow haze and blue mountains against a silver sky. Standing to his right, Lyana clasped his hand and held it tight. At his left side, Bayrin placed a hand on his shoulder and stared with him, solemn and silent. The wind blew their hair, cold and wet with rain, but Elethor thought he could scent the distant sands.

"What do we do now?" Bayrin said. "Do we stay here, hidden in the wilderness, and continue our search from this camp? Do we fly to Salvandos and seek sanctuary among the true dragons of the golden mountain? Do we fly east to Osanna and live among the men of the white halls?"

Elethor shook his head, watching the forest rustle and the rain sway in sheets.

"No, Bayrin," he said softly. "We will not flee. Not yet." He turned to look at his friend. "We collect what dragons we can still find among the ruins of Requiem. We fly to Tiranor. We rain fire upon them. If Mori is captive there, we will save her."

Bayrin nodded, lips tight. Elethor turned to look at Lyana; she stared back with green eyes that spoke of her loyalty, her love, and her fire that would forever light his darkness.

He squeezed her hand and whispered. "And we kill Solina."

They stood upon the mountain, holding one another, and gazed upon the southern horizon of forest, mist, mountain... and beyond them the cruel, endless desert.

The story will continue in...

A NIGHT OF DRAGON WINGS

Dragonlore, Book Three

NOVELS BY DANIEL ARENSON

Standalones:

Firefly Island (2007)
The Gods of Dream (2010)
Flaming Dove (2010)

Misfit Heroes:

Eye of the Wizard (2011)
Wand of the Witch (2012)

Song of Dragons:

Blood of Requiem (2011)
Tears of Requiem (2011)
Light of Requiem (2011)

Dragonlore:

A Dawn of Dragonfire (2012)
A Day of Dragon Blood (2012)
A Night of Dragon Wings (forthcoming)

KEEP IN TOUCH

www.DanielArenson.com
Daniel@DanielArenson.com
Facebook.com/DanielArenson
Twitter.com/DanielArenson

Made in the USA
Lexington, KY
11 December 2012